The Alex Chronicles:
WHAT MY FRIENDS DON'T KNOW

PART ONE

Cover Image
Mayer George/Shutterstock.com

ISBN: 978-0-9862933-7-5

To my first loves
God
Mommy and Dad

Acknowledgements

This may sound like a duplicate or repeat acknowledgement, because I need to thank the same group of friends from The Alex Chronicles Prequel. Those kind friends were there with the original versions of this series. Thank you for your honest critiquing of the first draft of The Alex series.

Mommy, Selma, Debra, Terryl, Yolanda and Michelle

I refer to this series as my baby. This is the first book I wrote and like most first books, it has undergone a lot of maturation. I'm so glad I listened to my mother and waited to release it. I like the way this series has grown up.

Thank you to my friends Barbara Byndon and Beverly Evans, who critiqued the rewrite and fell in love with these characters. And to Jeanne Cadeau, bless you for reading both versions. Thank you L.K. Campbell, for your patience.

My friend Rachele Turner, I miss your quiet voice and honest observation.

About the Author

Tracy is a woman who loves God, Cute Guys and Fashion. Sometimes those last two things fight for second place, when there's a great designer sale.

She calls herself a partial New Yorker due to the two and half years she lived there. She refers to her books as Steamy Christian Fiction. Her stories are filled with relatable characters in real life situations.

When she's not writing, she's working at her other passion, her lingerie store, The Pink Duchess. Like her characters, she's a small business owner waiting on that one cute guy, who loves God and understands her love of fashion.

The Alex Chronicles

is a series about women, friends, marriage, divorce, boyfriends, husbands, ex-loves, new loves, should have been loves, babies, children, in-laws, rules and the elusive, happily ever after.

It also asks an important question, "Do you really know everything about your closest friends?"

The Alex Chronicles:
WHAT MY FRIENDS DON'T KNOW

PART ONE

TRACY REED

This is how it started...

I SCANNED THE ROOM ADMIRING the Who's Who of Atlanta, all here to help me celebrate the opening of my new Alex Simone store.

My cousin Taylor offered to throw me a welcome to Atlanta party, sort of a pre-opening. She said it's the best way to entice the glitterati of Atlanta to come to the opening. This is so not my thing. If I weren't the guest of honor, I'd be gone.

I looked across the room and caught the eye of the most beautiful man in the room. I convinced myself he was smiling at me, until I realized my cousin Taylor was behind me.

She walked over and whispered, "Too bad he is so old."

"How old is he?"

"He's in our neighborhood."

"So now, we're old?"

"No girl." She laughed. "You know what I mean. I thought I'd try something a little fresher." She turned to her right and cast a big smile in the direction of this young, honey colored, bald man child standing in the corner. He was fine, but he still had milk on his lips. I redirected my attention to Mr. Dark Chocolate who was headed toward us.

He moved like a gazelle, slow and steady gliding across the room. Swagger...confidence...danger. As he approached, I saw the details of his face more clearly. His skin looked like smooth dark chocolate and he had the most incredible light brown eyes. I've never seen a man so dark with such light eyes. They didn't seem real, nor did he. He smiled and I felt something deep in my core. I don't care if he's only coming over to talk to my cousin. I'm grateful to stand here in his presence and lust...I mean admire him.

He stopped in front of us and my mind immediately filled with thoughts no good Christian girl should know anything about. I wonder what he looks like wet and naked. I looked around hoping I hadn't said that out loud.

"Hello, Taylor." He smiled.

Oh God, did You recycle Barry White's voice box and put it inside this beautiful package? My hormones and body went into a tailspin and I was ruined for any other man on this planet.

"Hi Moses. I'm glad you came."

He kissed the back of her hand and replied, "Thank you for inviting me. Good evening, I'm Moses Adair." He took my hand, turned it over and gently kissed it. I think my uterus just flipped over.

Moses, lead me to the Promise land. "Alexandra Miller."

"Are you *the* Alex?" He asked.

If I wasn't, I was now. "Which Alex would that be?" I replied with a smile.

"The Alex I've been hearing people talk about all evening."

"Depends on what you've heard." I'm trying to flirt and that's not something I'm good at. I wanted to tell him, "I'm whoever I need to be in order to keep talking to you."

"Excuse me," Taylor said and left us standing in the middle of the room.

"I heard a woman say she hoped the pink dress Alex was wearing would be available at the store, because she liked the way it..." He slowly looked me up and down. When his eyes met mine, he was smiling. I instantly recognized that smile. It's the same one I had when I first spotted him. "...framed her face."

I gave him the same smile he gave me. "Then, I guess I am *that* Alex."

As soon as the flirting started, it ended. I saw him looking everywhere, but at me. Time to move on. I should have known this gorgeous man wasn't interested in me. I'm going to hurt Taylor for leaving me with one of her castoffs.

"Excuse me, but I..."

He gently grabbed my hand. "Please..." I looked at my hand and then his face. Those incredible eyes, went from light to dark brown in a matter of seconds. A jolt hit my core and I almost fell down. "Please...don't leave me alone."

"What?"

He leaned in close and his aftershave traveled up my nose. He smelled like an expensive cigar that had been dipped in sweet plums and cardamon. I took a deep breath tattooing his scent in my mind. "May I tell you a secret?"

He can say anything he wants as long as I can hear that voice. I swallowed hard. "Sure."

"This really isn't my thing."

"Then why did you come?" He was still holding my hand. Part of me wanted him to let go before he realized how sweaty it was. The other part of me didn't ever want him to let it go. I looked down at my hand and back at him and he released my hand.

"I'm trying to be more outgoing. Meet new people."

"And how's that working out for you?" I asked with just enough sarcasm to be cute.

"I met one person so far," he joked.

"Uh-huh. Excuse me." I started walking away and he grabbed my wrist.

"I'm sorry, how long have you known Taylor?"

"She's my cousin, and you?"

"We dated briefly."

"Really?" I turned to face him.

"You sound surprised."

"I'm sorry, you just don't seem like her type." He looked across at Taylor and junior.

"I don't?"

"Did you know, when a woman meets a man, she can size him up in a matter of seconds."

"Really? Let's get a drink, while you explain women to me." He gently placed his hand on the small of my back and my body temperature tripled.

God, please let there be something wrong with him.

"What would you like?" he asked.

"A mineral water with lime."

"We'll both have mineral water. Thank you." He turned toward me and it felt like he was looking into my soul. I heard someone say, you know you've met the person you're supposed to be with when you look into their eyes and see all the generations you'll create. When I looked into his eyes, I saw our great grandchildren several times over. "You were saying?"

"It's simple. When a woman meets an attractive man, within thirty seconds, or less, she's picked out their china pattern, placed him at the altar, and given birth to their first child." The bartender placed my drink on the bar and nodded his head in agreement with me. "Thank you." I took a sip and continued. "He, on the other hand is just hoping she'll say hello."

"Thank you." He said to the bartender and took a sip of his drink. "Taylor doesn't strike me as that type."

"Taylor is the rule with a little exception. She can sum up if you're too old."

"Too old?" He looked surprised.

"Yeah, that's probably why it didn't work out between you two. She kind of has this thing for younger men." As soon as the words left my mouth, it hit me like a ton of bricks. Not only did I just betray my cousin, I just betrayed my sex and called him old. He looked at me and slowly turned his lips up into the most beautiful smile.

"Your insight is enlightening. However, I don't think that's why we stopped dating." He took another sip from his glass.

"Trust me."

"And here I thought it had to do with my wife."

"Your wife?"

Chloe

"MISS KENDELL, WHAT ARE YOU up to? Remember, Alex's mantra, you spill on it, you bought it."

"I know that's why I gave her a check when she dropped it off yesterday. How's the party going?"

"It's a typical Taylor party," I replied.

"I take it you met her young man?"

"You knew about him?" Alex asked.

"She told me about him a couple of month ago. She says she's tired of dating guys her own age. What does he look like?" Kendell asked.

"He's cute if you're into the will be handsome when he grows up type. You've got to see them. They are all over each other." I shook my head. "Personally, I don't see the relationship going anywhere. But what do I know? My husband woke up nine weeks ago and decided he didn't want to be married any more. So, what are we having tonight?"

"Orlando did what?" Alex asked.

"Orlando has decided we should spend some time apart."

"What?" Alex repeated herself.

"Kendell, everything smells so good."

"Thank you."

"Are those crab cakes or salmon croquettes?"

"Salmon croquettes," Alex jumped in. "What about Orlando?"

"What about him?"

"Did you say time apart?" Alex asked.

"Yes, time apart or I believe the court documents say legal separation. I think it's a great idea, because I was two-seconds away from poisoning his trifling behind."

"Excuse me?" Alex replied.

"It was a bad marriage and I'm over it."

"But you two seemed happy," Kendell replied.

"All an act."

"Why didn't you say anything?" Alex asked.

"I come from a family where you keep things like this to yourself." I took a deep breath and continued. "Look, I...we haven't been happy together for quite a while."

"When did this happen?" Alex asked.

"A couple of months ago. To be precise nine weeks, three days, sixteen hours," I looked at my watch, "...and twenty-three minutes."

"Where is he?" Kendell asked.

"I don't know. As far as I'm concerned, all that's left is a divorce decree. Please don't feel sad for me. For the first time in a very, very, very long time, I'm happy. Besides, it's a party and now that I'm semi-single, I want to have some fun."

I looked across the room and noticed a very handsome gentleman. I sauntered across the room and fixed my gaze directly onto the beautiful man with the dark olive skin and jet black wavy hair. He was talking with a couple of other guys, but looking at me.

I stopped and locked eyes with him. Once I knew I had him hooked, I headed towards the bar.

"I'll have a glass of champagne, thank you."

"Good evening, Marcelo Telles."

I turned around and shook his hand. His eyes were amazing, like coal with flecks of gold staring back at me. I told myself not to look into his eyes but they had me under a spell.

"Chloe Jacobs. Pleasure to meet you."

"The pleasure is all mine." The bartender placed the glass on the counter in front of me. "Thank you."

He started speaking in that soft, seductive tone reserved for old school Latin movie stars. Too bad I didn't have a clue what he was saying. I know Spanish, French and Italian, but that sounded like Portuguese. I trust God he didn't say anything obscene. If this encounter leads anywhere, tomorrow I'm buying Rosetta Stone CDs for whatever language he's speaking.

I looked at him and my legs tried to betray me. There were other parts of me already revealing my obvious attraction to him. I took a deep breath and replied. "That was beautiful. Unfortunately, I don't understand enough Portuguese…"

He nodded. "I apologize. The way you walk is like the women at Carnival."

"Somehow, I don't think that's what you said."

"No, what I said doesn't translate well. It's a poem mi Padre used to say to mi Madre. He said she was swaying to the music in her head when she walked." He smiled.

"Uh-huh, I think…"

"I'm sorry, I don't mean any disrespect, but you are very sexy." He leaned in a little closer. "Every man in here has been looking at you, but you've been ignoring them. I took a chance and came over to talk to you. We should have lunch."

"Lunch?"

"Yes. Coffee is too brief. Dinner will be our third date and the fourth date, will be your choice."

"What about the second date?"

"Breakfast after a night of dancing."

"I have never received such an intriguing and seductive lunch invitation. I have to be honest, I am very curious to know if the date will be as tantalizing as the invitation." I looked into those deep dark Latin eyes smiling back at me and answered, "I would be delighted to join you for lunch."

"How may I contact you?"

I grabbed a napkin and wrote my number on it. I can't remember the last time I did that. "Here." I handed him the napkin.

"Bom...Good. I'll call you in the morning with the details." He looked at the napkin before placing it in his jacket pocket. I wanted him to leave so the blood could get back to my feet and allow me to walk. "Adeus, Chloe Jacobs."

"Adeus, Marcelo Telles." He placed his glass on the bar and walked away. I turned and took a very big sip of my drink and let out a sigh.

The bartender laughed and said, "If you didn't agree to have lunch with him, I was going to slap you."

I WAS GLAD TO HAVE a little quiet time to myself. I love my girls, but when we get together, it turns into an extended slumber party. I slipped out of the party and snuck back inside and went upstairs.

After a restless night, I looked at my phone, it was six thirty and I had a lot to get done before the opening.

"His wife," those two words kept ringing in my head right next to that beautiful smile and those incredible eyes. *"God, why are you allowing a man like that to roam free among single women?"*

I got up, showered, got dressed and headed downstairs. When I walked into the kitchen, it was like being back at school, sitting around the table sharing about the night before.

"Good morning ladies." I stopped at the counter and poured a cup of coffee.

"Good morning Cuz, how'd you sleep?" Taylor asked.

"Fine. I see your kitchen is getting its quarterly workout," I teased.

"I'm not shame. I did this kitchen for show, resale and for Kendell," she announced.

"Trust me, she's telling the truth," Kendell replied. "I found everything just the way I left it."

"So what did I miss?" I sat down with my coffee.

"Chloe was just filling us in on her mystery man," Kendell informed me.

"As I was saying, the way he introduced himself knocked me for a loop. He looked straight at me and announced himself, 'Marcelo Telles', with such authority, immediately taking control of the moment."

"That's Marcelo," Taylor confirmed.

"Then he blew me away with something about me being in control and sexy."

"He's a good catch," Taylor added.

"Dish," Chloe urged.

"All I know is he's from Brazil, but was educated in New York and London, which explains his English. There's some family money. He's in town working on some development projects."

"And?" Chloe begged.

"That's all I know. I haven't heard about a girlfriend or wife. He'll probably be at the opening."

"I'll ask him this afternoon." She sipped on her cup smiling.

"Excuse me?" I asked.

"We're having lunch this afternoon," Chloe announced.

"What about Orlando?" I asked.

"Way to spoil my high Alex."

"I'm sorry, but aren't we going to talk about the bomb you dropped last night?" I looked around the kitchen.

Chloe exhaled. "What do you want to know?"

"What happened? How are you doing? Why didn't you tell us?" She wasn't looking at me, but at Taylor and neither of them was looking at me. I looked at Taylor. "You knew?"

"She told me a couple of weeks ago," Taylor confessed.

I looked at Kendell. "Did you know?"

"The first I heard about it was last night."

"Since when do we..."

"Alex," Chloe stopped me. "I didn't tell you because I was embarrassed. I married Orlando on impulse for what I thought were the right reasons, and it wasn't until I, we had invested some time in the relationship that things started to go sour. Now he wants out and I'm fine with it. That's what I get for not doing my homework. The next time I marry—"

"You still want to be married?" I asked.

"I love marriage, I just married a Bozo instead of a Boaz." We all laughed.

"Are you okay?" I asked.

"At first, I was upset. I thought about poisoning him, but he isn't worth the trouble. Although, I had come up with several clever ways to get rid of him that couldn't be traced back to me." She laughed. "I'm fine and I'll be even better when he files for divorce."

"What if he doesn't?" Kendell asked.

"He will." Chloe took another sip from her cup. "His side piece is putting the heat on."

"You didn't tell me that," Taylor jumped in.

"Oh yeah, he thinks I don't know and please don't tell Little Miss Sunshine about Orlando. The last thing I need is for Dionne to give me a dog." We all laughed.

Everything was going great. The store was packed. Quentin and Dionne did an amazing job with the press. I love it! I'm so glad I decided to wear the pink Dior instead of the brown Cavalli. I looked up and saw Bas headed towards me.

"Hey Boss, you look a little on edge." He kissed me on the cheek.

"I'm fine. How are the sales?"

"Let's just say, 'Welcome to Hot-lanta!'"

"That good?"

He grabbed two glasses of champagne from the waiter. "Here," he handed me one of the glasses. "I'd like to make a toast." We raised our glasses. "Here's to Hot-lanta, may it always be hot and prosperous." We clinked glasses and sipped. "I'm going to work the room and make sure everyone is happy and shopping."

I spotted Chloe in the shoe department with Marcelo. I guess lunch went well. Taylor was in accessories talking to the mayor's wife. I bumped into someone and almost fell backwards, but a strong hand grabbed my arm.

"Are you okay?"

I turned around to see who had rescued me from an embarrassing fall. I looked up and saw those incredible eyes. My heart started pounding and my stomach felt like a herd of fashionistas running to the Manolo Blahnik Summer Sale. I managed to get a few words out. "Yes. Thank you."

"The store is amazing…just like you."

It was Mr. Dark Chocolate from the party. My first thought was to flirt back, but why? Flirting with a married man, no matter how fine he is, isn't an option.

"Excuse me." I ran back to my office and closed the door. A few seconds later, a rapid knock on the door startled me.

"Alex."

I hestitated to answer. "Come in." I looked up and saw a friendly face and exhaled.

"What happened out there?" Bas asked.

"What are you talking about?"

"Did something happen with that guy you were talking to?"

"What guy??"

"Tall, dark suit. I saw you talking to him the other night. Who is he? Did he say something to upset you?"

"I don't know who you're talking about."

He closed the door. "Alex, I'm not stupid. I saw you

talking to him and then rush in here. What's going on?"

"Nothing."

"That wasn't nothing. That was definitely something."

"I don't want to talk about it."

"Do you want security to escort him out?"

"No."

"Do you want me to get him so you can talk?"

"No." I started pacing back and forth wringing my hands.

"What's going on?"

I stopped pacing. "I met him the other night at the party and…," I felt my mouth turning up into a smile. "We talked and…" Bas looked at me.

"Sleeping Beauty has finally woken up." He teased.

"What's that supposed to mean?" I folded my arms in front of my chest. I looked like a school girl fidgeting.

"It means you're ready." He smiled and kissed me on the forehead.

He opened the door and I saw the man responsible for my teenage behavior staring back at me.

I SAY IF YOU CAN'T fly on a private jet, first class is the next best thing. Once I cleared security, I headed straight for the VIP Lounge.

I searched out a couple of chairs by a window for Bas and me to relax before the flight. I dumped my bags and headed straight for the coffee station.

I reached for a cup and saucer and accidentally brushed up against someone.

"I'm sor...," I looked up and my heart jumped into my throat. I tried blinking but my eye lids were frozen. A rush of blood jump started my brain, telling my mouth to speak. "Terry."

"Lexi."

He looked as shocked as me. Of all the places to run into him. My God, this cannot be happening.

Why is it whenever you run into an ex you immediately run a memory check of how you look at that very moment? You want to make sure your memory hasn't failed you and that you look your best and your breath is great. Everything has to be right because the last time he saw you, you were a pathetic mess, but not today. There's nothing I can do or say to convince myself I look good. Looking at this man is like Superman holding a bag of kryptonite. I felt weak, confused and nervous.

"You look good." He stood up straight and looked me in the eye.

The last time I saw those eyes, they were accompanying a warm smile, wishing me a good day as I left for work.

"Thank you. So do you."

"My wife said she read you were in town."

"Your wife?" The second time in less than seventy-two hours, those two words have caused an uneasy feeling in the pit of my stomach. I needed to break away and get my hands on a dozen Xanax. Better yet, I think God would forgive me if I drank a bottle of Jack Daniels right now. My nerves were parked on a ledge waiting for the least little thing to push them over. "That's right. I read somewhere you married your college sweetheart."

"About that---"

"Please, don't." My hand started trembling. I looked up and coming towards us was *his wife*. Man, I wish I knew how to swear, because I would be on full blast.

"Alexandra, this is my wife, Blair."

Holy crap! Did he forget I know who she is?

"Nice to meet you. I've been reading about your store opening last night. Congratulations."

I know this trick did not just extend her hand towards me like she doesn't know me. "Thank you." As I spoke the words, I felt a big hand brush across the small of my back.

"Alex..."

Never in my life have I been so grateful to hear that voice.

"Let me get that for you." Bas took the cup and saucer from my trembling hand and placed them on the table. "Hello, Sebastian Deveraux." He extended his hand to Terrence.

"Terrence Pierce and this is my wife, Blair."

30

"Nice to meet you."

"Terrence and I...and Blair went to college together."

"I see."

"Sweetheart." How dare she call my man *Sweetheart*. "We better get going. You know how long it takes with the children." She turned and started walking away.

"Yeah. Uhm, it was nice seeing you again Lex...Alex. Sebastian." His lips turned up slightly.

I forced a smile.

"Terrence," Blair called out.

"Coming." He turned and walked away.

I couldn't move. That was the most uncomfortable experience I've ever had, much worse than my first pelvic exam. In fact, right about now, those stirrups are looking pretty good, because that would distract me from all the memories that brief encounter resurrected. It's been over twenty years and he still makes my stomach jump.

"Who was that man?" Bas asked.

I couldn't dance around his question like I did last night. "Uhm...did I ever tell you how I got the money to start my business?"

"Does it have anything to do with the couple we just met?"

"It has everything to do with them." I took a deep breath and continued. "My girlfriends know about Jonathan, but only a handful of people know about Terrence."

"Come on, let's sit down." He guided me back to the club chairs, we sat down and I stared out the window.

"I spent the summer before my junior year and my junior year of college working at Motif Magazine in Paris. The short version, Terrence and I met at the Louvre. We were both trying to see the Mona Lisa. Unfortunately, so was everyone else. Instead, we spent the afternoon exploring the museum and by closing time, we were in love. He was in Paris working for his father's company."

"That's your ex?"

"Have you ever wondered if it's possible to be married and no one know?" He looked perplexed. "Let me answer it for you. Yes."

"Excuse me?"

"Towards the end of summer we were hooked at the hip. We spent all of our free time together. Instead of going home for the holidays, I stayed in Paris and spent them with Terrence. Spring came and the air was filled with love. He proposed and two weeks after Valentine's Day we got married. When his parents found out, they came over and yanked him out of our apartment. The last time I saw him was that morning."

"What?"

"I finished my stint at the magazine and came home a month later. I tried blocking the entire incident from my memory. His mother thought another approach was better and mailed my copy of the annulment papers to my mother, that's how she found out."

"What!"

I couldn't bring myself to look at him. Bas and I are more like brother and sister. We talk about everything, but news like this is... "I know, it's..."

"You thought you could keep that from Miss Connie, how?"

"After the initial shock, she was disappointed in me and pissed off with them. I think things would have been fine if I hadn't been pregnant."

"What!"

"I found out I was pregnant, the same day the final annulment degree arrived."

"And..."

I cleared my throat and continued. "Mama was furious. She waited until I went out and called his mother to come over. I overheard their conversation. As far as his family was concerned, the marriage was annulled and therefore, it never existed. And if the marriage never existed then there was no 'by product'. She said

Terrence had moved on." I swallowed hard. "I still get a chill when I replay the conversation."

"Where was he?"

"I don't know."

"What about the baby?"

I tossed my head back to stop the tears from coming, but when I lowered my head, they trickled down. "I hid in the house and put in for medical leave from school."

"And?" He was on the edge of his seat.

"My son died."

"Alex." He reached for my hand.

"I was devastated...and then to see him here today, with his pregnant wife, talking about their children, it's a little much for me to handle."

"And the money?"

"His parents. They said it was for my trouble and the rent." I wiped my wet cheek.

"What!" He shook his head. "Did Jonathan know about him?"

"He and Terrence were friends and I felt he should know, so I told him everything. He said he understood because it was before we got together." Sniffling. "He knew I didn't love him like I loved Terrence, but he was willing to wait until I was ready. In time, I was able to open my heart to Jonathan. A month before he left for Europe he made me promise I'd marry him when he returned. But...," I reached inside my purse and pulled out an airline ticket and handed it to Bas. He opened the jacket and I watched as his eyes got wider as he read the ticket.

"This is dated---"

"The day before Jonathan died. My plan was to surprise him in Milan and elope."

"Crap!"

I STILL CAN'T BELIEVE I ran into Terrence and his pregnant wife. Of all the people in the world I could have bumped into, it would be my ex-husband. Even after two decades, it's still hard to say. Maybe that's because I never told anyone, so it's not a phrase I'm used to saying.

They say everyone has a secret, which is true. For some, it's bigger and more shocking than others. If the girls knew about Terrence, they would be all over me.

I looked at my watch and hesitated before picking up my phone. I scrolled through the contacts and before I could press the name, my phone rang. I pressed the Answer Call button to the sound of a panicked voice.

"Good morning Alex, I know you said don't disturb you, but I didn't know who else to call."

"Calm down Kim. What's the problem?"

"We have a VIP, and we don't have a VIP stylist available."

"Just call Bas...oh, that's right he isn't in today."

"The VIP isn't on the schedule."

"Are you sure it's a VIP?"

"Yes."

"Okay, I trust you to handle it. Put her..."

"It's a man," she interrupted. "He said he's here for his wife."

"Set him up in the Brown Suite and I'll be right there."

"Thanks Alex."

Our VIP service isn't like most stores. Our VIPs not only include celebrities and socialites. They also include the girl who happens to shop here quite frequently, and spends deep into the five figures monthly. As a courtesy, she can request a VIP appointment.

A VIP appointment includes two hours in a private dressing suite complete with refreshments and a stylist. We keep track of everything our VIPs purchase, which helps us to pre-select things for their appointments.

Meeting an unscheduled or new VIP unprepared can be horrible and a novice can't handle the pressure. A quick hair and makeup check and I headed downstairs.

My phone started ringing and I checked the screen before answering. "Yes?"

"Alex, who do you want assisting you?" Kim asked.

"Let me evaluate the situation first."

"Okay."

I approached the door, took a deep breath and put on my warm and friendly boutique owner face. I knocked on the door and let myself in. I entered and looked around for the gentleman. He wasn't sitting on the sofa, but standing off to the side with his head down. I closed the door, cleared my throat and he turned around.

"What the--"

"Hello Lexi."

My heart stopped at the sound of Terrence saying my name. "What are you doing here?"

"After I saw you at the airport, I couldn't stop thinking about you."

"Excuse me?" He started walking towards me. "Stop right there."

"You have every right to be upset with me."

"Upset is an understatement. I returned to our apartment and instead of my husband sitting on the sofa, it was your parents' attorney waiting to tell me you wouldn't be coming back."

"I'm sorry, but I had no choice. If I didn't do what they said, I would have been cut off. I had just promised to take care of you, and without money, I felt that might be a little difficult."

"But that wasn't your decision to make. We were married. I was your family."

"I'm sorry, but that's why I insisted on the trust."

"I don't know anything about a trust."

"I refused to sign the papers unless you were taken care of."

"When I was told to sign the annulment papers, Gerard gave me a check."

"A check?"

"He said it was from your parents to cover the rent and expenses."

"That's not true. I refused to leave Paris without your being taken care of."

"I was taken care of alright." I rubbed my forehead trying to absorb his words.

"I'm sorry about all of this."

"What do you want?"

"Seeing you yesterday brought back a lot of memories and feelings I thought were buried."

"What?"

"I thought we could —"

"What, be friends?"

"Why not?"

How could he just walk in here and think everything is fine? Look at him, tall, handsome, rich, perfect smile and educated. Everything a woman could ask for, including a scheming, manipulative family. Heaven help that poor girl he married. Oh, but I forgot, he married his *college sweetheart.* "I don't believe this."

"Lexi, I want you to know I really do hate what happened, but I had no choice. They said my family was in jeopardy of losing everything if I didn't marry Blair. Only thing is, no one told me." He started pacing back and forth shaking his head. "But…this is not the life I signed up for, yet, it's the one I seem to be stuck with."

"Why are you telling me this?"

"I was fine until I saw you at the airport. Never before in my life have I felt like such a failure. I thought I did the right thing, but looking at you, all I saw was what could have been. We…I mean…I should…my father…you know he…they said the marriage was the deal breaker. My family's entire existence hinged on that deal and the marriage. I had no choice. That's funny. We're not a family, we're a corporation. I didn't want to marry that woman."

Oh fabulous, now I really feel like a slug. I wish I could say he was lying, but I know him, or rather, the man I knew wouldn't lie to me.

"We all have what we feel are difficult choices to make."

"Do we? That's why I asked Jonathan to look after you."

"Look after me? What are you talking about?" He turned to face me and continued with his ramblings. "When my parents went to talk to their attorney, I called Jonathan and told him everything. He promised he'd look after you and be there for you."

"Excuse me?"

"He didn't tell you?"

"Tell me what?"

"He said you knew."

"Knew what?" This game of half statements and twenty questions is annoying. Not only am I confused, I'm very angry with the two men I thought loved me, but apparently used me in some sick version of Cyranno de Bergerac.

"Jonathan always loved you."

"I know that." This wasn't a shocking revelation.

"The moment Jonathan spotted you freshman year, he said

he was done looking. You were all he talked about."

"He never told me that."

"He said he was waiting for the right opportunity to approach you. He's the reason I tried to delay our return home. I didn't know how to tell my best friend I married the woman he loved." He pounded his fist in his hand. "He was a good man and deserved a much better person to call his best friend."

I couldn't breath.

"He never turned his back on me even though I betrayed him. I really miss him."

The sadness in his voice confused me. He sounded sincere, but even sincerity can be faked with practice. "Then, why weren't you at the funeral?"

"I was at the cemetery in the back."

"I didn't see you."

"You were wearing a brown suit with a ruffle lapel and the pin he got you in London."

"How do you know about the pin?"

"Who do you think told him you liked pink diamonds?"

"I don't want to hear anymore."

"I'm sorry, I didn't come here to upset you. I just…I should go."

I turned around and he was gone and my life was turned upside down.

Mama

THAT DAUGHTER OF MINE IS under the impression she's a grown woman. Just because she's not a teenager and I live in her house, doesn't give her the right not to check in with me.

Alexandra knows the rule, call me every morning when I'm out of town and check in. Not only do I need to know she's fine, I want to talk to her about the sales figures. I may not be as active with the stores as I once was, but I'm still in charge. So what if her name is on the building and she owns the company. I know she and Sebastian think they can handle things without me, but I know better.

I looked at the clock, she was almost out of time. I picked up my phone and it rang with a familiar ringtone. I presssed the Accept Call button before the second ring. "What's wrong?"

"Hi Mama, nothing's wrong." Her tone said otherwise.

When will my daughter learn she can't hid anything from me. The only person who knows her better than I do, is God and I have a direct line to Him when it comes to her. I spent a good portion of the night praying for her and I haven't been able to shake this uneasy feeling.

"You sound strange. What's wrong?"

"What makes you think anything is wrong?"

"You didn't call this morning like you normally do, and you've been on my mind all night. I was giving you ten more seconds and then I was calling to chew you out."

"I'm fine."

"No you're not."

"Are you calling me a liar?"

"No, I'm saying you're not telling me everything." I waited for an answer, but nothing. "Okay, if it isn't you then which one of your cousins or girlfriends did what, and to whom?"

"They're all fine," she feigned a laugh.

"I saw the figures from the opening. It was a hit, so I know that's not the problem. I know it's not boyfriend related because you don't have..."

"It's husband related."

"What are you talking about? You don't have a husband? Unless you went off and did something foolish like Chloe, which would explain..."

"I bumped into Terrence at the airport."

"Terrence." The reason for the uneasy feeling. "Did you shoot him? Is that why you're late calling me? Are you in jail because you shot that poor excuse for an ex-husband? Hang up and I'll call your uncle and have him..."

"Mama, stop it."

I took a deep breath trying to calm down. "I assume his mother was close by, considering the short leash she keeps him on. Oh, that's right, she handed those reigns over to that trifling shrew he married."

"Mama..."

"You know how I feel about him and his family. I know you don't like hearing it, but his parents' interfering was the best thing to happen to that relationship." Her sigh was an indication of her being upset with me. I really should try to be a little more sensitive. After all he was the father of my grandson. "Baby girl, are you there?"

"Yes."

"Are you okay?"

"Yeah."

"Why don't I believe you?"

"Seeing him brought back a lot of memories. I was up all night wondering what my life would have been like had we stayed together. Which brought on a whole grieving session complete with tears." She sniffled. "It's still hard, and then looking at him wondering what my son would have looked like." She sniffled again.

"I think I should come home."

"No, you've been looking forward to this time. I'm fine."

"No you're not. I can hear it in your voice. Go home."

"I can't. Bas isn't here."

"Where is he?"

"I gave him the day off." She sniffled again. "He came by the store today."

"Who?"

"Terrence."

"Did you kick him out?"

"No. I was going to and then he apologized."

"Twenty years too late."

"Mama…"

"I forgave him but it's hard forgetting what his family did to you. What did he say?"

"He said he knew Jonathan had been in love with me since freshman year and he was at his funeral."

"Uh-huh."

"He also told me he's the one that designed the pin Jonathan gave me with the pink diamonds."

"He did?" I know the brooch she's talking about. She was so excited when she showed it to me. It's a beautiful leaf shaped brooch made out of pink diamonds. I always wondered how Jonathan could afford something like that. Terrence probably paid for it.

"Yes."

"And you're okay?" I asked again.

"I'm fine."

Against my better judgment, I won't go home. I'll give her the space she needs to deal with this.

Alex

"HEY, ALEX, THANKS FOR THE day off, I really needed it. How was it around here?" Bas closed the door, walked over and sat down in one of the antique French chairs in front of my desk.

"It was kind of quiet except for my ex-husband stopping by."

"What!"

"Shocked me too. I have lived in this city most of my life and I've managed to avoid him for over twenty years. I was shocked to see Terrence the first time, let alone a second time and in my store, but..."

Bas' phone started ringing. "Excuse me. Hello...I'm with her...can't you handle it? Who is it? Did you tell her she was here? Okay, get her something to drink and tell her she'll be there in a few minutes." He pressed the button ending the call.

"Who is it?"

He looked at me and took a deep breath. "You're gonna love this. It's your ex-husband's wife."

"Not funny."

"Serious, she said Mrs. Terrence Pierce was in the Brown Suite asking for Ms. Miller."

I walked down the hall and took a deep breath. *God please hold my tongue.* I walked into the dressing room to meet my opponent. "Good morning."

"Ms. Miller, or is it Miller Pierce."

"It's Miller. What can I do for you?" I stood with my hands clasped in front of me.

"I understand my husband came to see you." She stood rubbing her swollen belly. Pregnancy wasn't agreeing with her. Or maybe it was that horrible dress she had on. Red really isn't her color.

"Yes."

"May I ask why?"

"You may," I acquiesced.

"Well?"

"Well, what?"

"Are you going to tell me what happened?"

"No. I said you could ask. I never agreed to tell you."

"I knew it was pointless coming here."

"Then why did you? For that matter, how did you know he came to see me? I know he didn't tell you."

"Let's just say, he married me, but he's always loved you." She coolly walked over to the sofa, sat down and crossed her legs at the ankle. "It's no secret my and Terrence's marriage is one-sided. It's been a long haul, but we're finally a family due to my convincing him it would be better for us to work as a team. He's a good father and he's accepted our marriage, as well as his responsibilities at the company. A couple of days ago, as luck would have it, we ran into you. In less than forty-eight hours you've managed to throw a monkey wrench into everything I've worked so hard to build up the past twenty-years." Rubbing her stomach, she cut me a hard gaze.

"I have a meeting to get to." I started toward the door.

"Do you have any idea how hard it is to get pregnant once, let alone three times by a man that despises you? Or, who for the first three years of your marriage, called out the name of his ex-wife every time he made love to you?" She stood up. "I have worked too hard to get the life I wanted, and I'm not going to let a chance encounter with you ruin everything."

"Are you finished?"

"Yes."

"I am only going to say this once. I don't want your husband and I would appreciate it if you and he both, never came into my store again. I don't know what kind of sick game the two of you are playing, but if either of you comes here again, I will call the police and have you arrested for trespassing and stalking. You know the way out. It's the same way you slithered in." I opened the door, turned and faced her with a smirk. "Isn't it amazing how, none of your scheming managed to wipe me out of Terrence's mind?"

"That's not true," she countered.

"You're right. It's not his mind where the memories of our marriage live. It's his heart." I walked out and closed the door behind me.

Kendell

I WAS WALKING ALONG THE beach and an incredibly sexy, tall, brown skinned man approached me. He smiled and a chill traveled the length of my body.

"Would you like some company?"

"That would be nice."

We strolled along the length of the white, hot sandy beach a while before he casually reached for my hand. His touch felt like I'd been shot with an electric jolt.

We stopped walking and he dragged his finger across my lips, down my chin, along my neck, just stopping at the apex of my breasts. I could barely breathe. I felt like a busty, frisky romance novel heroine. My eyes locked with his as he crushed his lips against mine, invading my mouth with his tongue. He tasted like pineapple and sweet wine. I wanted more. He pulled me closer as his hands slid down….Bzzzz…Bzzzz…Bzzzz…Crap!…Crap!…Crap! The alarm rang and I woke up soaking wet, with no memory of the rest of the dream.

I've been having this same dream once a week for the past three years. I have no idea what happens next because my alarm rings waking me up.

I was making my rounds in the restaurant and noticed a friendly face sitting at the worst table. I walked over and cleared my throat. He looked up, smiled and everything in me turned to hot jelly.

"Bas, why didn't you tell me you were coming, I would have—"

He stood up and extended his hand towards the empty chair on the other side of the table. "Please, sit down."

"Thank you, but I have to get back into the kitchen. I'm sorry about the table."

"This is my favorite table. I can see everything and everyone. And I can watch the chef at work." He smiled.

Is he coming on to me?

"So what do you suggest?"

"The salmon with fennel and sweet potato mousse is good."

"Sold."

"I wish all my customers were this easy. I'll tell your server." He sat down and I went back into the kitchen to prepare his order. About fifteen minutes later, I returned with his dinner.

"What a beautiful server."

"Thank you." I placed the plate in front of him.

I went back to the kitchen and peeked out the door as it opened and closed to see if he was eating.

The last seating was starting dessert and I looked out to see if Bas was still here. When the door opened again, I noticed he was gone. I gave final instructions and made sure the pastry chef had the dessert orders under control.

I went out to make my final turn around the main dining room and spotted the tall honey colored man with the wild hair and seductive blue green eyes sitting on the corner stool. It's been a long time since a live person made my heart race.

"I see you managed to find the second worst seat in the place." I smiled.

"I like this seat, too." He smiled.

I know his type, charming, confident, sexy, a womanizer in a designer suit. I'm not surprised he's here alone. I remember Alex said, he may be a Christian, but even they come with a little player in them. I told myself not to be fooled by his warm eyes and inviting smile.

"Can I buy you a coffee?" He motioned to the barista.

Don't look into his eyes. I knew if I looked into those blue green pools of ecstasy, I'd be a goner.

"Thank you very much." I sat down and crossed my legs.

"Can I get a coffee for the lady and a refill for myself. Thank you."

"Thanks Bobby."

"Nice touch with the chocolate chip cookies," he said, as he popped one into his mouth.

"Much better than mixed nuts I thought." I looked around. "Why are you here alone?"

"I was stood up."

I laughed before I knew it. "You've got to be kidding?" What woman in her right mind would stand him up? "I'm sorry."

"Apology accepted. Thanks to your cousin and our crazy schedules, the current love of my life has had enough. She said she's tired of Alex occupying so much of my time, job or not."

"You're kidding?"

"Nope."

"This one lasted six whole months. Just long enough to use my discount at the Zac Posen Trunk Show last month. It's my fault though. I haven't really been picking my companions for their intellect, but for their other attributes." He smiled. "It's the same story. They like the perks of my job, but not the hours or my relationship with Alex."

"I see."

"What about you? Is there anyone special in your life?"

"Yes," when I said that one little word, all the color drained from his face. "My restaurant." We laughed.

"Good one."

"The restaurant takes up most of my time. And now with me seriously considering opening one in Atlanta, I'm really stretched."

"How are you going to handle that? If you're anything like Alex, you'll want to be hands on."

I sat mesmerized watching him pop cookies into his mouth. I closed my eyes to clear my head before answering his question.

"That's why I'm not sure. The timing has to be right. I don't know how Alex is going to do it. She's already stretched pretty thin."

"I know. But I also know she wouldn't have made the move without thinking it through." He looked around the restaurant and it was almost empty. "I'm sorry Kendell, I didn't realize it was so late. Where's my bill?" He reached for his wallet.

"No," I pushed his hand back. "Dinner is on me. I know how painful it is to be stood up," I teased.

"Thank you for feeling my pain." He patted his chest. "I better go." He stood up, left a generous tip and reached into his pocket for his keys. "Thank you for dinner." He flashed that beautiful smile, put on his pimp stroll, and like a cloud of Tom Ford aftershave, he was gone.

I run a tight ship and my team knows my routine. Once they've closed up, I go behind them and double check everything. It's important we maintain our "A" rating. I checked the lock on the front door, grabbed my bags, set the alarm, and exited out the back door to my car. As I turned the key, I looked to my left and saw a familiar presence coming towards me.

"Bas?"

"Here," he reached for the key to lock the door, "let me."

"I thought you left."

"I was about to and I realized I hadn't thanked you for dinner."

"Yes you did."

"Here, let me take that for you." He reached for my bag.

"Thank you, but my car is right here." I pressed the remote, opened the door and tossed my bags onto the passenger seat. I stood up and noticed he was still here. "Is there something else you wanted?" He stepped closer and I was pinned up against the car.

"Yeah, this."

He grabbed me by the waist, pulled me to him and brushed his tongue across my bottom lip. The teasing made me want to taste him even more. My body almost betrayed me when he pulled me deeper into his space.

His sweet full lips brushed across my cheek up to my ear. My breathing escalated anticipating his next touch.

"I got tired of waiting on you to notice me." He pressed those gorgeous, sweet, full lips against mine and I felt my legs buckle and time stop.

He slid his hands down my back, and the heat from his fingers, penetrated my skin. I wrapped my hands around his neck, as my fingers sank deep into his wild thick hair. I wanted more. This surprise kiss was better than any dream kiss. He slowly pulled back and my eyes fluttered open taking in his beautiful face.

A soft sigh escaped my lips as I stared at him. What was that and can I have some more. I was in a daze. How was I supposed to drive home when I couldn't even stand up.

"I...should...," I licked my lips and grabbed the door handle. "I should be going."

He moved me to side of the door and helped me inside my car. I sat still a few moments and a sudden tap on the window broke the euphoria. I turned the car on and let the window down.

"Drive safe." He kissed me and walked away.

Alex

I HAVEN'T HEARD FROM CHLOE in a couple of weeks, and I'm starting to get worried. The last time she went missing this long, she came back with a husband.

I picked up the phone and it started ringing at the same time. I looked at the caller ID and pressed Accept Call. "Hey Chloe girl, where have you been?"

"Brazil."

"Excuse me?" *Oh God, please don't let her have done something insane.* "Did you get married?" I teased.

"Are you out of your mind? First of all, I'm still married."

"That's right. Why were you in Brazil?"

"You know the guy I met at Taylor's party?"

"The Latin Sweet Talker?"

"The Portuguese Dream."

"Excuse me." We chuckled.

"Marcelo invited me. He wanted to show me his family's ranch and *his* Brazil."

"Are you kidding?"

"No girl. It was incredible. He's incredible and dangerous."

"Dangerous?"

"Let's just say, if I weren't married, there's a good chance I would have come back with a husband." We laughed. "Anyway, have you heard from Taylor?"

"I was going to call her this afternoon. What's going on?"

"You know that young squirt she was hanging on to at the party?"

"Yeah."

"Okay, let me back up. Do you remember Gretchen Charles from school?"

"Third floor RA? Isn't she a judge? What about her?"

"You know it was always rumored she was older and had been married."

"That isn't her husband?"

"Nope, even better, her son!"

"You're kidding? How old is he?"

"Thirty-four. Can you believe it? Our friend is officially a Cougar." We laughed.

"No, I can't."

"I told her messing with those young boys was going to get her into trouble."

"How did she find out?"

"They were at his place and she noticed a picture of him with this woman that looked familiar. She asked who it was and he said his mother and that she's a judge. Taylor immediately recognized her from the alumni newsletter and girlfriend bolted."

"No."

"She's been dodging junior's calls. She said something about coming here."

"At least it wasn't a repeat of the Andrew incident." I tried containing my laughter, but it was just too funny.

After Taylor's divorce she dated this older very good-looking white man, salt and pepper hair, amazing blue green eyes, tight physique, oozing with charm and sex appeal. She called him, her sexy silver fox. He was about twenty-five years older than her. He mentored her business and introduced her to the finer things in life.

After spending an evening with them, I started thinking about dating an older man.

They were going pretty hot and heavy until he invited her to a family dinner where she saw her ex-boyfriend...his son, Neal. She immediately broke things off and went into hiding.

When she resurfaced, she swore she would be a lot more careful. I can't believe it happened to her again.

"I had forgotten all about her junior senior moment."

"I'm headed to Atlanta this weekend, so I'll get the details."

"Alex, it's not that serious that you need to go see her."

"I'm not. I'm going to check on the store."

"You just got back."

"Miss Brazil, that was almost a month ago."

"Oh...when are you leaving?"

"Friday afternoon. I want to observe the weekend flow."

"I'll see you when you get back. Tell the cougar she can run, but she can't hide." We laughed. "Bye."

"Bye."

JASON HAS BEEN CALLING ME every day since I bolted. He says all he wants to do is talk, but every time I hear his voice, I melt. His voice reminds me of a deep baritone angel. I can't talk to him, because I'll get lost in the beautiful sound of his voice and instantly forget why being with him is wrong.

I may like younger men, but I draw the line at dating a classmate's son. It's bad enough I dated my ex-boyfriend's father. Every time I think about seeing Jason's mother's picture, it re-enforces the fact that he is way too young for me, and that's a bad thing...but being bad can be very fun.

I picked up my phone and pressed Jason's number and stared at his picture. Call me weak. I pressed the button and before the second ring, my phone beeped with a call from my assistant. *Okay God, I get it. I'll leave him alone.*

"Hi Dylan."

"Oh good, I got you."

"What's up?"

"Where are you?"

"I'm coming down the street. Is the client there?"

"Yes, but I don't think....I mean, Monique called and she's a couple of blocks over and she could really use your help. I can handle things here."

"Dylan, I'm pulling into the driveway. Once I sign the papers you have for me, you go help Monique."

"But Taylor, I mean, boss, really it's no problem. I'm already here and we're almost finished with the walk-through."

I got out of the car and hurried inside. "Dylan, hang up." I pressed the button and ended the call. I walked to the kitchen. Trying to hide my anxiousness

I love this house. I actually considered selling my house and buying this one, except it's too big for me. Maybe if I had a family.

Dylan was standing in the doorway of the kitchen with a folder and a pen.

"Hey Taylor, sign where the tabs are and then you can go help Monique."

"Where's the client?"

"He's down the hall."

I took the folder and pushed past him. I put my bag on the counter and signed the papers. "Is there anything else?" I handed him the folder.

"Taylor, I really can handle this," he pleaded.

"Dylan, stop it."

I heard footsteps approaching. "Go help Monique and I'll be there as soon as I finish here."

"But..."

"Dylan...leave or find a new job." He turned and walked away.

I looked in the direction of the footsteps and saw a cute boy, tall, fair skinned, dark hair and gentle eyes. He looked vaguely familiar. Then, I heard a second set of heavier footsteps. I looked in the direction of the footsteps waiting on the client to appear.

"Hello Taylor."

"Jason..."

"I see you've met my son, Zach." He continued into the kitchen.

"Your what!" We dated for six months and he never told me he had a son. Let alone a teenager.

"Zach, why don't you check out the rest of the house, while I speak with Ms. Richards."

"Is this your idea of a joke?"

"No. I didn't know any other way to reach you. You won't take my calls or reply to my emails, texts or flowers. When you returned the bracelet, you left me no other choice."

"Jason..."

The last time I saw him I told him, well, actually, I didn't tell him. I just disappeared. I messed up this time. I generally don't pick my men for their minds but for their looks. But this one tricked me. I managed to find the one Harvard educated Muscle Head with the voice of a baritone angel and a few bucks to boot. Could it get any worse?

I folded my arms in front of my chest and looked at him searching for my next question. "You have a son?"

"Yes. It happened when I was seventeen. My girlfriend got pregnant and my mother insisted I marry her. It lasted eighteen months. She really didn't want to be a wife or a mother. She left and didn't fight for custody. My mother wouldn't allow me to put Zach off on anyone. She said the only reason she left me with my grandmother was because the school didn't have any housing for single mothers. So she made sure I had everything I needed and I saw her three times a week. I worked hard, earned a full scholarship and my mother and stepfather helped me with childcare. Zach and I spent the next four years in Cambridge."

I nodded my head and realized I wasn't dating a young man but a mature man with a plan I wanted to be a part of. I regrouped and got on the defensive. "When were you going to tell me about Zach?"

"When were you going to tell me you knew my mother?"

"Touché."

"The night you disappeared. And you?"

"I didn't know who your mother was until I saw her picture the night I...wait a minute. You knew I went to school with your mother?"

"Of course, Taylor, I'm not stupid."

"I didn't say you were."

"I like older women. I seem to have more in common with them." He gently grabbed my arm and pulled me closer. "What do you say I take you to lunch and we talk?"

"Talk? What makes you think I want to start things up with you again? Besides, now that I know this was a ploy to see me, I've got to find someone to buy this house."

"Where's the listing." I handed him the paper and he reached into his pocket, pulled out his phone and pressed a number. "Zach come to the kitchen." He ended the call and placed the phone on the counter.

A couple of minutes later I heard footsteps walking back towards the kitchen.

"Yeah, Dad."

"Son, do you like this house?"

"It's great."

"Fine. We'll take it. Full ask...in cash, providing the inspection is clean. Where do I sign?"

"Is this another trick?" I asked.

"No. Zach and I discussed getting a new place and this one is great."

"Okay then, sign right here and I'll put in the offer."

"Before I do that, I'll need a few things or there's no deal."

"You name it."

"A short escrow, a quick inspection, plus you need to rent my existing house, and lunch with me and Zach."

"You got it. I thought you would have suggested dinner." I retorted. "I need you to sign right here."

He leaned in close and whispered, "You get the seller to

agree to my offer, plus the first two things on my list by the end of lunch and I'll take you wherever you want for dinner." He signed the papers and handed them to me.

"Seems we're all done here."

"So where would you like to go for lunch?"

I smiled and looked at Zach. "Anywhere Zach wants to go."

"Dear God, please don't let today be one of those days when I wish I had my own plane."

I APPROACHED THE AIRPORT CHECK-IN counter in the VIP lounge believing God heard my prayer. The woman in front of me was going on and on about her trip to Atlanta, and how excited she was to see her new grandson. The shrill of her voice was working my nerves. The nightmare escalated when she turned and said, "I know you."

"Excuse me."

"I've been to your store."

"You have."

"Yes, and I have a complaint."

"Excuse me?"

"You have some beautiful things, but not everyone can wear those clothes and the prices are..."

"Ma'am you're all checked in straight through to Atlanta. Is there anything else I can do for you?" the concierge asked.

"Yes, if my friend here is going to Atlanta, can you please seat her next to me." She requested as she pointed to me.

"Thank you, but I'm headed to New York," I quickly blurted out.

"Maybe we can sit together from here to Dallas?" she suggested.

"I don't think that will be possible." I turned around to see who was rescuing me. *Mr. Dark Chocolate* from the party. "My fiancée and I have a lot of things to discuss." He kissed me on the cheek and continued to speak. "Honey, I'm sorry, my breakfast meeting ran a little longer than I expected."

"No problem." I tried not to look stunned at my handsome hero.

"Moses Adair and who's your lovely friend?" He extended his hand to the annoying woman.

"Mrs...I'm sorry, I didn't get your name?"

"Mrs. Randall," she quickly replied.

"Pleasure to meet you." He shook her hand and I stood back watching the middle aged woman melt when he smiled at her.

"Honey, she's on her way to visit her new grandson." I played along.

"Congratulations, Mrs. Randall. Thank you for offering to keep my fiancée company. However she's promised to spend the entire trip discussing wedding plans."

She giggled and replied, "It was no problem at all."

I couldn't believe what I was witnessing. Not less than thirty seconds ago, this woman was telling me how expensive the clothing is in my store. And now, she's flirting with my fake fiancé.

"Did you check in?" he asked me.

"No, I was about to."

"Give me your ticket and I'll get us checked in."

I handed him my ticket and nosey Mrs. Randall kept yammering on about the lack of affordable and practical clothing in my stores while eyeing Moses. Finally, my hero completed our check-in and turned to rejoin the conversation.

"Mrs. Randall, it was a delight speaking with you. If you don't mind, I haven't seen my fiancée all day, and I would really prefer she chew me out before we board the plane."

"Oh, sure," she giggled again.

I think if she were a little younger, she'd be trying to get with him. Too bad he's married, otherwise, I'd be trying to get with him.

"Have a good trip and congratulations on your grandson." I nodded my head and smiled as he placed his hand on the small of my back and guided me to a quiet section in the Lounge.

"Thank you for rescuing me."

"My pleasure. Let's sit here."

We sat in a couple of club chairs in front of a window with a view of the planes coming in and going out. I knew who my hero was and his timing was perfect. When I looked at his mouth while he spoke, all I could hear were those words he uttered at Taylor's party "my wife." Where is she? I kept waiting on her to appear or for his telephone to ring with a call from her reminding him to bring home a goody for the kids.

"You are the last person I expected to see at the airport. I thought you lived in Atlanta?"

"I was in Los Angeles on business."

"I see. Do you travel a lot?" He is definitely a reason not to want my own plane. I don't mind being body scanned or dealing with crying babies if it means I can sit next to him the entire flight. What am I thinking…he's married. *Forgive me God for lusting after another woman's husband, but she truly is blessed. Can I have one like him?*

"Not as much as I used to." He reached into his bag and pulled out a thick bound document and began reading.

"Your family must be pleased about that."

"I guess."

This is taking small talk to a whole new level. "I see you're a man of few words." I pulled a magazine out of my bag, copying his move.

"I speak when there's something worth commenting on." He continued his reading.

"So I'm boring?"

"Is there something you want to ask me?"

"Excuse me?"

"I sense there's something on your mind?"

"Where's your wife and did you stop seeing Taylor because your wife found out?"

"How long have you been sitting on that one?"

I looked over and nosey Mrs. Randall was looking at us. He put his document down and looked me in the eye.

"My wife died shortly after we were married. I foolishly let a friend set me up with Taylor after what I thought was a reasonable grieving period only to find myself talking too much about my wife. Something Taylor took offense to. I'm sure I wasn't the only man at the party she had dated." His tone was sharp and a vast contrast to his earlier behavior.

I cleared my throat. "May I please have my ticket?" He reached into his jacket pocket, pulled out a ticket and handed it to me. "Thank You."

"You're welcome." He redirected his attention back to his document.

I looked at my ticket. "I think you gave me your boarding pass." He reached inside his jacket pocket and pulled out the other ticket and read it.

"I'm sorry."

"No problem."

"I normally sit by the aisle, but I'm willing to let you have the aisle."

"What are you talking about?"

"Is that all you're taking?"

"I'm only going for a week. Besides, if I need anything else, I can always pick up something from my store."

"I didn't know you had a store in New York."

"I don't."

"Then I hope you have a gown packed in that small bag."

"What are you talking about?"

He looked at his watch. "We can get you a dress in the morning."

"Excuse me?"

"I figure since I rescued you from a few hours of Mrs. Randall, a suitable reward, would be for you to go with me to my sister's engagement party, in New York."

"Are you out of your mind?" I know why Taylor stopped seeing him, he's crazy.

"Or you can sit next to Mrs. Randall on your way to Atlanta."

"Or I can take a later flight."

"Everything is booked until tomorrow afternoon."

"But I think--"

He put his document down and aimed those mesmerizing light brown eyes at me. "I have to attend this family thing and I don't want to go alone. You would be helping me out by coming with me."

"As appealing as your invitation sounds, I don't think so. Up until a few minutes ago, I thought you were a cheating husband who dated my cousin. Thank you, but I need to go to Atlanta to check on my store."

I went back to the check in desk. Crap! It was just as he said. There were no flights available until late tomorrow. Crap! I If I go home I'm faced with the stalking antics of my ex-husband and his pregnant wife, or I can spend four plus hours listening to a crazy woman tell me how to restock my stores without benefit of a Xanax, or I can escort my cousin's gorgeous ex-boyfriend to his sister's engagement party.

I went back to my seat and didn't say anything.

"I take it you weren't able to change your flight," he smirked.

"Shut up."

"Now is that anyway to talk to your fiancé? You wouldn't want Mrs. Randall to come over here."

"You know I could have you arrested for kidnapping."

"And it would probably be a lot more fun than going to this party."

"Is crazy a family trait?"

"No, I think it skips a generation." We laughed. "I'm sorry. I should have told you about my wife and daughter, but it's a difficult subject for me. This family function is not something I'm looking forward to either."

"When did your wife die?"

"Eight years ago."

"And your daughter?"

"She would have been eight." He took a deep breath and continued his story. "Natalie died during childbirth. She had an aneurism and never saw the baby." His eyes began to fill with water as he continued. "My daughter's name was Allegra..."

"Allegra Adair?" I tried to stiffle my laugh.

He smiled. "I know it's strange, but my wife was an artist."

"Oh."

"Allegra lived two weeks. Natalie's parents live in Atlanta and that's where I buried them. I go there every year on Allegra's birthday to spend the day with my former in-laws. That's why I was in Atlanta that weekend."

He's sensitive. You can fake a lot of things, but the emotions he's sharing are real. I need to find nosey Mrs. Randall and send her a gift card to the store. Because of her annoying prodding, I might be in for the ride of my life.

"Well, seeing I'm headed to New York, I need to make hotel arrangements."

"No need, there's plenty of room at my house."

"Excuse me, Mr. Adair. I agreed to go to the party. However, I'm not in the habit of staying at the home of a man I don't know. Thank you, but I'll call the Surrey or Mondrian and..." I reached for my phone and he grabbed my wrist.

"It will be very late when we land, you can stay at my house tonight and I'll stay at the Surrey. If you still feel uncomfortable in the morning, I'll pick up the tab at any hotel you want. Deal?"

I hesitated before answering. "I must be out of my mind... deal."

"Now that that's settled, would you like something from the bar?"

"A mineral water would be nice, thank you." He stood up and nosey Mrs. Randall was staring at us. He leaned down and kissed me behind my ear and I felt an electric surge shoot through my body. I began smiling and at that moment, all I wanted was some ice to cool down.

Dear God, please help me not to do something insane. It's been a while since I felt like this for anyone, and I don't want to do something I'll regret. In Jesus' name, Amen.

I love the flight to New York, it's a great time to catch up on work. But this time it's a little different. I'm flying next to a beautiful man I know very little about, except he used to date my cousin, he makes my heart race, my body temperature soar and he's a widower.

During the flight, we continued the charade because Mrs. Randall was sitting across from us. Occasionally, Moses would lean over and whisper. By the time we got to Dallas for the connecting flight to JKF, I knew I was in trouble.

"Uhm, Moses, I really think it would be best if I stayed at a hotel." Just as he was about to speak, Mrs. Randall walked by.

"Sweetheart, I completely understand your concerns, but I wouldn't do anything to make you feel uncomfortable. Trust me?"

I looked into those mesmerizing eyes and smiled.

When we landed in New York, my stomach was in knots. We deplaned and Moses was quite the gentleman. I followed him out to the curb where a black Bentley and driver were waiting for us.

"Good evening, Son. How was your flight?"

"Excellent. Otis, I'd like you to meet Ms. Miller, she's going to be staying with us for a few days, I hope." He looked at me with a huge smile.

"Hello." I don't know what he and this old man are up to, but as soon as I'm safely in the city, I'm heading to the nearest five-star hotel and the first flight to Atlanta.

The drive from the airport into the city is one of two things, very long or very short. When your nerves are on edge, the ride is very long. Maybe we should have brought Mrs. Randall with us, because alone in the car, he didn't have anything to say. I caught him looking at me but he quickly turned his head.

I've been to New York hundreds of times, but never have I been this nervous. It was hard to hear myself think with the voice in my head telling me to run. I'm a grown woman and right now, I feel like a teenager on a secret date.

After what felt like hours, the car pulled up in front of a beautiful townhouse on the Upper Eastside. Otis got out and took care of our bags, while Moses helped me out of the car. We walked up the steps and there he was again with his hand on the small of my back. Every time he touches me, I feel faint.

Before we reached the iron door, it opened and a petite, dark skinned woman, with salt and pepper hair, glasses and wearing an apron appeared.

"Hi Son. How was your flight?" She reached up to hug him.

"Hi Mrs. Joseph, it was great. I see you're wearing your pink apron." He bent down and kissed her on the cheek.

"It's in honor of our guest. This must be Alexandra." She smiled.

"Hello." I returned the smile.

"We're not that formal. Come here baby and give me a hug."

What have I gotten myself into?

"Come on let's get you settled. Moses says you're a little concerned about staying here."

"Well, I thought…" I crossed the threshold and followed Mrs. Joseph up the stairs as she continued singing Moses' praises.

"Don't worry, he's a gentleman. Besides, he knows I don't tolerate any funny business, especially on my watch."

"And you would be?"

"I'm second in command. Here we go, the second door." She opened the door and I followed her inside and forgot how to speak.

The room was beautiful and just like being at home. The bed was made with crisp white sheets with pink embroidery on the edges. Vases of pink roses were everywhere…on both night stands, the bathroom counter, the desk and around the bathtub.

A small table next to the chaise, housed a stack of international fashion magazines, bottled water, Asian pears, almonds and dark chocolates…all of my favorite things complete with a hot bubble bath and my favorite Diptyque candles surrounding the tub. When did Moses have time to do this?

"Beautiful." I mumbled.

"What was that dear?"

"Nothing." I was trying to absorb all the details in this beautiful space.

"We usually put guests on the fourth floor, but Moses thought you might be more comfortable on the second floor, next to me."

"How many floors are there?"

"Six plus a basement. She walked over to the night table and pointed at the telephone. "If you need anything, you can reach me or Otis on line three."

"What about Moses?"

"His office is line five...that's all you need to know."

Her response was her polite way of telling me I'm not allowed past the second floor. "Yes ma'am."

She walked over and hugged me. "Sleep well." Code for take a bath and go to bed...alone.

"You too. Good night."

She closed the door and I exhaled. I peeled off my clothes and got into the tub. It was just what I needed. The water was very invigorating, like being in a rose garden. Moses was making it extremely difficult not to stay here.

After my bath, I quietly explored the downstairs and got distracted when I saw the kitchen. It looked like I was standing inside the pages of Architectural Digest. Large marble topped island surrounded by dark walnut stools, a large double Viking stove a wall sized Sub Zero refrigerator, two dishwashers and a deep fryer. Those were just the things I saw. I'm sure behind the dark cabinet doors, were enough gadgets and appliances to stock a William-Sonoma store.

I looked around and spotted a plate of chocolate chip walnut cookies. Tempting.

I walked over to the cookies and began to reach for one when I heard footsteps and someone clearing their throat. I looked up and saw Moses standing in the doorway with his arms crossed and smiling.

"Whatcha doing eating my snack?" he asked.

"I'm sorry."

"Everybody knows you can't eat chocolate chip cookies without milk." He walked over to the refrigerator, pulled out the milk and a couple of glasses out of the cabinet. "Mrs. Joseph knows I like to forage at night while I'm working, so she leaves me a snack. Sometimes, it's a plate of cookies, a slice of cake, a couple of chicken salad sandwiches or my favorite, banana pudding."

"These are so good. I thought you were gone."

"I have to pack. How's your room?"

"It's not a five star hotel...it's better." I smiled. "How did you know what I like?"

"That's my secret. I take it you're staying?"

"If you insist."

"Good. I better get upstairs and pack."

"You know, I was thinking. This place is huge and I think I'll be safe next door to Mrs. Joseph."

"Thank you. I'm exhausted. I just want to crash. Well, I better go. I don't want Mrs. Joseph on my case about keeping you up. Good night." He lingered in the doorway awhile before walking away.

"Can I ask you something?" Keep your cool girl. He's just a man. "What are you doing? Who are you? I don't know anything about you and against my better judgment I'm staying in your house. I appreciate the hospitality, but I would really like to know something about my date for the weekend." Man, I used the "D" word, that's not good.

"I kidnapped you, or rather, I asked you to come to New York because my sister is announcing her engagement this weekend with a huge party, and I didn't have a date."

"Which I find hard to believe."

"It's true. The women I've been dating are shallow, boring and looking for a sponsor. I didn't want to go to this party with some wannabe socialite. I wanted someone fun that would make this whole thing a lot easier."

"What if I'd said no?"

"Then I guess I would have gone by myself."

"Or you could have taken Mrs. Joseph."

"She has a date, Otis, her husband."

"Really?" I smiled

"Yes." He smiled. "Who am I? I'm a single man living on the Upper Eastside with a housekeeper and driver who have been with my family longer than I have."

"That's what you are. Who are you?"

He scratched his head, and sat on the stool.

"I grew up in the city and I have a younger brother and

sister."

"That's nice. But who are you?"

"I'm sort of the black sheep in the family. My parents forced me to study Finance and Economics, but I wanted to be a writer. While I was in college I wrote a book and managed to get an agent who shopped it all over town, but no one wanted it. My agent never gave up. Instead, he told me to keep writing and I told him to keep trying. My parents threatened to cut me off if I didn't join my dad's company. I liked my life, so I gave in and joined the family business. Everything was in place, all I had to do was show up. Two days before I was to start, my agent called with a three book deal."

"No way?"

"It seems the reader originally assigned to my manuscript left and my book was misplaced. When it finally resurfaced, the publisher liked it. Long story short, the book became a best seller and eventually a play."

"No way."

"Yeah way." He mocked me and laughed.

"I've written twenty-five books and four became plays. I was in L.A. to discuss turning one of my books into a movie. I'm very grateful for everything God has done for me."

"Wow."

"It's taken a while to gain my family's respect, but I never really cared what they thought. All that matters is what God thinks. So here I am, the black sheep in a townhouse on the Upper Eastside."

"Wait a minute, you aren't Darryl Moses…are you?"

"In the flesh." He smiled and bowed.

"You look different in person. I'm sorry. That didn't come out right."

"I get that a lot…it's the glasses." He teased.

"No, it's your face."

"Excuse me?"

"That didn't come out right either." He started laughing and I covered my mouth with my hands. "I mean, on your books you have a full beard and your eyes are much darker." In person his eyes seemed to dance and his smile was mesmerizing. "I'm sorry." I smiled.

He rubbed his smooth jawline. "That was my agent's idea, as well as the dark contacts."

"Taylor never told me she knew you. I've read all of your books. My favorite is "One Last Kiss." I love how the wife poisons her cheating husband by kissing him good-bye with mango flavored lip-gloss knowing he's allergic. He was so naive. Just goes to show how simple some men can...oh...that came out wrong. I seem to keep putting my foot in my mouth."

He laughed. "That's okay."

"I'm sorry, but come on, what made him think she really wanted him back, especially when she had that fine young man waiting in the wings?"

"I'm glad you liked it."

"Wow, Darryl Moses. So Mr. Moses, tell me, what you have planned for me this weekend?"

"It's Moses and that's a surprise." He took a sip of his milk and it turned his mustache white. He looked sweet and innocent. I laughed and imagined him as a child sneaking into the kitchen at night, looking for milk and cookies.

"What's so funny?" I reached over to wipe the milk, but he grabbed my hand. "Do I have a milk mustache?"

"Just a little one." I turned my glass up to give myself one as well.

"Twins." We laughed. "Now that you know a little about me, it's your turn."

"Me, I'm boring." I sipped my milk. "I didn't have the childhood you had. Mine was a little more traditional. Grew up in the suburbs, went to college in the south with my cousins Taylor and Kendell. That's where I met my other best friends, Chloe and Dionne. I love fashion and by way of a private investor, I received the money to start my business. I was engaged, but he died on a business trip a week before our wedding."

"I'm sorry."

"Don't be. I mean....that came out wrong. I think he loved me more than I loved him and that's what delayed our getting married." I felt my eyes tearing up. "We met in college. Maybe if I hadn't been so self absorbed...by the time my heart caught up to his, it was too late. He was gone and it's something I've been working hard to get over."

"But you can't, not on your own." A tear rolled down my face and he leaned over and gently wiped my cheek. "I mean you can, but you've got to be willing to give it up to God. Once you do, you'll be able to forgive yourself and move on."

"So tell me, who's the woman we're trying to fool?"

"What woman?" He smiled.

"The ex-girl friend your mother or sister invited."

"How did you know?"

"Female intuition."

"Vanessa Toliver, my ex-fiancée. I met her a couple of years after college. We dated about four years and again after Natalie died."

"So what caused the breakup?"

"Me. I loved her, but not like she wanted. You know sometimes, you have to hurt yourself in order to save someone else. As much as I loved her, I wasn't in love with her. What about you?"

"I already told you."

"Who was the guy that stopped you from marrying the fiancé?"

"What makes you think---"

"The fiancé isn't the cause of the heartache you're wearing."

"Am I that transparent?"

"Yes."

"That's a story for another time."

"Why?"

"It's too painful and I'm not ready to share it with myself let alone anyone else. Okay my turn, you said you dated Taylor briefly, please explain, because I can't ---"

"My relationship with your cousin lasted a total of one

coffee date, a brunch, two dinners and a charity event at my parents' place in Atlanta."

"What happened?"

"She's a good friend, but I realized we weren't right for each other. The few times we went out I think I bored her talking about my wife and daughter. So as a thank you, I asked her to be my date at a charity event my parents were hosting. She's fun and I knew she'd make the evening bearable. Plus, it was a great networking opportunity for her."

"Why didn't you ask her to be your date this weekend?"

"I didn't want to." Short, simple and to the point. "If you don't want to go, we don't have to."

"Excuse me? You kidnap me and now you say we don't have to go to the party? No mister, we're going."

"If you insist." There's that smile again. Now I know how Chloe ended up married after three days. Many a woman has done something impulsive because of a gorgeous smile, dancing eyes, hard chest and tight behind.

"Did you kiss her?"

"Why do you want to know that?"

"Because…"

"No." I wanted to smile, but I didn't want him to read too much into it. "My turn. Tell me about your parents."

"My parents are divorced. They had been married twenty-three years and the relationship just snapped. What was good turned sour. He became controlling and she didn't like being controlled. She grew and he didn't. I think they stayed together as long as they did because of me. When it fell apart it was wicked and it made me rethink my views on marriage."

"How?"

"I'm not sure if it's something I want to do."

"You're kidding?"

"Apart from the prior relationship, my Dad's behavior is my other reason for not wanting to get married. I figured I would be better off being inseminated and raising a baby by myself."

"Really?"

"But with a lot of prayer and a strong belief that a child really needs both a mother and father, is what got me over my fear and I finally set a wedding date, and you know the rest. What about you, is marriage something you want to do again?"

"I've always wanted to be married. My problem has been finding the right woman. My fiancée didn't really love me and my wife cheated on me."

"I'm sorry."

"But I've moved on."

"So what's your type? What are you looking for?"

"A good thing."

I know he didn't just say the magic words. Settle down girl.

"I want someone I can trust, that's supportive, she has to love God, and like chocolate chip walnut cookies," he smiled. "I'm not one of those people who treats dating like a hobby. I have plenty to keep me busy. After I broke up with Vanessa the second time, I asked myself why was I dating?"

"And?"

"I found out dating was really life mate interviewing and until recently, there was no one I wanted to interview."

I scratched my head. "It's getting late. I better get some sleep if I'm going to make your ex-fiancée jealous. Good night." I started toward the doorway.

"Good night and thank you."

"You're welcome."

Dear God, what is this You have presented me with? It's certainly an unexpected treat. I could easily see myself with this man or one like him. He's charming, funny and easy to talk to. I like him. It's been a long time since I felt like this. God, I'm trusting You to guide me in this new friendship. In Jesus' name, I pray, Amen.

Alex

IT'S A LITTLE AFTER SIX at home. I don't want to wake Bas, but I really need to let him know where I am. Maybe I can have him call Mama and tell her where I am. I dialed the number and hoped the right words would come.

"Good morning."

"Where are you?" When she didn't say hello, I knew I was toast.

"I'm in New York."

"Why? I thought you were headed to Atlanta?"

"I ran into a friend at the airport and they asked if I'd accompany them to a family function for moral support."

"Uh-huh."

"How are my aunties?"

"I'm at home."

"You are?"

"Yes. I would have come back sooner, but your Aunt Ada asked me to stay and help her with a project at her church."

"Oh."

"In fact, I was in your office when Mr. Adair from the hotel called to confirm your reservation and VIP request."

"That's how he did it," I mumbled.

"Did what?"

"Nothing. I'll be home Monday."

"You sure there's nothing you want to tell me?"

"No, everything's fine."

"I don't believe you...be careful...love you."

"Love you too, Mama. Bye."

"Bye baby."

I continued my walk down Madison and made a right onto Fifty-Seventh Street, stopping to pay homage to Chanel and Hermes, before heading across Fifth Avenue to Bergdorf's. Ten o'clock straight up. I popped inside and headed straight for Zac Posen. God knows it hurts my heart to pay full price for a dress. If I had an extra day, I would have had Bas overnight me something from the store.

I love being in this store. It reminds me of being in church. It's like you can hear the clothes calling you, unlike my store, where the music sets the tone enticing you to buy. An hour into my shopping trip, my phone rang interrupting my solitude.

"Hello."

"Good morning early bird." That voice.

"Good morning. How did you get this number? Wait let me guess, the same way you got the information about my favorite things?"

"I'm not saying. Where are you?"

"Bergdorf's."

"Checking out the competition?" He teased.

"More like supporting the economy. Remember, I need a dress."

"I was going to go with you."

"Why?"

"My treat since you agreed to be my date."

"Thanks for the offer, but..."

"Wanna grab lunch?"

"BG's at one?"

"Actually, I had some place else in mind."

"Where?"

"Meet me at the fountain in front of the Plaza at one. Have everything delivered to the house. See you later. Bye."

"Bye."

I checked my watch because I didn't want to be late. Is this a date? If I don't treat it like a date, I'll be fine. It's only when it's a date that it becomes scary.

I looked across the street at all the people having one of those great weekends in the city you hear about. Jonathan and I always talked about coming here for a spontaneous romantic weekend.

I like the person I am when I'm here. Relaxed, chic, culturally sophisticated. I really should consider opening a store here, maybe a petite atelier. Something very French, with a strong emphasis on personal styling and emerging designers with couture skills. I could buy a townhouse. I'd live upstairs and have the atelier downstairs...like Coco Chanel.

All this day dreaming and the light hasn't even changed. I looked across the street and spotted Moses sitting at the fountain reading a newspaper. I walked across the street with the crowd and stopped once I got in front of Moses and lightly kicked his foot. He looked up and flashed that beautiful smile.

"Good afternoon."

"Good afternoon."

"Did you find a dress?"

"I did indeed and a great pair of shoes too. So where are we eating, I'm starving."

"Here." He stood up.

"Here?" All I saw was the hot dog vendor. "Hot dogs? You've got to be kidding!"

"And what's wrong with a New York City hot dog?" I know he saw the confused look on my face. Then he started laughing. "I'm kidding. Come on let's get a taxi. "

Like the fool I am, I hopped into the taxi as this romantic adventure continued. Oh crap, I used the "R" word. A few minutes later, we were in the middle of Times Square.

The taxi made a right turn and we got out and walked down the block mid way to a diner in the theatre district.

We walked in and went to a booth in the back of the restaurant. We slid into the red patent leather booth under the most hideous green Formica tabletop. I looked around the diner surveying the hideous décor, hoping the food was a lot better.

"So, what's good?" I asked.

"Everything."

"You have got to be kidding."

"Trust me, the food is great. I come here at least once a week. It reminds me of my grandmother's cooking," he confessed.

"Okay, then what do you suggest?"

"I love the chicken fried steak."

"Well, my hips and that dress I just bought won't like it. What else?"

"Chicken pot pie."

"Really?"

He smiled. "Okay, what about the grilled cheese and tomato soup?"

"That was my grandmother's cure all."

"Then it's grilled cheese."

The waitress came over and took our order. While waiting for our food, I probed some more. "So tell me, what do you normally do on the weekend?"

"I've tried not working on the weekends, but it doesn't always work out that way. I make it a point to play golf with my dad and brother a couple Saturdays a month and Sundays are reserved for family."

"What about friends?"

"Between our crazy schedules, we get together for lunch or dinner during the week." He sipped his water. "What about you?"

"Work and church."

"You're kidding."

"What...I love what I do. I've poured myself into those stores. They're my children and I have to make sure they're taken care of. Being away from them this weekend is so out of character for me. In my circle, I'm the sensible one, the planner. Being spontaneous isn't my style. Going off to New York on a whim, isn't me. Going to New York for a planned buying trip, very much me."

"What about friends?"

"My girlfriends are my family. We talk daily and spend a lot of time together, and we go to the same church." I took a sip from my glass. "So, how many other women have you kidnapped?"

"It's not a habit if that's what you're thinking." He smiled. "I only kidnap women who make me laugh."

"You are so full of crap," we laughed.

"Seriously, when I met you at Taylor's, I knew you were someone I wanted to get to know, but--"

"Then--"

"Let me finish. I had my eye on you the moment you entered the room. It took me all night to work up the courage to come over and introduce myself. I enjoyed talking to you. You made me laugh."

"I'm glad I could amuse you."

"I think I became a work-a-holic so I wouldn't have to be around my ex so much. Somewhere along the way Vanessa stopped being fun. Our lack of communication drained us emotionally. We both had moved on, but neither of us was willing to make it official. Instead, I cheated on her with my work and she cheated on me with her ex-boyfriend."

"What?"

"I guess she thought if I saw someone else wanted her, it would move me to marry her."

"And?"

"That relationship was over the first time."

"Then why did you go back?"

"For the same reason it took you so long to agree to marry your fiancé, loneliness. I was very lonely and thought the comfort of someone familiar was the answer."

It was at that moment I realized, I was falling for him.

Dionne

FABULOUS, I HAVE THE DISPLEASURE of spending the afternoon with my mother-in-law. I love my husband, but his family is a horse of another breed. They are the perfect example of how having money doesn't equal class.

My sister-in-law, Regina, is hosting the annual clinic fundraiser at her house, or as I like to call it the annual snooze fest. The only reason she invited me is because Quentin asked her to include me in family functions. He really didn't have to do that. I would have been very comfortable spending the afternoon at the spa, or sitting in my lovely backyard with the latest Darryl Moses book, and a pitcher of sangria.

My sister-in-law has a beautiful house. It's tastefully decorated to suit her mother. Which means it's always party perfect. Everywhere I turn, I see one boring Botox injected face after another. I wonder... when these women blink, do their eyes close or do they just blink in theory. There's not one wrinkle in sight unless you count the ripples in the pool. Not to mention all the saline and silicone on display.

Standing across the garden overseeing everything is my mother-in-law, the queen bee. She actually told me to call her for an appointment. She said, "Dionne dear, you need to call the office and schedule an appointment so we can get you started on those fertility treatments. As if it would ever let her anywhere near my nether region."

I looked up and saw Chloe. Whenever she's around this society crowd she takes charge. Most of these women are friends of her mother which means Chloe tries to be on her best behavior, but occasionally, she slips up.

Every year she makes the same entrance. She stops by my mother-in-law's table and hands her a big fat check. That way, whatever she may do or say, the rest of the afternoon is a blur. My mother-in-law may not like me, but she loves my friend's money.

"Hey girl." Air kiss.

"Thanks so much for coming. I see you paid your admission."

"You didn't even have to ask."

"Where's Kendell? I thought she was coming with you?"

"She said she had a stop to make and she'd be a little late."

"Oh."

"That husband of yours must really be something special for you to put up with this every year. I commend you. The best thing that idiot head I'm married to did for me was file for separation. Now he can make me the happiest woman in the world by filing for divorce. Where's the waiter?" She looked around the garden.

"I thought you were seeing someone?"

"I was until my attorney said it wasn't good for my case. He said I need to play up the abandoned wife angle. Which means no fun for Chloe. What about you? Are you going to let your mother-in-law shoot you up with baby making juice?"

"Chloe!"

"What?" She laughed. "So where's Quentin?"

"Playing golf with his dad and brother-in-law."

I looked to my left and saw my sister-in-law walking towards us with one of her pampered, stuck-up friends. Please don't stop, please don't stop, please don't stop. Oh crap. They stopped.

She tries her best to say very little to me, let alone speak to my friends. So, why the change today?

"Good afternoon, Dionne."

"Good afternoon, Regina."

"Good afternoon, Chloe. Thank you for the donation."

"You're welcome."

"It's because of people like you that the clinic is able to do the work it does."

"Has anyone seen the waiter?" Chloe asked looking around the garden. "Twenty-five thousand dollars and I can't even get a glass of water." Regina turned and signaled for a waiter to come over with a tray of Bellinis.

"I'm sorry. We're using a new serving company this year." Regina apologized. The waiter walked over and handed each of us a glass.

"Thank you," Chloe said.

"Oh, forgive me, Blair Pierce, this is my sister-in-law, Dionne, and her friend Chloe Jacobs."

We all shook hands. "I see the caterer is signaling me. Excuse me ladies." She disappeared and left us with her friend.

"I asked Regina to introduce me because I believe we went to college together. You would have known me as Blair Abrams."

I think I would have remembered someone as pretentious as this woman. "Chloe, do you remember Blair Abrams?"

"No."

"I believe we had Humanities together. You probably remember my boyfriend or rather my husband Terrence Pierce… tall, dark, very handsome. One of his fraternity brothers dated your friend, Alexandra."

"That's right. Now I remember," Chloe nudged me.

84

"Dionne, you remember."

"Oh yeah." I played along.

"How is Alexandra? Is she here?" Blair asked looking around the garden.

"No," Chloe answered.

"I love her store. She has excellent taste, but I don't have to tell you that. You probably shop there all the time," she said, rubbing her belly. "I'm hoping to go on a little shopping spree there once this little one gets here. I told Terrence I have to experience the full VIP treatment. I've heard it's like having your own personal fashion godmother." She looked across the garden and waved at another Botox princess. "Excuse me. It was good seeing you. Bye." She turned and waddled away.

"Bye." We said in unison.

"Chloe, who was that?"

"I haven't got a clue." She sipped from her glass.

Her phone started ringing and she looked at the caller ID and smiled. I tried to look over her shoulder to see who she was texting, but she turned away.

"Is that him?"

"Yes." She smiled.

"I thought you weren't allowed to see him?"

"My attorney didn't say anything about texting. Besides, we're working on a deal."

"Be careful."

"I will."

YOU KNOW THAT SAYING, "WHAT happens in Vegas stays in Vegas?" Take it from me, that's a bunch of crap. What happens in Vegas packs itself up and comes home with you and I should know because that's what happened to me.

When I met Marcelo at Taylor's party, I really should have known better, but he is so fine. In the daylight he looked a lot different. You have to be careful when you meet someone in a place that isn't lit very well.

After seeing him in the light of day, it was worse than I imagined. This was a beautiful, sinful Brazilian dream...jet balck, wavy hair, green grey eyes and lips, I imagined doing things to me, Orlando couldn't even...my God. And thanks to my idiot head, hopefully soon-to-be ex-husband, I have to stop seeing him, otherwise I might lose the upper hand in any future divorce deliberations. But Marcelo would be worth it. I get all hot in certain places just thinking about him.

I told Marcelo all about Orlando and my attorney's

suggestion that I not get involved with anyone right now. However, my attorney should know when it comes to my personal life, I only do a fraction of the things he suggests.

So Marcelo and I are phone dating. At first I felt a little strange mixing business with pleasure, but Orlando left me. Which makes me single and free to see whomever I choose.

Marcelo keeps asking when I'm coming back to Brazil, but I just can't risk being seen with him in a social setting. Publicly, we have to remain distant business associates.

Once the deal is complete and Orlando and I are divorced, I'm headed to Brazil. Until then, I'll have to settle for texting, emailing, video dating and some great phone calls. I've been wearing my Rosetta Stone CDs out. I can almost order lunch and buy a bathing suit in Portuguese.

I walked inside and sitting in the family room was my albatross. I know I should have changed the locks. That's just another example of my incompetence when it comes to men.

I want Orlando out of my life, but it doesn't seem like it's going to happen without some prodding. I constantly tell myself to be nice because I want him to leave. I placed my bag on the table, took a deep breath and tried to be polite.

"Good evening."

"Hey."

"Where have you been?" I asked.

"Vegas."

"Vegas. Interesting. Alone?"

"No, me and the fellas."

"I see."

"And you?"

"Clinic fundraiser." My phone dinged and I reached inside my pocket and pulled it out. It was a text from Marcelo. The sight of him brought a smile to my face and a heat surge through my body. Man I gotta get back to Brazil. I sent my response and turned my attention back to Orlando. "Will you be staying for dinner?"

"You moved my clothes?"

"I thought you would be more comfortable in one of guest rooms since we're separated. Are you staying for dinner?" I asked again.

"I'll have it in my room."

"Will you be staying for a while?"

"Yes."

"And then?"

"What do you mean?"

Apparently my question confused him. I walked over and stood in front of the television and asked again. "What's your plan, your objective? You had to have something in mind when you filed for separation."

"Oh, my plan."

"Yes, your plan." My phone rang again and it was Marcelo. "Hold that thought." I diverted my attention from Orlando to read Marcelo's text. It was a photo of him steering his boat with an invitation, "Might be in Chicago in ten days. Would love to take you to dinner. Will send a plane. What do you say Carnival Queen?" I didn't hesitate to type my response. "I would love to. Send details."

"Put that thing down," Orlando demanded.

"As I was saying, what's your plan? I mean is this, the prelude to something else or is it a temporary arrangement. Should I include you in the family Christmas card or replace you with my mother's dog, Coco?

"So now I'm a dog?"

"You said that not me. A friendly reminder, just because we're sharing a house doesn't mean you're allowed guests or privileges. You might want to tell your little girlfriend, if I catch her here or hear that she has been in or near my house—"

"Your house?" He jumped up.

I got right in his face. "That's right, my house. If she even attempts to come within ten miles, you and she both will pray for death to ease the pain I'll inflict upon you." I cocked my head to the side. "Unlike you, I have a plan. Good night Sweetheart." I turned and started down the hall.

"Chloe, you're crazy," he yelled out.

I turned and walked back. "I know you would love for me to make a scene. But I'm not going to give you the satisfaction. You started this little game and I have no problem playing. You forgot negotiating and fact finding is what I do every day. I have a plan. Are you tough enough to see this through because that's what it's going to take."

"You don't scare me."

"Then bring it on."

He wished his bite was as good as his bark. I'm not a twenty-two year old child. I'm a grown woman who knows what she wants. And what I want right now, is him out of my life. He's playing in my backyard, by my rules. I give him thirty days, and he'll be begging me for a divorce.

Alex

OKAY, A QUICK CHECK IN the mirror. Everything was tucked where it should be.

I opened the door and heard my heart beating. I stopped midway on the staircase, leaned against the wall and took a deep breath. I stood up straight, and continued on my journey into the unknown.

My feet landed on the third to the bottom step, giving me away. Moses turned around and in my head, there was music and everything went into slow motion. He looked like he just stepped off a runway in Milan. I continued to the bottom and he extended his hand to help me.

"I'm a writer, and yet, I don't have the words to describe how beautiful you look."

Is he serious? "Thank you. I think we will be the best looking couple at the party."

"I agree. Ready?"

"Yes."

The party is in the Hamptons at Moses' parent house. Instead of driving, we flew via helicopter along with the Josephs. The train of my dress barely fit inside the helicopter. Soaring over the beautiful city and admiring the magic that is Manhattan, I felt calm.

I closed my eyes and a thousand thoughts bounced off the walls of my mind. Then the pilot told us to prepare to land. I braced myself for the landing and Moses grabbed my hand. I tried not to let it shock me, and continued staring out the window at the beautiful homes lining the beach. We landed and got into one of two cars waiting for us.

The drive to the house was quiet just like the helicopter ride. No conversation, just the sound of the tires rolling along the highway, and then he reached for my hand.

It reminded me of that scene in The Age of Innocence when Leland Archer went to the train station to pick up the love of his life, Ellen. Very sensual. He took his glove off, reached for her hand, turned it over to reveal the thing keeping him from his intended goal. He released the button and gently kissed her wrist. Then he slowly removed the glove, kissed her hand, and moved his lips up to hers. No words, just emotions resounding against the sound of the carriage wheels rolling in the freshly fallen snow. And then he tells the driver to pull over because it's too much. He needed air.

That's how this ride feels, emotions without sound bouncing off the windows of the car. Like Leland I want to tell the driver to pull over because I can't breathe, I need air. It's too much.

The gravel driveway, leading to the house started back at the edge of the highway and ended about a few hundred yards later under a carport hiding the front door.

I was shocked at the magnificence of the house. I thought we'd be driving past the mega mansions not going to one. I was expecting a classic brown shingle beach house like the ones you see on television or in magazines. Not this phenomenal piece of craftsmanship.

Who would have thought you'd find a French Chateau

smack dab in the middle of the Hamptons...I know I didn't. The house is gorgeous...antique grey brick, iron and glass doors and windows, surrounded by a low boxwood hedge.

The driver followed the directions of the parking attendants and I couldn't close my mouth. The last time I saw this many luxury cars in one place at one time, was when I went to the car show with Jonathan. It looked like a convention for luxury car owners... Bentleys, Porsches, Phantom Rolls Royces, Maserati, a Bugatti a couple of Maybachs, not to mention the Lamborghini, Teslas, Aston Martins and Batwing Mercedes.

Moses wanted to sneak into this grand event, but the simplicity of the automobile we were in stood out. He insisted the Josephs take the Maybach his mother sent for him. When I asked, he replied, "They're family."

Once we reached the front of the line, I saw a circular carport equipped with valets running everything with the precision of a luxury hotel.

When the car stopped, the parking attendant helped me out and Moses walked around to my side and escorted me inside the house. The silence had run its course. After all, we're supposed to be a couple, and how would it look if we weren't speaking to each other?

"What a beautiful home. It must have been fun growing up here."

"It's a beautiful house."

Okay that told me a lot. We walked through the white marble foyer complete with antiques, past the great room, and out to the courtyard where the immediate family was receiving guests at the end of the portico. We fell in line with the rest of the guests. I tried not to look surprised at the faces sprinkled around the party. Faces I'd only seen in magazines, newspapers, television or the movies.

The closer we got to his parents, the harder he squeezed my hand. His prior behavior didn't match up to the anxiety I was sensing. Any man bold enough to kidnap a woman falls into the category of either badass or stupid. And I know he's not stupid.

His parents are an odd looking couple. His mother, is very petite and his father, is very tall. I looked ahead in the receiving line, and saw his sister. She's a little taller than his mother and his brother is tall like him.

We inched our way to meet the wizard, and I saw his mother's face turn from plastered joy to obvious displeasure. I wasn't sure if she was perturbed he came, or if she was pissed he wasn't lined up with the rest of the family.

"Hello, Moses." Her voice had a little edge on it. He bent down, hugged her and she gently kissed him on the cheek.

"Hello, Mother."

"We were expecting you yesterday. What happened?"

"Clarice, this is not the time, the line is backing up. Hello son." His father hugged him and smiled.

"Hi Dad." He turned slightly and pulled me closer. "This is Alexandra Miller."

"Hello." I know I looked good. Zac Posen baby. I was wearing the hottest dress at the party. A hot pink strapless Zac showing every curve God gave me. Thank God they were able to fix the top of my dress. Otherwise, his parents would have seen more of me than they needed to.

"Alexandra, welcome to our home." His mother shook my hand and I felt a death chill riddle my body. Man that's one cold woman. I don't blame Moses for staying away. If I had a mother who could freeze water simply by looking at it, I'd stay away too.

"Thank you."

"Good evening Alexandra. Welcome to our home. I look forward to chatting with you later," his father said. He took my hand and his warm touch thawed his wife's frozen grip.

His brother was friendly, but his sister was imitating her mother.

Sitting at the end of the line was a beautiful grey haired woman tapping a cane as the cute waiters passed by. When she saw Moses, her face lit up like a Christmas tree. It was clear this beautiful chocolate woman with light brown eyes and a wide smile, was the one that mattered most to Moses.

"Hi Grams." He leaned down and kissed her on the cheek. When he straightened himself up, he was still smiling. "Are you behaving yourself?"

"Who's this?" she asked pointing at me.

"Grams, this is my date, Alexandra Miller."

His date. Oh crap. We were fine as long as neither of us said the "D" word. "Hello, ma'am," I replied.

"Alex, this is my grandmother, Emma Bartholomew or Grams."

"Hello, Alexandra."

I went to shake her hand and she extended her arms signaling for me to hug her, completely different from his iceberg of a mother. She must be his father's mother, because there is no way this warm woman gave birth to that petite ice machine.

"Moses, help me up, I'm getting stiff." She grabbed him by the arm and stood up.

We slowly walked towards the pool and she began dishing on everyone at the party. Starting with her daughter and granddaughter. Okay now I know whose mother she is. "You know your mother was expecting you yesterday," she reminded him.

"I know." He didn't seem to care that he had defied his mother.

"Be a good grandson and get me a glass of champagne while Alexandra and I have a little chat." We continued walking and she started questioning me.

"How do you like my house?"

"I'm sorry, I thought this was your daughter's house."

"Forgive me, you know it as Moses' house."

"Excuse me?"

"I love my grandson. When he decided to become a writer and turn his back on the family business, his mother persuaded his father to cut him off. He had nowhere to go so he came to live with me."

"That explains the Josephs."

"Mrs. Joseph was the children's nanny and when the last one entered high school, I asked she and Otis to come work for me."

"I see." We circled the pool and she continued.

"See that woman over there in the red?" She was pointing towards a giant woman dressed in a gorgeous tomato red body hugging Versace gown. I remember that dress from the show last Spring.

"The model looking woman?"

"Yes, the tall skinny one."

"Nice dress."

"I don't know what Moses saw in her." She looked me up and down. "Don't worry."

"Excuse me?"

"She's not the one you need to be concerned with."

"I think you---"

"I am the one you need to be concerned with. Moses is my favorite and I will cut your throat if you break his heart."

"Excuse me—"

"My dear, I may be old, but I'm not stupid. I don't know what you did, but you are all my grandson has talked about since he returned from Atlanta."

"Excuse me?"

"Do you know any other words?"

"Ex—huh?"

"My grandson told me all about you."

What was there to tell, we'd only met once a few weeks ago. It bore repeating, "Excuse me?"

"I'm surprised he got you here."

"Mrs. Bartholomew, I think you have me confused with my cousin?"

"No, let's see how did he put it. She's beautiful and her eyes dance when she smiles. She owns a chain of stores called Alex Simone. She has a great sense of humor and can be brutally honest in a matter of fact way and her favorite color is pink."

"We only met once."

"You met more than once. I agree you're beautiful, but unlike my grandson, I can't be swayed by a pretty smile. I need to know what your intentions are?"

"Excu——what?" We stopped and sat on a sofa near the pool where Moses could see us. The line at the bar was short, but the path to us was paved with well-wishers and nosey people, giving his grandmother and I plenty of time to talk.

"My grandson has been hurt and I will not allow that to happen again. I see how he lights up when he talks about you. Do you have feelings for him?"

"This is our first date." Did I just say that?

"And it's a good one isn't it?" She smiled.

I smiled. "It's pretty amazing." I just gave in to it. As much as I tried lying to myself, I knew it was a date, and the best one I'd ever been on.

"Do you have feelings for him? Because if you don't, then it won't be hard to leave, but if you do, and you want him, you can't be like Vanessa."

Moses didn't tell me his grandmother was a little off her bean. I don't know where any of this is coming from so I'll play along with her.

"Okay..."

"Did I catch you off guard?"

"Yes."

"I'm still trying to figure you out."

"What's that supposed to mean?"

"You are more dangerous than Vanessa."

"Excuse me." I don't care if I sound like a broken record.

"Vanessa is selfish and pampered and you're not. That girl has never worked a day in her life, and you are dedicated to your business. My grandson is the same way. Just like you, he isn't quick to let people in. So when he came home talking about this woman he met in Atlanta, I encouraged him to get to know her."

"Is that how I ended up here?"

"What do you think about my grandson?"

She blew me off. We looked across and saw Moses talking to the mayor. "He seems very nice." I cleared my throat, "But I don't really know him."

"And he's pretty cute, too." She caught me smiling. "Did I shock you?"

"Yes ma'am." I think my face is the same shade of red as that woman's dress.

"When you decide you care for him, I want you to ask yourself if you're ready for a relationship? More specifically, are you ready for this relationship?"

"But I have---"

"I am a very not young woman and one of the benefits of age is being able to speak your mind. I have always preferred the straight forward approach."

"Excuse me?"

"You know you say that a lot. Unlike my grandson, I had you checked out. I know you didn't think I'd let any chippie stay in my house."

"And?"

"I like you Alexandra. I think you'd be good for my grandson. You remind me a lot of myself at your age."

"Thank you, I think."

"You're welcome. I know Moses. He'll move heaven and earth to make you happy, if that's what you want. But at the same time, if I feel you don't feel the same, you'll have to answer to me. Do we understand each other?"

How do you respond to someone when they tell you something like this? We only met a couple of times and this is all a little much for me to take in. I think stunned doesn't really sum it up, but I feel, no, I know I need to say something. I searched my limited vocabulary for the right words and looked up and saw Moses approaching.

"I..."

"Let me give you a bit of advice. You have to be sure you

want this, because once he comes after you and he will, there'll be no time to think, just act. I've seen him in love. He'll fight for you and he won't let anything get in his way. Can you say that about any other man?"

Before I could answer, Moses was in front of us with drinks in hand.

"And how are my two favorite girls doing?" he asked as he handed each of us a glass.

"Thank you. Your grandmother has been bringing me up to speed."

"Grams..."

"What? I only told her what she needed to know," she confessed.

"Really?"

"Moses, take your best girl out there for a spin." He placed his glass on the coffee table in front of the sofa and extended his hand towards his grandmother.

"Would the most beautiful girl at the party do me the honor of this dance?" She looked at me smiling.

"How about asking the second most beautiful? Alexandra, would you please dance with my grandson?"

"It would be my pleasure," I smiled.

"No, it's mine." He extended his hand to help me to my feet and out onto the dance floor. Breathing was already a challenge in his presence, but dancing, required an oxygen tank.

He slipped his hand around my waist and slowly pulled me to his chest. We fit like two puzzle pieces...connecting and locking in all the right places.

He took my right hand in his left and I fought my body to calm down. I was glad he was holding me because I couldn't stand up on my own.

The music came up and my heart started pounding. I felt weak and found relief in resting my head against his chest. I closed my eyes and lost myself in his strong, spicy scent.

His heart was beating in time with mine. I wanted to stay

like that the rest of the night...possiby, the rest of my life. When the next song began we remained enveloped in each others arms, swaying to the soulful sounds of the band.

My mind drifted to my conversation with his grandmother. What I knew about Moses wasn't enough to fill a chewing gum wrapper. Let alone enough for me to make any life changing decisions, but it was enough for me to know I wanted to. Lost in the moment, neither of us realized we'd danced through four songs.

When the band announced they were taking a break, we pulled apart and joined the others in a round of applause. He took my hand and escorted me back to his grandmother who was talking to the woman in the red dress.

"Moses," the red dress woman said, as she walked over and kissed him on the cheek completely discounting my presence.

"Vanessa." His tone was curt and the tight grip he had on my hand, made it apparent he was uncomfortable in her presence. "Alexandra Miller," he looked at me smiling and then back at her, stone faced. "Vanessa Toliver."

She shook my hand with the enthusiasm of a woman being asked to shake hands with a leper.

Up close she wasn't nearly as intimidating as I had imagined. I was expecting Naomi Campbell's twin. Not this skinny over made up plain Jane.

"Moses, how about a dance for old times sake, that is if Alex doesn't mind?"

"It's Alexandra." I piped in and his grandmother winked at me.

"I'm sure your...date, wouldn't mind if a couple of old friends shared a dance." She stepped closer and patted his lapel.

I know this trick didn't just disrespect me by feeling up my date.

"I promised the next dance to my grandmother." He helped me sit down before helping Grams to her feet and out onto the dance floor.

I sat sipping my champagne, watching Moses and his

grandmother dance. I smiled and he smiled.

"Do you mind?"

The sound of that pretentious voice was like fingernails dragging on a chalk board. No wonder Moses left her. It was the thought of listening to that voice everyday for the rest of his life that made him leave. I ignored her hoping she would go away. Instead, she sat down on the other end of the sofa.

"I don't know if he told you, but we were engaged."

Playing cat and mouse isn't my thing, but what the heck, I'm supposed to be Moses' girlfriend tonight and that means dealing with scorned, trifling ex-girlfriends. "Yes, he did."

"Then you know how close we are?"

"Uh-huh." I sipped my champagne.

"Our families thought we'd be married by now. But you know how it is, people and things have a tendency to get a little off track."

"Uh-huh."

"When something is meant to happen, no one or thing can stop it."

If I was really involved with Moses, I'd be pissed to hear this trick calling my relationship a pit-stop on the way to her happy ending. "Wow, Moses was right, you really are something."

"Thank you." She sat up straighter smiling.

"He didn't mean it as a compliment," I clarified.

"What are you saying?"

"My mother has a saying, let me see how does it go, oh yeah. You would give your eye tooth, to be back with Moses."

"I beg your pardon, I don't understand your quaint colloquialism."

I know she didn't try to get educated on me. "I see you managed to pick up a few words while you were with Moses. Good for you. Too bad, you didn't realize what you had until he was gone. Now you want him back, not because you miss him, but because you miss the perks of being with him. When he came back the second time, you just knew he was going to marry you, but you underestimated him. You even started wearing your engagement ring hoping it would nudge him along, but it didn't. Instead, you should have tried being an asset instead of a liability. Here's a tip for your next relationship. No man wants a needy woman...no matter how nice *he* thinks the package is."

"You don't know me well enough to make such assumptions and to imply I'm still wearing my engagement ring," she protested.

I looked down at her hand and saw the simple diamond solitaire on her left ring finger. She quickly picked her hand up and folded it in front of her. "I would think if you and Moses were so *in love*, he wouldn't have bought you such a...*common* ring."

"You don't know what you're talking about."

"I know what Moses has told me and I believe him."

"Then he didn't tell you everything."

"Maybe he didn't, but he told me enough to paint a good picture of you."

"And what's that supposed to mean?"

"It means I know quite a few things."

"Like what?"

"I don't think you really want to know what I know."

"I'm sure whatever it is you think you know won't surprise me."

"Good, then there's no need for you to keep annoying me with these questions." I took a long sip from my glass.

"How did you meet Moses?"

"Through a mutual acquaintance."

"I see. I suppose he told you how we met?"

"I see you're one of those hard headed chicks that just won't leave well enough alone. So here it is. I know how you met, I know how long you were together, both times. I know you tried to get him to marry you. I know you drained him emotionally while he supported you financially. I know you're demanding and conceited. I know you cheated on him which I find amazing because you are so boring. I know you think you're better than him and that you feel he was lucky to have you, which in my opinion is in reverse, because he was and is too good for you. I know you conspired with his mother and sister to get invited here tonight. I know you came here alone hoping to rekindle things with him. I know the man you left him for treated you like trash. I know you regret your decision to leave Moses, and I know you still love him." I took another sip from my glass. "And I know if you don't stop flirting with him, I'll cut you and that's not just talk. Don't let this Zac Posen gown fool you sweetie, I carry a gun and a knife." I put my glass down, stood up and got in her face. "I'm not one of these Park Avenue society princesses. You don't scare me with your little intimidation tactics. I learned from the best. So, I strongly suggest you set your sights on someone else, because Moses is spoken for."

"I never said I wanted Moses," she countered.

"Oh but you did, with your actions." I straightened up, looked over at Moses and walked away.

Dear God, Please forgive me for losing my temper, but she was working my nerves. You know I was very prepared to knock the fool out of that Amazon. I can't believe she let a good man go. It could have been worse though. I could have pushed her into the pool, but the dress didn't deserve to be abused. Forgive me, God.

I stood quietly in front of the pink rose bushes in the garden, trying to calm down when I heard heavy footsteps walking towards me. No need to turn around, because I knew who they belonged to. As he approached, my heartbeat got louder. I told myself to breath.

Then, as magically as the footsteps entered the garden, they magically stopped. I asked myself if I was hallucinating. To confirm, I tilted my head and looked out the corner of my eye surveying my surroundings, and then I heard him clear his throat and the footsteps continued.

He stopped close enough for me to feel his breath on the back of my neck. My heart began racing and I wanted to breathe, but couldn't. He stepped closer and all manner of calm was gone and had been replaced with a strange eagerness. It couldn't be love, because I didn't feel like this with Terrence or Jonathan.

I needed to leave but my legs were numb. I was afraid if I tried to move I would topple over. I kept pleading with God, hoping Moses could read my mind and just leave.

"Do you want to tell me what happened back there with Vanessa?"

I just verbally assaulted a woman I don't know all for the sake of a man I've known about as long as my new shoes. I shook my head. "No."

"Okay."

The garden was blooming with unspoken emotions and intoxicating smells. Someone needed to say something, but what? I took a deep breath and addressed the pink elephant in the garden.

"I think we have a problem."

"Oh?"

"Yeah." I swallowed hard. "I think I made a mistake coming here."

"Why do you say that?"

"Because...your grandmother...she said...she asked me how I felt about you."

"What did you say?" I heard him step closer.

"I uhm..."

He brushed my hair back and placed a hot kiss on the back of my neck. The feel of his lips on my skin sent a surge through my body climaxing with a deep gasp. He slowly turned me around to face him. I looked into those incredible eyes and knew I was in trouble.

He eased his hand around my waist, gently stroked the side of my face and whispered, "Alex..."

The way my named sounded as it floated off his lips was

intoxicating. He brushed my lips with the ball of his thumb and I desparately wanted him to kiss me. I closed my eyes, took a deep breath and his mouth consumed mine.

He pulled me closer and every muscle in his chest and legs pressed against mine. This kiss and his touch was awakening feelings of desire and lust that had long been dead. He tasted like champagne and chocolate. I wrapped my arms around his neck, pulling him closer. His kiss grew more intense and demanding. His hands slipped down the small of my back and he pulled me deeper ito his space. We were locked together trading deep moans in between passionate kisses oblivious to everything around us.

He pulled back and I could barely breath. I felt his finger brush arcoss my swollen lips and I slowly opened my eyes. His incredible light brown eyes were now dark brown. The intensity of the moment was obvious. My body was shaking and I wanted him to kiss me again, although I knew it was a bad idea.

He stroked my cheek and the heat of his hand traveled the length of my body. I was on fire and felt my blood boiling. "Do you still think we have a problem?"

I swallowed hard, hoping for air to answer his question. "Most..." he kissed my neck. "Uhm...most...definitely." I tried opening my eyes, but they wouldn't cooperate.

"I don't."

He took my mouth again lighting a passionate fire so hot, I wanted to jump out of my skin. One of his large hands slid lower down my back, pressing me against his hard body. He buried his other hand deep in my hair, searing my scalp. My skin and mouth were on fire. Every inch of my body was aroused. The sensations flowing throw me were so intense, I could barely stand up. My body had long betrayed me. I needed a release, but I didn't want to end the kiss. As those words left my mind, his tongue continued to ravage my mouth, rendering me breathless while erasing the memory of every kiss before his. With one kiss, he had branded me his.

Kendell

THE DOORBELL RANG AND I froze. I took a deep breath and walked toward the door. The door bell rang again and I exhaled. I opened the door and standing in front of me, was *my boyfriend.* For the first time in a long time, I was excited about using that term.

"Hey." I felt like a giddy teenager. Bas leaned forward and gently pressed his lips against mine, no hands just his lips. He slowly pulled back and smiled.

"Hey yourself."

"Come in." I stepped to the side and watched as he walked inside. I closed the door and he pinned me up against the door and kissed me again, more passionately. I couldn't breathe. The smell of his aftershave traveled up my nose overwhelming me. The kiss was so...I think I blacked out momentarily. He pulled back and my thoughts were all jumbled. "Uhm...maybe we should eat." He released my hands and I started towards the kitchen.

"I'm starving. What's for dinner?"

"I thought we'd start with tuna and kale crostini with

yogurt dill sauce. Followed by five cheese soufflé and sautéed broccoli rob." I looked over my shoulder and smiled.

"That's serious cooking girl." He followed me into the kitchen. "Cheese soufflé is one of the things I make a point of eating when I go to Paris, so I'm expecting to be blown away."

"You will be."

"Listen to you." He kissed me and sat down. "What did I do to deserve you?"

"I've been asking myself the same thing." The obvious chemistry is a little scary. "Uhm, we better eat before it gets cold."

Bas' plate was empty and there was very little soufflé left. "So, did the soufflé meet with your approval?"

"Yes, it did." He patted his stomach. "I'll be at the gym early in the morning working this off. Having a girlfriend that's a chef, is good and bad."

"How so?"

"I can always expect a good meal, but I can also expect to over eat," we laughed.

"I didn't tell you to eat three servings."

"I couldn't help myself, it was so good."

"I'll pack the leftovers for you."

"Another advantage to dating a chef." He took a sip from his glass and I couldn't help staring at his lips. "So what's for dessert?"

"Dessert? I didn't make dessert."

"I know better. There's no way, you didn't make dessert. You can't just take my taste buds to the mountain top and leave 'em begging for more."

"I think I have some ice cream."

"Are you serious?" His smile was gone. "I'll take it, because knowing you, it's probably some amazing flavor."

"I'll check. I made it a week ago. It was an experiment I was thinking about for the restaurant." I walked into the kitchen, opened the freezer and pulled out the glasses of ice cream, placed them on the tray and joined Bas in the dining room. I put the tray on the table and sat down.

"What's that?" he asked looking at the tall glasses.

"Ice cream." I sat down and placed my napkin back in my lap. "Actually, it's a float."

"A float?" He looked vexed at my reply.

"Yes, and cookies." I placed the glass in front of him along with a straw. "It's fresh peaches, peach gelato, cassis and champagne." He took a sip and smiled. "What do you think?"

"This is good and the cookies hit the spot." He took another sip. "Girl, you are killing me. From now on, all I'm having is soup for lunch before coming over for dinner," he laughed.

"I'm glad you enjoyed dinner." He covered my hand with his and I felt a spark. "I want to ask you something."

"You sound serious."

"I know you're not really the monogamous type."

"Let me stop you."

"No, please let me finish."

"Okay."

"I've seen the women you've brought into the restaurant and it's been quite a few." I shifted a little. "I'm not exactly your type."

"My type?"

"The women I've seen you with are very beautiful and tall. I'm---"

"Petite and beautiful." He smiled.

"Thank you, but I haven't really seen you with one for a long period of time either." I looked at him trying to figure out the best way to ask my question. Those eyes. I could get lost in those beautiful blue green eyes. I bet there have been quite a few women who have succumbed to the temptation in those eyes.

"I see. You think this is a romantic pit stop?"

"Yes, I don't want to be something you do while waiting on the next best thing."

"You are the next best thing."

"Am I? I've had men fill my head with a lot of romantic

fantasies only to find out later, they never meant any of it."

"Kendell, I'm not looking to pass time. I'm looking for someone I can share my life with. I'm tired of fluff. I want substance. I want to be with someone who can stimulate my mind, my spirit and my body. If I just wanted someone to help me pass the time, I wouldn't be here."

"I thought it was my cooking that caught your attention." I teased.

"Baby, it wasn't your cooking that caught my attention. It was your cute little walk."

My face felt warm. "Uhm..."

"I know my reputation precedes me, but don't let that stop you from giving this, us a chance. I think we could be good together. Scratch that. I think we could be great together."

HIDING OUT IN MIAMI WAS supposed to help me clear my head. Instead, I spent the past three days replaying the weekend and that make out session in the garden with Moses. I probably shouldn't have left like I did or at least I could have left a note.

What was I thinking spending the weekend with him? He may not understand, but I know I did the right thing. *If it's supposed to be, God, I leave it up to You to work it out.*

I knocked on the door to my office and stepped inside. "Seems you two have everything under control."

"Good morning, sweetheart," Mama said, smiling.

"Hey Alex," Sebastian chimed in as he got up and hugged me. "How was your trip?"

"Fine." I walked over and kissed Mama on the cheek and noticed the flowers on the coffee table. "Beautiful flowers."

"Where have you been?" she asked.

"What do you mean, you know where I've been."

"No, I know where you were Saturday. Where have you been and why haven't you returned any of my calls?"

"Ma'am?" I walked over to my desk and noticed another bouquet. "Where did the flowers come from?"

"Alexandra Simone Miller, I gave birth to you, the only person that knows you better than me, is God. So, I am going to ask you one last time, where have you been since I spoke to you on Saturday?"

Mental note, whenever your mother calls you by your full name, no matter how old you are, you are required to answer whatever question she's asking.

"And don't bother trying to make up something, because we know." Bas jumped in.

"Know what?"

"You weren't alone," Mama announced.

"Did you pull a Chloe and run off and marry some strange man?" Bas asked.

"What! No." I sat down.

"Then where have you been and with who?" Bas asked.

"Sebastian, calm down. Let me handle this." My mother walked over and got in my face. "You have three-seconds to tell me where you've been and with who."

I'm a grown woman and yet when confronted by my mother about an impromptu break, I feel like a teenager explaining why I broke curfew. I swallowed hard and inhaled, trying to come up with an answer. "I..."

"And don't even think about lying because the man I spoke with on Friday, has been calling every couple of hours for the past two days looking for you, and asking if the flowers arrived."

I tossed my head back, hoping for an answer other than the full truth. I lowered my head and met her gaze. "Uhm..."

"So, who is he?" She demanded.

I swallowed again before answering. "Darryl Moses."

"The writer?" Bas asked.

"Actually, it's Moses Adair."

"This is bad," Mama blurted out.

"Mama you know who he is?"

"Of course I do. I've read all his books." She announced. "This is not good."

"Where did you meet him?" Bas asked.

"Taylor's party."

"The married dude?"

"What?" Mama shouted. "Have you lost your mind?"

"Will everyone calm down. He's a widower." The look on my mother's face went from crazed mother bear to a confused scowl.

"I thought you said the guy you met at the party was married?" Bas asked.

"That's what I thought."

"So, in a matter of a few weeks he went from being married to a widower. I'm not buying it." My mother protested.

I started to stand up and she cut me a death glance so I stayed seated. "He's a widower. His wife died giving birth."

"He has a child? Oh this just keeps getting better." She started pacing back and forth. "How old is the child?"

"She died shortly after being born." I looked at both of them and saw a look of compassion on their faces.

"I'm sorry to hear that. However---"

"Mama, nothing happened."

"Really, I've seen that man." She stopped pacing and folded her arms in front of her. "Now that we know who you were with, where have you been for the past three days?"

"Miami."

"I thought you were in New York?" Bas asked.

"I was and then I went to Miami."

Mama looked at me tapping her thumbs. That usually meant she was processing or scanning my body language for clues. She says she never asks a question without knowing the answer. "What happened in New York?"

"I was his date for his sister's engagement party. When was his last call?"

"Right after you called this morning. What happened in New York?" she asked again.

"Nothing I can't handle," I replied trying to convince myself.

"How did you end up in New York and later in Miami?"

"I was headed to Atlanta, but I got distracted at the check in counter when an obnoxious customer insisted on sitting next to me. She offered to explain how I could better stock my stores for the common woman. Before I knew it, I lied and said I was headed to New York. However, that didn't stop her and she kept insisting. Before I could lie again, Moses came in, overheard the conversation, and proceeded to pretend we were traveling together. I played along and the next thing I knew, I was on my way to New York for real. He had changed my ticket and when I tried to change it back, there was nothing available." I stood up. "I only agreed to stay at his house because it was so late when we got to New York, and he said he would stay at a hotel."

"That explains the phone call," Bas jumped in. "I thought it was the hotel."

"Nope, it was him."

"Brother's got game," Bas smiled.

"Long story short. I bought a dress, went to the party, met his family and came home via Miami."

"You bought a dress. You don't pay retail for clothes." Bas quipped.

"I know." I started pacing.

"Who did you wear?" he asked.

"Zac," I mumbled.

"Dang, Alex, you broke out the heavy artillery. He didn't stand a chance. So what happened?"

"Nothing."

"And you stayed at his house? I know I raised you better than that," Mama reminded me.

"He lives with his grandmother."

"Is that bit of news supposed to convince me nothing happened?"

"Don't you trust me?"

"You, I trust. It's the good-looking man I don't know that I don't trust."

"It's not like we were alone."

"Oh?"

I couldn't believe I was defending myself. I'm a grown woman sitting here trying to convince my mother and best friend, I did nothing to be ashamed of. "The housekeeper and her husband were there. Trust me, if I hadn't felt safe, I would have left."

"But you did."

I hate that Mother-knows-everything tone. The tone that implies she knows you did something and are ashamed to say what it is.

"Technically I left Sunday morning after we came back from the party."

"Alex, I gotta go, I've got a VIP coming in a few minutes." He picked up his iPad and left.

Once the door closed. "So is it as bad as I think?" Mama asked.

"Worse."

"What happened?"

"I got scared."

"Scared?"

"I told God what I wanted and..."

"Now that you see it in the flesh, it's scaring you."

"Exactly."

"I knew there was more to you fleeing New York than you said." She smiled and wrapped me in her arms. "Baby, that's how God works. In His time not yours." She stepped back and gently brushed the side of my face. "Kiddo, it's time for you to get on with your life. I know it's hard, but you have got to stop blaming yourself for Jonathan's death. It's the only way you're going to be ready for the next thing God has for you."

"Moses said the same thing."

"He did...hum...he might not be that bad after all." She looked at her watch, "Tell you what, why don't you catch up on things here in the office, and I'll go help Bas." She kissed me on the forehead, and like a puff of Hermes parfum, she was gone to do what she does best, look after me.

Mama

"MISS CONNIE, DON'T YOU THINK we should have told Alex about..."

"No."

"But what if...,"

"Sebastian, trust me."

"Yes ma'am."

Now, what room is mine?"

"The Brown Suite. I'll make sure Alex stays in her office."

"Thank you." I stepped back, took a deep breath, and pushed the door open. "Good morning, Mrs. Pierce." The average height, gray haired woman turned around. She looked the same, just a little more aged. The signs of time were beginning to show on her face.

"Mrs. Miller. I requested Alexandra."

"She's not available. So, what can I do for you?"

"I understand my daughter-in-law came to see Alexandra."

"And?"

"I need Alexandra's help."

"Looking for a party dress?"

"Maybe I'll come back when she's available."

"What is it with your family? We haven't heard from you in over twenty years, and in the last few weeks every time we turn around, one of you is here. And now you want my daughter's help. With what?"

"It really doesn't concern you," she sniped.

"My daughter told me all about her meeting with Terrence." I shook my head. "You should be proud."

"I am." She stood up straighter.

"He turned out just like you wanted...weak...broken... confused. On behalf of my daughter and myself, thank you for removing the burden of raising him from us."

"I beg your pardon."

"If he had been a fourth of the man he pretended to be, he wouldn't have allowed you and your husband to ruin his life."

"Terrence is a man of honor and integrity. He did what was best for his family and in the process there was some fallout," she retorted.

"That's the second time you've referred to his son as an afterthought. Do it again and you'll find my foot in a very uncomfortable place."

"Are you threatening me?"

"Of course not. I'm telling you what I'm going to do. Much like Alex did when she told the other Mrs. Pierce what would happen if she came here again."

"Keep that...daughter of yours away from my son."

"Your son?" I chuckled. "You better check the door on the cage you put Terrence in. Seems the lock isn't that secure."

"I don't know what you're talking about."

"You don't?"

She looked around, surveying her surroundings, "I see Alexandra bought an interesting life with my money."

"You know, I have often wondered how you managed to

persuade that boy to sign away his life."

"It wasn't that difficult once he saw that girl for what she really was."

I balled my fist. "Get out."

"Seems I hit a nerve."

"I said get out."

She started toward the door. "If your daughter knows what's best for her, she'll stay away from Terrence. He knows what is expected of him and there's no way he's going to throw it all away for a temporary trip down memory lane."

"How can she be a memory, if he never stopped thinking about her?"

"My son is happy."

"Maybe if you say it enough times, it will be true.

MY MOTHER AND BAS ARE right. It's time to stop grieving and get on with my life. Moses is everything I asked God for and although the thought of this relationship scares me, I have to trust God. I like being with someone not afraid to share his feelings.

My cell rang and I recognized the ringtone. "Hi Kim...no, I'm not...which room...give me five minutes, bye." I hung up and went down to the Pink VIP suite and knocked on the door, but there was no answer. I cautiously walked inside searching for the client, "Good afternoon and welcome to—"

"Alex."

"Moses, what are you doing here?"

"After I called every hotel I thought you might go to in New York, I figured you came home, so I started calling here every couple of hours looking for you. Why haven't you returned my calls?"

"When did you get here?"

"Yesterday, if you hadn't skipped out on me, I would have told you I was coming back, and we could have flown back together."

"Oh."

"Why did you leave without saying good-bye? Did I do something to offend you?"

"No. I just thought we got caught up in the moment and..."

"Wow, I can't believe I misread the signals. I'm sorry. Now that I've made a complete fool of myself, I'll be leaving."

"Have a good trip."

He walked past me and stopped.

"I'm sorry for whatever it is the other men in your life did to you, but you have got to stop punishing yourself. I know losing your fiancé was hard and it left a huge hole in your heart, but how much longer are you going to be using that excuse?"

"Excuse me? This coming from a man that--"

"I'm falling in love with you, and I need to know exactly what degree of crazy I'm dealing with."

"Excuse me?"

"You know you say that a lot." He smiled and stepped closer. "I said, as insane as it sounds, I am falling in love with you but you're making it difficult. Running from the future isn't going to make the past go away. It just puts the future farther out of reach."

His words hit me like a ton of Louboutins, and I plopped down onto the sofa. All this time I had been blaming myself for the inability to change the past. I felt that if I had been with Jonathan, maybe I could have gotten him help before it was too late. Or if Terrence had come back to the apartment, maybe we could have fought his parents together. But there's no way to know what could have or would have happened. I have to live with what did happen.

As I sobbed like a baby, he sat down and wrapped his massive arms around me.

"Shhh." He pulled out his handkerchief and patted the tears streaming down my face.

"Thank you."

"I think I should go home. When you're ready to start this relationship, call me and I'll be on the next flight. For me, there's no one else, but I'm not going to force myself on you. It bothers me that there's still something holding you back from moving forward."

"I told you I wasn't ready to talk about it."

"I know. And I respect your feelings, but you need to let go of the past and get on with your life." He gently kissed me on the lips, brushed the side of my face and stood up.

"Thank you for the flowers."

"You're welcome."

"What are you doing for dinner?"

"I hear the chicken on the late flight back to New York is pretty good. Why?"

"I thought you might want to come over and see what's in my fridge and maybe make some cookies?"

"What time?"

"Six-thirty. I'll write the address down for you."

"You know, now that I know you a little, I think it would be better if I waited downstairs and rode with you." He smiled. "I don't want you disappearing on me again."

"I deserve that." I smiled. "Give me a couple of hours."

As magically as he appeared, he was gone. I walked into my office and saw the two people who were probably responsible for tonight's impromptu family dinner.

"How was that last VIP baby girl?" Mama asked smiling.

"You tell me."

"She knows," Sebastian mumbled.

"I saw him going downstairs?" Mama announced. "His pictures don't do him justice."

"Which one of you is responsible for him coming here?"

"I knew you wanted to see him. Where did he go?" Mama asked.

"He's downstairs in the lounge. I invited him for dinner. So what are you cooking Mama?"

Dionne

QUENTIN IS OFFICIALLY IN THE doghouse. I can't believe he cancelled our date. I'm so mad I could poison him. Take that back, the one I really should poison is his mother. That old goat is demanding we have dinner with her and the coven...family. I swear Quentin and his brother, Adam, must be adopted or the result of someone's creeping around because they are nothing like their shrew mother.

So, instead of spending some much deserved quiet time with my husband, I'm headed to dinner at my in-laws. *God, what did I do to deserve this?*

We pulled into the driveway and parked the car. Quentin hopped out and before he walked over to my side, I was standing next to the door. To emphasize my displeasure in this impromptu dinner party, and to piss his mother off, I pulled out my secret weapon. A tight black Herve Leger that emphasizes my birthing hips as she calls them. It also served as a reminder to Quentin of what he wasn't having for dinner. I watched his eyes travel up and down my body as I adjusted my dress.

"Let's get this over with." I started walking in front of him and could feel his eyes watching every sway of my hips.

"You look nice."

No need to tell me what I already know. "Thank you." We walked up the steps and landed on the porch. He rang the bell and a few seconds later, the door opened. There she was, the bane of my existence, the high priestess of the Burke family.

"Hello son." She kissed Quentin on the cheek. "Dionne."

"Katherine."

We stepped inside and walked down the hall to greet the rest of the family. I looked around the room and asked myself, was being married to Quentin really worth all the aggravation and criticism I had to put up with from these people? Then I looked at Quentin and figured tonight wasn't the night to answer that question.

"Would you like something to drink, Sweetheart?" Quentin asked.

Something to drink? If we were at home, we'd be drinking that insanely expensive bottle of wine I bought yesterday. "I'll have a glass of merlot, thank you."

"That's an interesting dress Dionne, but is it really suitable for dinner with the family?" Katherine insinuated.

This coming from a woman who dresses like Endora on Bewitched. I thought about my reply. I wanted to say, is that black and gold kaftan suitable for dinner, considering you expect me to keep my food down? Instead, I replied, "It's Quentin's favorite."

"I see his taste in clothes has slipped just like his taste in so many other things."

Strike one.

"Now that Quentin is here, we can eat. This way everyone," she instructed.

We all followed her lead into the dining room. This is my least favorite room in this house. The beige color on the walls is so bland. There's no life in here, yet my mother-in-law is always trying to bring it to life with people. I've got news for her, it's hard to liven up a room when half of the people in it are as bland as the color on the walls. I think she painted the walls beige so her kaftans could stand out.

Katherine always uses place cards at family dinners, like we don't know who everyone is. And to reiterate her disapproval of our marriage, she never sits Quentin and I next to each other. Tonight, that's a good thing. He helped me with my chair and kissed my shoulder before he walked around the table to his seat. Grant it, the kiss did send a chill down my spine, but he won't be tasting anything else from the Dionne menu tonight.

"Everyone be quiet while Adam says the blessing." Katherine ordered.

"Thank you Father for this meal and time of fellowship with family. I pray there is nothing in this food that will harm our bodies, but will help to fuel them as we work the plans you have for us. In Jesus' name Amen." Adam leaned over and whispered, "I see my big brother has gotten himself into a little trouble."

"More like he let your mother get him into trouble." I placed my napkin in my lap.

"I see." He nodded. "That explains the dress."

"Is it too much?" I was confident in my decision to wear the dress, but seeing myself in the eyes of someone I respected made me think differently.

He handed me the serving plate. "Let's just say, if you weren't my sister-in-law, scratch that, if I was the old Adam, sister-in-law or not, you'd be going home with me." He smiled.

The compliment was just what I needed. "Good to see a little of the old Adam is still in there."

"I didn't die. I just traded in some of those old ways." We laughed. "Dee, go easy on him. I know he doesn't want to be here either."

I looked at Quentin talking to his brother-in-law and back at Adam. "He should have told her we had plans."

"You had plans?" he asked.

"Not so much plans, but...," I was embarrassed to tell my brother-in-law, my pastor what our plans were for the evening. "We uhm, we were...,"

"Let me guess. They were of the romantic nature." He smiled.

I think my face just turned the same color as the stuffed tomato appetizer. "Yes."

"Now I see the real reason for the dress." He looked across at Quentin. "My mother has always been a demanding person. I think that's why I did a lot of the things I did."

"And what's your excuse now?" I smiled.

"I deserve that." He sipped his water. "I refuse to let her get to me. Quentin on the other hand, is trying to be the good son. It's that oldest child syndrome."

"I don't think that's it. I think he's afraid to stand up to your mother."

He leaned closer. "If that were true, he wouldn't have married you."

"What?" I looked around to make sure no one could hear our conversation.

"She told Quentin not to marry you. If you don't believe me, ask him."

I looked at my husband, dumbfounded at Adam's confession.

The ride home was just as quiet as the ride to dinner. I looked at Quentin with Adam's words replaying in my head. After being together for three years, I still didn't know my husband.

We pulled into the driveway, and this time I waited for him to help me out. I stood up and faced him. I was too ashamed to apologize. I walked in to the kitchen and sitting on the counter was the bottle of wine I hoped we would be sharing tonight. He walked in taking his tie off, not bothering to stop. "I'm going to bed."

"Is it true your mother told you not to marry me?" I blurted out.

He stopped in his tracks and turned to face me. "Is that what you and Adam were talking about?"

"That and how he thinks you feel some sort of obligation to your mother because you're the oldest."

He exhaled. "Adam doesn't know what he's talking about."

"Is it true? Is that why she hates me?"

"She doesn't hate you."

"It's for sure she doesn't like me."

He exhaled again and walked over and stood next to the counter. "My mother feels it's her right to interfere in her children's lives."

"You're a grown man Quentin."

"I wouldn't expect you to understand."

"What's that supposed to mean?" Just when I was beginning to feel sorry for him and open the Dionne buffet.

"It means, I have spent my entire life trying to justify my choices to my parents."

"That doesn't make any sense."

"My parents aren't like yours, Dionne. Your parents support everything you do. Not mine. I didn't go to the school they wanted me to. I didn't become a doctor. I don't go to the same church. I didn't marry the woman they wanted. I have been fighting for my choices and I'm tired." He leaned against the counter, dropped his head and exhaled. "You're right, I should have told my mother we had plans, but it was easier to let you down than to fight with her. I'm sorry." He walked away.

A few minutes later I heard the shower running. I waited until it stopped before going upstairs. When I walked into the room, he was in bed. I took a shower and crawled into bed. The distance between us was vast, with him clutching his side of the bed, and me clutching mine.

My childish behavior had hurt my husband. I had no idea of the war he had been fighting. I thought I was the only one fighting, when in fact, he'd been fighting for us long before we became an "us."

I rolled over and got as close as I could, wrapped my arms around him and kissed his shoulder. "Thank you for being a fighter. I love you."

"I'M SORRY ABOUT THE GRILLING session. That wasn't what I meant when I invited you to dinner."

"I understand. Your mom is great." Moses smiled.

"Thank you."

"And Sebastian?"

I sensed his curiosity about my relationship with Bas. "Bas has been with me for years. He's a good friend and has seen me through a lot of tough things like Jonathan's death and the opening of all my stores. He knows me almost as well as my mom. He's the son my mom wishes she'd had."

I looked at Moses and saw the calm expression on his face. He caught me looking at him and smiled.

"What?"

"Let's take a walk." It was a little chilly so I threw my wrap around my shoulders.

"Nice night."

"I love the way it smells. I wish I could pinpoint the

scent." A few minutes into our walk we got quiet.

He reached for my hand and our fingers intertwined. "So, what's on your mind?"

I took a deep breath and began. "I spent my entire junior year and the prior summer in Paris and I met someone...Terrence. He was before Jonathan and very different. You remind me of him and that's what scares me. He was very charming and I fell in love with him very quickly. Shortly after Valentine's Day, we got married. His parents found out and immediately came to Paris and took him away."

"What?"

"My mother found out when his family sent my copy of the annulment papers to her. I can't believe I'm telling you this. When I returned home, I discovered I was pregnant. How's that for timing. No husband, knocked up and one year of school left. I never told him I was pregnant. I went into premature labor and three days later, my son died."

"I'm sorry."

"I went back to school and that's when I started dating Jonathan, but it wasn't the same. Eventually, I began to love him, but not like I loved my husband. He proposed and I accepted. Getting over my husband was difficult and Jonathan was patient. Before Jonathan left for Milan, he gave me an ultimatum, and I agreed to marry him when he came back." I felt a lump in my throat as I tried to hold back the tears. "He had a massive heart attack and I buried him on our wedding day."

"Oh my God."

"Up until a month ago," I wiped the tear I felt rolling down my face. "No one knew I was going to meet him to elope but something happened and...that's enough for now."

"Wow, that's a lot to take in."

"You said you wanted to know what level of crazy you were dealing with, does this help?"

"Yeah," he bobbed his head.

"I'll understand if it's too much crazy for you."

"I meant what I said. I'm falling in love with you and I want to be a part of your life, if you'll let me, crazy and all." He smiled.

"Okay, here's the rest? When we bumped into each other at the airport, I was running away."

"From?"

"My ex-husband. I bumped into him and his wife in the VIP lounge at the airport the weekend of the store opening."

"No way."

"The last time I saw Terrence was over twenty years ago the morning his parents came to Paris and took him away. That's how Bas met him. My girlfriends don't know any of this. They knew of him, because we all went to school together. To this day, they have no knowledge I had a relationship with him. I was told to never mention the marriage or contact him. When I got back from Atlanta, he showed up at the store. Very apologetic, begging my forgiveness. Then he confused me with all this stuff about Jonathan and how he knew we were married."

"My books don't have this many plot twists," he teased.

"You wanted to know it all and here it is. Then his pregnant wife showed up the following day with all this crap, about the past and I exploded. I knew I had to get out of town before his crazy mother showed up. I figured it was better to spend a little time in Atlanta instead of jail because I beat up an old lady."

"That's some story." He kissed my hand. "It's getting late. Let's head back."

The walk back was quiet. I opened the door and asked, "Do you want to come in?"

"It's late, I better go."

"Okay." I turned to go inside and he grabbed my arm.

"I'm going to stay in town for a while."

"That would be nice."

"Can we have dinner tomorrow?"

"I'd like that." He leaned in and gently pressed his lips against mine. I was instantly transported back to that night in the garden, kissing him. He slowly pulled back and greeted me with a beautiful smile. "That was nice." I smiled.

"I'll call you in the morning. Good night."

"Good night."

THIS JOURNEY, AS BAS CALLS it, has been wonderful. I really want to tell my girlfriends about us, but we agreed to wait a little longer.

Although we've known each other for years, I still don't know him. I only know Bas, Alex's assistant that occasionally escorts us to events, or sits with us in church. I don't really know that much about Bas, my boyfriend. I know he likes my cooking, is a hard worker, loves God, always looks like he just stepped off the pages of a magazine, and has the most amazing blue green eyes. Oh yeah, and he has dated enough women to fill a small country. That's what scares me.

He knows all the right things to say and probably has some amazing moves. However, I don't need someone who will say and do all the right things. I need someone who understands what it means to partner with someone else and not be selfish. I don't think that's too much to ask.

My phone rang with a familiar ring tone. I pressed the

answer call button and tried to calm my voice.

"Hey Babe."

"How's my girl doing?"

"Fine."

"I know it's short notice, but I was thinking, could we do dinner and a movie tonight at my place?"

This entire relationship isn't what I expected. I thought because none of Bas' relationships appeared to be long term, that there was a problem with him. On the contrary, he's a nice guy, a gentleman.

I think the problem has been his style. He has a lot of swagger which some women read as edgy, tough or cocky, but that's not him. He's kind, compassionate, and romantic. I can tell he's been hurt and all the women were probably his way of not dealing with the hurt. I like his gentleness…that's what's behind those blue green eyes, gentleness.

"Depends on the movie."

"You pick, but no chick flicks."

"Please, I don't do chick flicks."

"Stop lying. I know better," he laughed.

"Busted." I laughed. "Okay, I'll bring over two orders of…"

"No need. I got you."

"Are you sure, because it's no…"

"I got this."

"Okay, I'll bring dessert?"

"I've got that covered too," he announced. For this to be a last minute date, it seemed like it had been well planned. "I'll see you at six."

"I'll be there."

I walked up to the door, took a deep breath, and knocked. After a few seconds, the door opened and there he was, my boyfriend.

"Hey Babe." He pulled me close and greeted me with a soft kiss. "Welcome to Casa Devereaux." I walked inside and he closed the door. "Here, let me take your jacket."

I slipped my jacket off, handed it to him and he hung it up in the closet by the door. "Thank you."

"Come on, let me show you around."

He took my hand and gave me a guided tour of his home. It was nothing like I imagined, but it was just like him. Warm, inviting, quiet with little shocking touches. There were childhood pictures of him and his grandmother. A photo of a beautiful couple on their wedding day. They must be his parents. I remember Alex saying his parents were killed in a car accident when he was a baby, and that his grandmother raised him. That would explain the quilt on the sofa in the office.

"It's very you." I stood next to the island looking around the kitchen. Very masculine, unlike mine. Stainless steel appliances, dark cabinets and very little on the counters, except for a large black binder on an easel. "Your kitchen is…"

"Not like yours, but it works for me."

"It's nice. You have all the essentials and that's what matters. What's with the binder?"

Not looking up from the stove. "Recipes."

"Recipes?" Definitely not the answer I was expecting.

"My Nana wanted to make sure I had a little bit of her cooking whenever I wanted it. I have to confess, I can't make half the things in there." We laughed.

"What can I help you with?"

"Nothing."

"Are you sure?"

"Yes. I may not be a great chef like you, or a great cook like my Nana, but I can muddle my way around the kitchen."

"So what are we having?"

"Chili."

"Chili?"

"It's my Nana's recipe. She believed a good pot of chili was just as comforting as chicken soup."

"I see."

"I know it's a little different from what you're used to, but I thought you might like something a little different." He looked over his shoulder smiling.

I was already experimenting with something different, I was seeing him. All this time I thought he was a commitment phobe, when in reality, he's a great guy looking for someone to partner with.

"Different is very good. How do you think I come up with most of my recipes? I like experimenting."

He filled two bowls and turned off the stove. "Come on, let's sit down." I followed him to the table and sat down. He blessed the food and I took my first spoonful. "So, what do you think?"

"This is amazing." I put another spoonful into my mouth, closed my eyes while savoring all the flavors. "Uhm.....this is really good. You might want to hide Nana's recipe."

"I'm glad you like it."

"This would be good with cornbread and…"

"I'm sorry." He jumped up, went into the kitchen and came back with a cutting board and a small skillet of cornbread. "I'm glad you said something. I almost forgot the best part."

"Is this Nana's recipe too?"

"Yes, she always makes her cornbread in a cast iron pan." He cut a piece and placed it on the saucer for me.

I broke a piece off with my hand and popped the warm bread into my mouth. "Oh my God, this is amazing. I need to hire your Nana."

"I'm glad you like it."

We continued eating and I wondered how many other women had been the recipient of his Nana's chili and cornbread. I tried not to give in to the myriad of questions in my head.

"What's with the smile?" He asked.

"This isn't what I expected."

"What do you mean?"

"When you invited me over for dinner, I was expecting take-out."

"Really?"

"Yea, you just never struck me as the type of man that…I mean, this is so normal and you…"

"What?" He looked a little anxious waiting on my response.

"You don't look normal. You look make believe."

"I don't follow." He got up and started clearing the table and I followed behind him. He meticulously scraped the bowls and loaded them into the dishwasher.

"See what you just did." Pointing to his handling of the dishes. "I wouldn't expect you to be like this, a regular guy. I see you as this suave dude in the designer suit and shirt, perfectly put together, in a sports car and sunglasses, smelling incredible. Not this guy with a box of dishwasher detergent and a sponge cleaning up the kitchen. He washed his hands and pulled a pie out of the refrigerator and placed it on the counter. "What's that?"

"A chocolate pie."

"You made a chocolate pie?"

"No, I bought a chocolate pie. I had my hands full with the chili and the cornbread." He laughed.

"Thank God."

He placed the pie on the counter. "Kendell, what's going on?"

"I'm not used to this. I've always been the one doing this, in the relationship."

"I'm sorry. I didn't mean to over step my bounds."

"You didn't, it's me. You are really way more than I expected."

He walked over, wrapped his arms around me. "Is that all?"

Now was my chance to ask the question that had been sitting on my lips. "How…I don't…"

"Let me help you. No, you aren't the first woman I've

cooked for, but you are the first one to appreciate it."

"I am?"

"Yes. Usually, when they see this side, they don't like it."

"I don't understand." I like this side of him.

"Most of the fluffy women I've been with, even the Christian ones, don't want a sincere, real man. They want the guy in the designer suit and sports car and the fancy dinners. Don't get me wrong, all of that is very much me, but so is this." He looked around. "This is the me I've been wanting to share. That's why I invited you here for dinner. I wanted you to get to know my other side." I nodded. "So what do you think?"

He was definitely not the man I thought I knew, but the man I wanted to know. "I like this side a lot."

Alex

I LOOKED AT MY WATCH, one o'clock and I still hadn't heard from Moses about dinner. Maybe he changed his mind. Maybe I had a little too much crazy for him to deal with. That can't be possible, because he said he was going to stay around for a little while. Maybe that was just talk...

My phone rang interrupting my self-doubt party. I looked at the caller ID. It was a New York area code.

"Alex Miller."

"Hi beautiful." My heart jumped into my throat. He didn't forget. As soon as I hang up I'm putting this number in my contacts and committing it to memory.

"Hi."

"I'm sorry, I wanted to call you earlier but my meeting ran a little longer than I expected."

"That's okay." She's here. The fourteen-year-old schoolgirl, excited that the cutest boy in school just called her.

"Are we still on for dinner?"

"Yes."

"Is there any place special you want to go?"

"I'll leave it up to you."

"Okay, how about I bring dinner and we can talk?"

"Okay." I'd agree to fried bologna sandwiches if it meant spending the evening with him.

"What do you like? Better yet, what should I avoid?"

"No shellfish."

"Okay. I'll see you at six. Bye."

"Bye."

Five fifty, the phone rang and five minutes later, Moses pulled into the driveway. I opened the front door and saw him walking toward me with a couple bags from Whole Foods.

"I see you've been to one of my favorite places."

"We have it at home, so it seemed like a good choice."

"What did you get?" I asked, trying to peek inside the bag.

"Stop that." He smiled as he walked past me and into the kitchen. I closed the door and followed him. I sat at the end of the counter and watched as he took a bottle of wine out and placed it on the counter. "Where's the corkscrew?"

"I'll do that." He handed me the bottle.

"Thank you."

"So, what are we having?" I walked around the counter, opened the drawer and pulled out the corkscrew. I scooted past him and took two wine glasses out of the cabinet.

"Nothing jumped out at me, so I decided to cook."

"You cook?" I smiled.

"Yes, Miss Miller, I cook."

"Okay, so what are you cooking?"

"I thought I'd grill some steaks and asparagus."

"That's not cooking, that's grilling." I teased.

"Okay smarty, how about tomorrow I make baked ziti?"

"Are you asking me to dinner tomorrow?"

"Yes, I am."

"Okay. I'll meet you here at six."

"It's a date. But tonight, we're eating steak."

"Yes sir."

Our dinner conversation consisted of our trading stories about our family, friends and work. Everything, but the one question I really wanted to ask, *What are we doing?*

"What's on your mind?"

I wish he would have asked *what are we doing?*

I looked at him and the answer to his question was sitting on the tip of my tongue. *What's on my mind?* I'm wondering how you look naked…how your lips would feel touching a few delicate spots on my body…how your skin would feel pressed against mine. As the possible answers bounced off the walls of my mind, I couldn't stop the smile rising on my face. I wonder if his chest tastes as sweet as his lips?

"Uhm…," This is insane. I can't believe I'm sitting here lusting after this man. What is wrong with me? I jumped up and walked around the sofa. I needed a few deep cleansing breaths and I couldn't get them with him looking at me. *What's on my mind?*

"Alex…Babe…"

He got up and stood behind me. The heat from his body was overwhelming. I figured standing up would calm the hormonal war raging in my body, instead it made it worse.

He stepped closer, eased his hands around my waist, pulled me to his hard, warm chest and I went limp. My defenses were down. I knew at that moment, if he asked, I would have gladly let him make love to me. I know God would forgive me and I'd feel guilty afterwards, but my body would enjoy the ride.

I turned around and rested my head on his chest. His spicy, exotic scent, made him smell strong, sexy, powerful. I bet he could find my joy spot on the first try, unlike my ex-husband. It took him three and a half weeks and that was with me giving him directions.

His hands gently rubbed my back. I'm sure he thinks this is settling my spirit, calming me so I'll tell him what's on my mind. But it's doing the opposite. This sweet gesture is exciting me even more.

I pulled back and looked up at him. Biting my lower lip, I was all set to answer him, when he brushed my lips with his finger. That simple gesture took my breath away. He teased my lips with soft pecks before crashing his mouth against mine.

His kiss was demanding and strong, like him. I eagerly followed his lead, wrapping my hands around his neck enjoying his lips. He pulled me closer as his tongue invaded my mouth, leading me in a dance of passion. Trading deep moans with each kiss, my body was reacting in a way I hadn't experienced in years.

His hands slid down my back and pulled me so close I could feel every muscle in his body reacting to our dance. Lost in the moment, his hand slid down my behind and pulled me closer. I rose up on my tiptoes and pressed my body deeper into his.

Suddenly, I couldn't breathe. I didn't want him to remove his lips, but I needed air.

I pulled back and folded my arms across my chest. It had been a while since a kiss affected me like his. I didn't need to look down, because I felt my nipples pressing against the lace cup of my bra. Looking at him with those dangerous lips. I tried to speak. "Uhm…I…,"

He eased his hands around my waist and pulled me back to him. "What's wrong?"

How do I tell him, I enjoyed that kiss so much, my breasts are about to explode.

"I uhm…maybe we…your lips are…," I brushed his lips with the tip of my finger. "That kiss was…," It seems every time we kiss, it becomes more intense. He leaned down and took my lips and devoured every inch of my mouth climaxing with a deep moan I felt in my core.

There are a few traditional things my mother does, and one of them is Sunday dinner. The first Sunday of every month is Family Dinner, and it always includes Bas. He loves it, because he comes over after church, stuffs his face and loads up enough leftovers for a couple of days.

With Moses in town, Mama had another man to stuff today. She spent all day yesterday cooking. I tried to warn Moses, but he wouldn't listen. I think he and Bas were competing to see who could eat the most…Bas won. There was baked chicken, pot roast, mashed potatoes, string beans, mac and cheese, black-eyed peas, hot water cornbread, banana pudding and a sweet potato pie.

After dinner, Bas and Moses went out to the patio for guy talk while Mama and I cleaned up the dishes.

"Baby girl, I like him."

It only took Moses a few days to get Mama's seal of approval. Not that he needed it.

"So do I," I whispered.

"How long is he going to be in town?"

"I don't know, all he said is he's going to be around for a little while."

"I see. Do I need to disappear again tonight?"

"Funny, but that won't be necessary."

"I don't want to be a third wheel," she joked.

"You're not."

"It's good to see you happy."

"It's him. I like having him around and I like who I am when I'm with him."

"I'm going to get Bas packed up and out of here so the two of you can spend a little time together."

"Mama you don't have to do that."

"Shhh…Bas," she called.

"Yes, ma'am." He walked into the kitchen.

"Son, I have you all packed up. It's getting late."

"But Miss Connie…oh, I got you." He turned and yelled out to Moses. "Hey, Moses, I'll catch up with you later." Moses walked inside.

"You leaving?"

"Yeah, man." They shook hands. "It's been a long day."

"It was good talking with you."

"Same here. How are you at pool?" Bas asked.

"I know my way around the felt."

"Cool we'll set something up."

"Get my number from Alex."

"Definitely. Alex, I'll see you Tuesday." He walked over and hugged me. "Miss Connie, dinner was great as usual. Thanks for taking care of me," Bas said as he hugged her.

"Come on, I'll walk you out."

They walked out the front door and we sat at the counter talking. Mama came back into the kitchen and we both got quiet.

"Moses."

"Yes, ma'am?" He stood up.

"Sit down. I have enjoyed your company today, but I am exhausted."

"Mrs. Miller, the pleasure has been all mine. It reminded me of Sundays with my grandmother. Thank you. Everything was excellent. I'm stuffed," he said patting his stomach.

"I'm glad you enjoyed it. Alex told me you like banana pudding, so I put some in a bag along with a few pieces of chicken for later."

"Thank you."

"Good night." She kissed both of us on the forehead before going upstairs. "Alex, don't keep him up too late."

"Yes ma'am. Good night."

"My door will be closed," she shouted back.

"Mama…," I was mortified. "I'm sorry." I looked at Moses

and smiled.

"Let's go outside." He helped me down from the stool and we walked out to the patio and looked up at the sky. "It's a beautiful night." I rubbed my shoulders. "Are you cold?"

"No, I'm fine."

"Dance with me." He stood with his hand extended and a huge smile on his face.

"There's no music."

"Wait right there." He went inside and came back with his phone, pressed a button, placed the phone on the table and suddenly there was music. I was shocked at his selection. He turned around smiling, and started dancing towards me with his hand extended, singing along with the Gap Band. "The time has come for us to stop messing around. Don't you know I like having you around…Come on, dance with me."

"I'm a horrible dancer."

"I know better. Come on." He pulled me to him and we started swaying to the sounds of the Gap Band's, Yearnin' For Your Love. It felt good to let go. He spun me out and back into his arms. "You can't keep running in and out of my life. I need to have you as my lover and my wife…my heart is yearnin' for you…let me inside your love." He spun me out and back into his arms again. "You can't keep runnin' in and out…oh baby. Come on, show me what you got." We traded old school dance moves. "I thought you said you couldn't dance?"

"I said I'm a horrible dancer."

"Well, we'll have to work on that." He put his arm around me and led us in the chai chai. "Back and forth…you got it. Okay I'm going to spin you, one, two, three." He spun me out and back to his side as he sang. "I need to have you as my lover and my wife…you can't keep running in and out of my life…be my friend, my lover and my wife…my heart is yearnin'…let me inside…" He spun me out again and back to him.

I rested my head on his chest, inhaling his scent. He smelled like tobacco and exotic spices. I closed my eyes, inhaled again, savoring the aromas. This is what a strong, confident man smells like. He pulled me closer into his space and I felt safe. I held him tighter, enjoying the embrace. He gently stroked my hair as we swayed to the music. It felt strange, but it also felt right. I looked up into those incredible eyes staring back at me and knew this was where I belonged…in his arms. He gently traced my lips with the tip of his finger. "You're beautiful."

My face felt hot and my blood was boiling. My body was on the verge of betraying me. He pulled me closer, slid his hands down my back and I sank deeper down the rabbit hole. His intoxicating scent was clouding my judgement. I had never been with a man that had so much power over me.

I closed my eyes and my mind drifted to a lustful place. Then he kissed my neck and nothing made sense. I tried to open my eyes, but I couldn't. I felt his lips travel up my neck followed by a sweet, wet pinch on my ear and my breath caught in my throat. He brushed his hot lips across my cheek before capturing my mouth. I wrapped my arms around his neck and fell deep into a hot embrace trading soft moans stroking the fires of passion.

Every muscle in his chest was pressed against my breasts and the discomfort was overshadowed my the pleasure of being so close to him. The firmness of his body pressed up against mine awakened comatose feelings of desire. I pulled back and covered my mouth with my fingers.

"What's wrong?"

I shook my head smiling. "Nothing."

He pulled me back to him. "Did I do something you…"

"No."

"I'm confused."

I patted his chest and it felt like I was pounding on carved marble. "I like kissing you, it's just…,"

He stroked the side of my face. "You want to slow down?"

"Yeah, do you mind?" He exhaled. "Now you're mad."

"I'm not mad. I don't want to do anything to make you uncomfortable."

Uncomfortable wasn't the problem…more like lustful, sinful, unforgettable…I mean regrettable. "Thank you."

He turned off the music. "Come on, walk me out."

"You're leaving?"

"I thought…"

"I don't want you to leave. I just want us to slow it down."

"Come here." His hands eased around my waist and he pulled me to his chest. "What's going on?"

"I've never been kissed like that."

"Excuse me? Because just the other night…," he smiled.

I playfully socked him on the arm. "I've been kissed like that, but not with so much…passion."

"Passion?"

"Yeah. I felt more than your tongue with that kiss."

"I thought I was doing a good job keeping things under control." He joked.

"Funny."

He tucked my hair behind my ear. "I like you too, and sometimes I get a little carried away." He gently pressed his lips against mine letting them linger before pulling back. "Come on, walk me out."

He took my hand and we went inside and I helped him with his jacket. Brushing my hand across the contours of his shoulders, a wicked thought popped into my mind…how would his naked body look raised above me as we made love? I quickly removed my hands.

"Oh, don't forget your bag." I went back into the kitchen, got Mama's care package and handed it to him.

"Thank you." He leaned in to kiss me and I backed away.

"You better go."

"I have meetings tomorrow. How about lunch on Tuesday?"

"I'd like that."

He slipped his hands around my waist, pulled me to him and kissed me with such passion, I almost fell backwards. He eased his hand up my back and pulled me closer to his chest. My blood was boiling again as I forgot my plea to slow things down. His tongue sunk deeper into my mouth exploring and re-igniting the fire I thought was out. His hands slid down my back lifting me deeper into his grasp.

Suddenly a thud broke the mood. We pulled apart and saw the bag on the floor. He picked it up and looked inside. "All clear." We laughed.

I brushed the side of his face. "I guess that's your cue to leave."

He kissed the inside of my hand and whispered, "My heart is yearnin…be my lover and my wife…" He pressed his lips against mine and those feelings were stirring up again. He slowly removed his lips followed by a gentle brush of his thumb across my bottom lip. "Uhm…I better go. I'll call you tomorrow."

"Okay." I stood in the doorway and watched him get into his car and drive off.

I closed the door and walked back out to the patio and stared up at the sky. *Thank you God for bringing Moses into my life. And thank you for self-control.*

My phone rang with his ring tone. I pressed the button and before I could say anything, he started singing.

"The time has come for us to stop messing around. I like having you in my life."

I smiled. "I like having you in my life too."

"Good night, beautiful."

"Good night."

I WAS SURE DYLAN GOT the message wrong. Why would this woman be calling me?

Instead of having Dylan place the call, I did it myself. I closed my office door, sat down and dialed the number. After the first ring, someone picked up.

"Hello, this is Taylor Richards returning Mrs. Bartholomew's call." I know her first name but women of her position expect a certain level of respect.

"This is she."

I was shocked. I wasn't expecting her to answer the phone. I thought I'd have a couple of seconds to brace myself.

The little I knew about Emma Bartholomew could be written on the inside of my palm. I know she's a widow, has one daughter who's married to Eli Adair, has three grandchildren, is quite powerful on the Manhattan social scene and, she's very rich.

"I'm returning your call. How may I help you?" I felt like I should be standing up for this call.

"I'm Moses Adair's grandmother."

How could I forget who she is. When we met, she made it perfectly clear she felt I was not a suitable choice for her grandson. I will never admit it to her, but she was right. I thought the same thing after our first date, but knew it for sure after our second. Moses is more settled and I'm not trying to settle down, yet. He's looking for someone he can give the fairy tale to and I don't believe in fairy tales.

"I know who you are. What can I do for you?

"Alexandra Miller, what do I need to know about her?"

"Excuse me?"

"Young lady, I don't have time for games." Her tone was curt.

I hesitated to answer her question. "When I told Moses there was someone I wanted to introduce him to, he wasn't very receptive. However, I persuaded him to attend a party I was throwing for Alex. I thought they'd be perfect for each other, but I was wrong. He left the party early and alone."

"Is that all?"

"He called me later and asked if I had a problem with him asking her out and that was it. I haven't spoken to Moses since he called a few weeks ago."

"What about Alexandra?"

"I haven't spoken to Alex in a couple of days. Why?"

"I overheard a conversation and I thought…never mind. Thank you."

"I thought when Moses called, he was going to ask her out, but I guess he changed his mind."

"Why do you say that?"

"I know my cousin. If he had called her, she would have called me. We have an agreement, no dating each other's ex-boyfriends without asking."

"I see."

"So even if he did call her, it doesn't mean she agreed to see him. It's a shame because I thought his call meant he was ready to stop grieving and get on with his life."

"Young lady, I…thank you for trying."

Her gratitude shocked me. "You're welcome. Moses is a great guy. I'll tell you the same thing I told my Aunt Connie about Alex, don't push. When Moses is ready, he'll open his heart to love again."

"Good bye." Click.

That was bizarre. I thought about calling Moses, but I wasn't sure what to say. I know his grandmother is a little overprotective, but he's a grown man. At the same time, like Alex, he needs to stop grieving and get on with his life.

I scrolled through my contacts and pressed the button. Before I could process the call, my phone rang. I immediately recognized the ring tone and I pressed the Answer Call button. "Hey baby. How's your day going?"

"Very well. What about yours?"

"Interesting."

"How so?"

I thought about explaining, but stopped myself. "Just some rather interesting phones calls. Are we still on for tonight?"

This was our night with Zach. This new dating paradigm was very outside of the norm for me. This is the first time I've dated a man with a child. What am I saying? Zach is a five-foot-eight teenager. I have made it a point not to get involved with a man who has children. I don't have time for baby mama drama, and I thought myself too selfish to share my man with anyone, even his kids.

However, God surprised me. Zach is a good kid and Jason has done an amazing job raising him.

On these family dates, we allow Zach to pick the activity we do. We've gone to the batting cage, go kart racing, and I've seen more slasher movies than I care to mention. But it's been fun.

"That's the other reason I'm calling."

"Canceling on me?"

"On the contrary. We're going on a double date."

"With who?"

"Zach and Melissa."

"Excuse me? Since when did Zach start dating?" I was shocked. How could this child be dating?

"Since she moved in next door."

"Uh-huh." I really wasn't feeling this. "I think Zach is a little young to be…"

"Listen to you sounding all motherly." He teased.

"No, I'm not. I just think it's a little soon for him to be dating."

"Honey, it's just burgers and a movie."

"Really? I remember my first burger and movie date."

"So do I, that's why you and I are going." He laughed. "So what do you say? Would you like to go on a double date with me tonight?"

"Only if I can have extra butter on my popcorn."

"Deal."

"I'll pick you up at six."

My phone beeped and I looked at the screen and recognized the number. "Babe, I've got to take this call. I'll see you later, bye." I pressed the answer call button. "Hey Alex, what's going? I thought you were coming for a visit."

"I changed my mind," she informed me. "I went to Miami instead."

"And you didn't call me?"

"I needed a break. The opening really took it out of me, and you would have had me running all over South Beach," she laughed.

"And you know it." I laughed. "So what's going on?"

"Nothing much, just work. What about you? How are things with Jason?"

Alex is more like a younger sister than a cousin. She's constantly in my prayers. "Things are better than well with Jason. In fact, tonight, we're going on a double date."

"A double date…with who?"

"Zach and his little girlfriend."

She started laughing. "You're kidding!"

"No. Jason just confirmed it."

"I don't believe it."

"Believe it. Jason, told Zach the only way he'd allow him to go on a date was if we went too. So tonight, I'm going for burgers and a movie with my boyfriend and his son and his date. What has happened to me?"

"It's called a mature relationship."

"Don't say that. I've been trying to avoid one of those." I laughed.

"Too late, it found you." She laughed.

"What about you, when are you going to let one of those mature relationships find you?"

"Soon."

"Cuz, you've been saying soon for the past few years."

"I've been out there."

"Alex, I'm not talking about that weirdo you dated right after you broke up with Quentin."

Alex dated this handsome corporate lawyer. He wasn't exactly her type. He was about five nine; brown skinned, a little stalky, but he had a nice smile.

All the men Alex has dated had one thing in common, a great smile. She'll never admit she has a "type" although she does. Her type is a little under six feet, brown skinned, fit, not too muscular, dark eyes, a warm smile and no facial hair. Her fiancé, Jonathan, had a slight swimmer's build and like Quentin, he was more mocha in color.

She says, a man that knows how to dress his body to show off his best assets is a man who will understand her passion for clothes, and what she does for a living. That's why we couldn't understand why she went out with Bradford, and why I thought Moses would be right for her.

I know Moses isn't really her type, but he's very good-looking, looks good in everything he wears and has a great smile. So he's dark chocolate and a little over six feet, that's what stilettos are for. I think Bradford is the reason she's dragging her feet about getting back into the dating game.

"I beg to differ. Bradford was not weird. Strange maybe, but not weird." We both laughed.

"Alex, the man asked you to adopt a dog with him on your second date and took you to couple's counseling on your third date."

"That doesn't make him weird. It makes him special."

"Special? Alex, the guy was nuts. Did you forget when you broke up, his mother accused you of pet abandonment." We laughed harder.

My cousin is beautiful inside and out, and it breaks my heart to see her so closed off to dating again. I really was hoping things would have worked out with her and Moses.

"Did I tell you the funny part of that whole thing? His mother called and asked me if I had plans to sue for visitation for the dog." She continued laughing.

"How funny." I was laughing so hard, I started crying. "Seriously though, do you remember my friend, Levi?"

"The mortician?"

"Yeah. The cute short guy with the bright smile."

"Yeah. What about him?" she asked.

"He asked me if you were seeing anyone. And wanted to know if he could call you?"

"No, thank you."

"Are you sure? He'd be a nice companion for you here in Atlanta."

"I'm sure he would be, but no thank you."

THE PAST FEW WEEKS DON'T seem real. It's like I stepped into someone else's life. Moses is everything I wanted with a few extras I didn't even know I needed. I wanted to tell Taylor about him, but I wasn't sure how to tell her I might be falling in love with her ex-boyfriend.

My phone rang interrupting my thoughts. I looked at the caller ID and pressed the button to answer the call.

"Hey Chloe girl, what's up? How was Chicago?"

"It got pushed back. Where have you been?" she barked. "And why do you sound so strange?"

"What are you talking about? I sound like I always do." I relaxed my voice a little hoping to convince her there was nothing to be alarmed about. "What's going on with you?" I got her off me and on to herself.

"I know better, but I'm feeling too good about my latest deal."

I'm really not paying any attention to her, but her rambling

153

is just the sedative I need to send me back to my patio with Moses dancing and kissing. As I gave into the teenage girl who's been waiting on her dream man, Chloe said something that caught my attention. "What did you say?"

"I said, congratulate me. I just landed a big fish."

"Congratulations. Tell me all about your big fish."

"It's funny, I almost missed this one."

"How is that possible?" That girl could sniff out a potential client two continents away.

"My mother strongly suggested I attend the library fundraiser this year instead of sending my usual check and that's where I met this woman. Seems her husband has been looking for a way to cut down on the cost of executive housing for some of his long-term senior managers. We started talking and she said she'd have him call me. Long story short, I met him yesterday and if the numbers work out, he'll be getting the last three units in that New York building I've been trying to sell. Plus he wants one in the Houston and Vegas properties. And, he said he needs a pied-`a-terre in Paris as a gift for his son and his wife, something with a view of the Seine. Girl, this is some major money. He wants to turn them into suites so he can house multiple employees."

I heard the elation in her voice, but something about this mystery man sounded familiar.

I asked the multi-million dollar question. "What's his name?"

"Here's the ironic part, I just met his daughter-in-law at the Clinic Fundraiser. His name is Pierce…Thomas Pierce. Turns out we went to school with his son Terrence and his wife Blair. Do you remember them?"

Of course I remember them. Man, if I knew how to swear I'd be on full blast right now. My insides were boiling. I couldn't believe Blair would go to such extremes. I thought I'd made myself clear on where I stood with Terrence. I guess this deal is supposed to be a message for me. First, a visit, and now an attempt to expose my past to my friends.

"Congratulations," I tried feigning excitement.

"Thank you. So you know what that means. A little shopping to be followed by dinner at Kendell's. What time do you want me to pick you up?"

"Sweetie, I can't tonight. I have plans."

"Okay, what about tomorrow?"

"Let me check my calendar and I'll call you later."

"Cool. I'll probably stop by later this afternoon and do a little shopping."

"What time?"

"I'll call you when I'm on my way."

"Okay, see you later." I pressed the button ending the call.

All right, I see Blair is feeling a little threatened and felt the need to call in re-enforcements.

The knock at the door disrupted my much needed mini quiet time.

"Come in," I shouted.

"Alex, these just came for you." Kim walked in with a large arrangement of Casablanca lilies. "Where do you want me to put them?"

"On the credenza. Is there a card?"

"Yes, here." She removed the card and handed it to me.

"Thank you."

Meet me at Wesley's at one o'clock. Moses' schedule must have changed.

I followed the maitre d' to the table and he helped me into the booth. "Thank you." My phone rang before I could get comfortable. I recognized Bas' ring tone and immediately answered. "Hello...I see...my lunch date is here, bye." I pressed the button ending the call and greeted my lunch date. "Gerard."

"Alexandra."

I stared at him remembering the last time I met with him and how that meeting changed my life forever. I could leave and let him think I'm scared or I can stay and listen to what he has to say. He slid into the booth and the server magically appeared.

"May I get you something to drink? " the server asked.

"I'll have a mineral water and the lady…"

"Nothing, thank you." I waited for the server to leave. "What do you want Gerard?"

"I understand you and Terrence had a meeting."

"Is that a question or a statement?"

"This will be a lot easier, if you cooperate."

"Cooperate?" I smiled. "The last time I cooperated, it earned me an annulment, a broken heart and a check."

"The family needs your help." I laughed out loud. "Did I say something amusing?"

"The entire statement was funny. According to your boss' wife, I was never part of the family. A fact made perfectly clear when you presented me with annulment papers."

"I was merely doing my job," he retorted.

"Which you seemed to enjoy." His face went blank. "What do you want?"

"Ever since Terrence saw you, he's been a little distracted and it's causing problems."

"I see you've been talking to Blair."

"She may have mentioned coming to see you."

"I'll tell you the same thing I told her. It was just a coincidence that I bumped into her and Terrence."

"According to Mrs. Pierce…you're still in love with her husband."

I laughed. "I see Blair managed to paint her own picture of what happened. What I said was, you never forget your first love." He pushed an envelope towards me. "What's this?"

"The family needs you to not be so available the next time Terrence contacts you."

I opened the envelope, looked inside and saw a check for five million dollars. "I guess you thought this situation required more zeros." I closed the envelope and placed it back on the table. "As I told Blair, I've kept up my end of the agreement and stayed away from Terrence. If you don't want Terrence to see me, then you better get him on a shorter leash. Now if you'll excuse me, I have a meeting to get to." I stood up and left.

I opened the door to my office, walked inside and looked around. Mama and Bas were looking out the window, and Moses was pacing back and forth. I closed the door and everyone turned around.

"What's going on?" I asked.

"Kiddo, you had us worried," Mama said as she ran over and hugged me.

"I'm okay." That statement was more for me than for her.

"Alex we——" Bas jumped in.

"I'm fine, thank you for the call."

"If anything had happened….," Bas quipped.

"I told you, I'm fine." I looked across the room. "Moses."

"Alexandra." The formalness of his tone was more scary than my surprise lunch meeting.

"Baby girl, what happened?" Mama asked.

"Who was the mystery person?" Bas asked.

I placed my bag and jacket on my desk, took a deep breath, and crossed my arms in front of me. "Gerard." Moses looked at me, not smiling.

"Who's Gerard?" Bas asked.

"The ex's family lawyer. What did he want?" Mama asked.

"Five million dollars worth of cooperation."

"What the crap!" Bas yelled.

"Not again," Mama replied.

"Yep."

"All of this because Terrence came to see you, doesn't make any sense." Mama said what I assume everyone was thinking. "What exactly did the lawyer say?"

"He said I needed to not be so available. That Terrence has been a little distracted since he came to see me. Oh yeah, and his wife accused me of still being in love with him."

"His mother said something similar."

"Mama, what did you do?"

"I didn't do anything. She came here looking for you and got me instead."

"Mama...," She walked over and kissed me on the forehead.

"What else did Gerard say?"

"Nothing. I left."

"Now what?" Bas asked.

"Nothing. I mean, I could call my ex and tell him, but why?"

"It could put an end to the madness," Bas replied.

"I doubt it." I took a deep breath. "I don't want to talk about it anymore. "

"Come on Bas, let's go check on things downstairs." Mama grabbed Bas by the hand and pulled him toward the door.

After the door closed, I looked at Moses. "You're very quiet. What's on your mind?" He hadn't looked at me since I said Gerard's name.

"Nice flowers."

"I thought they were from you."

"When I heard you had gone to meet me for lunch, I was terrified." I walked over to him and kept my distance. "I felt helpless," he continued. "I immediately asked God to protect you. I knew if anything happened to you I..."

I eased my arms around his waist and laid my head on his wide back. His heart was beating, like a tribal drum. He took my hands, placed them on his heart, and I could feel his heartbeat slow down. I exhaled and felt my heartbeat get in step with his. The tribal beat became a slow and easy thump. We stood quiet, not moving, just breathing in sync.

Dionne

I SAT ON THE SOFA replaying the events of this afternoon. I knew it was just a matter of time before Quentin got home. I tried calling him, but all I got was his voicemail. I know that shrew mother of his had probably called him, and that's why he wasn't answering my calls.

I poured myself a large glass of wine and sat on the sofa wondering how I was going to explain my side of the story. I took a long sip and tossed my head back. It could have been worse. I could have shot her with that little gun Chloe gave me for protection. Considering what she did, any jury would rule it self-defense.

I looked at my watch. Seven o'clock and still no word. I went into the kitchen, opened the refrigerator, and pulled out the leftover chicken and broccoli. I made myself a small plate, drank another glass of wine, and sat staring out the kitchen window.

I pressed Quentin's number again. Voicemail. I didn't bother to leave another message. I went upstairs, took a shower, climbed into bed, and turned on the television. Even with two glasses of wine and a warm shower, I still couldn't sleep.

I picked up my latest Darryl Moses book and tried losing myself in the story. About an hour later, I heard footsteps coming towards the bedroom. I looked up and saw Quentin walking through the door. He didn't look at me. He went straight into his closet. A few minutes later, he climbed into bed and turned off the light.

I started not to say anything, but it was clear there was a lot that needed to be said. I closed my book and braced myself. "Are we going to talk about what happened?" Silence. So I poked the bear. "I know you know, and that's why you've been avoiding my calls." He exhaled loudly. "Quentin...Quentin...fine."

I turned the light off and laid down. I tossed and turned for quite a while before finally dozing off. The sudden shift of the bed woke me. I sat up and realized I was in bed alone. I got up and went searching the house for Quentin. I went down to the kitchen and found him sitting at the counter with his face in his hands. "What is going on with you?"

I exhaled. I could either ignore him and the direction this conversation could go or I could just answer him. "There's nothing wrong with me."

"I don't understand why you keep playing into her hand."

"Are you serious? She's the one who...I don't want to get into this right now." I turned and started out of the kitchen.

He lowered his hands. "Where are you going?"

"Back to bed because I see where this conversation is headed and I don't want to go there."

"You've been calling me all afternoon saying you wanted to talk and now that I do, you don't."

"I don't think either of us is in the right frame of mind for this conversation."

He nodded. "Don't you see what she's trying to do?"

"Do you?" No answer. "Fine, you want to talk Quentin, let's talk." I walked back into the kitchen and stood on the other side of the large, white marble counter staring at him. Sitting in front of me wasn't the man I married, but my mother-in-law's son. Right now it felt like he was on her side and not mine. "I get that you're tired of fighting, but so am I. It seems I've been fighting a war all by myself. Since when did you stop fighting with me?"

"What are you talking about?"

"When it comes to your family, it feels like I'm all alone."

"That's what you think?"

"That's how it feels." Silence. "I have tried being nice to your mother, but she's constantly attacking me."

"So you felt the best way to handle her was to play into her hand. You gave her exactly what she wanted."

"What she wants is to break us up. And today she proved just how far she's willing to go to make that happen." My voice was starting to escalate. "My God, Quentin, she brought that woman to our home."

"All you had to do was ask her to leave." His voice was starting to meet mine.

"She shouldn't have been here in the first place. Instead of chastising me, it's your mother you need to talk to."

"My mother isn't going to change."

"So you expect me to spend the rest of my life fighting this woman?"

"That's what I've been doing."

"So when we have kids, are they going to be expected to just, deal with her meddling as well?"

"Unfortunately, yes."

"Now I see what Adam meant."

"What's that supposed to mean?"

"It means you are a grown ass man still trying to gain your parents' approval. I've got news for you Quentin, if you don't have it by now, you never will." I stormed out and went upstairs.

The next morning, I checked into the Viceroy. I guess Katherine won this round.

Kendell

I SAT STRAIGHT UP IN bed. The dream seemed so real. It's been a while since I had a visit from Rêve. I looked at my phone. It was three o'clock. I tried going back to sleep, but I couldn't. Every time I closed my eyes, Rêve's face kept appearing. I thought the dreams were the result of something lacking in my life. Tonight's visit negates that idea. My life is perfect. My restaurant is doing well, the relationships with my family and friends are well, and I have an amazing man in my life. So what could be triggering this latest visit?

I lay staring at the ceiling, contemplating another attempt at sleep. I drifted off and woke up after what felt like hours. What woke me, was Rêve. He was standing in front of me with tears streaming down his face. It was as if someone had died and he was grieving. I tried to console him, but he pushed me away. I sat straight up again and looked at the clock, three-thirty.

I climbed out of bed, picked up my phone and headed into the kitchen. I scrolled through the address book until I found the number I wanted to dial. I pressed the button and waited for someone to pick up. After the first ring, a voice on the other end answered.

"What's wrong? Who's dead? Who's in jail? I'll be there as soon as I can get a flight."

"Calm down Taylor, everyone is fine."

"Girl, you scared me. The only other person I know up at this hour is Jason and I know he's not calling because he's making money."

"I'm sorry."

She cleared her voice. "What's wrong? Is everyone okay?" she asked again.

"Everyone is fine."

"Then why are you calling at this time of morning? It had better be important."

"I couldn't sleep."

"So you thought you'd call me?"

"Three hour time difference. I figured you'd be up."

She cleared her throat again. "So, what's on your mind?"

"I had a bad dream."

"Kendell Denise Martin, I know you did not call me because you had a bad dream. What's wrong?"

"I've been seeing someone."

"Couldn't this have waited, I don't know, two more hours?"

Taylor has never really been much of a morning person. Even in college, she made it a point to take all late afternoon or evening classes. While we were in class she was sleeping in. Then she'd party, study a little and crash. To this day, I don't know how the girl graduated Magna Cum Laude with that schedule.

"I'm sorry, I can call back." I started to hang up.

"That's okay. I need to get up anyway. I promised Jason I'd meet him for breakfast later. So tell me about the dream."

I recalled the details of the dream as I could remember them. "It was very clear. It felt like he was saying goodbye.   So what do you think?"

"He was."

"You think?"

"Not to be all psychological, but your sub-conscience or sleeping mind created this man to fill a void you thought needed filling. Instead of trusting your love life to God, you tried to handle it yourself and that's where this Rêve came from. What's changed in your life?"

My first response was to lie, but I couldn't. "I started seeing someone." I confessed.

"Well, there's your answer." She didn't seem surprised. "How long?"

"Almost two months."

"Really? Is it serious?" She asked the same question I've been wanting to ask.

"I think so."

"Your subconscience is telling you it's time to let the fantasy go."

"You think so?"

"Is it serious?"

"I've been too afraid to ask."

"You don't think he feels the same?"

"No, I'm terrified he does."

"And that would be a bad thing?" She sounded confused. "I don't understand you Kendell. For years you've been saying you want the fairy tale…the complete package…the husband, children, Sunday dinners and birthday parties. Now you have someone who just might…"

"He says he's tired of fluff and wants substance."

"And you don't?"

"I do, but…"

"Not with him?"

"His reputation precedes him. He hasn't always been the type to…I've never pictured him as the husband and father type. Not that he probably wouldn't be great in either role. Maybe it's all moving a little fast. Let's be real, my last few relationships were not the best."

"People change."

"I know that."

"Look at me. I never would have thought I'd be dating a man with a teenager. Not only am I seriously dating him, I'm picturing a future with him."

Now it was my turn to be shocked. "Excuse me?"

"If you tell anyone I said that, Kendell Martin, I will walk to California and slap you." We laughed.

"This is Taylor Richards I'm speaking with, right?" I teased.

"Shut up. I know, I can't believe it either. I got involved with Jason, because he was young. I figured after a few months, I'd toss him back into the kiddie pool. Instead, I discovered he's more mature and focused than any other man I've known. And the way he cares about his son is amazing. Zach is his priority, as it should be. At the same time, he's made it clear he wants more, and more includes Zach."

"So you're dating them both?"

"You joke, but yes, I am. I honestly believe if Zach and I didn't get along, Jason would be gone."

"You think?"

"I know."

"So is it love?" I asked.

"So tell me more about this new man."

"Ah, the well timed subject change." I felt myself blushing. I hadn't told anyone about me and Bas. We agreed to wait a little longer, but I needed to tell someone. "He's amazing, kind, compassionate, has a great sense of humor, and loves God. I think this time I got it right. Like I said, his reputation…"

"Is in the past." She reminded me.

"You're right. That's who he was. We've decided to wait before telling anyone."

"How long?"

"A little while longer."

"I see."

"I know it sounds strange, but it's a good thing, and I agree."

"Why?" I sensed her reservation.

Bas and I wanting to keep our relationship a secret doesn't make him sound very trustworthy. "Taylor, he's a good man and he's not seeing anyone else."

"Are you sure?"

"Yes."

"Kendell, Sweetie, your track record hasn't been that great and I don't want to see you get hurt again." Her concern was genuine. "If he's insisting you keep your relationship a secret…"

"It's Bas." I blurted out. She was quiet. "Say something."

"I don't know what to say. Definitely not the name I was expecting to hear."

"Please don't tell anyone," I begged.

"Are you kidding? I'm still trying to process it myself."

"So am I."

"Talk about going against type. You're right to want to take it slow. I love him, but his reputation does precede him."

"So am I nuts?"

"Honey, only you can answer that question."

Chloe

MY TRIFLING, GOLD-DIGGING HUSBAND really is a piece of work. We've been at this game of clever cat and dumb as dirt mouse for a few weeks. I have to give him credit, I thought he would have been gone by now, but he's still here. I know him better than he's willing to admit. His strategy for getting me to cave is typical.

I suspected at some point he'd bring that trampy little girlfriend of his around my friends, but I had no idea he'd bring her to church.

Sunday's move completely changed the game. It really was the grace of God that kept me from making a scene. Although I wanted to snatch that ratty weave off her head and cut his throat, I kept my cool and acted like I didn't even see them.

He's trying to bait me and I refuse to play his game. I lowered my standards once and that was one time too many. Time to adjust my strategy because playing nice isn't working. Instead, it's making me look weak, and I'm anything but weak.

He probably thought I was going to retaliate a few days ago. Just because I've threatened to knock him into next week doesn't mean at this point in our "relationship" that I'd actually do it. Nor would I cut him off financially. Both are too predictable. No, this situation requires something a little more simple and unexpected. Kindness. Treating him like everything is fine, like we're still a happily married couple. That simple move will do more damage than anything else I could think of.

Orlando has been running around like he's cock of the walk. Coming in at all hours of the night and passing out all over the house. This is a new day with a new set of rules...mine.

I looked up from my iPad in the direction of the haggard footsteps coming towards the kitchen and there he was, the man I married on impulse. I knew Orlando wasn't expecting to see me, which was evident from his lack of a robe.

When I met Orlando, it was his looks that drew me in. It's only been in the past four years that he's slowly turned from the man I fell in love with, to this man I can't stand to be around.

I wish I could say I'm ashamed of what happened the other night when I helped him into bed, but I'm not. I was friskier than a cat in heat. He had passed out in the hall, and I tripped over him when I went to set the alarm. My immediate reaction was anger, but then he smiled, stroked the side of my face, and kissed me. Instead of resisting, I gave in, right there in the hall. When he finished, he called me by her name and it brought me back to reality. I got up and left him lying there like the dog that he is.

"Good morning, Sweetheart," I said with a smile.

He almost stumbled over his open mouth looking at the breakfast spread. I know one of the things Orlando loves is a big breakfast. In the past, he would work out and come back and load up before heading to work. Once this battle started, and he began spending his mornings elsewhere, I had Mrs. Andrews stop making breakfast. Instead, I'd grab a smoothie or some fruit after working out.

This morning marks the beginning of a new plan, one that

includes breakfast. I had Mrs. Andrews make all of his favorites, buckwheat pancakes with blueberry compote, herb scrambled eggs, fresh fruit, bacon, salmon croquettes, honey apricot muffins, fresh cucumber juice and coffee from that little French place in Manhattan Beach he likes.

"What's all this?"

"Just a little something I had Mrs. Andrews whip up. Hungry?"

"Uhm…"

"Sit down." He pulled out a chair and sat down. "Coffee?"

"Yeah, thanks." I got up and poured a cup of coffee and placed it in front of him.

"How did you sleep?"

"Fine."

"I had Mrs. Andrews take that pile of clothes you had stacked in the corner of your room to the cleaners. I was at Neiman's yesterday, and I got you some new underwear and socks." I poured myself another cup of coffee and sat down.

"Thank you."

Kill him with kindness. If he hauls me into court he won't be able to say I wasn't performing all my wifely duties even if he can't remember some of them. "Good….full schedule today?"

"Why are you being so nice?"

"Honey, that's what wives do. They send their husbands off to work with a good breakfast, they inquire about their work, and they buy them new underwear."

"Chloe, I don't wanna play this game."

"What game? I want to make sure you're full and prepared to tackle your tasks for the day and have clean underwear. Oh, I ordered the fight for you and the fellas, and Kendall is going to send over some food." I attempted some small talk, finished my breakfast but all I got were grunts. I looked at the clock on my iPad…eight-thirty. I've wasted enough time. I stood up, walked over and kissed him on the cheek. "Have a good day sweetheart," and left.

If I were Orlando, I'd be scared. Grant it, I would never hurt him physically unless I was provoked. It's the mere fact that he has no idea what to make of my behavior that has him off his game. A con always thinks he has the upper hand, but Orlando forgot who he was dealing with. Little gestures like this keep him confused and weaken his strategy, giving me the upper hand. He's a formidable opponent and his little girlfriend is probably coaching him, but neither is really a challenge. I could win this fight with one hand tied behind my back wearing Loubos two sizes too small, and not even break a sweat.

I got in the car, plugged my phone into the charger and started the engine. I pressed Taylor's number and by the time I pulled out of the driveway the phone was ringing. After the second ring, she picked up.

"Hey girl, what's going on?"

"Got a few minutes?"

"Sure, let me close the door. Okay, what's going on?"

"I need you to tell me why poisoning my trifling, cheating husband is a bad thing." Her laughter was contagious. "I'm serious, Taylor. I want to hurt this fool so bad, my hair aches."

"For starters, you look horrible in orange." We laughed harder. "What did he do now?"

"Girl, I just knew he would have left by now."

"I've got to give him credit, I didn't think he had it in him. You've probably made it a little too comfortable for him."

"Yeah, and giving him a little taste didn't help either."

"What! When?"

"Girl, I wish I could say I was drunk, but I was just frisky. Hey, we're still married."

"You better be careful. I know someone that did that and now she and her ex are fighting over visitation. Did you protect yourself?"

"It happened so fast."

"Oh, I'm sorry."

"No fool." We laughed. "That part was actually good.

Seems his little girlfriend has taught him a few things."

"I'm not condoning infidelity, but seems it improved one part of your marriage," she joked.

"Not funny Taylor."

"I'm sorry girl, just trying to make you feel better. Back to my original question. Did you protect yourself?"

"No." Now I was even more ashamed of what happened. "I know Orlando. He's so paranoid, he wears condoms with me even though I'm on the pill."

"But he hasn't been with you, he's been with her."

"And I know he doesn't want kids."

"What?"

I felt tears gathering. "In the beginning I felt the same, but..."

"You changed your mind."

"Yeah. I think that's why I was so careless."

"Chloe, you have to be careful. It's not just you two anymore. It's you, him and her."

I wiped the tear rolling down my face. "I know."

Bas

WHEN I ARRIVED AT THE restaurant, Moses was sitting at a table in the corner looking like a man with the weight of the world on his shoulders.

"Bas." When I shook his hand all I heard was Alex asking me what I was doing.

Some assistant and friend I am. Let's sum up a few of my betrayals. First, I've been sneaking around with her cousin and asked said cousin not to say anything. Then, I didn't tell her that her boyfriend asked me to meet him to talk about her. Oh yeah, and I didn't tell her that her ex-mother-in-law and mother almost got into a fight at the store. If she worked for me and did what I did, I'd fire her. So I know what she'd do to me if she found out.

"Thanks for coming." We shook hands and I sat down. "Coffee?"

"Thanks." He filled my cup. I took a big sip, and braced myself for this conversation. "So, what's on your mind?"

"Man, where do I begin?"

Betrayal is a booger just waiting to be picked at. "Do you love her?"

"Yes, what about you?"

"Like a sister. Did you tell her you love her?"

"I told her I was falling in love with her."

"Bad move," I disclosed.

"Why? Don't you think she loves me?"

"I know she loves you, but—"

"But what?"

"She's not ready to admit it." We all know it's time for Alex to stop grieving and get on with her life. But until she's ready, nothing is going to happen.

"Why?"

"Because she's scared."

"That's what she said."

"I bet if you bring it up again, she'll get defensive and try pushing you away."

"She already did…how long have known Alex?"

"Twelve, no, fourteen years."

"So you're somewhat of an authority on her?"

"Second to her mother."

"So what do I do?"

"Nothing. I'm a little protective of her. But I gotta be honest. This whole Terrence thing threw me for a loop. I don't know how she managed to keep it a secret for so long. Between you and me, if we hadn't bumped into him she probably still wouldn't have told me." I sipped my coffee. "I think this is something she planned to take to the grave. Did she tell you about the plane ticket?"

"What plane ticket?"

"Then, I guess you don't know about the funeral either?"

"No." He sipped his coffee and placed the cup back on the saucer.

"Everyone suspected she and Jonathan were finally going to get married, but we didn't know she planned to surprise him in Europe so they could elope. I only know because she showed me the plane ticket. She's still carrying that thing in her purse." I disclosed. Now I am officially the worst friend ever. I wouldn't have said anything except I think he really cares about her.

"Why?"

"I think it's her way of blaming herself for what happened to him."

"Her being there wouldn't have necessarily changed things."

"I know, but in her mind she thinks if she'd been there she could have called for help."

"And what happened at the funeral?"

"When Terrence came to the store, he told her he was still in love with her and that he was lurking in the background at Jonathan's funeral. He told her he and Jonathan talked constantly, that's how he kept tabs on her."

"What!" I could see the anger on his face. "That explains a lot."

"Turns out he married his best friend's dream girl."

"You're kidding?"

"Nope." He shook his head. "Oh, but it gets worse. Her favorite gift from Jonathan is something Terrence helped him design and probably bought."

"I don't want to hear anymore. This guy is a piece of work." He shook his head. "He let his family manipulate him into annulling their marriage, and yet he couldn't seem to stay away from her."

"Tell me about it."

"No wonder she's so guarded and confused." He tapped his fingers on the table.

"Exactly. So what do you think they want from her?"

"I don't know."

"I overheard Alex talking to one of her girlfriends about Pierce Holdings. Something about an IPO."

"That would make sense. A good portion of what goes on

with an IPO is image. If word got out the future CEO is having problems in his marriage, it could make possible shareholders a little nervous. No one wants to invest in a company where the CEO is involved in a messy divorce. It also weakens his perceived ability to run the company. Worst of all, it could lower the opening stock price. They have to present a united front and be the perfect corporate family."

"How do you know all of this?"

"I have an MBA and do some consulting for my dad's company. They can't afford a scandal right now. From what I've heard about this guy he really hasn't been that involved with the company. His biggest contribution was his marriage. I told Alex he's probably looking for closure. But there has to be more. They're scared about something and whatever it is, she's the key."

"HEY ALEX, GOT A MINUTE?"

"Sure, Bas. What's on your mind?"

"There's something I've been wanting to talk to you about. With all the craziness going on, I really haven't had a chance. And I'm not sure how you're going to react."

"The best way to find out is to just tell me."

"I met someone."

"Again?" I laughed. "Have a seat and tell me all about the new Ms. Right Now."

"No, this time it's different. Remember when you hired me, you said your friends, family and customers were off limits?"

"Uh-huh."

"I kinda broke the rule."

"Who is it?"

"It's not a customer."

"Okay."

"It's Kendell."

"My cousin, Kendell?" I removed my glasses so I could see who I was talking to. It sounded like Bas, it looked like Bas, but the words didn't make sense.

"Yeah."

"Where is this coming from?"

"Please don't get mad. I've been watching you and Moses and, it got me thinking about my life and what I want." He was sitting on the edge of the chair with his hands clasped together.

"Kendell is what you want? Isn't that kind of out of the blue?"

"Not really. I've always had a thing for Kendell, but because of that stupid rule," I smiled and shook my head. "I kept my distance. You know, I've dated quite a few women, but none of them was ever serious. I've been going to her restaurant twice a week since it opened. Every time I'm there, she stops by and says hello, but nothing more. Honestly, I didn't think I had a chance. I'm not really her type."

"Is that a little insecurity I sense?" I smiled.

"No. I've seen some of the guys she's been with and I'm nothing like them."

"You're right. You're what she needs, not what she wants."

"Thanks."

"So when did this romance happen?"

"A few weeks ago."

"A few weeks?"

"About the same time as you and Moses."

"Really?" Talk about a well guarded secret.

"She wanted to tell you, but I said I broke the rule and I have to face the consequences, not her. So here I am. Wearing my heart on my sleeve and hoping you don't fire me."

"I don't know what to say." I sat with my arms folded in front of me trying to wrap my head around everything he said.

He stood up. "Okay, then. I'll clear out…"

"Sit down. I'm not going to fire you. Right now I'm not in a position to tell anyone who they should or shouldn't date. I caution you. My cousin can be a little..."

"I think I know what you're going to say."

"You do?"

"You'll kill me if I break her heart."

"No, I'll kill her if she breaks yours."

I was staring out the window thinking about my conversation with Bas. Still trying to wrap my head around his confession. Bas and Kendell. I didn't see that coming. Now if he had said Chloe, I wouldn't be surprised because they have a weird love-hate relationship which usually leads to something more.

The knock on the door interrupted my one-sided conversation. "Come in." I called out. "Yes?"

"Lexi..."

I immediately turned around to confirm the reflection I saw in the window.

"Terrence...how did you get in here?" I didn't know if I should run over and throw my arms around him or get my gun. "Whoever let you in, is fired."

"No one let me in." He closed the door. I picked up the phone and began dialing. "Please, I just want to talk to you."

I hesitated a few seconds before hanging up the receiver. I closed my eyes, and for a brief moment I was back in my apartment in Paris, looking at the man I loved apologize for being late for dinner. "What do you want Terrence?"

"I don't know."

"You don't know? You risk being arrested for, I don't know? Please."

"Lexi, I...I thought seeing you again would help me figure out some things." I folded my arms in front of me. "But it didn't.

I'm miserable and I'm not sure who I'm more angry with, me or you."

"Me?"

"Yeah, when Gerard returned and said you took the money, I was shocked. I expected him to say you threw it in his face. I thought you'd come after me, and when you didn't, I knew they'd won. While Gerard was with you, I called Jonathan and confessed everything. That day I lost my wife and my best friend. When Jonathan forgave me, I encouraged him to pursue you. One of us deserved to be happy and I'm glad it was you."

"Happy? You think my life with Jonathan was happy? I was miserable. Our entire relationship was the worst emotional roller coaster ride of my life. We never really understood each other. It was a lot of wasted time neither of us admitted to."

"I didn't know." He stepped closer.

"Your best friend made me feel horrible." I felt myself getting angrier by the second, but refused to give him the satisfaction of a scene.

"I don't understand. He said everything was fine. He was excited about marrying you."

"He was also excited about the other women."

"You knew about that?"

"Yes, I just never knew how involved until he told me about his son."

"You know about JJ?"

"He introduced me to him and his mother before he proposed the last time. He said he wanted to come clean and lay everything out on the table."

"He swore to me you didn't know."

"Chalk it up as another one of Jonathan's many lies."

"If I'd known, I would have…"

"What, told me? That's funny. To think, all these years I've been feeling guilty about taking that money. Like I was betraying us. But it was you who betrayed me. You and your best friend played with my heart and lied to me."

"No, we didn't."

"I asked Jonathan if he ever spoke to you and he said the last time he spoke with you, was a week after your wedding. Now I know that wasn't true." I shook my head. "Lying sack of crap."

"He loved you."

"I don't want to hear it."

"It's the truth."

"No, it isn't. He was in love with being like you and he succeeded. He hurt me just like you did, and I was the fool that allowed it to happen."

"Don't say that."

"It's the truth. Everything that happened, I allowed. I could have fought for us, but I took the easy way out. I knew if I hadn't, I would have spent the rest of my life fighting for our relationship."

"That's not true," he demanded.

"Yes, it is. I can't help you. You made your choices and you have to live with them." I walked around my desk to the door and opened it.

"Lexi…"

"Please leave or I'll call the police."

He started toward the door and stopped when he got next to me. "Lexi…I'm…,"

"Leave." He walked out and I slammed the door. I wrapped my arms around myself breathing hard. I felt tears just waiting on permission to fall, and I didn't know why. I wasn't in love with him anymore, but after twenty years he still had a piece of me.

I stood in the middle of the room quiet. A rapid knock on the door broke the silence. I turned around and headed to the door, opened it and looked up and saw Moses. I tried faking a smile, but tears came. I quickly covered my eyes and fell into his chest, sobbing. He wrapped me in his arms and walked me back inside my office and closed the door.

"Hey, what's going on?" His gentleness made me cry harder. "Shhh…shhh…shhh, Beautiful. What's going on?"

I pulled back and he took out his handkerchief and patted

my face. "What are you doing here? I thought you left."

"Come on, let's sit down." We walked over to the sofa and sat down. I got as deep into his side as I could and we wrapped our arms around each other. "What's going on? What's got you so upset?"

I took a deep breath and thought about my answer. If I told him the truth, he would go after Terrence and I didn't want a scene. "I don't want to talk about it."

"You don't? You're shaking and crying, and you don't want to talk about it?" He continued rubbing my back. "Does it have to do with the man I passed in the hall?"

"I don't want to talk about it." I sniffled. "I thought you were leaving this morning."

"I changed my plans." He tucked a stray hair behind my ear.

"Not because of me?" I looked at him and everything about him said he cared about me. I believe he would fight for me, for us. I wouldn't have to be the strong one, he would gladly take on that role. "That was probably Terrence you saw." He jumped up and started toward the door. "Where are you going?"

"To have a talk with him." I jumped up and got in front of him. "Move, Alexandra."

"No." I stood my ground. He reached for the doorknob and pushed me to the side. "Moses, stop it." He ignored me.

"Alexandra, move. I'm going to have a chat with Mr. Pierce."

I placed my hand on top of his. "Moses, please don't." I looked up and saw the anger in his eyes. Those beautiful light brown eyes were black as coal. I gently stroked the side of his face. "Let's sit down, please…" I took his hand and led him back to the sofa.

"You're right. A scene would be bad for business. I'll go over to his office and talk to him." I looked at him and a huge smile covered my face. "What's so funny?"

"You." I gently stroked the side of his face.

"Me?"

"I love that you want to defend me," he started to speak. "I can take care of Terrence."

"He made you cry."

"No, I made me cry. I let him get to me."

"That's why I shouldn't leave. How am I going to protect you from him and his family?"

"You can't."

"Then I'll hire you a body guard."

"Are you insane? I don't need a body guard. Besides, I have security and he still got up here."

"Exactly."

I covered his mouth with my finger. "You keep your plans and let me handle this."

"I don't agree."

"I know you don't. He's harmless. Like you said, he's probably looking for closure."

"Then call him up and the three of us…"

"The three of us?" In that moment I realized I could love this man.

"Yes, the three of us will meet and let him speak his peace and we'll be done with him."

"It's not that simple."

"Why not? You said you were over him."

"I am, but you yourself said, he's really not the problem, his family is."

"All the more reason for you to have more security."

"I don't want to fight." I kissed him.

"We're not done with this."

"Yes, we are, and you are not going to his office."

"Are you trying to tell me what to do?" A slight smile appeared on his face.

"No, but I don't want to make this any worse than it is. I'm done with Terrence Pierce." He pulled me to his chest and wrapped me in his arms.

I walked into my bedroom and sitting on my nightstand was a huge bouquet of pink peonies. I recognized the white envelope with the chocolate brown monogram. I quickly opened the envelope and pulled out the card. *I want you in my life. Counting the days until I come back. Moses.*

I hate the way I left things with him this afternoon. My phone rang with a familiar ring tone. I pressed the answer call button.

"Hey there, Beautiful."

"Hi." That voice was just what I needed to hear right now. "The flowers are beautiful. Thank you."

"I thought they might cheer you up."

"They did and the note made me miss you even more. How was your trip?"

"Quiet. I missed my travel buddy. I didn't have anyone to talk to," he chuckled. "I was up working, and I just wanted to check on you."

"I was going to do the same thing."

"So much for space," we laughed.

"What kind of treat did Mrs. Joseph put out for you?"

"I didn't go home," he confessed.

"You didn't?"

"No. I needed a little time to myself. Away from Grams, the Josephs, the play, New York and—"

"Me?"

"Only because you asked."

"So where are you?"

"That's a secret."

"But what if I need you?" I stretched out on the bed.

"All you have to do is call and I'll come running."

"I feel like a teenager sneaking a late night call with her boyfriend."

"Your boyfriend?"

"You know what I mean."

"No, I heard what you said. Is that what I am?"

"I thought you were my fiancé?" I giggled.

"Okay, let's do this right. How was your day?"

When did I become a teenager again? This sort of behavior is not suitable for a grown woman. What is happening to me? "It was good. It started off a little rocky but it got better. My assistant is dating my cousin."

"Please tell me it's not Taylor." We laughed.

"No, it's Kendell."

"Really?"

"He says he's had a thing for her for quite a while."

"Good for him."

"So how was your day?"

"Good. I met with some producers about turning one of my books into a movie, had a business lunch and bought Grams a present. The highlight of my day is right now, talking to you. Low point of the day was seeing you cry," he sighed. "And you?"

"Highlight of the day, right now talking to you, low point letting you leave." I sat up and started pacing. "I was thinking about our conversation."

"What?"

"Well, I know I asked for a little space. However..."

"What's on your mind?"

"I was thinking, I'd really like it if...I mean, it would really be nice if we agreed to two phone dates a day."

"You sort of lost me."

"It would be nice to hear your voice in the morning when I wake up and at night, right before I go to bed. You know what, forget it. In my head, it made sense, but saying it out loud..."

"So you want to change our agreement."

"It's not so much changing our agreement. It's more like

amending our agreement. You know what, never mind."

"Beautiful…"

"Yes…"

"Call me in the morning. Good night."

"Goodnight.

Chloe

I CAN'T BELIEVE ORLANDO HASN'T cracked. I've been doing the kindness dance for three weeks and I'm tired. Seems my new strategy has been met with a little opposition. However, I've done a little tweaking and the ball is back in my court. I believe the envelope I messengered to his office will be the catalyst required to get him to take our relationship to the next level.

I sat at my desk reviewing notes for a conference call when my cell rang with a familiar Latin tune. I looked at the screen, and was presented with a picture of Marcelo's beautiful speed boat. I pressed the answer call button and was immediately greeted by a deep, sexy Latin voice.

"Bom, Chloe."

"Bom, Sweetie. How are you this morning, I mean afternoon?"

"I am doing well. How is my Carnival Queen feeling?"
The sound of his voice was music to my ears. I felt a huge smile rise on my face. "Even better now that I'm talking to you."

"When am I going to see you again?"

"I thought next month, but things aren't going as I had planned."

"He hasn't left?"

"No, and I've tried everything."

"Be patient, Sabella. It won't be much longer."

"I hope not, because I miss you."

"Did you get the contracts?"

"Yes. My legal team should be done with them by the end of the week."

"You know, they finally cleared all the debris off the site. Maybe you should come and see for yourself?"

His offer was very tempting and it would be a professional visit. "My attorney is adamant we keep our relationship professional. Hold on." I pressed the hold button and yelled out. "Tucker."

"Yes?" He shouted back.

"Come here."

"What's up?"

Tucker is my assistant and occasional bodyguard. He graduated magna cum laude from Morehouse and has an MBA from Stanford. Why is he working as my assistant, and not the head of some Fortune 500 company? I don't know.

I know he's good at what he does. He's able to anticipate my every need and, I know I can trust him with the utmost private business dealings and my personal life. He never complains or questions the tasks I give him, and it doesn't hurt that he looks more like a WWF contender rather than the typical overly groomed male executive assistant. Bottom line, I trust him, and that's all that matters.

"I'm thinking about disappearing for a few days. How does my schedule look?"

"Depends. Where are you going?" He stood in the doorway.

"I need to check on the Brazil project."

"Really," he said smugly.

"Yes. Now when can I leave?"

He looked at his iPad. "I might be able to juggle some things around giving you about three days week after next and that includes travel time."

"So, I'll have a couple of days?"

"More like thirty-six hours."

"Crap. Thanks." He walked back to his office. I exhaled and pressed the button taking the call off hold. "I thought I might have been able to sneak away, but it's just not possible."

"Sabella, I understand. I'll send you images of the site. We'll talk later. Adeus."

"Adeus, Sweetie." I pressed the button ending the call and yelled out again. "Tucker…" No reply and no Tucker. I called out again. "Tucker." I looked at the wall standing in front of my desk.

"Why are you yelling? This is a place of business."

"I'm yelling because you vetoed my trip."

"You'll thank me later."

"We'll see. Anyway, I need to inform you of something. My low-life gold-digging husband will be calling and I don't want to talk to him."

"Got it."

Later that afternoon, I heard loud voices. I buzzed Tucker, but there was no answer. I ended my call and went out to see what was going on and to find Tucker. I opened my door and Orlando barged into my office.

"Chloe, what's this crap?" he asked waving a piece of paper in my face.

Where did all that testosterone come from. He looked a little hot and sexy all fired up. If we were at home, I might have been a little tempted to settle this in bed. I backed away and collected my thoughts.

Tucker walked in behind him. "Ms. Jacobs, can I send those papers to Y.T. Iruces?" he asked.

When Orlando started acting strange, Tucker and I developed a code. Y.T. Iruces is security spelled backwards. And my answer dictates his next move.

"Yes." He exited my office leaving the door half-opened.
"What are you talking about Orlando?"

"This." He handed me a piece of paper.

"This is an invoice for your portion of the monthly expenses."

"Are you kidding?"

"No. If you recall, I said you can stay in my house but since we are legally separated, so is everything else. Now if you choose to utilize the services of Mrs. Andrews, then you will need to pay her. Or you can do your own laundry, clean your own room and bathroom, and fix your own meals once you've earned kitchen privileges."

"I see."

"You chose to drink the skim milk instead of the rich cream that was at home."

"Why are you doing this? Just the other day you were offering me breakfast and being all sweet. Almost like the Chloe I married. What changed?"

"You."

"Me?" He squinted his eyes trying to intimidate me.

"If you're not happy with the way I'm treating you then do something about it. You made this mess, and you can change it."

"So I'm the reason you work late? I'm the reason you never have time for me? I'm the reason your parents don't like me? It's all my fault." His voice was escalating.

"Grant it I do work late, but I don't see you complaining about the benefits of my job. No, you just sit around complaining about how neglected you are, how we never spend any time together. In actuality, you're the one who's always gone."

"Me?"

"Yes, you're either at the house hosting a party or flying your boys to Vegas or AC. If anything, I should be the one complaining about being neglected. Truth be told, you checked out of this marriage long ago."

"Are you kidding?"

"Did I stutter?"

"You left me no choice Chloe."

"So it's my fault you took up with that child?" I shouted back. "Why didn't you just get a hobby?"

"I did, and she doesn't work late."

"How can she when she hasn't gotten her work permit yet?"

"You know Chloe, I'd leave, but you're right, I like being Mr. Chloe Jacobs. It suits me." He reached into his pocket, pulled out his checkbook and proceeded to write a check. "Here, I believe this is the correct amount. Oh, and I threw in a little something extra for the other night, when you thought I was drunk."

"You son of a…get out!"

He walked toward the door and stopped. "Tell Mrs. Andrews to get some more of that coffee. Thanks, doll. Oh yeah, what time is dinner tonight?"

"Get out!"

"Now, now, Sweetheart, you wouldn't want people to talk."

"Get out!"

"See you tonight." He walked out and passed the security guards…about three minutes too late.

I LEFT THE STORE A little early and went over to Kendell's restaurant for dinner, and to talk to her about this thing with Bas. Who'd have thought Bas and Kendell? I still can't believe it.

I pushed the glass and mahogany door open and walked into the beautifully appointed restaurant, complete with chocolate brown leather chairs, white linens, and vases of orange roses on each table.

The patio is filled with petite tangerine trees, and when they're in bloom the aroma is amazing.

She's done well, and I see why her dad jumped at the opportunity to front her the money to get this place going. When you open the door, your nose is instantly held captive by the exotic aromas emanating from the kitchen.

As a thank you, the bill comes with a plate of bite sized chocolate chip cookies with a hint of tangerine flavoring.

I headed to my favorite seat at the end of the bar. I think it's the best seat, but Kendell would disagree. I like it because it gives you a view of everything and everyone.

"Good evening, Alex," Bobby said.

Bobby is Kendell's assistant and her muscle. He's a former Marine and is always smiling. I asked him why he was so happy? He replied, "After my three tours, I'm just happy to be alive. I could have stayed in the Marines, but I'd seen enough. I wanted the opposite of that life. This job gives me peace." He pulled a menu from under the counter and placed it in front of me along with a glass of the house burgundy.

"Is she expecting you?"

"No. I thought I'd pop by and see what's on the menu tonight. Tell me what looks good besides you?" I love teasing him. I get a kick out of watching this giant black man gushing.

"White sausage with grapes in a balsamic vinegar and red wine sauce, on a bed of garlic parmesan mashed potatoes."

"Sounds good, I'll take it."

"I'll put your order in and let the boss know you're here." He took the menu and went into the kitchen.

I like these moments when there are no customers or employees begging for my attention. It's my time to relax with a book and a glass of wine.

Bobby came back and placed a white envelope in front of me. "The gentleman in the corner asked me to give this to you."

I looked across the room to where Bobby was pointing. I'd never met him, but I could tell by the eyes who it was. He and Terrence had the same eyes. Only his eyes radiated anger and Terrence's eyes screamed loneliness. He stood up and I saw that height was another thing he and Terrence had in common. He walked over and sat next to me.

"I was told this is your favorite restaurant. I also heard you were not a very friendly person and slow to warm up to strangers."

"But you're not a stranger." I sipped my wine.

"They didn't tell me you had such a quick wit."

I ignored him and kept reading my book.

"I was also told I'd be wasting my time coming here, but

I chose to ignore all attempts to dissuade me." Out of the corner of my eye, I could see he picked up a menu and began reading. "Everything looks good, what do you suggest?"

I know he doesn't want me to answer that question.

"Seems you have shaken things up in my world."

I heard him tapping the unopened envelope.

"Aren't you curious to see what's inside?" I took another sip from my glass. "I apologize for sending my lawyer. I should have come myself. I think you'll find this envelope more to your liking."

Curiosity killed the cat, but what about the snake that's sitting next to me? I picked up the envelope and looked inside trying not to let the amount surprise me. I closed the envelope and pushed it toward him. "I see my value has gone up. Your attorney had a fifth of that amount. Impressive, but I'm not for sale."

"Young lady, do you know who I am? I buy and sell people all day. With one phone call I can destroy your entire world."

"I can do the same thing to you with one call to Terrence about that check." I took another sip from my glass and continued. "I believe this is what they call having the upper hand. I'm having the white sausage but I think you might be more happy with the shark tartar."

"I don't know what my son sees in you."

"Your son?" I smirked.

"What's that supposed to mean?"

"Mr. Pierce, I think some statements are self-explanatory, don't you?"

"This isn't over."

"I'm sure it isn't. Is the Paris apartment supposed to be for me? Because if it is, I would much rather prefer a house in Tuscany."

He picked up the envelope and left taking all of his toxic energy with him. I took a deep breath, finished my wine in one swallow and exhaled. My insides were shaking. That body guard Moses offered was looking like a good idea right now.

I lifted my empty glass towards Bobby, signaling for a refill. A few minutes later someone tapped me on the shoulder and I jumped.

"Hey Alex, are you okay?" Kendell asked.

"I was engrossed in my book. " She placed the plate on the counter in front of me and kissed me on the cheek. "Thank you. Sit down."

"Congratulate me." She was smiling from ear to ear.

"For what?"

"I just booked a huge wedding weekend for three hundred people with a mega budget."

"Congratulations." I reached over and hugged her again.

"Thank you. I'm so excited. I'm doing the rehearsal dinner, wedding breakfast, reception and they booked the restaurant for the bridal shower."

"Congratulations. Who?"

"Anthony Gerard. It's for his daughter."

"Gerard?"

"He's an attorney and the wedding planner said, his daughter loves my food and insisted I cater everything."

"That's great," forcing a smile.

"Yeah. I can use the money to set up Atlanta."

"It's that much?"

"The budget is huge. The planner says if this goes well, she'll refer me to more of her brides."

"That's good. I'm happy for you. This sausage is amazing" I wiped my mouth. "Bas and I had a nice conversation. Is there anything you want to add?"

"What did he say?" Her wide smile answered my question.

"He said he's been coming here twice a week for a while waiting on you to notice him."

"True."

"And that you two have been seeing each other for some time." Her smile got wider. "Well, I can tell by the look on your face that it's all true."

"He's not what I expected. I thought he was going to be all suave and slick, but he's not. He's sweet, kind, funny, compassionate, and an incredible kisser. I mean wow. Boyfriend has got skills."

"Okay, okay. I'll take your word Bas is a good kisser. Remember I have to work with him. I don't need a mental image of the two of you kissing floating around in my mind."

"But I thought you were fine with us as a couple?"

"I am. I'm just not ready to hear about the two of you kissing." I smiled.

"Okay, but don't tell the girls yet. I want to see where this is going."

"Okay." I hugged her.

"Thanks, Alex."

It's nice being courted. Having someone send me flowers, cook for me, call just because, be concerned about my well being and want to be my friend too.

I loved Jonathan, but romance wasn't his thing. He would send flowers on my birthday and Valentine's Day, and when he thought he had messed up. But never just because. I sent him flowers once but he didn't like it, so I didn't do it again. Some men come by romance naturally and some need help…Jonathan needed help. He had great taste in jewelry. At least that's what I thought until recently.

Compliments weren't his thing either. My girlfriends wondered why we were together if there were so many things lacking in our relationship. It was comfortable. I know he loved me, and I guess I fooled myself into thinking the way he treated me was good enough. Even worse, I thought it was love.

In the brief time I was with Terrence, he said and did all the right things and maybe with Jonathan, subconsciously I was punishing myself for what happened with Terrence, so I settled. Now, I have someone in my life that does and says all the right things and more, and it's a little overwhelming, but I like it.

I pulled into the garage and my phone started ringing. The ringtone confirmed it was my phone date. I got out of the car and pressed the answer call button.

"Hey, Beautiful."

I sigh every time he calls me that. I know that greeting is just for me. He makes me feel like a geeky schoolgirl secretly dating the cutest boy in school. "Hey, yourself."

"You sound out of breath."

"I just walked inside. I went to Kendell's for dinner and we started talking and I stayed longer than I planned."

"Do you want me to call you back later?"

"No."

"How was your day?"

"It was okay until my ex-father-in-law showed up." I walked into the kitchen.

"Are you okay? I knew I should have gotten that bodyguard."

"Calm down, I'm fine and no, you shouldn't have gotten a bodyguard." I lied, I wish he had.

"What happened?"

"He tried to give me another check." I sat my phone on the counter and hit the speaker button.

"What!"

"Calm down." The silence was deafening. "Moses."

"How much?"

"Twenty-five million," I mumbled hoping he didn't hear the amount.

"What! I'm on my way back. I'll be there in eight hours."

"No, you don't need to come back." I lied again. I really want him here, but it's best he stay away right now. "I can handle this."

"Why don't you want my help?"

"I can handle this."

"I can have a bodyguard at your place in less than an hour."

"Are you insane? I'm fine."

"Do me a favor, don't go to dinner by yourself again. Take one of your girlfriends, your mother or better yet, take Bas."

"Are you serious?"

"It's that or a bodyguard."

"I promise to be careful and I'll eat at home. How's that?" I tried making a joke.

"Better but, I still think I should come back or…"

"Honey, I'm fine. I'm going to talk to my uncle and see if there's something he can do."

He exhaled. "I guess it's pointless arguing with you."

"Yes, it is," I exhaled.

"Fine."

"How was your day?"

"I got a lot of work done and my agent called about the movie."

"Is it good or bad?"

"There are some things I'm not sure about. So we decided to put it on hold."

"Are you okay with that?"

"Yes, because I'm getting ready to start a new play, and that would mean two plays running at the same time, plus a movie. That's a lot. I would rather have one or two major projects going at a time. I can write anywhere, but it's difficult when you have three major projects in two different locations happening simultaneously."

"I understand. Fashion month is coming up and I was thinking about coming to New York a couple of days early so we can spend a little time together."

"Just tell me when and I'll have your room ready," he sounded excited.

"I don't think that's such a good idea."

"Why not?"

"Because things are different now."

"So you would rather I be seen going in and out of a hotel in a city where more people know me as opposed to you staying at the townhouse with Grams and I where we have a lot more privacy?"

"When you put it that way…I'll let you know when I'm coming. Will I see you before then?"

"Do you want me to come get you and we go to New York together?"

"I'll let you know."

"Okay. Sweetheart, it's getting late and I want to finish editing this chapter before I go to bed. You call me in the morning. Good night."

"Good night." I pressed the End Call button.

I walked into my office and a large bouquet of pink peonies was waiting for me with a simple note. *Beautiful, are you sure you don't want me to come back? Moses.*

I WAITED UNTIL AFTER READING my investigator's report before signing the contracts on the Brazil project.

After being so impulsive with Orlando, I wasn't about to trust Marcelo with my money or anything else. Brazil was nice… wonderful, but I can't afford to be impulsive again. Marcelo knew my involvement in this deal was contingent on the due diligence.

Our personal relationship was contingent on my investigator's report. Now I know everything I need to and then some. There's an ex-wife and a son that he has custody of, his parents left the ranch to him and his sister, and all of his business dealings appear to be legitimate. And, unless I'm mistaken, he scores high marks for integrity and character. All the things I wanted in a man but failed to look for with Xavier or Orlando.

I'm no stranger to being pursued by wealthy men, but one so unselfish, is a little strange. The other reason I was a little hesitant is because I'm not quite sure what's going on with Orlando. Seeing he's hardly ever home and we're legally separated. I think it's safe to say, I'm technically a single woman. Making it perfectly fine for me to enjoy the company of a nice man. My girls are great, but let's be real, a sister likes a little male attention from time to time.

Dating again isn't something I thought I'd be doing. But here I was, separated and contemplating going on a date. My nervousness didn't make any sense. After all, I spent a week at Marcelo's ranch. But in my defense, that was business…sort of. I told Alex about my date and like the proverbial mother hen that she is, she suggested I not go. I assured her I knew what I was doing. She told me to be careful and have a good time…but not too good of a time. Instead of being excited about my date, I spent the ride to the airport second-guessing myself.

Part of me felt like I was cheating on my husband, and the other part felt like this was my new beginning. I kept reminding myself that Orlando and I are separated…that he walked out on us. He's moved on and so should I. The driver opened the door and helped me out of the car. I left my fears behind and took the stairs to my new life.

Once seated, the flight attendant walked up behind me and asked, "Would you like a glass of…" That voice sounded familiar. I turned around and saw my flight attendant was also my dinner companion.

"What are you doing?" The sight of him brought a smile to my face. He leaned down and kissed me. His kiss confirmed I was doing the right thing or at least it felt like it was.

"What would you like to drink…cranberry juice, red wine, mineral water…you name it."

"I'll take the red wine. Thank you." He disappeared into the galley and returned with a glass of wine. He called the pilot and told him we were ready for take-off. Ten minutes later, we were taxiing down the runway and headed to dinner.

"Sabella, why you look so nervous?" The sound of that voice coming out of that beautiful package made me forget why I was nervous.

"Eu não sei…I don't know."

"I see your Portuguese is getting better." His compliment on my effort to learn his language made me blush.

"Obrigado. I mean…I started not to get out of the car. But…"

"Sim…yes, I understand your concerns."

"What are you talking about?" He got up and went into the galley and came back with a pizza box.

"That is why I brought dinner…fresh from Pizzeria Uno in Chicago. We'll eat dinner on the way to San Francisco for dessert."

"You are making this very easy," I smiled.

"Sim, that is my plan." He pressed his lips against mine before slowly pulling back. "Now eat your pizza."

I did as instructed. "Uhm, this is good." I wiped my mouth. "You surprised me."

"That was my intention."

"I expected you to do something romantic, but this…"

He nodded. "I made reservations at three restaurants, but could never decide which one would be perfect for our date. I did not want you to feel you were being watched."

"Thank you."

"Instead, I asked my friend's assistant to get me two pizzas and a bottle of wine."

"Good choice for dinner." I wiped my mouth. "Very good pizza."

"Very good company."

My face felt hot. "So what's for dessert?"

"It's a surprise I found in San Francisco."

"Really?"

'Really." Followed by a kiss.

Dear God, what am I doing? I don't want to do anything impulsive. Please help me keep my sanity and make good decisions. In Jesus' name, Amen.

Alex

THE DARK MAHOGANY AND GLASS door compliments the stonework beautifully on this house. Walking up the steps leading to the door, my stomach filled with butterflies.

I've been to this house hundreds of times, but today, was different. I felt like a goat being led to slaughter. Every tap on the door elevated my heart another inch higher into my throat. Knock, knock, knock…the door finally opened to reveal a small woman with dark hair wearing a maid's uniform.

"Good afternoon, Miss Alex. He's been expecting you."

"Thank you, Iris," called the voice. Crossing the threshold, I heard the heavy footsteps of a man's shoes and the trotting sound of a dog crossing the mahogany wood floor.

"Baby girl." He smiled with outstretched arms.

"Hi Uncle Wallis" Uncle Wallis isn't a blood relative, but he's always been there for me, like an uncle.

"Down, Dempsey, Alexandra doesn't want you jumping on her."

"He's all right."

"I know better," he said shooing the dog away. "Iris, please take Dempsey. Thank you." She grabbed the chocolate lab by the collar and walked him toward the kitchen. "Come on, let's go out back."

Out back is a beautiful garden with views of the Pacific Ocean.

Uncle Wallis lives on a hill in Newport Beach, California. It's more of a mansion on a private street. The nearest neighbor is about a quarter mile away. It's secluded and peaceful, just the way he and Aunt Myrtle like it.

"I saw your mom at church Sunday. She said I should expect a call from you. Have a seat. So what's on your mind?"

I repeated the story of my secret marriage and son. "There you have it."

"Wow, that's some story, but I'd already heard it."

"What…when?"

"Your mother came to me when it happened. She needed help with the papers. I thought everything had been settled."

"So did I."

"What do you want from me?"

"I'm not sure. I needed to talk to someone that wasn't emotionally attached to the situation to tell me what to do."

"I'm sorry, I can't do that." His eyes were deadpan.

"Why not?"

"Are you asking as my niece or as a client?"

"Both."

"Not possible."

"Why?"

"As your Uncle, I'd say let's call this guy I know and order a beat down. As your lawyer, I'd say, let's examine this from all sides and find the right course of legal action. You can't have it both ways."

"Okay, as my lawyer can you call that guy you know and order a beat down?" I joked.

"Very funny."

"Okay, as my lawyer, what do you suggest?"

"Do you love him?"

"What does that have to do with this?"

"Everything."

"I love who he was. But I don't know who he is now. From what I've seen so far, he's nothing like the man I knew and loved, but an aged man with the weight of a troubled life on his shoulders."

"Then you don't love him?"

"No."

He nodded. "So why are we discussing him?"

"It's his family. They think I want him back, and they keep threatening me."

"Threatening you, how?" His lawyer hat was on.

"It's more like stalking me through my friends."

"I don't understand."

"They've been popping up when I'm not around and asking about me."

"I see." He nodded.

"I guess it's their way of letting me know they're watching me."

"Sounds like they're scared."

"That's what Moses said."

"Really?"

"He said I should call their bluff, but I don't want to hurt Terrence."

"So you do still care about him?"

"Part of me always will, but that's the past."

"So tell me about Moses?" He sat back and crossed his legs. "Your mother said he's a great guy in spite of his kidnapping you." I started laughing. "Please explain."

"It has to do with our first date."

"So far, I'm not sure if I agree with your mother about him. I like his books, but his books aren't dating my niece."

Uncle Wallis and my mother grew up together. When she moved here, she stayed with him. He met my Aunt Myrtle when she came over to pick my mom up. They were headed to a party. He says, it was love at first sight. Three months later, they were married.

My mom met my dad at their wedding. She always says that second piece of cake was a good example of not listening to God. She said if she hadn't gone after that second piece of cake, she wouldn't have met my Dad, but she also wouldn't have me, so she got the good with the bad.

"What do you want to know?"

"What do you want me to know?"

"He's the opposite of Jonathan."

"How?"

"He makes me feel safe. I trust him. He pushes me to step out of my comfort zone."

"And that's a good thing?"

"Yes, but he also scares me."

"How?"

"When I'm with him, I can't breathe, it's very overwhelming and intoxicating. It's like I'm not me, not Alexandra, but Al."

"Do we like Al?"

"I don't know. I told him the chemistry overwhelms me. He rescued me from an awkward situation at the airport and, that's how I ended up in New York with him and that's not me."

"Ah, the kidnapping," he smiled. "I see Al is impulsive. I don't know if I like her. She sounds a little wild."

"She is, but I'm not. I don't know what it is."

"It's passion." He nodded, leaned forward and rested his elbows on the table.

"That's what I said. That's how it feels when he kisses me." My face felt warm. I couldn't believe I just said that to my uncle.

"It happens to everyone at some point. It happened to me," he confessed.

"With Auntie?"

"Love is nice, but when you mix it with passion, wow." I

started laughing. I've never seen my uncle like this. "You laughing at me?" He smiled.

"Who are you?"

"Hey passion isn't just for the young." He stood up. "Come on, let's walk. I'd known your aunt for a while, but that day something just clicked. When I saw her, it was like magic. That smile drew me in. All I heard her say was, 'Hi.' You know this story."

"Not the details."

"Myrtle and your mother were headed to a party, but they never left the house. I fried up some catfish and we stayed in, talking and playing cards. Connie put us down around ten. Myrtle and I sat up way into the early morning talking. When the sun came up, I took her home and three months later, we were married."

"You sat up all night talking, really?" I looked at him, and his smile said otherwise.

"Well, there may have been a little lip action going on." He wrapped his arm around my shoulder. "Don't tell your aunt I told you that."

"Oooh, Uncle."

"Hey, what can I say, I had her at hello." We laughed. "Baby girl, I know what you're experiencing. It's intoxicating. The attraction is so strong it can be a little overwhelming, and when they aren't around, you sense the void. At the same time, you still feel safe."

"Exactly."

The phone rang blasting Heather Headly's "He Is." I knew exactly who it was. I thought it was the perfect way to describe Moses. He is everything I asked God for and so much more. I pressed the Answer Call button.

"Hey, Beautiful." I love the sound of his voice.

"Hey, Good-Looking."

"You sound good."

"I feel good."

"I take it things went well with your uncle."

"Yes, they did."

"That's good to hear because I was a lot concerned about you."

"My uncle said as long as Terrence doesn't bother me, I probably don't have to worry about his family. But if any one of them shows up again, he'll file a restraining order."

"Good. What else?"

"He knows the whole story. Seems my mother told him everything when it happened, and he feels this is the best way to handle things. So, what's going on with you?"

"Just working. I think I'm going to head back to LA soon."

"Don't come back because you think I need a baby sitter."

"Sweetheart, I know you don't need a baby sitter."

"Good, because I don't want you to come back until this thing is settled."

"I thought your uncle said everything was fine." I sensed a little irritation in his voice.

"He said as long as Terrence doesn't come around—"

"Is there something you're not telling me?"

"No."

"Then why don't you want me to come back?"

"Because I want to wait until they launch the IPO, then I'll feel better."

"Is that the only reason?"

"Now you're angry."

"I'm not angry. I just don't trust your ex-husband."

"I miss you, too." I heard him exhale.

"I'll call you in the morning, Beautiful. Goodnight."

"Goodnight.

After a sleepless night with lots of prayer, I knew what I needed to do.

I picked up my phone and pressed the programmed number. After the third ring a deep familiar voice answered. "Baby girl, is everything okay?"

"Uncle, I need my lawyer."

A few hours later, I was sitting in my uncle's conference room questioning my request. Uncle Wallis reached over and patted my hand. "You're doing the right thing."

"Am I ?"

Before he could reply, the door opened. I looked up and, standing in the doorway was my ex-husband. Long gone was the handsome young man I met one rainy afternoon at the Louvre. He'd been replaced with a mature man carrying the weight of a life he didn't want. I understand why Moses thinks I need to confront my ex-in-laws. However, they aren't scared of me, but of Terrence possibly walking out on them and their plan.

"Have a seat." Uncle pointed to the chair in front of him.

"I don't understand, what's this about?"

"I'm, Wallis Landry. Alexandra's attorney and uncle. Seems your visits to Alexandra have made a few people nervous."

"I don't understand. No one knew I came to see you."

"Alexandra, do you want to handle that one?"

I took a deep breath and began. "Your wife is having you followed."

"What!"

"When she came to visit me—"

"She came to visit you? When?"

"The day after you came to see me the first time."

"Lexi, I'm sorry. I had no idea." His apology seemed sincere.

"I gathered as much. But it gets worse. Seems she's taken a page from your parent's playbook. She told Thomas you came to see me. And he and Gerard tried to give me money to disappear."

"Why?"

"Uncle, would you give us a minute, thank you." He cut Terrence a sharp look as he walked out. "I know I told you to leave me alone, but—what is going on with you?"

"I don't know. I was fine until I saw you. When I looked into your eyes, I didn't see what I saw when we were married. Instead, I saw hurt, disappointment, anger, but no love. I know I told you I was sorry, but when I let you go, it seems I let the fighter in me go as well. And that's what I can't forgive myself for. I knew you were the strong one in our relationship, but I didn't know that without you in my life I would lose my desire to fight."

He looked lost. I wanted to go over and wrap my arms around him. For a brief moment, he was that sweet young man I married in Paris. "Uhm, what do you know about your grandfather's will?"

"Why are you asking me about that?"

"Please, just answer the question."

"My dad was the only child, so he inherited everything."

"Not exactly." I hit the buzzer for Uncle Wallis to join us. "Your grandfather wasn't your grandfather, he was your father."

"What!" he shouted. My uncle walked in and took a seat next to me.

"Uncle, please explain everything."

"Son, sit down. When Thomas returned from London, he discovered his father had married a much younger woman. Unfortunately, she died about a year after giving birth to you. Your grandfather, I mean father, was distraught and asked your brother and his wife to take you for a while. From what I've been able to ascertain, it was always his intention to raise you after he got himself together, but your brother and his wife took you and moved to Paris for a few years."

"None of this makes sense."

"When they returned to the states, your father had remarried again and his new wife didn't want any children, so your father and brother never said anything to her about you. She died shortly after Thomas went back to Europe, not knowing the truth about you."

"I can't believe…"

"Thomas convinced your father it was best if you stayed with him, and not disrupt your life by telling you the truth. Fast forward to Paris, you and Alexandra and a marriage that upset everything." He sat still as Uncle Wallis told the hidden details of his past.

"I don't know what to say. So what does this have to do…"

"Here's where it gets even more complicated. Your father and uncle were equal partners."

"That's correct. When our father died, Thomas got forty percent and I got ten."

"That's not correct."

"I don't understand."

"Somehow, Thomas managed to get a copy of your father's will and changed it."

"You're right, I'm confused."

"You were to receive forty percent and Thomas ten."

"Which would mean, I'd have controlling interest in the company."

"Not exactly."

"Please explain."

"Thomas and your father had a huge fight before he died and he cut Thomas out of the company."

"What?"

"Your father didn't want Thomas involved with the company. So he left his half of the company to you. He did however, equally divide his personal holdings between you two."

"Why are you telling me this now?" He asked.

"I want these people to leave me alone," I answered.

"Will you excuse us again sir?" Uncle Wallis left again. When the door closed, Terrence stood up and walked over to the window. "On some level I knew there was a problem. Things were always strained with my dad, I mean brother. That sounds so strange. How long have you known?"

"My mother received a letter from your Uncle Royce, apologizing for what Thomas and Lillian did. He promised her that he would correct the wrong done to Vernon's other son."

"So he knew?"

"Apparently. After Royce died, his attorney sent her another letter and it said, 'It's handled.' Nothing more."

"What did he do?"

"I don't know, and we probably never will."

"You must think I'm the biggest idiot you've ever met."

"No, but I do feel sorry for you."

"I don't know who to trust. I can't believe the very people…I did what they wanted and this is how they treat me. I trusted them and they lied." Shaking his head, "I don't know what to do."

"Confront them."

"It's one thing to say confront them, it's another to do it. My dad, I mean, my brother is very powerful and I don't know how to fight him. Do you think your uncle would help me?"

"I'll ask, but…you're not his favorite person."

"What about you?" He turned to face me. "Do you still hate me?"

"I don't hate you."

"Then will you help me?"

I looked into his eyes and saw him reaching for a lifeline. "I just started seeing someone and, I'm not quite sure how he'll feel about me being buddies with my ex-husband, especially since I told him all about you."

"I understand."

"You had no clue about any of this?"

"In the back of my mind, I always knew things weren't right. I could have stood up to them, but I took the easy way out and look at me."

"I'm going to talk to my uncle."

I walked out and leaned up against the wall trying to fight the tears gathering in my eyes. I swore I would never let that man make me cry again. Just as I said the words, a tear rolled down my face. Crap!

I CAN'T BELIEVE I AGREED to have dinner with Jason's family. I have never done well with my boyfriends' families. Throw me in a room full of potential clients, and I'm the brightest star in the room. This dinner is even more problematic because of my history with his mother. Back in college she didn't like me because she caught me making out with one of her professors. Now that I'm dating her son, I'm pretty sure there's no chance her opinion of me has changed.

I picked up my phone and pressed Jason's number. Before the call connected, Dylan buzzed.

"Taylor, I have Gretchen Phillips on line one." A plethora of four letter words filled my mind. "Taylor, did you hear me? Do you want me to put the call through?"

"Yes, thank you." I took three deep cleansing breaths and pressed the button. "Hello." I wasn't sure what to call her.

"Taylor, let's cut to the chase. This dinner my son wants isn't going to happen," she announced.

"Excuse me?" How dare she cancel on me. I was calling Jason, to do the exact same thing.

"There's no way I'm going to have dinner with you," she informed me.

"What makes you think I'm jumping at the chance to break bread with you?" I retorted.

"Are you finished?"

"You called me."

"I know my son is infatuated with you and to be honest, I was glad when you left him. However—"

"What do you want?" A five letter word just appeared in my mind and it's not judge.

"Seems my son wants us to talk. I feel lunch between the two of us would be better than a family dinner. Are you available next Tuesday at one?"

She shocked me. I thought she was calling to threaten me. "One thirty would be better." There's no way I'm giving her the upper hand.

"That won't work. I have a heavy schedule next week. Look, we can play this game all day. I'll meet you Thursday at Theodore's Grill, six-thirty."

"That's bold to assume I don't have plans."

"Seeing that's the night you were going to come to my home for dinner, I took a chance."

Crap! "What about Jason?"

"I'll explain to Jason. Good-bye." Click.

Was that a meeting or a sentencing? I pressed Jason's number, after the third ring, he answered. "Jason Bishop." The sound of his voice was soothing.

"I'm sorry, I was hoping to speak with my boyfriend," I teased.

"Hey babe, I'm sorry. How's my girl doing?"

"Fine, considering I just got off the phone with your mother."

"My mother?"

"Yeah, she said she needs to cancel dinner."

"What! I knew she was going to pull something like this." He exhaled. "I'll talk to her."

"No need."

"No Babe, she knows how important this dinner is. I told her I wasn't…"

"Sweetie, calm down." His exasperation was sweet. "She and I are going to have dinner, alone."

"Alone? When?"

"Same day…just us girls."

"I'm not sure that's a good idea."

"I know it's not a good idea, but I also know how important this is to you, so I'm willing to meet with her." He was quiet. This is what happens when you get serious with a man. You start doing all sorts of crazy things, like have dinner with his mother who has the power to lock you up literally, just for the heck of it. "Babe… Babe…are you there?"

"Yeah, I'm here. Are you sure you want to do this?"

"I'm sure I don't want to do this, but I will."

I pressed the button and waited for the voice on the other end to answer. Voicemail. Perfect. I reluctantly left a voicemail. "Hey girl, it's Taylor, where are you? I need some advice. Please call me."

I pressed the button ending the call. An hour later and still no response. I picked up my phone and dialed the number again. And like last time, voice mail. I left another message. Finally, around nine the next morning, my phone rang.

"Hey girl, what's wrong?"

"Where have you been?" It's not like Alex to not return a call right away. I didn't even waste my time texting her. She hates texting. She says she likes human contact. She's the only person I know who still writes letters.

"Is everything alright?"

"No it isn't." I was at my breaking point.

"Calm down, Taylor. What's going on?"

I took a deep breath. "Girl, I foolishly agreed to have dinner with Jason's mother."

"Why?"

"Because he asked me to."

"I see."

I recognized that tone. "What's that supposed to mean?"

"This my dear is your vetting. In your case, maybe it's your sentencing. I've got bail money, but…"

"Not funny. My vetting? What are you talking about?"

"How have things been going with you two, I mean three." She teased.

Her comment was in reference to my relationship with Jason's son, Zach. I've sort of stepped in as his mother figure, a role I never saw myself doing. In addition to our family dates, I cheer him on at his baseball games and occasionally, do the school chauffeur thing.

"Things are going great."

"Uh-huh…sounds like Jason might be getting ready to pop the question."

I laughed out loud. "That's funny. No one has said anything about marriage."

"Girlfriend, think about it. He introduced you to his son. He bought a larger house…"

"That house was for him and Zach."

"Please, Zach will be headed to college in a few years. No, girl, he bought that house for you and him and your family."

"Family?"

"Yeah, Zach's little sister or brother or both."

"Please, we haven't even…I mean he did bring it up."

"And?"

"I conveniently skirted around it."

"Well, Cuz, I hate to be the one to tell you, but it seems your young cub is getting ready to propose."

"I've already done the marriage thing and it didn't work."

"That was a mistake and you know it. So it doesn't count." She teased. "I wasn't too sure about Jason at first, but after spending a little time with him, I like him and I think you..."

"Don't say it." I felt a warm sensation come over me.

"Why, because you know I'm telling the truth?"

"No because, I'm too scared to admit it. Alex, do you think I'd be a good wife?" I trust Alex's opinion. I know she'll tell me the truth, that's why I called her.

"Sweetie, you are a good thing, loaded with favor just waiting for the right man to share it with."

"Thanks." I exhaled. "Now what about you?"

"What about me?"

"It's time to open your heart."

"I know."

That was the first time she didn't fight me on the subject. I think she just might be ready. I only wish Moses was ready, because I still think he would be perfect for her.

Alex

"WHERE HAVE YOU BEEN?" ASKED Sebastian.

"Last time I checked, my name was on the building." I barked back as I walked into my office.

"I see. We have the displeasure of Evil Alex's company today?" he sniped back.

"Tell, uhm," snapping my fingers trying to remember my junior assistant's name. "Shoot, what's her name?"

"Kim?"

"Thank you. Tell her I'm not available if anyone asks."

"Okay. Anything else?"

"Call Moses and tell him I need to see him tonight." I looked at Bas and he looked shocked at my statement. "That's right, I know he's in town and, I know you've been talking to him."

"Oh."

"And consider me invisible." He walked out and closed the door. I was catching up on paperwork when the buzzer rang. I pressed the buzzer and shouted, "I said consider me invisible!"

"No need to bite my head off. Mrs. Pierce is here to see you."

"Which one?"

"The wife," he replied.

"Crap. Send her in."

The door opened and walking towards my desk, was the thorn in my side...my ex-husband's pregnant wife. After babysitting her husband for the past twenty-four hours, I'm really not in the mood to deal with this trifling woman. "Alexandra."

"Blair." I see we're going to attempt a formal tone with this meeting. "Excuse me, before you start, there's something I have to do." I dialed the number and pressed the speaker so she could hear my conversation. "Sebastian?"

"Yes, Alex."

"Would you please have Travis call the police and tell them we just caught a pregnant, overdressed shoplifter. Thank you."

"Will do." I pressed the button ending the call.

"Apparently, you forgot our last conversation, so I'll just remind you. I said, if you came back, I'd call the police. By my calculations, it will take the police about four minutes or less before they get here."

"I understand you saw my husband recently?"

"Are you asking me or telling me?"

"I know you've been in contact with him, and I want to know where he is," she demanded.

"That sounds more like a question for the private detective you have following him."

"How dare you imply—"

"Please, ask the one you have on me how he liked that trip to the gynecologist last week?"

"I don't know what you're talking about. Are you going to tell me where my husband is?" She demanded.

"No. If he wanted you to know where he is, he would have told you."

"You may think you're helping, but you're interfering with

my marriage. This is between Terrence and me. It has nothing to do with you."

"On the contrary, you put me in it when you came to see me the first time. Tick tock, you've got three minutes."

"What about his children?" She asked rubbing her swollen belly.

"What do you want from me?"

"My husband."

"I can't give you something I don't have."

"Why are you doing this?"

"Because unlike some people, when a friend takes me into their confidence I respect their request. I may not agree with what he's doing, but I respect him for taking control of his life."

"What's that supposed to mean?"

"Figure it out."

"Fine. I'll leave. Oh, the next time you see Chloe and Dionne tell them it was great talking with them at the Clinic Fundraiser."

"I suggest you leave or figure out how to explain your mug shot on the evening news to your in-laws." She stormed out, slamming the door behind her. Knock, knock. Does anybody know what the word invisible means? "Yes!"

The door opened and Bas walked in and closed the door. "Where were you yesterday?"

"I was with Terrence."

"What!"

"It's not what you think."

"Then what was it?"

"I wish I could tell you, but I gave my word, I wouldn't say anything. All I can say is, he's in real trouble and I'm helping him."

"We all say that to get women to do what we want."

"No, it's not like that. He's dealing with something very serious and I told him he could count on me to help."

"And Moses?"

"I'm hoping he'll understand."

"Are you high? No man let's his girlfriend hang out with her ex-husband."

"Did you find Moses?"

"No. I tried every number I have and nothing."

"Crap! I have to disappear for a few days and I need to speak to him before I leave."

"I hope you know what you're doing," Bas asked.

"I don't, but thanks for the support."

"Alex, Moses is a good guy and he really cares about you. As your friend, I'm begging you not to mess this up."

"It may not seem like it, but I'm doing this because of him. Please keep trying to reach him."

I sat down and my phone rang with a familiar ringtone. I took a deep breath and pressed the answer call button.

"Hey, Beautiful."

"Hey."

"I missed talking to you last night and this morning. Are you upset with me?"

"No. It was late when I got home last night. And I was talking to Taylor when you called this morning."

"Is everything okay?"

"I need to see you."

"I'll be there in…"

"I know you're in town. Meet me at my house in an hour."

"I'm on my way.

The knock on the door wasn't unexpected, but it startled me just the same. I stood in front of the door, trying to convince myself I was doing the right thing. I took a deep breath, counted to three, grabbed the matte gold knob, opened the door and asked myself, was confiding completely in Moses worth the risk?

He took his sunglasses off, looked me in the eye and smiled. "Hey, Beautiful." He's definitely worth the risk.

"Hey." I stepped to the side and he walked in. I closed the door and he pulled me to his chest and crushed his lips against mine. The passionate kiss reinforced my decision.

"I missed those lips."

"Me too. Let's go into the kitchen. Do you want something to…"

"Alex, I'm sorry about the bodyguard, but I…"

I stopped and turned around. "What bodyguard?"

"I thought that's why you wanted to see me."

"No, but…thank you."

"You're not upset?"

"Of course I am, but I know you did it because you care."

"What's going on?"

"Do you want something to drink?"

"No, I'm good."

"It's Terrence." He braced himself against the counter. "First, I want to thank you for understanding my need to handle this on my own. Since you have a bodyguard following me, you know where I've been the past twenty-fours."

"I haven't spoken with him today. Where were you?"

"My uncle's house with he and Terrence."

"I see. Should I be saying congratulations?"

"No, it's not what you think. I only told you part of the story behind our annulment. There's another part even he didn't know, and that's what I've been dealing with."

"Okay." He took his jacket off, placed it on the back of the stool, and listened as I told him the whole story. He scratched his forehead as if he was looking for an answer. "Is that all?" he asked as he folded his arms in front of his chest.

"Yes, that's why I suggested the break. I thought given enough time, my ex in-laws would see I didn't want anything to do with Terrence and they'd leave me alone. Instead, they've been stalking me, giving my friends jobs, and leaving hints they want me to disappear. That's why I didn't want you around. I didn't want them to harm you. But it seems I've made it worse, and the only way I know how to clean it up, is to help Terrence fight his family."

"Uh-huh."

"I know you probably don't want to hear this, but I need to extend our break until this is resolved. And to complicate things even more, I think I'm falling in love with you, and you're probably angry with me because I want to help Terrence."

"Is that all?"

"Yes." He walked over, gathered me up in his arms and gently pressed his lips against mine. I lost myself in the kiss and suddenly pulled back and smiled.

"I've missed those lips."

"Is it me, or is it a little warm in here?" I smiled.

"When I said I wanted to love you more than any other man, I lied, I already do."

"You do?"

"Yes, I have loved you from the moment we first kissed, but I didn't want to press you." He took a step back and asked, "So what are we going to do? What do you need me to be in agreement with you for?"

"We?" His statement confused me.

"I'm sorry, I thought we were dating. If you want to get old school, I'm your boyfriend, right?"

"Uhm, yeah. I guess. I never really thought about it like that."

"Like what?"

"That I'm your girlfriend. I thought we were just…I didn't know we…"

"Is there a problem with me defining what's going on between us?"

"No, you just caught me off guard."

"How?"

"I'm sorry, I'm not use to having, what did you say, my boyfriend, ask me what I needed him to be in agreement with me for or want to help me."

"Where I come from, that's what you do. If we're a couple then that means I support you, and you support me, right?"

"Yes, I'm sorry. It's just, Jonathan never did that. If I wanted him to stand in agreement with me or help me, I had to ask. I'm not used to having someone assume that's their place."

"Did I overstep my bounds?"

"No. I...I uhm..."

"Okay, so what are we going to do? Because I know you didn't think I would knowingly be fine with you going away with your ex-husband. I'm understanding, to a point."

In the back of my head, Bas' words were replaying.

"Terrence has been hiding out at my uncle's house. Not contacting anyone, which has his wife freaking out. He and my uncle have been brain storming and researching for the past twenty-four hours. Tomorrow, I'm supposed to meet them at my uncle's office. He's chartered a plane to take the three of us..."

"The four of us."

"The four of us," I smiled, "to his place up north. So we need to leave at..."

"We need a distraction."

"What?"

"Tell your uncle to order four Town cars and a black mini van. Have one car go to his office and park in the garage. A couple of hours later have one pick you up here, have one pick me up, and send the fourth one to the store to get your mother and Bas."

"The store? Why?"

"They'll think it's you and the ex with glasses and hats on. Then, have your car and your mom and Bas' car go to your uncle's building. Have your uncle and ex-husband get into the mini van. Once you get there, get into the mini van with them. Have your mother take one car and Bas take the other one and let the first car go empty. Have all the cars leave at the same time, going in different directions. Wait about an hour and then leave. If you are being followed, they'll only be able to follow two of the cars and won't give the mini van a second thought when it pulls out. Hopefully, they'll tail the cars, and I'll meet you at the airport."

"You've got to be kidding."

"Baby, I get paid a lot of money to write this stuff."

"Okay, if you say so." I teased.

Dionne

I PRESSED THE VOICEMAIL BUTTON and listened to the message. It was the fourth message that morning. I wasn't ready to talk to Quentin. I was still too angry. Instead, I called the one person I knew would understand. I pressed the call button and waited. After the third ring a familiar voice answered.

"Chloe Jacobs."

"Hey, Chloe, do you have a minute?" I tried to hide the sadness in my voice.

"I'm about to…hold on. Tucker," she yelled. "Call Marcus and tell him if it looks like it will work, I'll look at it later this afternoon. And hold all my calls. Thanks. Okay, I'm sorry about that. What's going on?"

"Quentin and I had a big fight and I left," I blurted out.

"Excuse me?"

"I left him," I repeated my response.

"Is this a joke? I told you why I didn't tell you about me and Orlando. I thought…"

"It's not a joke."

"Where are you?"

"The Viceroy."

"I'm on my way."

"No, you don't need to come."

"Are you sure? Because, I'll pick up Alex and we'll be there in thirty minutes."

"You don't need to come, and please don't tell Alex."

"Tell me what happened."

I replayed the incident with my mother-in-law, and mine and Quentin's fight. "He's been calling all morning. So what should I do?"

"Wow. I don't know what to say. Why did you call me?"

"I thought maybe you could help me."

"Honey, our situations aren't the same. Besides, I'm in no position to give anyone marital advice."

"But..."

"Your husband loves you. He's just having mother issues. If my situation were as easy as a meddlesome mother-in-law, I'd throw money at her and be done."

"Okay, thanks. I'll talk to you later."

"Hold on." She stopped me before I could hang up. "You love him, right?"

"Of course I do. It's his family I'm having issues with."

"Call him and invite him over to talk. Apologize for threatening his mother. Then ask him to help you figure out a way to deal with her."

"Okay."

"And if that doesn't work, then make love to him, and he'll forget all about the fight." She joked.

"I don't think sex can fix this."

"Honey, there isn't any marital problem that can't be fixed with sex." She laughed. "You're right. You might need to throw in a good meal as well."

"Chloe..."

"I'm sorry Dee. It's just you and Quentin are perfect for each other. This fight seems huge because you're letting it be. There isn't a married woman alive who hasn't competed with the ghost of past girlfriends. It's all in how you let it affect you."

"She brought her to our house."

"Chances are that woman has no clue what your mother-in-law is up to."

"You think?"

"Honey, this amazing relationship Quentin had with her is all in Katherine's head. Think about it, if Quentin wanted her, he never would have broken up with her. When were they together?"

"College."

"Hang up Dee."

"What?"

"You're letting some college crush ruin your marriage. Hang up. This chick is probably married and not even thinking about Quentin. If it will make you feel better, call her and tell her you want to talk. Find out where her head is."

"Quentin won't like that."

"Do you like living at the hotel and sleeping alone?"

"No."

"Then call this woman and talk to her." She exhaled. "Would you feel better if I was there?"

"Yes."

"Fine. Make it for tomorrow afternoon."

"Thanks."

"See you tomorrow, bye."

I sat waiting for this woman who has caused a disruption in my marriage. I called Chloe and told her she didn't need to come, but I promised to call her as soon as my meeting was over. I alternated between sips of coffee and water, trying to gather up my courage. I don't particularly like confrontation, but in order to get my life back, this is what I needed to do.

I looked up and saw the hostess escorting Stacey to the table. I looked at her, wondering what attracted Quentin to her in the first place. She was average height, pretty but no great beauty, like Katherine eluded to. When she turned to sit, I checked her out. We definitely didn't have similar figures. I guess Katherine was right, Quentin's taste had evolved. I believe for the better.

I smiled. "Hello, Stacey."

She smiled, "Hello, Dionne."

"Would you like something?"

"I'll have what you're having."

I'm sure she would. Seems she wants everything I have. I raised my hand to get the server's attention, and pointed to my coffee cup and he nodded. A few minutes later, he placed the white cup and saucer on the table in front of her. "Will there be anything else, Miss?" he asked.

"No, that will be all, thank you." I took another sip of coffee and dabbed the corner of my mouth. "I asked you here so I could apologize. I realize, I involved you in a family matter." She nodded. "Katherine and I have been…mother-in-laws can be difficult."

"Yes, they can," she sipped her coffee and placed the cup back on the saucer.

"Excuse me?"

"Cherie, I could tell you mother-in-law horror stories."

"I thought…the way Katherine keeps bringing you up, I thought you and she were conspiring to break Quentin and me up."

She laughed out loud. "That's funny." She covered her mouth with her napkin. "That's insane. I am happily married to a wonderful man."

"Really?" I was beginning to relax.

"Pierre Duchamps."

231

"Is he French?"

Her smile covered her face. "Oui. We've been together eight years, but married only four."

"Does Katherine know this?"

"I thought she did." She sipped again from her cup. I apologize for just showing up unannounced. I wasn't given all the details. I do quite a bit of charity work and I thought I was attending a committee meeting. My husband and I are often asked to sponsor events. Katherine mentioned the clinic and…"

The only people I know that sponsor events are people with a lot of money. People like Chloe and her family. "So you thought…"

"I thought I was coming to hear a presentation about the clinic. I was prepared to write a check. I had no idea what she was trying to do." She patted her chest. "Cherie, I apologize. Pierre and I are expecting our first child so no, I do not want your husband. If you want, I will speak with Katherine."

"Thank you, but, I'll take care of her."

"Cherie, when Pierre and I were dating, my mother-in-law constantly paraded his ex-girlfriends in front of me." She shook her head. "I just laughed because it was clear, he was tired of vanilla and wanted a little spicy chocolate." We laughed.

"Stacey, I'm glad we talked."

"So am I. The four of us should have dinner."

"I'll check with Quentin." Once I apologize and get him to speak to me again.

I CAN'T BELIEVE MOSES' PLAN worked. I walked out of the restroom and took the first seat. Thumbing through my magazine, I heard the flight attendant talking to Moses outside.

I stood up and looked at the door, waiting on him to board. He entered, walked over, gently kissed me on the lips and then behind my ear. He pulled back, put his arm around my waist and pulled me to his side.

"Uncle Wallis, Terrence, this is Moses Adair." All three men shook hands.

"Thanks for your help," Terrence said.

"I did it for Alex."

"Son, I've heard a lot about you and I've read all of your books. Come sit with me. I've got an idea for a book. The lead character is an attorney." As they walked to the rear of the plane, Moses looked over his shoulder, winked and smiled at me.

"So that's him?" Terrence asked as he sat down.

"Him who?" I asked as I sat down and strapped myself

233

into my seat.

"Is that who you're seeing?"

"If you're referring to the tall, handsome man that helped orchestrate your escape from your scheming, manipulative family? Yes, it is."

"Looks a little cocky, if you ask me."

"I didn't."

"What do you see in him?"

"A man that loves me so much, he's willing to put aside his feelings about you to help."

"Exactly. If he trusted you he wouldn't be here."

"He trusts me. It's you and your whacked-out family he doesn't trust." He was quiet the rest of the flight.

My uncle's place is a boutique vineyard in Napa. Actually, his place is in St. Helena. His winery is considered boutique because he doesn't produce as many cases a year as some of the larger wineries. And because he also offers a more personal relationship with his customers. I love his Moscato and the blush sparkling wine. I like both with popcorn.

His place looks like something out of a movie. A Tuscan style villa surrounded by a few other buildings used for his winemaking. The property is even more beautiful during harvest season. Everything is green and lush, and the air is filled with the smell of grapes. The main house sits just off the road and the back is filled with grape vines.

Although he only produces a few cases, his wines are being requested in some of the best restaurants in the region. He told me he was shocked when he and Aunt Myrtle were on vacation in Maui and he noticed his sparkling wine was on the wine list.

I was glad Moses insisted on coming with me. Walking around the grounds with him was very romantic. Definitely not something I did with Jonathan.

When we would come up to spend time with my uncle and aunt, he'd sit on the patio working while I relaxed. But this is like being in a dream. This is how I wanted Jonathan to be… peaceful, relaxed, removed from work.

"This place is amazing," Moses words brought me back to the present.

"I love it here. After my parents' divorce, Mama and I would come up here every chance we could. It's the kind of place where you can gather your thoughts and dream. Me and God have had quite a few talks out here amongst the grapes."

He reached for my hand and I felt like I was twelve years old touching a boy's hand for the first time. Our fingers entwined gently swinging in the air. My boyfriend. I repeated the words in my mind and it still sounded strange.

"It's intoxicating. It feels like we're in Tuscany taking an evening stroll in search of gelato and espresso."

"Thank you."

"For what?"

"Everything."

"You don't have to thank me." He brought our clenched hands up to his mouth and gently kissed mine.

"But –"

"If I didn't want to help, I wouldn't have." He took a deep breath before addressing the pink elephant in the room. "So what's the plan?"

"I'm not sure, that's what my uncle and Terrence are at the house discussing."

"Oh."

I know he doesn't like what I'm doing, but I feel this is something I need to do.

"You know, deep down he's a good man. He just got caught up in something he had no knowledge about. What he needs now is to regroup and figure out what he wants to do."

"How do you fit into his quest to find himself?"

"I don't. We're just two people that were married to each other. Nothing more, nothing less. Right now he needs to be alone. I don't know, maybe I could introduce him to Vanessa."

"Not funny, but they could be—no, even I'm not that mean." We laughed.

"I'll help him up to a point, but I don't want him getting the wrong impression. Besides I have a boyfriend." I smiled.

"You do?" He smiled.

"Yes."

"Tell me about him."

"He's tall, dark, very handsome, has a great smile and a warm heart. He's a writer, lives in New York and he loves God more than me. I think my mom has a little crush on him."

"I don't know about this guy. What else?"

"He cooks for me and sends me flowers. And for our first date he took me to New York to meet his family. Don't tell anyone, but I let him kiss me on our first date."

"What? I don't know if I like this guy."

"Too bad, because I like him, a lot."

"You do?"

"But it's a secret." I held my index finger over my lips. "I don't want him to know how much I like him yet. He kissed my hand. "What about you, do you have a girlfriend?"

"Yes, I do."

"What's she like?"

"She's beautiful inside and out. Her family and friends are very important to her. Her mother is adorable. My grandmother likes her a lot. She's stubborn and I love that about her. She's very compassionate, has a big heart and the most incredible lips." He looked at me and my face felt hot. "There's another man, but I'm cool with it, because I love Him too. And if it wasn't for Him, we wouldn't be together. She lives in California, but she's coming to visit for the first time since we started dating and I'm a little nervous."

"Nervous, why?"

"Because I really like her and I want to show her a good time."

"What else you got?"

"She's a successful business woman and she treats her assistant more like a brother. And she kissed me on our first date."

"She did what! I don't know if I like her…the little tart."

"Watch it, that's my girlfriend you're talking about." We laughed.

"We better head back to the house." We started towards the house and suddenly stopped. "What's wrong?"

He looked at me with those incredible light brown eyes and they started to get dark. He wrapped his arms around my waist, pulled me to his chest, covered my lips with his, kissing me passionately. Every muscle in his chest pressed against my breasts. I was so aroused, I could barely stand up.

I wrapped my hands around his neck and pulled him closer. Trading deep moans in between sensual kisses. This was one of my fantasies, kissing my boyfriend amongst the grapevines. He slowly pulled back and smiled.

"Do you kiss your girlfriend like that?"

"Every chance I get." He pecked my lips again.

We continued back to the house and walked inside searching for my uncle and Terrence.

"Where have you two been?" Uncle Wallis asked.

"I wanted to show Moses around."

"Sir, your home and vineyard are beautiful. It reminds me of Tuscany."

"Thank you."

I looked at all the papers scattered on the table. "Uncle, do you really need me and Moses?"

"No, not really. Terrence and I pretty much have everything under control. You two want to go out?"

"No. I think we're going to leave."

"What?" Moses sounded surprised.

"Excuse me." I left and returned a few minutes later. "What was I saying?"

"You said we're leaving," Moses repeated my statement.

"That's right. Uncle Wallis has everything under control and we'd just be in the way. I asked Henry to call a car for us. It should be here in less than an hour."

"Are you sure?" Moses asked.

"Yes."

"Moses, come with me." Uncle Wallis said and they left and I followed behind them.

"I was wrong," Terrence blurted out.

I turned around. "Excuse me?"

"I was wrong. He's a nice guy."

"I know."

"You seem happy."

"I am." I folded my arms in front of my chest. "Now if you'll excuse me."

"Lexi…" He stood up. "Thank you."

"You're welcome." I almost felt sad for him.

"Miss Alex," Henry called out.

"I'm in here, Henry."

He walked into the room. "They called and the car will be here in twenty minutes."

"That was quick. Thank you. Excuse me, Terrence." I walked down to the kitchen. "Hey Baby, the car will be here in twenty minutes." I looked at the crowded island countertop. "Uncle, what are you doing?"

"We're having a little impromptu wine tasting. I was going to do this after dinner, but since you're leaving…"

I stood next to Moses and he kissed me on the forehead. "Babe, this is good. Sir…"

"Call me Wallis."

"Wallis, are you only local or can I get this at home?"

"How about I send you a case?"

"Thanks. Just tell me how much and…"

"It's on me."

"Sir, I couldn't," Moses protested.

"You put a smile on my niece's face. It's the least I can do."

"Thank you."

I walked over and hugged and kissed him. "Uncle, we have to go."

Once inside the car, I finally felt free from the noose. I rested my head against Moses' arm and he lifted my hand to his mouth and kissed it.

"Sweetheart, why did you change our plans?"

"I wanted to spend time with my boyfriend before Fashion Month starts."

"Works for me."

The ride to the airport was long and filled with the kind of small talk couples exchange when they are about to be apart for a while. Three weeks. That's how long before we would see each other again.

Last night, Moses planned a very romantic evening for us. He told me we were going out for dinner followed by dancing. Instead, we had an intimate dinner at the townhouse, followed by dessert and dancing on the patio. The evening went way into the early morning, capped off with my favorite chocolate chip walnut cookies and milk.

I looked at him, smiling.

"What's on your mind?"

What's on my mind? I'm thinking I don't want to leave. I want to stay here with you sharing intimate dinners and kisses under the stars.

"You'll think it's silly."

"Try me."

"I was replaying our kiss last night."

"Which one?" He teased.

"Ha, ha." He lifted my hand up to his lips and kissed it. "When you walked me to my room." He smiled and nodded. "It was filled with…" I looked up and noticed we were headed into the parking lot. "You missed your turn."

"No, I didn't."

"The parking lot?" He pressed the button lowering the window, reached out and took the parking ticket. "Moses, what are you doing?"

"Help me look for a parking space."

We rode around several rows looking for an empty parking spot and settled on one a couple of rows from where we entered the parking lot. He parked the car, got out, walked around and helped me out.

"What's going on?" He smiled and closed the door. "I'm not moving until you tell me what's going on?"

He stepped closer and I backed up against the side of the black Bentley with my arms folded in front of my chest. "What do you want to know?"

I swallowed hard before answering. "Why did you park the car? Are you coming with me?"

"No." He leaned in close and whispered, "I parked because I wanted to kiss you good bye." He stepped closer and the heat from his body surrounded me.

"What are you talking about? You could have kissed me at the curb like most people do."

"We're not most people."

He unfolded my arms, stepped closer, slipped his arms around my waist, leaned in and whispered. "Three weeks." He kissed my neck right behind my ear and my temperature shot up. Passion. That's what my other relationships were missing. He continued speaking. "That's how long this kiss has to last me."

He teased my lips with gentle pecks, before capturing them between his. He pressed his body into mine as he covered my mouth with his. I could barely breathe, just like last night. He tasted sweet, and the feel of his tongue dancing with mine was more intense than our kissing last night. He slid his hands down the small of my back, pulled me closer and the kiss intensified.

He gently bit on my bottom lip before ravaging my mouth again. My hands wrapped around his neck, pulling him deeper into my space. We were one, locked together by passion and our lips. My heart was racing and I didn't want to let him go.

He slowly pulled back and I brushed my finger across his swollen lips. God, my boyfriend is gorgeous.

"That was some goodbye kiss."

"That wasn't a goodbye kiss." He smiled.

"It wasn't?"

"No, it was a reminder kiss."

"A reminder?"

"Yea, when those slick European dudes start hitting on you, I want you to remember what's waiting for you at home."

"And what's that?" I smiled.

"Me."

He took my lips again and we stood in the parking lot making out until my phone rang and interrupted us. I immediately recognized the ringtone and pressed the button. "Yes…I'm here… outside…as soon as I get checked in…okay." I pressed the button ending the call.

"Bas?"

"Yeah."

"I guess it's time."

"Yeah."

He loaded my bags onto the cart, locked the car and we walked over to the terminal. Before I left for my gate, he kissed me one last time followed by two words, "Three weeks."

I wanted to say it, but I couldn't, not yet. Instead I replied with one word, "Passion."

"Exactly."

Dionne

I STARED AT THE PICTURE on my phone wondering if I should make the call. This is the longest we've gone without speaking. We were both very angry and said some things we probably shouldn't have, but needed to be said.

I called the office and Tanya said Quentin has been biting everyone's head off. She asked when I was coming back to the office because some of the staff were threatening to call in sick until Quentin and I stopped fighting. It's difficult to be angry with your husband when you work together because everyone knows. At the same time, I can't let our personal relationship effect our business relationship.

Maybe I shouldn't have left, but I felt we both needed some space. This isn't how I pictured marriage. I thought it would be filled with sweet talk, constant romance and the occasional misunderstanding. Not this petty crap we seem to be dealing with on a regular basis. Selah. Quentin is right, I have to ignore his mother. I know she would love to have me out of the picture, but

I'm not going anywhere.

I looked at Quentin's face on the screen of my phone and remembered why I agreed to marry him, because he said he loved me and wanted to share his life with me. Then I thought about what Adam said, "He married you against our mother's insistence that he didn't." That meant I was his choice. He was willing to give up his family to become a family with me.

I pressed the Call button and he picked up after the third ring. "Hello."

"We need to talk. I'm at the Viceroy."

"I'll be there in an hour." Click.

I got dressed and paced back and forth praying. I probably should have told him to meet me at home. The knock on the door startled me. I felt my insides jump. Another set of rapid knocks. I took a deep breath, shook out my hands and walked to the door. I grabbed the knob, took a deep breath and opened the door. Standing in front of me was the most amazing man in the world. I was hoping to see his beautiful smile, but he was stone faced.

"Come in." I stepped to the side, clearing the path for him to enter. When he walked past me, his cologne trailed behind drawing me into his space…citrus, sandalwood and chocolate with something spicy. He always smells good. I told him his cologne distracted me when we first met and that's why I agreed to go out with him. I inhaled his scent and, the memories of the first time we met flooded my mind. I exhaled, closed the door, and followed him.

He stood next to the desk and I positioned myself across the room. "You wanted to talk."

I see he's not going to make this easy. I took a deep breath and blurted out, "I'm sorry." I waited for a reaction, response, something. He looked at me with that same stone face that greeted me. How are we supposed to fix this, if half of the we won't help? I stood copying him, staring with no expression until I couldn't take it any longer. "I don't know what you want from me. I apologized and apparently it's not enough, but unless you tell me what you want, I can't fix it."

"That's the problem." Finally, he speaks. "It's not for you to fix."

"Excuse me?"

"I thought we were a team."

"We are."

"Then why do you insist on trying to fix things by yourself?"

Again, he caught me off guard with his question. "I'm not try…"

"We are one, at least I thought we were."

"We are."

"You say that, but your actions say otherwise."

"Quentin, I'm trying to follow you, but you're not making any sense."

He stepped closer. "I know my mother can be a handful."

"That's an understatement."

"I know how she feels about you. There are days when I think she doesn't love me, but I know better."

"Wait a minute. Your mother treats me the way she does, because she loves me?"

"No, she really doesn't like you, but that's not the point." He stepped closer. "I am in love with you and that's all that matters. I don't know why my mother likes to bring up Stacey. That was a long time ago. And for the record, we only dated a few months."

"I talked to Stacey."

"You did."

"Yes, I wanted to apologize for my behavior. I felt it was the best thing to do."

"You know you don't have anything to worry about."

"I do now."

"How could you think I'd be interested in another woman?"

"Your mother said…"

"This is all my fault." He stepped closer. "When my

mother hurts you, she's hurting me...us."

"I thought you were siding with her? You said it was easier to let me down." I reached up and wiped the tear rolling down the side of my face.

"I was wrong to say that, and it was wrong for me to do that." He stepped closer. "You're my wife, my partner, my lover. I should never let you down, because that means I've let us down." I felt more tears coming. "Forgive me?"

I nodded. "Yes."

He lifted my chin, patted the tears and gently pressed his lips against mine. "Now about that gun."

Now it was my turn to apologize. "I'll get rid of it."

"Do you have a license?"

"What?" His question surprised me.

"Do you at least have a carry permit, because our attorney will need to know for the future."

I was looking for a smile, but there wasn't one. He was serious. "What are you talking about?"

"I know my mother likes to push your buttons...threaten you almost. I just need to know, if you're licensed to carry that thing." He smiled.

"Very funny, and yes, I do."

He kissed me again. "I've missed you."

"Me too. I'll get my things and we can..." He grabbed my hand as I started to walk away. "What?"

"I'm thinking, the room is already paid for..." There's that beautiful smile. "I mean, I did promise you a little break."

"You promised me three days in Maui, not three days locked up in a Beverly Hills hotel room." I smiled as he pulled me to his chest.

"It really doesn't matter where we spend our three days, the plan is going to be the same." He brushed the side of my face.

"Really?" My face felt hot.

He leaned in close and whispered in my ear, "It doesn't matter where we are as long as we're together."

"I see, but I was looking forward to…"

He kissed my neck and continued. "I want to stay here for the next three days making love to my wife. Is that all right with you? Or are you going to pull that gun out on me?"

"Only if you don't keep your promise."

I AM EXHAUSTED AND EXCITED. I love Fashion Month, but I'm glad it's over. The thrill and excitement of looking at all the beautiful clothes and accessories for the upcoming season is a treat for my eyes.

I'm also glad I got to spend time with Moses before the madness started, because it made the rest of my trip a lot more enjoyable.

Moses had flowers waiting for me at each hotel I stayed in during my trip, along with some of the most romantic notes I've ever read. Having a writer for a boyfriend has its advantages. Every time I looked at the flowers, it was like having him there with me. Our main source of communication was texting. And every night before I went to bed, I was treated to a video call. When I was in Paris, he surprised me with a video date complete with chocolate chip walnut cookies and milk.

I stopped in Atlanta for a few days and the plan was for him to meet me. Unfortunately, there were some problems with his new play and he wasn't able to get away. Instead, I spent the time with Taylor. She and Jason took me and Bas around to all of their favorite spots, and introduced us to a few people. I forgot how exhausting it is hanging out with her. I told Bas not to mention anything about Moses. I know it's been four months, but I'm still not ready to share him with my girlfriends.

I sat in the airport contemplating going to New York instead of home. Staring out the window thinking about Moses, I looked at the screen. The next flight to New York was in two hours.

"So are you going home or to New York to see your boyfriend?" Bas startled me with his question.

"What?"

"I saw you looking at the screen."

"Thinking about it, but that's insane, right?"

"Not if that's what you want to do." He handed me a glass of mineral water.

"Moses is busy with the play and…" My phone rang with his ringtone. I pressed the Answer Call button. "Hey, Baby…no, we're sitting in the airport…I was thinking about coming to see you…why not…what…when…do you want me to pick you up… okay, I'll see you Friday…I miss you…me too…bye." I pressed the button ending the call.

"I guess you're headed home?"

"Yes, and he'll be there Friday." I smiled.

"Hey Beautiful," there's that deep voice I love.

"Hey."

"I was on my way to the airport, but it doesn't look like I'm going to make it."

"What's going on?"

"This new play isn't going as well as I would like. It's been one attack from the devil after another. I thought I would have been able to come for the weekend, but it's not going to happen. My leading man just got a movie and now I have to recast him, and my second choice is already committed to another project."

"What do you need me to pray in agreement with you for?"

"Thank you Sweetheart. I need another strong leading man who isn't going to cost me an arm and a leg."

"You got it."

"Unfortunately, I don't know when I'll be able to come see you."

"I understand if you have to put us on hold to take care of your business."

"What are you talking about?"

"You and me. I understand if we need to take a break."

"I didn't say that. I just don't know when I can come see you. I'd ask you to come here for the weekend, but I know you just got home," he exhaled. "I've got to go meet the director. I'll call you later tonight."

"I understand. Now it's you that needs time."

"That's not what I said," he sighed. "I don't want you to think I need a break from us. Just because we don't see each other every day, doesn't mean we're done. I lo—I'm in this for the long haul. Okay?"

"Yeah."

"Just because I'm having work challenges doesn't mean we're having challenges. It just means that kiss has to last me a little longer," he teased.

"Me too."

"I'll call you later."

"Okay."

"I've got to go. Bye."

"Bye." Crap.

Kendell

"I BROKE OUR AGREEMENT." **I** blurted out my confession waiting for his response. I had been trying not to fall back into my old habits with this relationship and now it seemed I'd done the same thing again.

Bas stepped back and nodded. "What agreement?"

"The one not to say anything to anyone except Alex." I was wringing my hands waiting on him to yell or something. After all, I did say I wanted to wait until we had been together a while longer before telling anyone.

Between the two of us, we don't have the best track record when it comes to relationships. Bas has enough ex-girlfriends to fill a small country. And the list of losers or bad choices I've been involved with is the equivalent of an NBA team roster. We seem like complete opposites, but we aren't. We understand each other. I feel like I can share anything with him, without his judging me. It's no secret I've had trust issues in the past, but I think he trusts me and I'm learning to trust him.

"Who did you tell?"

"Taylor." I was still holding my breath waiting on his reply.

"Okay." He smiled and kissed me. "Do you want to order a pizza?"

Excuse me? I just confessed I broke an agreement between us and he's talking about pizza. "You're not upset?"

"No, should I be?"

"Yeah, I mean, we did agree not to say anything."

He folded his arms in front of his chest and stood firm. "Honey, it's no big deal. So you told Taylor we're seeing each other. What did she say?"

"She was surprised and said I had a right to be concerned." Oh crap, I let that slip out.

"Concerned...about what?"

Now I've gone and done it. "I think she was referring to my past behavior." I quickly got it off of him and put the caution on me. "I have a tendency to get a little attached and over think things."

"Honey, I already know you have issues." He laughed.

"Not funny."

"So do I." He kissed me. "I'm sure she's just looking out for you. I know I'm not the poster boy for long term committed relationships, but I'm trying to change."

"I know, and I've seen a difference from when I first met you, but it's just, my last serious relationship left me with a lot of scars and..."

"That's the past. You and me, we are the present, maybe even the future." He pulled me close and the smell of his cologne traveled up my nose. At that moment, I didn't care if he was old Bas, New Bas, Shifty Bas, I just liked being in his arms watching his lips move.

I closed my eyes and exhaled, clearing my mind so I could continue the conversation. "What are you saying?"

"I agree with you, taking it slow is the best thing to do,

because I want this relationship to last."

That sounded like a marriage declaration. "Are you talking about marriage?"

"Maybe."

I stepped out of his grasp. "Bas, can we not talk about marriage."

"Why not?"

"I have had too many men talk about marriage only to discover that's all it was. So, can we agree not to talk about marriage? For one thing, it's way too soon. Heck, I'm just getting used to having a boyfriend that wants to go to church with me. I don't want to get my head full of possibilities that may never occur."

"I don't understand. I thought you'd want to know how I felt about marriage."

I didn't have a suitable answer. He's right. I do want to know how he feels about marriage, but I don't want his answer burned in my mind. What if he says he doesn't want to get married? Then I'll spend all my time waiting on the other shoe to fall. And if he says he does, then I'll start having fantasies about being married to him. "I do, but I don't want your answer stuck in my head like some bad love song."

"Excuse me?"

"No matter what you say, it will haunt me, and I don't want it messing up what we have. I know me and I'll dwell on it and..."

He stepped closer, wrapped me in his arms and gently pressed his lips against mine. His strong intoxicating scent traveled up my nose, clouding my thinking. At that moment, I was powerless. He slowly pulled back and whispered, "Whatever you say."

I opened my eyes and saw my future. If the eyes are the window to the soul, then I saw something in him I'd never seen before in any other man. I saw his heart. I saw someone who wanted to love me. He didn't care about my past. Heck, he was willing to lose his job because he cares about us. I think he could be the one, but I can't dwell on that.

God truly does go above what we expect and give us something more. I never would have thought it possible that a man like Bas would be interested in me. He's my complete opposite. He's suave and sophisticated and I'm a girl happy to be in the background. Maybe it's time I stepped up to the front row.

"Thank you."

"So how do you eat your pizza?"

THE DRIVE HOME SEEMS EVEN longer with this tragic music framing my thoughts. I should turn the radio off and drive in silence, but that would be even worse. The silence is the gateway to thoughts. Thoughts of Moses kissing me, touching me, singing to me, holding me and his scent. God I miss him. I should turn around and go to the airport. Fly to New York, grab a kiss and fly back. Now I sound like a junkie in search of a fix. But isn't that what I am...a passion junkie.

What is happening to me? I've never felt like this with any man I've been involved with. It's like he's branded me or injected me with a drug. And the only cure is him. I seem to crave him all the time. The phone calls are nice, but they're just like throwing salt on an open wound.

I should have taken him up on his offer for a weekend visit both times, but I couldn't. There was just too much going on at the store for me to get away. I was hoping to see him during the holidays, but that idea was killed because of the demands of his new play. So now, I've got to wait until January, when I go to New York for the beginning of Fashion Month to get my passion fix.

I looked at the clock on the dashboard and noted the time...seven thirty. Just enough time to get home and relax before my nightly phone date.

I thought about ending things with Moses, because I'm no good at the distance thing. But every time I try to form the words, they won't come and I know why...because I'm in love with him. I've tried denying it, but it's true.

I pulled into the garage remembering the last time I touched Moses, and how his body felt pressed against mine as he kissed me. And his smell. I've never met a man that smells like he does. It's like sweet plums and tobacco.

I got out of the car and headed toward the door and realized I forgot my bag and phone. I went back to the car, reached inside the passenger side, picked up my bag and the phone started ringing. I knew the ring tone. I looked at the screen and it was a picture of Moses.

I pressed the Accept Call button. "Hey, Baby."

"Hey, Beautiful. You sound strange. Where are you?"

"The garage. I forgot my phone in the car." I looked at my watch. "I wasn't expecting to hear from you until later." Any questions I had about staying in this relationship, just disappeared.

"I know, but I'm meeting a friend and the only time they were available was late and I didn't want to break our phone date."

"You could have called me later tonight or waited until tomorrow."

"I know, but after breaking our date for the holidays, I wanted to make sure I kept my promise to call you every night before turning in."

I tossed my head back, fighting the tears my confused emotional state was causing. This is why I can't break up with him. Why can't he show no remorse for canceling on me. Instead, he's...

"I told you I understood about the holidays."

" I know, but I feel like I let you down."

"You didn't…I…" I didn't know how to respond.

"Baby…Baby…"

"I'm here." I sniffled. "How was your day?" I pressed the garage door button and the loud rumbling of the door made it difficult to hear his answer.

"Beautiful, I have to go, my friend is here."

"Where are you?" I pushed the door open and walked inside.

"Your kitchen."

I looked up, dropped my bag and phone, ran over and crushed my body against his. He cupped my face in his large hands and took my mouth in a passionate, scintillating kiss I felt deep in my core. His hands slid down my back pulling me deeper into his space. The only air we inhaled was the air we drained from each other's lungs. He pressed me harder against his body and everything I remembered from our last kiss was there… his smell…his touch… his warm body.

The doubts had been replaced with the lustful and salacious thoughts I fight off after every one of his calls. His hands slid down my back cupping my behind as he lifted me up and sat me on the counter. We never broke the kiss. He moved in between my legs and I threw myself deeper into the kiss. Kissing frantically, trading deep moans and groans. He dug his fingers into my hair and the heat from his fingers penetrated my scalp, sending a surge of passion coursing through my body.

I pulled him closer, absorbing every piece of him. His lips slid from my mouth to my ear and his hot, sweet breath gave birth to one word, "Passion," followed by a kiss behind my ear.

"Exactly."

He brushed his finger along my lips. "I missed these lips."

"Me too." He gently kissed me. "Meeting a friend?" I smiled.

He leaned back. "My girlfriend." He smiled as he brushed my cheek.

"I guess you're the reason why my mother offered to cover

me at the store tonight."

"I called Miss Connie last week and…"

"Last week?"

"Yes. I called and told her I was coming for a few days." He grazed my lips with the tip of his tongue as he tucked a loose hair behind my ear followed by another gentle peck on the lips.

"And Bas?" Now things were starting to make sense. Bas told me he would handle things if I wanted to take a couple of days off to rest up before the holiday rush.

"It took a team to pull this off." He smiled.

I looked around and noticed a pink box on the counter. "What's that?" I smiled.

"What?"

"The box."

"Oh, that's for you."

"Really?"

"Yep." He reached over and picked up the box and handed it to me and I shook it.

"What is it?"

"Open it?"

I ripped off the wrapping and opened the box. Inside was a sterling silver picture frame with a photo of us at Courtney's party. I brushed my hand over the picture. "It's perfect."

"Let me see." I held it up. "Nice."

His reaction didn't make any sense. "Didn't you see it when you wrapped it?"

"This isn't from me."

"It isn't?"

"No. It's from Grams."

"Oh." I put the box on the counter and kissed him. "Thanks for being the messenger."

"You're welcome." He smiled.

"Uhm, I wasn't expecting company for dinner. How do you feel about pizza…it's not what you're used to but, it's close."

He tilted his head and raised one eyebrow. "Pizza…that's an

option. Or we could eat the dinner I made."

"You made dinner?" I smiled.

He lifted me off the counter and placed my feet on the floor. He took my hand and I followed him into the dinning room.

"I hope you don't mind, but I thought it would be nice to eat in here."

I was shocked at the attention to detail he had taken to make this night romantic. The table was dressed with my good china, crystal and lots of candles. I leaned back against his chest and he eased his hands around my waist. "You did this?"

"I had a little help. Miss Connie, took care of the table and I cooked." He pulled the chair out and I sat down. He pushed my chair in and kissed me on the neck before sitting at the head of the table. He looked very comfortable, like the chair and position were made for him. He took my hand, said grace, and we enjoyed dinner.

"I'll be right back." I went into the family room, came back and handed him a black box with a red satin ribbon."

"What's this?"

"Merry Christmas." I kissed him. "I was going to mail it because I didn't want to wait until January."

"You didn't have to get me a gift." His smile said otherwise. "And all I did was come for a surprise visit."

"That's all the present I need. Open it."

He opened the box and his eyes got wide as he stared at his gift. He lifted the cover and his mouth dropped open. "It's a signed first edition of Shakespeare in Harlem by Langston Hughes. He's one of my favorites."

"I know." My smile was almost as wide as his. "Read the book mark."

He pulled out the sterling silver book mark and read the inscription out loud. "Moses, thank you for kidnapping me. Merry Christmas, your girlfriend, Alexandra." He leaned over and kissed me. "Thank you, Beautiful. Now I really feel bad. I guess tomorrow I'll be doing a little shopping."

"Baby, having you here is all the gift I want."

"I wasn't raised like that. I should have gotten you a little something." He kissed me again, but more passionately. When we pulled apart, I noticed a small black box with a fuchsia silk ribbon sitting in front of my plate.

"What's this?"

"A little something."

"You didn't have to get me a gift." I said the words, but the way I attacked the wrapping said otherwise. I opened the box and inside was a pink alligator and rose gold Chopard Happy Sport Watch with floating diamonds. "Oh my God, it's beautiful…but, I can't accept it."

"Aren't you my girlfriend?"

"Yes, but—"

"Where I come from, jewelry is the expected Christmas gift for a girlfriend. Do you like it?"

"Yes."

"Read the inscription."

I turned the watch over and read the sentiment out loud. "Alexandra, it's time we stop messing around. Merry Christmas, your boyfriend, Moses." I brushed my finger across the words. "It's beautiful. Thank you." I leaned over and kissed him.

After dessert we went into the family room and snuggled on the sofa. This is how I imagined the holidays with Moses. I laid my head on his chest inhaling his enticing masculine scent. I really missed being like this with him. Tonight makes up for the months we've been apart.

It also took every ounce of self-control I had not to do something I'd regret. Just as the thought was on its way out of my mind, his hand slid down my back, resting on the crest of my behind. The subtle gesture brought the thoughts I'd been wrestling with back to the forefront of my mind.

His large hand pressed against my body, guiding me deeper into his space…our space. I looked up and he gently stroked the side of my face. "What's on your mind?"

What's on my mind? I'm too embarrassed to truthfully

answer him. I don't want him to know I'm wondering how his naked body would feel pressed against mine, doing things I need to keep locked deep in the corners of my mind.

"I'm thinking, I missed being like this." I traced his lip with my finger. "What were you thinking?"

He looked at me and his eyes started getting darker. "I was thinking…" he crushed his mouth against mine as he eased me down on the sofa. He covered my body with his and my hands traveled down his back, grabbing his behind, pulling him deeper into my space…our space.

I didn't need to give him permission to take possession of my mouth. The way his tongue broke through my lips capturing my tongue was savage. His hard body pressed against mine as his tongue dove deeper inside my mouth leading us in a kiss so erotic my body began to shake. I have never experienced a kiss so passionate.

His hand slipped down my back under my behind pressing me against him. His body's excitement was obvious as our kiss grew more intense…both of us breathing hard and moaning. Suddenly, I felt him pulling away.

I opened my eyes and he was leaning above me staring and breathing hard. His lips were swollen and his light brown eyes were now the color of coal. We were frozen in passion. I wasn't sure what to do. I couldn't move, not with two hundred plus pounds of solid hot chocolate man on top of me.

"Is that what you were thinking?"

"Not exactly." He still wasn't moving, but his body was speaking volumes. He stood up and adjusted his clothes. "Dance with me." He extended his hand to me.

I took his hand and stood up. He eased his hand around my waist slowly pulling me to his chest. I looked into his eyes, searching for a clue to what he was thinking, and why the sudden change in behavior. His hand slid down my back, pulling me to his chest. His eyes were still the color of coal and he was stone faced. We slowly swayed to the soulful sounds framing the room.

I wanted to say something, but what. I rested my head

against his chest following his lead, listening to the beat of his heart. The heat from his hands penetrated my skin raising my body temperature even more.

"I'm sorry."

Not what I was expecting to hear. I looked up and his eyes were still dark. His statement bore asking for clarification. "Sorry about what?"

"I got a little carried away." He brushed the side of my face and smiled.

"Me too."

"Passion?"

"Exactly."

Taylor

EVERY YEAR AUNT CONNIE INVITES me to spend the holidays with her and Alex, and I always decline. I keep hoping this will be the year my dad invites my brother and me home to spend it with him. Since my mom died, the holidays just aren't the same.

Once my dad married Agnes, she made it perfectly clear, things would be different. Instead of a traditional family Christmas, she and my dad go on a cruise.

My brother Tyson and his wife Mia, usually spend the holidays with her family. He says I can spend it with them, but she's never made me feel like it would be okay for me to join them. He and I exchange gifts, and he calls me twice a day between Christmas Eve and New Year's Day to check on me. He says, "One of these years, we'll be together again as a family, I promise." But that's what big brothers are supposed to say. Then he adds his big brother jab, "When are you going to settle down and give me a brother-in-law?" We laugh and I reply, "As soon as a man as good as you finds me."

The days leading up to Christmas are filled with social obligations. I spend Christmas Eve in my big gourmet kitchen eating from the gift baskets and other gourmet gifts I receive, while looking at pictures from Christmases past.

I miss watching my mom cooking Christmas dinner, and my dad sitting around the table telling stories, opening presents, eating until the zipper bursts on my skirt, and sitting in front of the fire roasting peanuts.

By noon on Christmas Day, I've made all my calls, eaten my grocery store dinner, and have settled in for an evening of opening presents from my family and friends, and watching movies.

This year I could have spent Christmas Eve with Jason and his family, but I passed. I prefer to stay at home, alone, as opposed to spending it with a woman who despises me.

I thought about calling up a friend, but most of my girlfriends are spending the evening with their loved ones or significant other, and any male friend would get the wrong impression. That's what I get for falling in love with Jason.

I should have taken him up on his offer. I mean, how bad would it have been to spend the evening with a woman who thinks I'm not only a cougar, but a bad influence? Okay, maybe I shouldn't have let Zach drive my car. Everything would have been fine, if she hadn't pulled up next to us. Hey, the experience made me very cool in Zach's eyes. Since then, we've limited his driving lessons to streets in my neighborhood, because I know Gretchen isn't coming over to this part of town.

I can't believe I'm dating a man with a child...a teenager. That wasn't part of my plan, but he's a great kid. I miss both of them.

I looked at the clock on the wall, nine-thirty. I wanted to call Jason, but I didn't want to come off as a needy, depressed, single woman.

To heck with pride. I picked up my phone and pressed Jason's number, but it rang with a familiar ringtone before the call connected.

"Hey, Baby. How was dinner?"

"Fine."

"What does your mom have planned for you and Zach tomorrow?"

"The usual…breakfast, early dinner and then she'll spoil Zach with a bunch of stuff I told her not to buy, before filling him up with massive amounts of sugar."

"Sounds like fun." I felt my heart aching as I said the words. I should have taken him up on his offer.

"I can pick you up in the morning and you can spend the day with us."

"Jason, I told you. I don't want to intrude on your time with your family."

"Okay. I'll call you later. Bye."

"Bye." I ended the call, took a deep breath, and verbally chastised myself. I picked up the phone and pressed his number. As the phone rang, I tried to figure out what to say.

"Hey, pretty girl."

"I was wondering…I mean, you did say, I could…I mean…I know how your mother feels about me, but this is a good time for me to prove I'm…"

"Taylor…"

"Yes?"

"Open the front door."

"What?"

"Open the front door." I walked to my front door, looked out the side vent and saw Jason and Zach. I opened the door and standing on my doorstep was the one man that never listens to a word I say, and his little helper.

"I gotta go, you're on the porch." I pressed the button and ended the call.

"Merry Christmas." He leaned forward and gently kissed me on the lips.

"What are you doing here?" Zach walked inside and Jason followed him.

"It was Zach's idea," Jason confessed.

"Miss T, we couldn't let you spend Christmas Eve alone," Zach admitted.

"What?"

"When Zach gave me his Christmas list, spending Christmas with you was the second thing on the list."

"What was the first thing?"

"A car." We laughed.

"What about your mother?" I'm already on shaky ground with her. I don't need any more problems. Holidays or not…I don't want to spend New Year's Eve in jail sharing a kiss with Big Sal at midnight, because Jason decided to spend Christmas Eve with me.

"She told us to bring you over tomorrow for dinner."

"Really?"

"Yes. So, I think it's time Zach and I show you how to use your kitchen, starting with a late dinner tonight, and breakfast in the morning."

"I see." I was trying not to cry.

"Zach, take the groceries into the kitchen and Taylor and I will handle the presents."

"Okay Dad. Merry Christmas, Miss T," he kissed me on the cheek, and I wiped the tear that escaped my eye.

"Merry Christmas, Zach." I followed Jason into the living room. His hands were loaded with shopping bags. "I don't know what to say."

I watched him taking charge and placing presents under the tree. It started to feel like those Christmases I had with my family.

I remember my dad would wait until he thought Tyson and I were asleep before putting the presents around the tree. We would sneak downstairs and watch our parents drinking eggnog and kissing like newlyweds.

"I hope you don't mind, but I brought Zach's presents with me."

"No, that's fine." He stood up and put his arms around me pulling me close. "I can't believe you did this."

"It was all Zach's idea. He didn't want you to be alone tonight. I was just going to come by for a little while tonight, and bring you breakfast in the morning. It was Zach's idea to stay over tonight and cook for you. He even brought sleeping bags. He wants us to camp out here by the tree like a family…number three on his Christmas list."

"A family? Wow. Uhm…"

"I know, he's a pretty special kid. But I think he might be trying to take my girlfriend." We laughed. He cupped my face in his large hands. Staring into those warm, dark brown eyes, I saw a lifetime of love and a great future. "I love you and…"

"You love me?"

"Yes, Ms. Richards, I love you."

"I-I…" He pulled me to his chest and I could feel his heart beating. When his lips touched mine, I forgot about all the Christmases when it was just me sitting alone wishing I had someone to spend the day with. He pulled back and I whispered, "I love you too, Jason Bishop. Merry Christmas."

Thank you God, for making this a great family Christmas.

Chloe

IF ANYONE HAD TOLD ME last year I would be spending the holidays in Brazil with my hot Brazilian boyfriend, I mean business associate, I would have had them arrested for impersonating a sane person. But the tan on my body and the smile on my face, says otherwise.

My first visit to Brazil was mostly business, but Marcelo and I did manage to sneak in a little fun. So this time when he invited me for New Years, he made it perfectly clear it was going to be all leisure.

However, my attorney feels a relationship with Marcelo could hurt me during divorce proceedings. Although things haven't escalated to that point, I know that's where Orlando and I are headed. I don't feel bad, because Orlando stepped out on me first. Just because I got married without a prenup...I'll never let that happen again, doesn't mean I have to put my life on hold waiting for the other shoe to drop. That's why I said yes to Marcelo's holiday invitation.

I told him what my attorney thought and he agreed with him. However, he also agreed with me. He said it was the thought of me in a bikini that convinced him to side with me. So, he chartered a jet to fly me to Brazil and put me up in one of the guesthouses on his ranch.

My itinerary said day one would be spent sailing. When he came down to the house to get me, he had a frown on his face. I was wearing a tiny, bright blue Agent Provacoteur bikini and a sarong.

"Why are you so covered up?"

"Covered up?" I looked at myself and actually thought Brazil was seeing too much of me.

He shook his head and said, "Those curves deserve to be seen. Come. Let's go shopping."

I have spent the past four years trying to get rid of some of my curves because Orlando said I was starting to get a little wide. So in an attempt to please my husband, I hired a trainer. Isaac and I have a love-hate relationship. My feelings toward him and his assignment to keep me in shape, vary depending on how I look in my clothes at the time. Marcelo's compliment, means I love my trainer.

Marcelo patiently sat there as I modeled swimsuits… interesting, the smaller the suit the wider his smile. After two hours of watching me try on swimsuits and rendering his opinion, I left with three thong bikinis, two teeny string bikinis with tops that barely accomodated my breasts and this killer one piece that I believe if I wear it at home, I'll be arrested for indecent exposure. Thank God, I had the forethought to get waxed.

I left the store wearing a tiny white thong bikini with a top that barely covered my nipples, a beautiful orange and white sarong, and the widest straw hat in the store. As soon as we got on the boat, Marcello graciously volunteered to apply sunscreen to my back. You haven't vacationed until you've had a gorgeous Brazilian man with large soft hands apply sunscreen to your bare backside…my, my, my.

The past ten days were amazing. We danced, went sailing on his boat, horseback riding, took long walks, swam, talked a lot and made out like teenagers under the stars. For New Years' Eve, he arranged dinner on the beach. When midnight came and the moon was right over us, he sang "Auld Lang Syne" in Portuguese, followed by one of those amazing kisses I've grown to love. Man, it's been a while since I spent time with a man that's my equal in every way, and who knows how to treat me the way I deserve to be treated.

I was shocked at some of the things he shared with me that God had brought him through. He said if it hadn't been for his relationship with God he wouldn't have had the courage to fight his ex-wife for custody of his son, or confront his sister about her drug problem. He said it broke his heart to put her in rehab, but he loves her too much to watch her slowly kill herself. He said it's like he has two children.

This trip showed me a side of Marcelo that surprised me. This could turn into something I might want to seriously pursue, once I'm divorced. But until then, I have to be content with video dating, over-the-top dates and occasional trips like this. If my girlfriends saw me running around Brazil in a thong, they'd lock me up.

When I got home, my husband or rather roommate, wasn't there. Thank God. I walked inside and the smell almost knocked me out. It smelled like a frat house. The stale beer, reefer and funk, were overwhelming. Orlando's feeble efforts to cover up the smell failed. It looked like he and his little girlfriend had been playing house while I was gone.

I walked around and surveyed my house. Nothing appeared to be broken, and there were no signs of Orlando or Tasha. Instead of settling in, I had Russell take my bags back to the car. I called a locksmith and had the locks changed. I should have done that a while ago. Then I went to my parents' house for a couple of hours. When I returned, the black Maserati was parked in the driveway. I walked up to the window, looked inside and found Orlando asleep and drooling like an old drunk.

I banged on the window and he jumped up. He let the window down and he smelled like a brewery. I'm surprised he was able to drive home. "Why are you sleeping in your car?"

"My key won't work." He wiped his face with his hand. "When did you get back?"

"What's wrong with your key?"

"I don't know, I tried to open the door, but it wouldn't work." He got out of the car and could barely stand up.

"Are you sure?" I walked up to the door, put my key in the lock, turned the knob and walked inside. "My God, are you so drunk you don't know what key opens the door?"

"What are you talking about?" He walked inside rubbing his head and slurring his words. "I guess I used the wrong key."

"Let me see your keys." He handed me his keys and I pretended to look for the house key. "I guess it would help if you had the house key."

"I don't understand? I had it when I left last night." His words were slurring more and he smelled like a combination of cheap cologne, whiskey and reefer. I shook my head in disgust.

"Does your little girlfriend have your key?"

"Uhm…uhm…"

"Great, now on top of everything else you've done, I have to wonder if you've left your key somewhere, and be concerned some stranger is going to just walk in here and attack us?"

"I must have left it at…" He rubbed his head again as he reeled from side to side trying to stand up straight.

"Great." I threw my hands up in the air laughing to myself. This is too easy.

"Would you stop yelling. The sound of your voice is making my headache worse."

"It's not my voice making your head hurt. It's that cheep weed your little girlfriend has you hooked on."

His eyes got wide. "What do you know about some weed?" He turned his mouth up in a crooked smile.

"Baby Boy, I know more than you think."

"Please, like you and your stuck up friends know anything 'bout gettin' lit up."

"What you don't know about me and my friends would crash the internet."

"Just talk." He threw his hand up in the air. "I'm going to bed." He walked down the hall and tripped on the rug. "Oh, my bad."

I shook my head and watched as he barely made it to his room.

Later that night, I quietly walked into his room and switched the house keys. Now let Tasha try to get in while we're not home.

This is a new year and, I have new insight on how to handle my husband and his girlfriend.

MY UNCLE CALLED AND SAID he was meeting with Terrence later this week at his place in Napa and asked me to join them.

I immediatley replied, no. Moses was still here and our plans for the rest of the week didn't include spending them with my ex-husband. But when my Uncle insisted, I knew I had no choice.

I told Moses and he quickly made wine out of grapes and said it would be a beautiful drive. He also said, if I drove, he'd read his book to me. How could I refuse such an offer.

I think when we get back I'll tell my girlfriends about him. He's been very patient and I feel now is the time to fully integrate him into my life. I love the private times we have, but it's time to bring this relationship out of the dark and into the light. Besides, it's not easy hiding a six foot three man who loves to stand up in church and praise God.

He needs to know I'm not embarrassed to be with him. I think once I tell my friends about him, I'll be able to tell him I love him. But first, I need to get rid of that albatross ex-husband that seems to have attached himself to my feet.

We all gathered in the den with Ed, my uncle's investigator, and a large blank white board.

"I have to say this has been the most exciting case I've worked on in years." Ed was almost walking on air.

"Calm down Ed. Did you find something new?" Uncle asked.

"Did I. Miss Alex, has anyone from Pierce Holdings ever contacted you?"

"No, why would they?"

He clapped his hands. "As I was digging, it occured to me to check the other will."

"You did that, remember. That's how we found out it was fake," Uncle Wallis replied.

"I'm talking about Royce's will."

"Why would we check Royce's will?" Terrence asked.

"Oh man, this is good."

"Ed..." Uncle Wallis urged.

He flipped over the white board and all our mouths dropped open. "What the crap!" I shouted. "Is that correct?"

"Let me explain. Royce had a child."

"Holy crap!" Terrence shouted. "That can't be right."

"But it is. Your mother and Royce were lovers."

"What the crap!" I shouted.

"This is so good." Ed stood rubbing his hands.

"How is that even possible?" Terrence asked.

"Before your mother died, she gave her maid a stack of

letters. The maid hid the letters. Several years later, before the maid died, she sent the letters to Royce. They were his response to your mother's letters and in one letter, she told him you were his son." He pointed to Terrence.

"This is the third father I've had in..." Terrence shook his head.

"Listen son, this, is the truth. Your mother was married to one brother, but in love with the other. When she became pregnant, she assumed her husband was the father, but he wasn't."

"Oh my God," Terrence replied.

"She never told either brother."

"That's why Royce started visiting me so much and spending time with me."

"I don't mean to sound selfish, but what does this have to do with me?" I asked.

"Here's the really good part." Ed was salavating. "Royce suspected Thomas had done something shady, but according to the will as he knew it, everything was in order. So he decided to right things for his son."

"Ed..." Uncle cut him a look.

"Royce hated what Thomas did to you two. He knew he was dying, so he did the only thing he knew would piss Thomas off. He left Miss Alex ten percent of the company."

"Excuse me?" I asked. Just when I thought I was done with this mess, I've been sucked in deeper.

"The ten percent that Thomas took really belonged to Miss Alex."

"You're telling me, I own ten percent of Pierce Holdings?"

"That's correct. Are you sure no one ever contacted you?" Ed asked.

I closed my eyes scanning my memory. "Oh my God." I jumped up and walked to the white board and looked at Royce's picture. "I remember a very well dressed man with a cane and a sweet smiled who came into the store about three times a week for three months. He always paid in cash. I just thought he had a crush on one of the stylists." I looked at Royce's picture. "It was him. Was he spying on me?"

"Who knows," Ed replied.

"A nice gesture, but I don't want the shares."

"Now I get it," Uncle Wallis said as he looked at the board.

"Get what?" I asked.

"See, if you two pool your shares, you have controlling interest and can stop the IPO."

"This is insane." I walked over to the sofa and sat next to Moses and he rubbed my shoulders. "I don't want the shares."

"Babe, it's not that simple," Moses finally spoke up. "Ed, what does the will say about Alex's share?"

"She can only sell them to Terrence or give him her proxy."

"This is too much to deal with." I rubbed my forehead. "Is this why these people are stalking me?"

"What's she talking about?" Ed asked.

I got up and went outside.

I heard footsteps and turned around. "You okay?" I shook my head and started crying. Moses pulled me to his chest and wrapped me in his arms. "Calm down."

"I don't want any of this." He rubbed my back and it seemed like it made the tears come harder.

"I know. We'll figure something out."

The quiet up here is magical. It allows you to hear everything you're trying to block out. I was content being alone with my thoughts when I heard the door open and close followed by heavy footsteps and a familiar voice.

"This has all been a lot to take in."

"I don't want anything to do with your family. Whatever

I need to do to..."

"I'm sorry about all of this. You've got to believe me, Lexi."

"I believe that you didn't know anything about Royce, but that pre-nup...please."

"Okay, I knew about that, but..."

"Seven hundred and fifty thousand dollars."

"What?"

"That's the amount of the check I was given after I was forced to sign the annulment papers."

"That's not right. Gerard assurd me..."

"If you divorce Blair, she'll receive one hundred and twenty million dollars. She probably doesn't even love you." I felt tears trying to come, but I wouldn't allow myself to shed one more tear behind this man.

"What are you saying?"

"No matter what we thought, I was an obstacle. A gnat Thomas was eager to squash."

"That's not true."

"Isn't it?" I turned and faced him. "Maybe if you had been concerned about your own life instead of stalking me with Jonathan's help, you would have known about all of this."

"I guess I deserve that."

"And more."

"Before you completely write me off with your pity pen, I have something to say." He stepped closer. "There hasn't been a day, an hour, a minute or moment that you haven't been in the forefront of my mind. When I said I loved you, it wasn't a line to get you to help me, it was the truth."

"I don't want to hear your lies."

"Lexi..."

I started towards the door. "What?"

"I promise to fix this mess. I'll do whatever I have to, to get my family to leave you alone."

"Thank you." I grabbed the handle on the screen door.

"I know you have someone in your life, but I will not let

another day pass without telling you how much I love you. Lexi, I'm sorry. You're right, I should have stood up to my family. I should have given you a chance to help me. I should have been the man you knew I could be, but I was scared. I felt I didn't have a choice. I didn't know if I could take care of you, when I barely knew how to take care of myself. If you forgive me, I know I can be the man you fell in love with. I'm begging you for another chance."

Dionne

I BRACED MYSELF BEFORE KNOCKING on the door. I stood staring at the name...Chloe Jacobs. I've never understood why she doesn't use her married name. I like it...Kingston. It sounds regal. Seeing the way Orlando has been behaving, it's probably a good thing she still goes by her maiden name.

I can't believe the stunt Orlando pulled last night. Not only did it make the local papers, it's circling the internet as well. Turns out Orlando's little girlfriend's ex-boyfriend is some wannabe rapper, and he and Orlando got into a huge fight last night at a club on Sunset. I think his little posse posted the pictures on the internet.

Then on his way home, he was pulled over for speeding. When he didn't pass the field sobriety test, the police hauled him in and charged him with a DUI. They impounded his car and threw him in jail. Some genius in booking put the two incidents together and bam. Orlando is today's internet darling. Quentin's phone has been ringing off the hook with reporters looking for a comment from Chloe.

I knocked on the door and waited for an answer.

"It better be important," she barked back.

I pushed the door open and poked my head around the door. "I think it is." She looked up. "What are you doing, hiding?" I teased.

"Hey Dee. Come on in." No reaction to my little joke. A definite sign she was upset.

I closed the door and walked toward her desk. "Got a minute?"

She put her pen down, lifted her hands above her head stretching and let out a sigh. "Not if you're coming to talk to me about that trash in your hand."

"So, I take it you saw the paper this morning?"

She stood up, walked around the desk and hugged me. "Yes, and so has everyone in the building. Tucker's been fending off calls all morning. Come on, let's sit down." I followed her to the sofa and sat down. "Worst of all, my father has given me twenty-four hours to fix the problem."

"What are you going to do?"

She scratched her head and sighed. "I don't know."

"I can have Quentin issue a statement."

"No, that would just be adding fuel to the fire. What I want to do is..." She got silent. "How are things with you and Quentin?"

I tried hiding my smile, but it was on full blast. "Good."

She looked at me smiling. "That explains the glow."

"What glow?"

"Girl, you are beaming from head to toe. I might need to get my sunglasses," she teased.

"No I'm not."

"Please Dee. I know it's been a while since I glowed, but I recognize the look." My smile got wider. "Not to mention that smile on your face. Good for you."

"Thank you."

"I'm happy for you."

"Now back to you. Quentin will be upset, if I return without an answer from you."

"So he sent you to do his dirty work."

"Sort of. I told him it would be best if I talked to you. First of all, where is Orlando?"

"I don't know."

"Excuse me? I thought he was in jail."

"So did I until my attorney went to bail him out. Seems his little girlfriend got him out."

"With what money?"

"I don't know. I checked all of our accounts and nothing has been touched, so maybe she had a few dollars stashed."

"And you haven't heard from him?"

"I tried calling but all I got was voicemail."

"Wow. So what do you want to do?"

"I don't know."

"I have to ask, is there any chance for reconciliation?"

"You sound like my attorney. I'll tell you the same thing I told him, no."

"Are you sure?"

"Just because I was going to bail him out and we had sex."

I immediately cut her off. "Hold up. What did you say?"

"We had sex. He was a lot drunk and I was a lot frisky." She had a strange smile on her face. "We always worked well in the bedroom. Not to mention my dad's jet, Orlando's office, the pool deck at the beach house and..."

"I get the point."

"It's over." She opened up the folder and looked at the picture. "Can you believe this is what he wants?"

I saw the hurt in her eyes. "Are you sure there's no chance of reconciling?" I asked again.

She hesitated before answering. "I thought it was until I saw them together." She dropped her head so I couldn't see her face. "She's in his blood. I saw it in his eyes."

"Don't say that." I patted her hand.

"It's true. No matter how angry I am at him, it's not going to change anything." She lifted her face. "He doesn't love me anymore."

I didn't know how to respond to her statement. Quentin and I may disagree on a few things, but I know he loves me and would never do what Orlando has done. He told me he felt guilty about going out with me because of his past relationship with Alex. Before our second date, she told me he called her and asked if she had a problem with us dating. She told him she thought we would be good together that's why she introduced us.

Quentin has integrity and that's one of the things I love about him. I know he would never disrespect me. Heck, he basically told his mother to kiss off when she didn't approve of him marrying me.

"Are you sure?"

"Yep." She nodded. "I looked in his eyes and the only other time I saw that look was the first time we met." She dabbed at the tear sitting on the corner of her eye.

"But that doesn't mean..."

"Dee, I appreciate your optimism, but my marriage was never like yours. Quentin loves you and my husband loves someone else. Grant it she may not be old enough to vote," we laughed. "But she's old enough to take my husband."

I've never seen my friend like this. I see the hurt in her eyes. "So, what do you want to do?"

She shrugged her shoulders. "I don't know. You're my publicist, what do you suggest?"

Seems our roles had changed. Instead of me asking her for relationship advice, she was looking to me for help.

"I've got my gun." I teased.

She wiped the tear that escaped her eye. "So do I."

Alex

"WHAT'S THIS?" MOSES ASKED STARING at the two carat diamond solitaire engagement ring sitting in the black ring box on my desk.

"My wedding ring."

"Your what?"

"My wedding ring." It's been more than twenty years and the words are still difficult to say.

"Where did it come from?"

"Terrence."

"Why?"

This was an unfamiliar tone and it scared me. " I don't know." That was a lie. I knew Terrence sent it to confuse me.

"So he came to see you?"

"No. It came by messenger, along with this note." I handed him the note and watched his face. His jaw grew tight. He looked at me and his eyes were as dark as coal.

"He says he's still in love with you and wants you back...

and that you didn't answer his question. What question?"

I was scared to answer him. I stepped back, took a deep breath and answered. "When we were at my uncle's house, he told me he still loves me and wanted to know if I felt the same."

"What did you say?"

He asked me a simple question that deserved a simple answer. Unfortunately, I knew the answer I had would make him angrier. I braced myself and owned my response. "Nothing."

"Nothing?"

"How do you respond to something like that? I mean he was apologizing and I...it was like every old feeling came alive. At that moment, he was the Terrence I fell in love with. It felt like I was twenty-one years old again back on the streets of Paris."

"So what are you saying...you want him back?"

"It's not that simple. We never really had a chance. I mean, one day we were newlyweds walking the streets of Paris and the next day I was alone and pregnant and now I find out Jonathan kept things from me that could have changed everything."

"What things...are you saying you would have settled for a relationship with no future?"

"No. I'm saying—"

"I have to go back to New York," he blurted out.

"What?"

"There's a problem with the play. That's what I came by to tell you."

"When are you leaving?"

"Tonight."

"When are you coming back?"

"I don't know." He stepped closer, pulled my face close and kissed me. The kiss felt nothing like his kisses in the past. It felt like it was the last one. He pulled away and gently wiped the tears rolling down my face. "I love you, but I can't be here right now. Call me when you decide what you want."

I covered my face with my hands so I didn't have to watch him walk away.

Dear God, I don't know what to do. For the first time in my life Lord, I don't know what to pray for. I know I need help but, please God, protect my heart and keep me from making the same mistakes again. In Jesus' name, I pray, Amen.

"Bas, come in. I need to go over things for our trip." I continued reading until I heard the door open and slam shut. "First off---"

"Excuse me Alex." I looked up. "Are you okay?"

"I'm fine." I lied. I was up all night crying and praying.

"You don't look or sound fine."

"I don't want to talk about it."

He nodded. "When you talk to Moses, tell him to call me. I need to know if we're still on for the game?"

"You better call yourself."

"What are you talking about?"

"Seems there was a problem with the play that only he could solve, so he left." I turned my attention back to the papers on my desk.

"I don't understand."

"He left me."

"What?"

I refused to look at him because I knew he would be able to read the look on my face and I'd start crying again.

"Alex, I know you. What happened?"

I looked up. "Terrence sent my wedding ring back to me."

"What!"

"Along with a note telling me he still loves me and wants me back."

"And you told this to Moses?"

"Yes."

"Why?"

"Because the ring and note were sitting on my desk when he came by to see me."

"I don't believe you. Are you trying to sabotage your happiness?"

Bas has never raised his voice to me and right now, he's acting as Moses' best friend. If he didn't know me, I think he'd slap me and I'd deserve it.

"I can't believe you did that." Shaking his head. "Does Miss Connie know what happened?"

"No. I know, it's bad."

"No, Alex, you don't."

"Since you're the authority on all things Moses, then you tell me. What should I have done?"

"This is one of those times when you shouldn't have said anything."

"I'm not going to lie to him."

"I'm not saying you should have lied. I'm saying you should have just sent the ring back and that would have been it. Unless—"

"Unless what?"

"Unless you love Terrence?"

"I don't know."

"You don't know?"

I reached for a tissue and wiped the tears before they had a chance to wet my desk. I didn't know what to say. If he had asked me this question four days ago, I would have immediately answered "no". But now, I don't know.

"Alex, if you love Terrence, forget about Moses, forget about your ex-in-laws and go get him. But if you don't love him, you need to tell him. Trust me, it's the only way you're going to break the hold he has on you."

"What about Moses?"

"If you want Terrence, then forget about Moses."

"But I—"

"What, love him? I doubt that." His words felt sharper than a paper cut.

"What makes you say that?"

"Because you haven't let go of Terrence. All this time I thought it was Jonathan you were still in love with, but it's Terrence."

Dearest Moses, I'm sorry. I don't know what I was thinking. You're right, I should have answered Terrence's question, but he caught me off guard. I had been waiting over twenty years for an apology from him and when it came in the form of a confession, it shocked me. Please forgive me. I miss you, Alex.

Mama

FOR THE PAST FEW WEEKS, I've been sharing a house with "Evil Alex". She's my daughter, but I can't stand the person she becomes when she refuses to deal with what's troubling her. For my own sake, I have got to do something. I am about three steps away from knocking her into next week.

Bas told me he's been in contact with Moses and from the sound of it, he's still angry. However, he got the impression Moses' feelings for that fool daughter of mine hadn't changed. Which means there's still a chance I can clean up this mess. However, I'm going to need help.

It's a mother's prerogative to interfere in her child's life. Especially when your adult daughter is being stubborn and pigheaded.

I would never tell Alexandra, but as angry as I was about what Terrence's family did, it was for the best. I'm sure Terrence is a nice man, but he has no back bone. Alexandra doesn't need just a "nice man." She needs someone not afraid to stand up to her and be the leader. Terrence wasn't that man. Moses on the other hand, cares about her, isn't afraid to stand up to her and is a strong leader. He's what she needs.

I decided to go with Alex and Bas to New York for Fashion week. It's been a while since I traveled with them, but I had an alterior motive.

I told Alex I wasn't feeling well and suggested she go to the afternoon shows without me and asked her to have Bas stay with me. After she left, Bas and I left for our appointment.

We stood in front of the beautiful Upper Eastside townhouse. It's just like Alex described. Grey stones and large pane windows. It looked like something out of an old movie.

We walked up the steps and were instantly greeted by a petite, brown skinned woman with salt and pepper hair. She gave both of us a hug and ushered us inside to the main parlor. Breathtaking. I instantly understood why Alex didn't want to leave, it was beautiful. I looked at Bas and he looked sad.

"What's wrong?"

"I miss her."

"Who?"

"Alex. If this goes as planned...Alex has been my longest female relationship."

I shook my head smiling.

"Don't just stand there," cried out a voice. We walked in the direction of the voice to a space where a petite, cholocate colored woman with grey hair and a strong voice was sitting.

"Good afternoon, Mrs. Bartholomew. I'm Alexandra's mother, Constance Miller." I walked over and shook her hand.

"Pleasure. And you, young man?" She smiled.

"Sebastian Devareux. Pleasure to meet you," Bas shook her hand.

"Have a seat. What can I do for you?"

"Mrs. Bartholomew, it seems my daughter and your grandson are...do you have any idea what is going on between them?"

"Do you mind if I call you Connie?"

"No, that's fine."

"Connie, I'm not exactly sure. I know he came back abruptly from Los Angeles and when I asked what happened he ignored me. I've been living with a grumpy old bear for the past few weeks. When he's not at the theatre, he's locked up in his office. How have things been on your end with Alexandra?"

"She's been evasive. All she'll say is she messed up and he left because of production problems."

"That's not true."

I looked at Bas. "Bas, what haven't you told me?"

He looked at Mrs. Bartholomew and back at me. "Uhm... the fight was about her ex."

"What about him?" I asked.

"He sent her a letter apologizing along with her wedding ring."

"And?" I asked.

"She said the ex asked her to forgive him and give him another chance."

Nothing he said should matter to Moses unless... "Tell me, Bas, did Alexandra tell Moses any of this?"

"She showed him the letter and the ring."

I exhaled and rubbed my forehead. "I don't believe this."

"Anything else son?" Mrs. Bartholomew asked.

"Moses asked her was she still in love with the ex."

"And?" Mrs. Bartholomew asked.

"That's all I know."

"I had no idea it was this bad." I got up, folded my arms in front of my chest and started pacing.

"I think they're both waiting on the other to call," Bas confessed.

"Now that's just silly and childish," Mrs. Bartholomew announced.

"So what do we do?" Bas asked.

"Son, leave this to me and Connie. The less you know

about our plan, the better. " Mrs. Bartholomew said.

"I'll text Alex and let her know I'm feeling better and that you're on your way to meet her."

"Are you sure?" he asked.

"Yes."

"I'll have Otis take Connie back to the hotel before he picks up Moses."

"Mrs. Bartholomew, it was a pleasure meeting you. You're as charming and beautiful as Alex said," Bas smiled.

"And you're as cute as she said. If I were twenty years younger I'd have to rewrite my will." She smiled and winked.

He kissed us both on the cheek, "Miss Connie, I'll see you back at the hotel. Goodbye, ladies." He walked out and closed the door.

"Now that the boy is gone, let's talk. What the boy said confirms what Moses said. He came back ranting and raving about her still being in love with the ex-husband. You're her mother, has she said anything to you?"

"No, nothing. May I call you Emma?"

"Yes."

"I know the ex-husband's family has been throwing money at her to disappear."

"Really, how much?"

"First time they sent the family attorney with a check for five million dollars. Then the second time the father showed up with twenty-five million dollars. And don't ask me how I know this, but they have been sending messages through her friends in the form of large contracts and donations."

"You lost me."

"They bought some properties from her friend that's in real estate development and want them renovated. I believe that cost them around forty-five million. The attorney booked my niece to cater a wedding to the tune of two hundred and fifty thousand dollars. My niece in Atlanta told me she was asked to be the sole broker for a new luxury housing development they're building in Atlanta. And the other friend's mother-in-law's clinic just received a two hundred and fifty thousand dollar contribution for their clinic along with some much needed medical equipment."

"Who are they?"

"Thomas and Lillian Pierce. Pierce Holdings. And the wife is-- "

"I know of the Pierce family and I know the Abrams family. Both families are a nasty piece of work. Do they know about Alexandra and Moses?"

"Terrence met Moses in Napa. How do you know them?"

"I knew Blair's grandfather, Sherman Abrams. He and my husband were friends. His son has done a pretty good job with the company, but it could be better. Anyone getting involved now can expect to make a fortune in the future."

"Blair's dowry was forty percent of the company in exchange for Terrence. When Pierce Holdings goes public, Terrence will be named CEO."

"How much did that cost them, apart from the boy's life?"

"At the time, it was worth one hundred and twenty million dollars and after the first year of marriage, Pierce Holdings got seven radio stations."

"Wow, that's interesting. Abrams Industries has never been the best peg in the Media game, nor is it the best division of Abrams Industries. It's riddled with debt and a lot of bad investments, and they expect Terrence to fix that mess? He must be a genius, because that's what it's going to take to bring that division back."

"Excuse me?"

"My portfolio includes five percent of Abrams Industries my husband and I received it as a first year anniversary present from Sherman. You know, first year paper."

"You've got to be kidding!" I sat back with my mouth open trying to digest everything.

"Tell me Connie, do you think she's is still in love with Terrence?"

"No. I know she loves Moses, only she's too scared to admit it. She's using this mess as a way to protect her heart. How much of what happened between Terrence and Alex did Moses tell you?"

"Unfortunately everything," she confessed.

"Then you know about the baby?"

"Excuse me?"

"The summer before her senior year of college, she had a baby but she never told Terrence."

"Then maybe she should."

"She won't. She didn't even know she was pregnant until some spotting occurred. The doctor put her on bed rest and she delivered prematurely. The baby lived three days. In her mind for a brief moment, she was a single mother and feels he doesn't need to know."

"She needs to tell him so the tie he has on her will be broken and she can get on with her life. It might hurt at first, but it's what she needs to do to get control. I like Alexandra and I like what she's done for my grandson. After his wife died, he became very distant and took up with his ex-fiancée. When he met Alexandra, he became his old self. Of all my grandchildren, he is most like my husband. His grandfather was kind, generous, passionate, protective, impulsive, stubborn and focused."

"He and Alex are a lot alike. I love that she still believes in the fairytale, but she's as stubborn as a mule. The past few weeks have been unbearable." Sigh. "So what do we do?"

"Invite them to lunch," Emma declared.

"Lunch? They aren't speaking to each other."

"You invite Moses to lunch and I'll invite Alexandra to lunch. We won't bring up either one of them."

"Temptation without confrontation."

"Exactly.

Alex

BAS AND I WERE IN Soho checking out some boutiques, trying to steal ideas, when my phone rang. The call was coming from a familiar Upper Eastside number. I pressed the button and tried not to sound too anxious, "Alexandra Miller."

"Hello Alexandra, it's Emma Bartholomew."

Crap! Not the person I was hoping to speak to from this number. "Hello Mrs. Bartholomew. How did you get...never mind. What can I do for you?"

"I need to talk to you."

"Is this about Moses, because--"

"Of course it isn't. I'll be at Central Park on the Fifth Avenue side close to Sixty-First Street at one fifteen. You'll see me."

"I have--"

Click.

I stood at the park entrance and looked at my watch. I have got to be out of my mind. I felt like I was being called into the principal's office for misbehaving. At least then, the worst I could expect would be detention for a week.

I walked inside the park and looked ahead a few yards and saw the sweet looking grey haired woman sitting on the bench, feeding birds.

It was the longest short walk in my life. I stopped a few steps short of the bench. I took a deep breath, continued and stopped next to the bench.

"Good afternoon, Mrs. Bartholomew."

She looked up at me, stone faced. "Grams. Call me Grams."

"Grams."

"Good afternoon. Sit." I did as told. "Before I forget, here," she handed me a small Bergdorf's bag. "Mrs. Joseph and Otis send their love and these. I understand they're your favorite?"

I looked in the bag and found warm homemade chocolate chip walnut cookies. Thank God, something to ease my nervousness. "Tell her thank you and I miss them both."

"Alexandra, when we met, I thought I made myself clear about how I felt about my grandson."

So much for the niceties. "I thought this wasn't about Moses?"

"This is not the time to talk."

"Ex..." She cut me a sharp look. I was tempted to leave. Instead, I reached inside the bag for a cookie and started eating.

"In case you have forgotten some part of our conversation, I'll say it again. Moses is my favorite and I will not allow anyone to hurt him. He's been a bear to live with since coming back from California. He hasn't fully disclosed what happened, but I'm convinced it has something to do with you and your ex-husband. You have one chance to tell me what happened."

This woman scares me. I equate sitting here like going through the security scanner at the airport. I think if I tried to lie, a buzzer would go off signaling my deception and I'd end up in jail, sitting next to some idiot wearing an aluminum foil hat and matching gloves, counting the hairs on her toes.

I swallowed the last of my cookie and wiped my mouth.

"He asked me about a conversation I had with Terrence in Napa."

"About what?"

"I don't think that's any of your business." That cookie amped up my blood sugar, making me bold enough to stand up to her.

"See, that's where you're wrong. Anything concerning my grandson's well being is my business."

In one short phrase, she zapped all of my boldness. I suddenly had diarreha of the mouth. "Terrence sent my wedding ring back to me along with a note asking my forgiveness and another chance because he still loves me."

"And what did you say?"

Here's that question again. "Nothing."

"Nothing?"

"Yes, and that's when Moses said he was having problems with the play and left."

"First of all, there was no problem. He's preparing for previews and everything is going well. Second, are you out of your mind? You don't tell a headstrong man like Moses you said nothing."

"Why? He asked and I wasn't going to lie to him."

"Do you remember when we first met, I told you I would tell you how you ended up at that party.

"Yes, ma'am."

"You have Taylor to thank for you being at that party."

"Taylor? Why would Taylor..."

"Moses did something I have never known him to do. He called an ex-girlfriend and asked if she would mind him asking her friend...cousin, out."

"He did?"

"She told him she thought the two of you would be perfect for each other, that's why she insisted he attend the party. If you ask her, she'll probably deny it. You were all Moses talked about when he returned from Atlanta. It was Taylor who told him you were on your way to Atlanta."

"But how did I end up in New York?"

"Destiny. God. You pick. Moses was headed home for Courtney's engagement party, and then to Atlanta the following morning to see you. He was doing what he swore he would never do again, chase a woman."

"I didn't..."

"So when you say you said nothing to his question, it cut. He didn't want to hear your reaction. He wanted to know if you wanted your ex-husband back. By saying nothing, even if you were stumped by your ex-husband's confession, made him think you did. All he wanted to know was who you loved, him or the other one? So, what's the answer?"

"I love Moses, but part of me feels things aren't finished with Terrence."

"Alexandra, I like you so I'm going to tell you something no one knows. I was married long before I met Moses' grandfather."

"Excuse me?" She looked at me and my mouth was wide open.

"His family didn't approve. When he stood up to his parents, they turned their backs on him and we eloped. We moved to Indiana and had a beautiful baby girl. I knew he was unhappy, so I convinced him we should go see his family. It took quite a bit of prodding, but he finally agreed to go see them. We loaded up the car and headed home. On the way we were hit by a truck. My husband and daughter were killed."

I sat still looking at her staring at the birds as she continued to share her story.

"While I was in the hospital, I sent his mother a telegram telling her what happened. Once I was discharged, I went back to our apartment, picked up four things...my daughter's birth certificate and photo and my wedding photo and marriage license. Then I took the first train to New York. Three years later, I met Earl Wesley Bartholomew."

She turned and caught me patting a tear in the corner of my eye. "What has..."

"I told Earl everything. He said I needed to forgive myself

before I could forgive my husband's family. He said he wouldn't marry me until I settled things with them. I went to Chicago and did just that and once I did, the burden of guilt and the anger I'd been holding on to, left. When I came back to New York, Earl met me at Grand Central Station, and we were never apart again until I buried him eighteen years ago. I loved my first husband, but I was in love with Earl."

Now the tears were really coming. I was about to use my coat sleeve, when she handed me a handkerchief. "Thank you."

"I understand what you're going through. Those people are never going to leave you alone as long as they think there's a chance you could come in and upset their plans."

"But Grams..."

"You've got to get closure, and shift the balance of power. This I know for sure, my grandson is in love with you. If he didn't believe you were in love with him, he wouldn't have helped you. He wants what's best for you, but he won't push you. If you decide you want to get back with your ex-husband, he'll respect your decision. But if you want Moses, you are going to have to clean up this mess. Moses isn't going to chase you and he won't enter a fight he knows he won't win. So I'm going to ask you again, who are you in love with?"

After my meeting with Grams, my focus was off. All I could think about was Moses. I wanted to call him, but I couldn't. She was right. Before I move forward I have to take a couple of steps backwards.

> *Dearest Moses, I miss you. You have every right to be angry with me, but I hope you aren't. I don't know who was more upset with me, my mother, Bas or me. When you left, I stayed up all night crying and praying. I wanted to call you today, but I didn't know what to say. Thank you for the flowers and the bag. I've asked God to show me the best way to fix this mess. Please be patient. Alex*

Mama

HOW DO YOU PLAY CAT and mouse when the cat nor the mouse are in the same room? You taunt them with the possibility of their opponent entering the game. Mrs. Bartholomew, Emma, is very clever. She's everything Alex said. I wasn't too sure about her plan, but I'm willing to do whatever it takes to make my daughter happy.

I waited for Alex to leave before calling Moses and putting my part of the plan into action.

"Moses Adair." The strong deep voice on the other end of the phone responded.

"Moses, it's Constance Miller."

"Good morning Mrs. Miller." The tone instantly changed from stern businessman to warm friend.

"I'm here in the city doing a little buying for the store and thought I would take you to lunch."

"Now how can I resist having lunch with such a charming tourist?"

"Thank You."

"I'll have Otis pick you up."

"That won't be necessary. I'll meet you at Fred's at one."

"Perfect. See you then."

Fred's is one of Alexandra's favorite restaurants and I know Moses will think he's meeting her instead of me. I patiently waited for my lunch date, being careful not to miss him exiting the elevator.

The elevator dinged, signaling the arrival of my lunch date amongst all the chic men and women exiting the elevator. I stretched my neck looking for the man I hoped would become my son-in-law. When the last person exited and the doors closed, my heart filled with sadness when I didn't see Moses.

I sat back and heard the other elevator ding. The doors opened and there he was. Alex is right... he has a beautiful smile.

"Hello Mrs. Miller," he said as he kissed me on the cheek.

"Hello, son." Call those things to be.

"I'll see if our table is ready." I saw him searching the waiting area. He walked over to the hostess and shortly thereafter, he called out. "Mrs. Miller."

I joined him and we followed the hostess to our table. We placed our lunch orders. During our conversation his eyes kept searching the restaurant and staring at the entrance.

"Son, you seem a little distracted."

"No ma'am, I'm not." He shifted in his chair. "How are things at the store?"

"Business is well. Bas is really adjusting to his new position."

"He mentioned Alex had given him more responsibility." He took a sip from his coffee cup.

"He and Kendell are doing great, but you already knew that." I smirked. I know he's been checking on Alexandra. I overhead a phone call between he and Bas.

"Yes."

"He said you persuaded him to act on his feelings for her."

"I wouldn't say that." He smiled and I saw why my fool daughter fell for him. He's charming, humble and those eyes are mesmerizing.

"How's the play coming?" After all, that's the reason he cited for his quick departure a few weeks ago.

"It's been a little rough. Would you like to see a rehearsal before you leave?"

"I'd love to."

"How about tomorrow?"

"That would be great."

"Then it's a date. Will you be coming alone?"

I see my opponent is very clever. I quickly responded, "Yes."

"Oh." His smile faded. "Maybe afterwards we can get dinner?"

"That would be nice. So when are you coming for a visit?"

"Mrs. Miller—"

"Mom." I reminded him.

"Mom, I know what you're doing."

"I don't know what you're talking about."

"Did Alex put you up to this little fishing expedition?"

"I don't know what you're talking about. Alex doesn't know I'm here, but since you brought her up..."

"Mrs...mom, I don't want to talk about her."

I nodded. "Is that why you've been watching the entrance?"

"I don't know what you're talking about." He shifted in his seat.

"Uh-huh."

"If you think I'm looking for Alex, you're wrong."

"Uh-huh."

"Just because I sent her a gift..."

"A gift? I saw *the gift*. Where did you find that bag?" Referring to the vintage pink Chanel handbag that was delivered to Alex on Valentine's Day.

300

"I saw it while I was out one day and thought she'd like it."

"Uh-huh. That was a well researched gift. It's a combination of two of my daughter's favorite things, the color pink and Chanel. Only someone who knows her very well and cares about her would go to the trouble of selecting a gift like that."

"Mom--"

"You don't have to explain." I sipped my coffee and placed the cup back on the saucer. "While we're on the subject, Alex would have a fit if she knew I was meeting with you."

"Can't two friends have lunch?"

"But we're not just friends. I'm your girlfriend's mother." I reminded him.

"My girlfriend?"

"Yes and she's miserable."

"I'm sorry but that's not my fault." He wiped his mouth and shifted in his chair again.

"Are you in love with my daughter?"

"You went right for the jugular."

"Are you in love with my daughter?" I asked again. "Not do you love her, because Bas loves her, her girlfriends love her, her employees love her. And from what I understand that idiot head ex-husband claims to love her. I want to know if you, Moses Bernard Adair, are in love with her. And if you are, what do you plan to do about it?"

"I...uhm..."

"Here's a little advice, if you don't go after her and Terrence gets free, she'll marry him and it won't be because she loves him. She'll do it because you left her no choice."

"When I asked her if she wanted him back, she didn't answer me."

"Let me tell you something and if you tell Alex, I'll deny it. I knew she was going to Milan to surprise Jonathan." He looked surprised at my confession.

"She said no one knew."

"She's wrong. I knew. I know everything that goes on

with my daughter." I looked at him with a raised eyebrow. "I wanted to stop her, but I couldn't. Jonathan was selfish, jealous, a liar and he cheated on her. He wasn't in love with her. I think he only wanted to marry her, to prove to Terrence that he could. If they'd gotten married, it wouldn't have lasted."

"Mom--"

I looked him straight in the eye. "Are you in love with my daughter?"

"God help me, but I am and I don't know what to do."

"The first thing to do is admit you have a problem." I smiled.

"My name is Moses Adair and I'm in love with Alexandra Miller." He smiled.

I patted his hand. "Good. Now we need a plan. First things first, don't call her."

"But you just told me..."

"My daughter is stubborn and from what I've heard, so are you. If you want her back, you've got to make her come to you. She'll come. It's just a matter of how long you're willing to wait."

"I've been waiting over a month."

"No, you've been sulking, not waiting. She's not coming to you until she cuts Terrence loose. And truth be told, you aren't completely free of Natalie. I suggest you use this time to finish the healing process. The two of you need to start with a clean slate." I wiped my mouth. "And buy a ring, because when she comes back, you'll only get one shot and it had better be a knock out."

"Is that all?" He smiled.

"Yes."

"So I take it I have your blessing to marry your daughter?"

"Not that you need it, but yes."

"Thank you." He leaned over and hugged me.

"Please don't let it be this difficult getting grandchildren from the two of you."

"Yes ma'am," he laughed.

Dionne

"I HAVE SOMETHING TO SAY and I don't want you to say anything until I finish." That's how I prefaced my next statement...or confession. "I'm pregnant and I'm not sure I want to be." I looked at three of my best friends trying to read the looks on their faces. They looked like the three monkeys statue on my grandfather's desk...see no evil, hear no evil and speak no evil. I'm not sure who was more in shock, them or me. "Okay say something."

"We can speak now?" Chloe asked.

"Yes."

"What the crap!" She shouted. "I thought you said you and Quentin were waiting?"

"Chloe calm down," Alex jumped in.

"How did this happen?" Kendell asked.

"Really, Kendell?" Chloe fired back.

"I mean, I know how it happened. I mean, like Chloe said, I thought you guys were waiting? What happened?"

"Ladies, stop it. It's not like she's some teenager confessing a mistake. It's our married friend. We should be congratulating her. Instead we sound like we're trying to figure out how to fix a problem," Alex replied.

"Excuse me, but was I the only one that heard her say, she's not sure if she wants to be pregnant?" Chloe asked.

Alex turned and faced me. "Is that what you said?"

I nodded. "Yes."

"What the crap, Dionne?" Alex exclaimed. "I thought you wanted a baby? In fact, ever since I've know you, that's been at the top of your list. What changed?"

"Me."

"You?" Kendell asked.

"When Quentin and I had that huge blow up a few months back, I had time to think and I realized, we were nowhere near being ready for a baby. I'm doing good remembering to feed my dog."

"And you wanted to get me a dog," Chloe spit out.

"Chloe...," Alex jumped in.

"I'm just saying, a dog is a huge responsibility," Chloe replied.

"Are you finished?" Alex asked.

"Go on."

"Dee, Sweetie, what did Quentin say?" Alex asked.

"I haven't told him yet."

"Are you kidding me?" Chloe jumped up. "Why are we even discussing this? She's getting us all worked up and she hasn't even told Quentin."

"Chloe please calm down," Kendell begged. "You know what, why don't you go get us some coffee."

"Coffee...this calls for something dark and strong and it ain't coffee."

"Then sit down and let her explain," Alex continued. "Go on Dionne."

"Like I said, I'm pregnant and I'm not sure how to tell Quentin."

"When you two talked about children, how did you leave it?" Kendell asked.

"We agreed to wait until next year before trying again."

"So what happened, I mean apart from the obvious?" Alex asked.

"After our blow up, we did the thirty day sex challenge."

"Excuse me?" Chloe replied.

"You know, sex everyday no matter how you feel for thirty days."

"Whatever. Aren't you using protection?" Chloe asked.

I was embarrassed to answer her question. "Uhm...I...uhm..."

"Dee, it's a simple question," Kendell piped in.

"What happened is...I was...I mean I am, but...his mother interrupted one of our sessions and to stay on track, Quentin surprised me with a weekend getaway."

"I'm not following," Chloe replied.

"He packed my bag and forgot a few things."

"Excuse me?" Alex jumped in.

"He didn't think to grab my diaphram and by the time I remembered..."

Chloe started ranting again. "Dionne, you forget your toothbrush, your lingerie even, but never forget you birth control."

"Chloe, settle down," Alex yelled out. "Dionne honey, how far along are you?"

"Eight weeks. What are we going to do?" I asked with tears streaming down my face.

"This ain't a we situation girlfriend. It's all on you. What are *you* going to do about it?" Chloe shouted.

"Chloe, go make some coffee," Alex instructed. "Dionne you need to go home and tell your husband you're pregnant."

"But, Alex—"

"Stop crying. How are things between you and Quentin?"

I felt a smile coming. "Really good."

"So why haven't you told him you're pregnant?" Kendell

asked.

"I don't know."

"Dionne, I know better," Alex piped in.

"How could you not want children?" Kendell asked.

"When I didn't get pregnant right away, I just put the baby on the back burner. I like my life, annoying in-laws aside."

"Trust me, you may not have planned this, but it's a good thing. I think you'll be a wonderful mother." Alex tried to convince me.

"Can I come back in the room?" Chloe asked.

"Only if you behave," Kendell shouted back. Chloe walked back into the room with a glass of wine.

"What are you drinking?" Kendell asked.

"I found a bottle of Merlot."

"Chloe...," Alex chimed in.

"What...it's not like Dee can drink it." She took another long sip. "Dionne, listen to Alex. You'll be a great mother. But don't ask me to babysit until the kid can drive," Chloe joked.

Kendell cleared her throat. "Well, I've got something to say."

"Are you sure, Kendell?" Alex asked.

"Yes. I've been seeing someone," Kendell confessed.

"Good for you," Chloe cheered and sipped from her glass. "Who is it?"

"Bas," she announced.

"Bas? Bas?" I repeated the three letter name.

"Bas, Alex's Bas? Oh crap, no! Are you out of your mind? Alex did you know about this?" Chloe shouted at her.

"Yes, he asked if it was okay to break the pact, and I said yes."

"Why would you do that?" Chloe shouted.

"Because Dionne is married and knocked up by my ex, you're separated and dating the Brazilian and he's not rich enough for Taylor," she reminded her.

"Oh yeah," Chloe said, smiling from ear to ear. She took

another sip from her glass. "Kendell, we're all very happy for you. So, is he a good kisser?"

"Chloe!" Alex shouted.

"What? Have you seen his lips? My God." Chloe announced.

I shook my head. I couldn't believe her. Kendell looked at Alex before answering Chloe's question. "Go ahead."

"Oh my God. I told Alex, I should send all his ex-girlfriends thank you notes, because the boy's got skills."

"Really..." Chloe smiled.

"So what about the pact?" Dionne asked.

"I think we can all agree the pact is dead. I mean Dionne's married and knocked by my ex, Kendell is, oh my God, dating my assistant. I think it's safe to say the pact is dead," Alex clarified.

"I move we abolish the family pact. All in favor raise your right hand," Chloe raised her glass. All of our hands went up in the air. "Family pact is dead. So does this mean Kendell's baby brother is available?"

"No." Kendell quickly replied.

We all laughed.

Kendell

I TAPPED ON THE DOOR waiting for approval to enter. "Come in," called the voice on the other side of the door.

I opened the door, walked in, and saw a familiar face staring back at me. "Hey, Alex."

"Miss Kendell, what a surprise." She stood up and walked over and hugged me. "Have a seat. What brings you here?"

I sat in the antique French chair sitting in front of her desk. "Lunch with Bas. Got a minute?"

"Sure, I could use a break." She stretched her arms up and exhaled. "So what's on your mind?" She was smiling, but it seemed forced.

"I haven't seen you since last week and I wanted to thank you for backing me up."

"I told you I would. Do you want some coffee?"

"No, I'm fine."

"And from the look Bas has been wearing the past few months, I'd say fine is probably an understatement."

"He's a great guy. If you had told me six months ago, I'd be dating someone like him, I'd have called you a liar. And if you said I would be dating him, I would have booked you a room at the nearest padded room spa." We laughed. "He brought up marriage."

"Really? That's a first. I've never heard him mention marriage."

"I told him it was too soon to bring it up."

"Don't you want to know how he feels about it?"

"I'll tell you what I told him...I don't want to know. I want to concentrate on getting to know him. I want to take it slow. Talking about marriage, just makes things tense and I'm having fun getting to know him. Did you know he can cook?" I felt the corners of my mouth turning up into a smile.

"Yes, remember he stayed with me for a little while."

"That's right."

"I'm glad things are going great. Is that what you wanted to talk to me about?"

I took a deep breath and continued. "I wanted to compliment you on your performance the other night."

"What are you talking about?"

"Did you forget I know about Terrence?"

"Oh my God." Her mouth dropped open.

"I've kept my godson a secret for over twenty years."

"That's right. I forgot."

"I never said anything because you asked me not to. But after you told Dionne she needed to talk to Quentin, I felt that was a little hypocritical of you."

It was a bold move calling my cousin a hypocrite, but it was the truth. Her telling Dionne she needed to tell her husband about her pregnancy was no different than her not telling her ex-husband about their son.

"You're right."

"Did you ever tell his father?"

"No."

"Why not?"

"After Terrence died I didn't think he deserved to know."

"Why not?"

"Because he…"

"Left?" She nodded. "Honey, he was young and he did what he thought was right. I know you don't like what happened, but, he still deserves to know about his son." I saw the tears welling up in her eyes. "I think you didn't tell him, because you were too scared to admit it was over."

"Of course I knew it was over. You're not making any sense."

"Hear me out. You two were in love, and then they came in and took away your fairytale, and as long as you never told him about your son, part of you was still living that fairytale." She wiped the tear before it reached the corner of her mouth. "Did you try contacting him?"

"Funny you should ask. I bumped into him last year at the airport," she confessed.

"And?"

"He came to see me."

"And?"

"He apologized. Said he still loves me…that being with me was the happiest time of his life. He offered to leave his wife and children and give us another chance at being happy."

"Wow."

She nodded her head and I could tell by the look on her face, there was more to it. "After Christmas he sent my wedding ring back along with a letter asking me to take him back."

"What did you say?"

"I sent it back without an answer."

"How could you not answer him?"

"It wasn't until recently, that I figured out what I wanted."

"And what's that?"

"I want a husband and children, but not with Terrence. I may not like what happened to me, but I refuse to be the reason another woman has to raise her children alone. I could never be with a man that would be comfortable doing such a thing, either."

"Will a husband and children make you happy?"

"They'll add to my happiness."

"But what about his happiness? If he's not happy, doesn't he deserve the right to be happy, too? Don't his children deserve a father that's happy and fulfilled in his life?" I asked.

"Yes, but he can't expect anyone else to make him happy. That's his responsibility."

"Let me ask you something. If he didn't have children and his parents weren't in the picture, would that make a difference?"

"I asked myself that same thing."

"And?"

"No."

"So you don't love him?"

"I love the memory of being with him, but I don't love him. Whoa."

"Are you okay?"

She was smiling and it was different from the way she was smiling when this conversation started. "Yeah, I just realized why I couldn't answer Terrence's question."

"Why not?"

"It wouldn't make sense to you, but it's clear to me."

Alex

OUT OF THE MOUTH OF two or three witnesses....that's what the Bible says. Grams and Kendell both said the same thing. I need to air my dirty laundry so I can get my life back.

"Uncle Wallis, I need you to set up a meeting for me...call Terrence and his family, and have them meet me in your office this afternoon. Have Terrence meet me an hour before everyone else and I'll handle it from there...trust me, I know what I'm doing... thanks...love you."

I stood quietly praying and turned around when I heard the door open and close. I looked up and saw my ex-husband. Over twenty years ago I thought I was prepared to change my life and be the wife he thought he wanted. Now, looking into those sad brown eyes, I see a life that would have been filled with heartache, disappointment and very little love.

"Hi Terrence." He walked over and hugged me, and I didn't feel the warmth and excitement I thought I would...confirming there were no feelings left. In the past year since we bumped into each other, that's the first time we've had any physical contact. The last time he touched me was when he kissed me goodbye as I was leaving for work, the morning both our lives changed. I thought I'd feel something, but…nothing. We pulled apart.

"Hi Lexi."

When he smiled, his eyes didn't dance, they just seemed dead. "Lexi and Terry. I almost forgot that's what we called each other." I smiled at the memories dancing in my mind. "That was a long time ago when we were happy. We were happy, weren't we?"

"I thought so."

"Do you think we would have had a good marriage? I mean if Thomas and Lillian hadn't shown up and you had told me the truth about Jonathan?"

"Yes, I believe so."

"That's what I thought, but now I don't. I think we would have ended up divorced. Not because we didn't love each other, but because you would have felt pressured to please your family and I would have resented you."

"I disagree."

"No, hear me out. We were young and naïve living in the city for lovers and foolishly thought nothing could destroy our relationship, but it did. I believe eventually you would have regretted your decision and it would have caused us to break up."

"I don't agree. I believe we would have and still can make it work. I love you Lexi and I want to spend the rest of my life with you."

"That's easy to say now, because you have a little leverage. If you had to make the decision and not have it forced on you, I think you would have done the same thing, because your family is important to you. No matter how badly they've treated you, you wouldn't have been able to turn your back on them." I stared into those sad eyes looking for that young man I loved, but he wasn't there.

"Lexi, don't say that."

"Please, our bumping into each other happened for a

reason. Maybe it was so you could learn the truth. Or maybe it was so we could get closure and move on to the next thing God has for us. Or maybe it was so both of us could grow up. Or maybe you had been looking for a way out and I just happened to bump into you at the right time. I do know it wasn't so we could get back together."

"That's not—"

"Let me finish. When you saw me you said it reminded you of who you used to be, and you wanted that man back. That's not possible because he didn't come back to the states. He's still roaming the streets of Paris with that young woman he met at the Louvre and they're happy. You need to figure out what you want to do with the rest of your life. But first, you need to clean house and then admit to yourself that you're not in love with me."

"Lexi—"

"I know you love me, but you're not in love with me, and there's a difference. And that's okay, because I'm not in love with you, but I do love you." I took a deep breath and continued, "I need to tell you something. Did you know Lillian came to see my mother?"

"No, when?"

"About a month after I returned from Paris, I found out I was pregnant."

"You were pregnant?"

"Yes and my mother felt you should know. She thought if your family knew it would change things and they'd let us get married. But Lillian said, since the marriage was annulled, you and I weren't pregnant, I was pregnant. She said I was on my own."

"What!" For the first time, I saw life in his eyes.

"I had a baby boy," I confessed, fighting the tears.

"And she knew?"

"Yes."

"Where is he? Where's my son, I want to meet him."

I took a deep breath and answered. "Terrence Miller Pierce died three days after he was born." There, I said it.

"Oh my God!" He plopped down in the nearest chair.

"Are you okay?"

"Yeah." I poured him a glass of water and handed it to him.

As he drank his water, I continued my confession. "I wasn't sure you deserved to know, but recently I spoke to someone I admire, and she told me how she dealt with something similar. She said until she confronted the cause of her anger she knew she wouldn't be able to get on with her life. I felt betrayed and abandoned, and thought I still loved you. By keeping our son to myself, I was keeping us alive, that's why I couldn't marry Jonathan."

"I'm sorry."

"I buried our son and marriage over twenty years ago, and buried Jonathan ten years ago. But I didn't stop grieving until a month ago. Now that I'm in control, I have to apologize to you for not letting you know about our son."

"I forgive you, but only if you forgive me."

"Yes."

"Your family doesn't seem to understand we're done."

"What do you mean?"

"For the past year, your family has been using my friends as leverage in an attempt to make me disappear."

"I don't understand."

"Thomas and Lillian have been buying real estate from one of my friends. Thomas even said he needed a place in Paris overlooking the Seine for you and your wife. I know he meant me. Because that's where…"

"Our place overlooked the Seine."

"Gerard hired my cousin Kendell to cater his daughter's wedding."

"Gerard doesn't have a daughter."

"Well, he gave her two hundred and fifty thousand dollars. He and Thomas hired my cousin Taylor to be the sole broker for a new housing development in Atlanta. And your lovely wife donated a nice little sum of cash and equipment to my friend Dionne's family's clinic."

"I had no idea about any of this." I handed him an envelope. "What's this?

"Inside are copies of the restraining orders I filed this morning against Thomas, Lillian, Blair and Gerard. If either of them violates the restraining order, my uncle will have them arrested." I reached into my pocket and pulled out a small photo and handed it to him. "Here."

"Is this him?"

"Meet your son, Terrence Miller Pierce." I watched his expression as he stroked the photo.

"He had my smile." He looked up and his eyes were filled with tears. He wiped his eyes. "Lexi, I—"

"Shhh," I put my hand over his mouth. "Will you help me?"

He nodded and removed my hand. "They took my father, my child, my life, my wife...of course, I'm helping you. What do you want me to do?"

"All four of them will be here shortly, I told them it was time we settled things" Biting my bottom lip. "After today, I need you to leave me alone."

"But I thought we might--"

"What?"

"Now that you're back in my life I'm not letting you go even if it's only as friends."

"I need time before we can be friendly. After I help you get your life back, I have to work on getting my own back."

※ ✳ Ⓦ ⚘ ⚜

An hour later, I was standing in the conference room facing the four people hell bent on destroying me.

I cleared my throat. "Good afternoon, everyone. Thank

you for coming." I waited to see if anyone was going to say hello. "You're all probably as eager as I am to be done with this entire mess. I promise after today, you will not have me in your lives. Uncle."

Uncle Wallis handed each of them a manila folder with their name on it. I waited for them to open the folders and look inside. "You're probably wondering what you're looking at? All of the contents are different except for the last page." I waited for them to get to the last page.

"Gerard, can she do this?" Thomas asked.

"According to this restraining order, she can stand on her head in the middle of your office and you can't come within five hundred feet of her."

"This is insane. How much is it going to take to get rid of you this time?" Thomas asked.

"This isn't about money," I replied.

"Everything is about money. How much?" he asked again.

The door opened and Terrence walked in and stood next to me.

"What's he doing here?" Blair blurted out.

"I thought this was a board meeting," Terrence replied.

"Then why is she here?" Blair asked. "She's not on the board." Terrence and I looked at each other. "Terrence, did you do something stupid? Did you give her shares?"

"No, I didn't, but someone else did," Terrence replied looking directly at Thomas and Lillian.

"What is he talking about Thomas? Lillian?" Blair turned her head and looked at Gerard. "Someone better tell me what's going on. Why is this woman here?" Blair asked.

"Be quiet, Blair," Thomas demanded. "What do you want?"

"I demand to know what's going on," Blair shouted.

I looked around the table and all of them were silent.

"I'll help you Blair." Terrence cleared his throat. "Seems there was a little discrepancy with the distribution of my father and uncle's wills."

"I don't understand?"

He looked at Thomas and Lillian. "Do you really want me to tell her?" They turned their heads. "Okay." He walked over to the large white board at the end of the conference room. He took the black marker and started to draw a diagram of the company shares and distribution.

"What is all of this? Why is her name up there next to yours?" Blair asked.

"It's quite simple, isn't it Thomas?"

"I demand to know what's going on," Blair yelled out.

"Thomas and Lillian, are not my parents. My mother was married to one brother, but was in love with another. In plain English, my mother had an affair with Thomas' father."

"What?" Blair shouted.

"My mother thought Thomas' father was my father. After I was born, I was hospitalized with pneumonia. While I was in the hospital, my mother had a paternity test done and only shared the results with her doctor. Shortly before she died, she gave her maid a stack of letters from Royce along with one last letter from her to him. That letter told the truth about me. The maid held on to the letters. Before she died, she sent the letters to Royce."

"This is a lovely fairytale, but…" Lillian jumped in.

"Royce's attorney verified everything my mother told him."

"So Thomas isn't your father?" Blair asked.

"No."

"But what does this have to do with her?" She pointed to me. "And why is her name up there next yours?"

"Royce suspected Thomas and Gerard had done something shady, but didn't have any proof."

"Wait a minute. Vernon, never knew you weren't his child?" Blair asked.

"That's correct."

"But Thomas did?"

"Yes."

"Oh my God…oh my God…I can't…they told me…," She covered my mouth.

"My uncle and Thomas had a huge fight and he left his half of Pierce Holdings to me along with half of his personal estate."

"Thomas gave me five percent of Pierce Holdings when we were married. He said, combined, we'd…"

"That was a lie and those shares belong to me."

"But my father said in exchange for me marrying you…"

"I'm sorry, but you don't have any Pierce Holdings shares."

"What about her?" she pointed to me.

"Royce suspected the other will was fake and decided to correct things on my behalf."

"Oh my God…"

I thought Blair was going to faint. The only thing this meeting was missing was popcorn and a bottle of my uncle's sparkling wine. I sat down and looked at the distraught faces looking at me.

"Royce left his shares to me and Lexi."

"That means…she owns more of this company than I do?" Blair asked.

"Not quite." I smiled. "She owns a piece of this company, but you don't."

"What about the deal…my father's radio stations? Thomas got those in exchange for my marrying you."

"I haven't been able to find any paperwork about a deal like the one you're talking about."

She looked at Thomas. "You bastard! You'll pay for this."

"What do you want?" Thomas looked at me.

Terrence walked over and sat down next to me. "I'm not quite sure."

"That's a lie. You wouldn't have put on this little performance, if you didn't want something."

"I'd like to know why you stole my birthright. Why you ended my marriage and made me marry Blair? Why you lied to me?" He looked at Lillian. "Why you kept my son from me?"

"What?" Blair jumped up. "She has your son? That's a lie. How?"

"Shut up Blair!" Thomas bellowed.

Terrence looked at him. "You knew?"

Thomas didn't blink. He sat stone faced. "Yes, I knew. What…do…you…want?"

"Why did you do it?"

Thomas stood up. "Are you done?"

"Effective immediately, you are retired from Pierce Holdings."

Thomas walked toward the door, grabbed the knob and looked at me. "I don't know what he sees in you!"

"And you never will." I felt a chill run through my body.

He opened the door and left taking his little minions with him.

Dearest Moses, I severed those old ties. I told Terrence all about our son and he forgave me. I wish you were here so we could celebrate. I really miss you, Alex.

I SAT IN MY CAR for twenty minutes trying to talk myself out of going inside. I took a deep breath, got out of the car and walked inside. There was no one sitting at the desk. So I tapped on the cream colored wood paneled door. "Hi, Pastor Ray."

The handsome, grey haired gentleman turned around and the look on his face spoke volumes. "Chloe, this is a surprise. What brings you here?"

"I really need someone to talk to."

"Come in. Have a seat. Can I get you a cup of coffee?"

"No, I'm fine." I sat down, crossed my legs and tried to get comfortable.

"So, what's on your mind?" He sat down behind his desk.

I thought about his comment before responding. "Everything we discuss is confidential, right?"

I was raised to keep your personal life to yourself. After my little wild spurt, it was drilled into my head that staying out of the papers was a surefire way to keep the upper hand in business. Orlando being arrested for a DUI wasn't that bad compared to his being the latest You Tube darling. So the last thing I need is to have the details of this meeting spread across the blogosphere.

"Of course."

"A friend confided she's pregnant. Although I'm excited for her, I also feel..."

"Jealous?"

"I wouldn't say that."

"Then what is it?"

"Fear possibly?"

"Fear?"

"Pastor, my life has been a little like a reality television show. My husband left me for a much younger woman and surprised me with separation papers. As if that wasn't humiliating enough, he was arrested for a DUI and a club fight which can be seen on You Tube. In an attempt to make myself feel better, I started seeing someone."

"Really."

"Don't look at me like that. I didn't break my vows, but I thought about it. "

"Chloe..."

"I'm pregnant," I blurted out. That was the first time I'd said it out loud since my doctor gave me the news.

"Is it..."

"I said, I didn't break my vows." I took a deep breath followed by a long sigh. "No, my husband...he was a lot drunk and high as a kite and I was a lot frisky and...it just happened...five times."

"Five times?"

"You know if I wanted to be judged I could have paid someone or gone to one of my girlfriends."

"I'm not judging you. I'm just asking did it *just happen*?"

"You think I planned this?" I jumped up and walked around the back of the comfortable chair staring off to the side. "The first time, I thought he owed me."

"And the other times?"

"I was frisky and wanted to have sex."

"So you let your lust take over?"

There's that tone again. "I thought I still loved him."

"And you don't?"

"No...I...the feeling passed." I contemplated my response and felt tears gathering in my eyes. I blinked and a tear escaped my eye proving me a liar. "And don't take the tears as some sort of sign."

"Did I say that?" He walked over and handed me a tissue.

"No, but I recognize that look."

"What look?"

"That questioning look. The one that says I'm fooling myself about how I feel about my husband. I've been seeing it every morning since my doctor told me I'm pregnant."

"And how do you feel?"

His calm attitude was getting on my nerves. "Unsure, confused, scared..."

"Sure it's not the pregnancy or..." He looked at me waiting on a reply. "Love."

"I thought it might be, but when I look at him, I don't see the man I married. I see a selfish, son of a---"

"Chloe."

"I'm sorry." I wiped my forehead and adjusted my belt. "It's just, he makes me so angry. How could he do this to me? I've been faithful and it's not like I didn't have the opportunity to cheat. I spent the holidays in Brazil with the most amazing man who..." I looked up and caught myself. "I'm sorry."

"I understand you're hurt, but you cannot stoop to his level. If you two aren't willing to work on your marriage, then..."

"I should leave?"

"I didn't say that. My suggestion would be to pray and ask God what you should do."

"It feels like He hasn't been listening."

"Maybe it's you that hasn't been listening."

I patted my belly. "I guess listening could be helpful."

Dionne

WE'RE HAVING A BABY. NO matter how you say it, it still doesn't sound right. I'm not ready for a child. I don't like my mother-in-law. I'm not sure my marriage can survive a baby. What if Quentin isn't ready for a child? I don't know anything about raising a child. How do you change diapers? Breast or bottle milk? What is formula? Disposable or cloth diapers? Is organic baby food really the best? What's the best pre-school? I can't find a good housekeeper, how in the world am I going to find a nanny? And buying a stroller is more taxing than buying a car.

Oh my God, how do I tell Quentin? "Hi honey. You knocked me up." Or maybe we'll go with, "We won't need your mother's baby making juice." Or "One of your little soldiers infiltrated my camp and now they've got a hostage." Then there's the demure 1950's way, "I'm with child" or "I'm expecting."

Or I can blame it on the wine and that surprise date he planned. "Remember that impulsive romantic getaway at the W Hotel and you said we didn't need to buy the little protection kit in the mini bar? Well, maybe we should have because we brought home a little something extra and it wasn't towels." And then there's the classic. It's short, sweet, quite effective and full of information. "Quentin, I'm pregnant."

"You're what!" He dropped his brief case.

I turned and faced him. I wanted to speak but my mouth wouldn't move.

"What did you say?"

"I'm with child, I'm expecting, you knocked me up, we should have used protection. No matter which one you choose the answer is the same. I'm pregnant."

"How did this happen? I mean, I thought we agreed to wait until late next year to add to our family?"

"Remember when we escaped to get away from your mother and you suggested we try that bottle of wine, then the champagne and you said we'd be fine without any protection?"

"Yeah, because you have a diaphram."

"Remember you packed my bag and forgot to pack my diaphram and you said we'd be okay, it was just one time and you'd get the little protection kit later. But one time turned into an all night love fest."

"But we got the protection kit. I know we did, because I remember questioning the charge on the bill."

"That was after the wine and the champagne. Remember the following morning, you went looking for aspirin?"

"Vaguely."

"Do you remember the mimosas?"

A smile covered his face. "Yeah. We had mimosas in the bath and I told you that was something we needed to add to our repertoire." He stood silent for a few moments and the smile slowly disappeared. "Oh my God, but it was just one night."

"And a day."

"So you're telling me...at some point during...uhm..." He turned around and faced the hall. When he turned back around, his brow was furrowed. "We're having a baby."

I nodded. "Yeah."

The corner of his mouth slowly turned up. "We're having a baby." He started jumping up and down. "Thank you, God!"

Not quite the reaction I was expecting, but I'll take it. "I take it you're happy?"

"Are you kidding?" He picked me up and started turning in circles.

"Baby, please put me down."

"Oh, I'm sorry. Do you want to sit down? Want some milk...ice cream...pickles? How about a car?"

"A car?" I laughed.

"It was the first thing that popped into my head."

"No, I'm fine but I reserve the right to revisit that car thing."

"Wow, okay, tell me everything. What did the doctor say? When? Is it a boy or a girl?"

"Okay, hold on. I'm due in February. The doctor says I'm doing fine. It's too soon to know what it is."

"Come on, let's sit down. This is great, if it's a boy let's go with Carson and if it's a girl, Shelby."

"Aren't you getting a little ahead of yourself? What about your mother?"

"Wouldn't it be great if it's twins."

"Twins?" He went from elated to insane.

"Yeah, they run in both our families."

"What about your mother?" I asked again.

"What about her?"

"How's she going to take it knowing we didn't need her help?"

"She'll get over it."

"Quentin..." I was shocked.

"We'll invite everyone for dinner Sunday, and tell them then."

He paced backed and forth. "Man, I can't wait to see the look on my mother's face. We're having a baby." He kissed my stomach.

Chloe

I DIDN'T WANT TO MEET with Orlando anywhere I might be recognized. Instead I booked a suite at a hotel by the airport.

Knock, knock. My heart jumped into my throat. I opened the door to the longest first date in history asking myself, "What was I thinking?"

"Orlando."

"Chloe."

"Come in." He crossed the threshold and headed straight to the sofa. "How have you been?" I walked over and sat down on the opposite end of the sofa.

"Why are we here? I know it's not because you wanted a romantic weekend."

This smug son of a...he can't even pretend to be civil. "Why did you marry me?"

He hesitated before answering. "I loved you."

"And now?" I was hoping to find a piece of the man that swept me off my feet.

"Is this why you asked me here?"

"I've been thinking about us a lot since you filed for separation. Asking myself that question over and over."

"What did you come up with?" He asked smugly.

"Nothing, because I've been obsessed waiting for the other shoe to drop."

"Meaning?"

"Divorce."

"Divorce?"

"Let's face it, neither of us has been happy for quite some time. Although I don't like how you did it, I agree with the separation. It was the best thing to do." I got up and walked over to the window. "When we got married it was romantic, impulsive and exciting. We brought out the best in each other. I loved your spontaneity and zest for life."

"And I loved your energy and passion."

That's the first compliment he's given me in two years. "But, things changed and I don't like who I am now."

"What do you mean?"

"I'm suspicious, negative, snide, impatient and not as compassionate as I know I can be. All because of you."

"Sorry."

I turned and faced him. "See, that's what I mean. I heard you say it, but I know you didn't mean it. The man I married would have been a little more compassionate. He wouldn't have treated my feelings so carelessly and he wouldn't have disrespected our marriage the way you have. What happened to us?"

"I don't know." He stood up and walked over to the window. "Everything was fine and then one morning I woke up and nothing in my life seemed to make sense. The thing with Tasha just happened. It's not like I left home one day with the intention of finding someone to have an affair with."

"I don't believe you."

"Are you calling me a liar?"

I met his gaze head on. His intimidation stare never was one of his strongest weapons. I looked into those eyes the color of dark chocolate, searching for a hint of the man I married on a whim and he wasn't there. He had been replaced with a selfish, cocky, idiot with a heart of stone.

"I guess I am. Our marriage may not have been great, but after a few years I can read you and you're trying to be polite."

He took a deep breath. "I'm tired of coming in a distant fifth to your career, your friends, your family. Oh yeah, and God. Some men may like being low man on the totem pole, but I don't. Ironically, I met Tasha at Barneys' while shopping for you. She helped me, we flirted a little and the next thing I knew I was asking for her number."

"Hearing this convinces me I made the right decision."

"What are you talking about?"

"I'm tired and I don't feel like waiting on you to wear me down hoping to gain a lot from a messy divorce."

"But I—"

"Orlando please, I know you." A loud knock on the door interrupted my speech. "Come in," I called out.

"Chloe," called a man's voice.

"We're in here." The tall fit man entered the room. "Orlando, you remember my attorney, Walter Douglas?" They shook hands. "Do you have everything?" Walter nodded and sat down at the table.

"What's he talking about?" Orlando asked.

"I took the liberty of having divorce papers written up, all you have to do is sign them and we'll go our separate ways."

"Shouldn't I have a lawyer?" Orlando asked.

"It's less messy this way. Besides it's fair." Walter continued laying the papers out on the table.

"What about a settlement agreement? What about the house?" Orlando asked.

"I wasn't going to bring it up, but since you insist," I replied.

"Yes, I insist."

Walter handed Orlando a two page document. He read

the papers shaking his head. "Is this a joke? There has to be a mistake."

"No, it's correct." Walter confirmed.

"How is it possible I owe her alimony? She makes more and is worth millions."

"Correction, Chloe's mother is worth millions. Not Chloe."

"Excuse me?" He sounded shocked as he walked around the room re-reading the papers.

"Everything belongs to her mother. Chloe is merely an employee who draws a salary of one hundred dollars a month. The house and its contents, belong to her mother. Your car belongs to Mr. Jacobs' company. The credit cards are from Mr. Jacobs' personal account. And the cash you're referring to is a trust, not to be touched until her fiftieth birthday."

"You've got to be kiddin'? Who has a trust fund they can't access until they turn fifty?" he shouted.

"Me. My parents have always been supportive, but when I started college, I wasn't the most responsible person. Couple that with quite a few bad relationships, a botched engagement, a stint in jail for some traffic tickets and a wild period in Mexico. My father came up with this as a way to keep me from losing my inheritance and I agreed. I asked for money to start my own company and he refused. He said it was work for my mother or nothing. Nothing wasn't appealing, so I took him up on his offer in exchange for him covering all of my expenses."

"Don't feel bad Orlando, anyone marrying Chloe would have encountered the same fate," Walter stated.

"What if I contest?" Orlando asked.

"Then the two of you will battle it out in court."

"I guess I'll see you in court." He said throwing the papers down on the table.

"Going to court means quite a bit of digging and prying. Are you sure you want to do that?" Walter asked.

"I got nothing to hide."

"I hope Tasha sees it that way," Walter remarked.

"Excuse me? This doesn't concern her," Orlando quickly replied.

"Yes, it does. She's the reason for the divorce, therefore she'll have to testify to the details of your relationship. If you insist on taking this to trial, our defense will be mental anguish as a result of infidelity, and prolonged alcohol and drug use. I don't think any judge will respond favorably to a cheating, junkie husband seeking alimony."

"I'm okay with that," he announced.

"Alright, since you filed separation papers you are saying the marriage is over. When you were married you were given certain rights or privileges," Walter declared.

"What are you talking about?"

"You were given a place to live, credit cards, office space, a small stipend, use of the corporate jet and the beach house. All of which effective immediately are no longer at your disposal. I'll need your keys to both houses and your office and your credit cards."

"Chloe this isn't fair," he begged.

"Oh, and the car." When Walter uttered those words, all the color drained from Orlando's face. He loves that car more than he loves me or any other woman. He would rather give up his girlfriend than his car.

"What about my car?"

"Your car belongs to Mr. Jacobs' company, remember? If you wish to keep the car, you will need to contact Mr. Jacobs' attorney about buying it."

"You've got to be kidding me! Chloe--"

"Mr. Kingston—"

"Mr. Kingston, what happened to Orlando?"

"That was before this became a formal legal matter. And I'll have to ask you to address any questions you have to me, and not to Mrs. Kingston."

"Mrs. Kingston. Six and a half years of marriage and she's never been called Mrs. Kingston. I file for separation and now she's Mrs. Kingston."

"Mr. Kingston, I must advise you that you are entitled to counsel during this discussion."

"You have got to be kiddin' me with all of this, Chloe?"

"I'm very serious. You left me. I'm a good woman and yet you chose to be with trash. Let the little girl you left me for put a roof over your head and a car under your trifling, sorry, pathetic behind."

"Chloe, can't we work this out?" he pleaded.

"No. It's over," I walked over to the table and signed the papers. "I've had all of your things packed and they're in the bedroom. Walter will arrange for you to stay here for a month, if you sign the papers. If you don't, you and your things will be removed from the hotel immediately. The decision is all yours as it has been since you filed for separation." I picked up my bag and headed towards the door. "The house has been leased. Don't bother trying to contact me, I'll be out of the country."

"Mr. Kingston, in the interest of all parties involved, it would be best if you just signed the papers," Walter urged.

"Chloe, please. I'll leave Tasha and come back home," he pleaded.

"Home? That's a joke. You should be happy, now you won't have to be, what did you say, oh yeah, a distant fifth in my life anymore."

"Chloe—" he tried to give me a threatening look but I didn't budge. "Fine." He walked over and dropped his keys and credit cards on the table. "Give me a pen. You amaze me Chloe. I didn't think you had it in you."

"Orlando, this is what it means to have a plan. Goodbye."

"It's done, you're a free woman. Where do you want me to send your copy of the papers?" Walter asked.

"Thanks Walter. You can send them to my parents' house."

"It bears repeating, I don't agree with you not telling Orlando about the baby."

"Walter, you're my lawyer not my conscience."

"How do you plan on explaining your situation?"

"A.I."

"A.I.?"

"Artificial Insemination."

"Are you serious?" He chuckled. "Why don't you just say you adopted the baby? It would be a little more believable."

"I'll think about it."

"When are you due?"

"February twenty-fifth."

"When do you want things put back?"

"I think I'm going to leave it like it is for a while. But I need you to change my will. Add the baby, remove Orlando and add Alex as the guardian."

"Anything else?"

"No that'll be all."

"Chloe, speaking as a father and your friend, despite how you feel about Orlando, I feel strongly he needs to know about the baby."

"Walter—"

"Hear me out. Say, twenty years down the road, your child unknowingly starts dating his or her sibling, what are you going to do?"

I laughed at his extreme attempt to get me to change my mind. "A little farfetched but I see your point. However, I don't want Orlando anywhere near me or my child."

"You may not want him around, but he should be allowed to decide if and how involved he wants to be in his child's life."

"What if he does want to be involved?" I countered.

"Then you'll have the law on your side. Don't let this become a side show because you're angry."

"I'll take all of what you're saying under advisement. But you have to understand my side. I may not have known the man I married, but I know the man I was married to. The only reason he'd want our child is because it might be the golden ticket to financial independence. If his past motives and feelings had been pure, I'd have no problem telling him, but all he wants is money. Besides there's no law that says I have to tell my ex-husband I'm pregnant. Plenty of women have kept post divorce pregnancies a secret."

"Now you're like other women?"

"No, I'm just saying I have an option and I'm exercising it. At some point, I'll tell Orlando, but not right now."

"But—"

"Walter, I've made up my mind. As my attorney and friend, I'm asking you to respect my decision."

"Fine."

"Thank you."

"HEY ALEX." **THE FAMILIAR VOICE** sounded a little strange.

"Hey Chloe girl, what's up?"

"Can we reschedule dinner?"

"Sure, what's up? Got a hot secret date?"

"No. I'm just not feeling very socialable."

"What's going on?"

"Nothing really, I just..."

"Let me guess, Orlando? What did he do now? Do I need to come over for a strategy session on how to hide his body?" She didn't laugh. A sure sign something was wrong.

"Funny, Alex."

She said the words, but her tone said otherwise. "What's going on?" I repeated my question.

"He signed the the papers."

"What papers?"

"The divorce papers."

"When did he serve you with divorce papers?"

"He didn't. I did."

"Back up...explain, because the last time we talked about this, you wanted him to suffer." I was confused. Chloe is very meticulous when it comes to strategizing and researching her opponents and this move seemed out of character for her. "What happened to make you change your mind?"

"I realized no matter how much he complained, he liked the benefits of being married to me, but he didn't want to be married to me."

"Chloe..."

"It's true. I know my ex-husband is an idiot head, but I don't have to be one too. Trust me, this is for the best. I'm already on the mend. Besides, if I hadn't done anything, it would have dragged on for months, years even."

"How's Orlando taking it?" I know it's not standard girlfriend protocol to ask about a friend's ex, but...

"He wasn't happy about the settlement but he has no one to blame but himself."

"And you?"

"I got over being angry days ago." She let out a loud sigh. "Where did we go wrong?"

The sound of her voice reminded me of a sad teenager who just found out the dress she saved all year for is also being worn by half the senior class to the prom. "It's not that we did anything wrong. I think we just failed to make good long term decisions."

"I disagree. You had a good man. It wasn't your fault he died."

I never disclosed Jonathan's truth to my girlfriends. If they really knew the truth, I think they'd dig him up and burn his bones.

"I know."

"What did you say?" She sounded shocked.

"I know it's not my fault Jonathan died."

"What have you done with my friend, the grieving almost widow?" She joked.

"She decided it was time to start living again and stop kicking herself for something she had no control over. I finally realized, even if I had married Jonathan, that doesn't mean what happened wouldn't have happened."

"That's what we've been telling you for years. If you weren't ready to receive it, you weren't ready. Sometimes what we want for our friends, isn't what God wants. If I hadn't been so impulsive and insistent I knew better than God how to ease the hurt and embarrassment Xavier caused, I wouldn't have run off and married Orlando and gained membership in the Starter Marriage Club."

"The Starter Marriage Club...Chloe where did you hear that?" I laughed.

"On television. Apparently it's a big club for women divorced after less than ten years of marriage. It could be worse, I could be in the Two Under Fifty Club."

Now she was starting to sound like her old upbeat self. "I give up what is the Two Under Fifty Club?"

"Two divorces before turning fifty."

"Do you regret it?"

"My marriage?"

"Yes. Even though it wasn't what you thought it would be. Do you regret having been married or has it sullied you on marriage?"

"No, I don't regret it. I'm a little upset I didn't pick up that phone call from God. If I had, I wouldn't have wasted six and a half years of my life. But I trust God will restore the time."

"And now?"

"Now I'm going to take the wisdom and good judgment I use in business and apply it to my love life. I know there's someone out there for me, but I've got to work on me. I don't feel I'm marriage material right now. There are a few things I want to work on before getting involved in another relationship. I need to get to know Chloe."

She sounded like someone else I know. "Does that mean Marcelo is out of the picture as well?"

"I'm not sure. He's a nice companion with very strong lips." She laughed. "But I'm..."

"Free to see him." I teased.

"I like Marcelo, but I'm not looking for anything serious. At least not right now. True, I miss having a man in my bed and in someplace else." She giggled. "But, I need to know what caused me to abandoned my core belief system and marry someone so obviously wrong for me."

"So it's au revoir to the handsome Brazilian."

"I didn't say that." She laughed. "Marcelo and I are working on a deal together, which means a few trips to Brazil and a lot of hot, hard kisses from those full sexy lips. My, my, my..."

Her tone changed and she started to sound like my wild friend. "Settle down, girl."

"I was just remembering the last time he kissed me. Uhm, what was I saying?"

"A few trips to Brazil and lots of kisses."

"Oh yeah. He wants me to come for the ground breaking."

"When?"

"Next month."

"For how long?"

"I'm not sure. He's suggested I stay until the project is complete."

"Wow. Be careful and don't come home with another husband."

"I should come through this phone and choke you." That's the girl that helped me lose those last five pounds before the Spring Formal.

"What?"

"Don't come home with another husband...not funny."

Mama

"I'M HOME." HER ANNOUNCEMENT REMINDED me of when she was a teeneager coming home from school. She'd burst into the kitchen excited to tell me about her day.

I know it's kind of odd living with my grown daughter, but she wouldn't have it any other way. I've tried to move out on numerous occasions, but she won't let me. However, I believe the time is coming when this little arrangement will become part of our history. I'm waiting to hear those three little words, "I'm getting married." In the meantime, I savor this time I have with her.

"Hi Kiddo."

"What's that I see on the stove?"

"A few of your favorites, fried chicken, macaroni and cheese, green beans and hot water cornbread."

She walked over and picked up a small piece of cornbread, sliced it open and put a chunk of butter inside. Then she bit the bread and licked the melted butter running down her arm followed by another bite. "Hmmm..."

"Ever since you were a little girl that's been your favorite way to eat cornbread."

"This is so good."

"I'm glad you like it."

"Oh yeah. This hit the spot. There's nothing like your mother's cooking to make you feel better."

"How was your day?"

"Fine. A little busy. We're getting things ready for the charity fashion show next month. I could eat a plate of this bread all day. It is so good."

"Well, I'm glad you're enjoying it."

"Oh yeah."

"So do you want to tell me what happened today?" I can read that girl like one of Moses' books.

"What do you mean?"

She looked tense and stressed. "Put the bread down and tell me what happened."

"Chloe divorced Orlando."

"What? How's she doing?"

"She says she's fine, but I can tell from the sound of her voice she's not."

"I thought she wanted a divorce?"

"She did. She said this makes her a member of the Starter Marriage Club."

"And you wanted to tell her you were one too."

"Yeah, but I knew I couldn't." She wiped her hands on the towel sitting on the counter. "Mama, it's so hard keeping this secret. Every time one of my girlfriends talks about their marriage or in-laws, I want to say, 'hey, I understand. I can tell you horror stories about marriage and in-laws'."

"Do you regret not telling them?"

"Part of me does, but I think if I had told them, they wouldn't have understood."

"That's what you think?"

"Yes, I think I would have lost their respect."

"Interesting. I always thought you didn't really care what people thought about you."

"I don't. We agreed it was the best thing to do."

"No, I told you I would support you no matter what you decided to do." I love my daughter and trust her judgment. However, I never liked that she didn't tell her best friends about her marriage or son.

"Are you saying I should have told them?"

"I'm saying maybe, after some time and you finished grieving, yes, you should have."

"So because I chose not to say anything, I'm doomed to a life of constantly looking over my shoulder waiting for the other shoe to drop?"

"That's not what I'm saying."

"Then what?"

I know she thinks she did the right thing, but her decision to keep both Terrences a secret was made out of anger. The reality is, she's been mourning a life that was never going to happen no matter how much she wanted it to.

"It's time for you to stop grieving and start living." I gently stroked the side of her face. "Honey it breaks my heart to see you moping around here like your dog died. How's Moses?"

"Fine, I guess."

"What does that mean?"

"We kind of had a fight." She walked over to the refrigerator and pulled out a bottle of water.

"When was the last time you spoke to him?"

"January, when he came for New Year's." She sipped her water.

"What is going on with you?" I shouted.

She jumped up. "He said to call once I settled things with Terrence."

"You did that almost two months ago." My voice was escalating. This child is working that last tolerable nerve I have for her love life. I'm trying to be on her side, but she's making it difficult. I don't know whether to hug her or knock her upside the head. "Are you in love with Moses?"

"Why does everyone keep asking me that question?"

"Are you?"

"Yes, but…"

"But, what? And don't tell me you're scared, because I know better." I felt like jumping across the counter and wringing her neck.

"Not until recently did I figure out what I wanted from marriage. I love him, but how do I know he's the one or…"

"Did he propose?" This is news to me. Emma and I have been in constant contact and prayer over these two and she never mentioned a proposal.

"No, but I know that's…"

"Honey, I think you're jumping to conclusions." The only way for me to get a straight answer out of her was to calm down. "What did he say?"

"He said to call him once things were settled with Terrence and he'd be on the first available flight."

"You don't make any sense. I take that back, you've found comfort in feeling sorry for yourself and I won't have any part of it. If you want to be alone, fine. If you want to be married, fine."

"That's not true. I don't feel sorry for myself. It's…you more than anyone, knows how hard marriage is. From what I've seen it can be very one sided. I don't want to look up one day and realize I'm doing all the giving and sacrificing and my husband is sitting back taking and dictating. I saw what happened to you and Daddy and I don't want that. I know I want to be married, I just don't know if I'm ready to be married."

"I'm sorry."

"For what?"

"For making you doubt your relationship. Marriage to the right person is wonderful. Don't use your father and me as a measuring stick. We were an example of marriage done the wrong way. We knew early on that we shouldn't have been married but we were too scared to admit it. If we had called it quits earlier we might have stood a chance at friendship."

"I thought—"

"We loved each other but it wasn't enough to maintain a marriage. You and Moses are in love each other and have something your father and I never had..."

"Passion."

"I couldn't quite put my finger on it, but that's what it is. It's the same thing I see when I'm around Wallis and Myrtle. That's something your father and I never had." I reached over and wiped the tear rolling down her face. "No matter how much Moses misses you, he's not going to force himself on you. And he's not going to beg you to take him back. Call him."

"Mommy, I can't...I don't know what to say."

"Tell him the truth, that you love him and miss him."

She sniffled. "And my son?"

"I think it's time you told his story." I kissed her on the forehead and went upstairs.

Alex

THERE ARE THINGS MY FRIENDS don't know about me and there are things I don't know about them. I think we all need to come clean or a little cleaner than we have been with each other.

I took a deep breath and looked at each of my friends. I had rehearsed my speech, but now that it was time to give it, I wasn't sure I could. I cleared my throat and stood up.

"Uhm...how do I say this. There's...I have, uhm..."

"Alex, are you sure you want to do this?" Kendell asked.

"Yes." I closed my eyes and blurted out, "I was married."

"I knew it. I knew you and Jonathan were married," Dionne shouted.

"It wasn't Jonathan, but he knew."

"Excuse me?" Chloe chimed in.

"I was married and I had a baby."

"Oh crap no!" Chloe jumped up. "Kendell did you know about this? What am I saying, of course you did."

"And you never said anything?" Dionne questioned.

"When? Because we've known you since your freshman year," Chloe's follow up question.

"When I was in Paris."

"To who? And where's the baby?" Chloe fired back and started pacing back and forth talking to herself. "Oh my God, she said you used to date her husband's best friend and she kept talking about you...but he wasn't there when you started dating Jonathan...and his father asked for an apartment overlooking the Seine and that's where your place was. I remember those pictures and the view overlooked...that's right...and when I asked about those men's clothes, you said..."

"What Chloe?" Dionne looked at her.

Chloe looked at me. "It was Terrence Pierce."

"The time I spent in Paris was amazing. I learned a lot, saw a lot and did a lot."

"No kidding," Chloe blurted out.

"We met at the Louvre. We were both trying to see the Mona Lisa, but there were too many people. Instead we found ourselves seated in front of this painting called the 'Wedding Feast' how ironic. He surprised me when he said he recognized me from school. We spent all our free time together and we were married three and a half weeks."

"What?" Dionne looked at me with her mouth wide open.

"When his parents found out, they flew to Paris and took him away while I was at work. When I got home, instead of my husband it was the family lawyer, informing me my marriage was over. I came home and when I found out I was pregnant, I tried to get him back, but his parents blocked all of my efforts."

"And the baby?" Chloe asked.

"Terrence Miller Pierce died, and his father never knew." Saying his name still conjured memories of him in my arms quietly dying. Only two people know the details of his passing. My mother who held me as I rocked him until his little spirit was gone and the man I love.

"That's the picture on your desk," Dionne surmised.

"Jonathan knew?" Chloe asked shaking her head.

"Yes."

"Does Taylor know?" Dionne asked in a soft voice.

"I called her before you guys got here."

"So why are you telling us now?" Chloe asked.

"I bumped into Terrence at the airport in Atlanta after the opening."

"That was over a year ago and you're just now saying something," Dionne remarked.

"I've been trying to--"

"Is that why you asked me about Pierce Holdings," Chloe interrupted.

"It's very complicated, but his family thought I wanted him back."

"You could do worse," Chloe declared.

"I don't want him. Besides that, he's married. We've met and decided it's best to be distant friends."

"Why didn't you tell us when it happened?" Dionne walked over and rubbed my back.

"I was embarrassed."

"Honey, we love you. Did it ever occur to you that maybe we could have helped you?" Chloe smiled.

"No. I thought--"

"No Sweetie, this just makes you a member of the club," Chloe joked.

"What club?" Kendell asked.

"The Starter Marriage Club." Chloe laughed.

"Does anyone else have anything to say?"

Chloe cleared her throat. "Orlando and I are divorced."

"What! When?" Kendell finally had something to be shocked about.

"Last week." She took a deep breath and continued. "I'm pregnant."

"What!" I almost passed out at Chloe's announcement.

"I'm pregnant," she announced again.

"Oh my God!" Dionne was jubilant. "We're going to be mommies together."

"Slow your roll, girlie," Chloe quickly clipped her excitement.

"How did this happen?" I asked.

"The first time was a couple of months after Orlando and I separated and the other four times..."

"You guys reconciled?"

"No."

She ran her fingers through her hair and walked over to the window so we couldn't see her face.

"I tripped over his drunk behind lying in the hall when I was headed to the kitchen. I helped him get to bed. One thing led to another and...I can't believe I let this happen." She turned to face us with tears in her eyes. "He didn't even realize it was me. He thought it was Tasha. What does that say about me?" She wiped her tear stained cheek. "I just laid there and allowed my husband to screw me thinking I was someone else."

"Oh my God." I walked over and hugged her.

"So, I might be pregnant, but I'm not sure I'm mother material right now," she confessed.

"Of course you're mother material. What are you talking about?" Kendell asked.

"I got married on a whim and now I'm pregnant because I couldn't control myself. Not exactly the perfect mother."

"You've got to be kidding, you'll be a great mother," I chimed in. "Wait a minute, is that why you're headed to Brazil?"

"I figured I'd hide out there until the baby is born, away from..."

"Who, us?" Dionne asked.

"Orlando."

"Wait a minute," I jumped in. "Orlando doesn't know?"

"No."

"Chloe, you've got to tell him," Kendell begged.

"No, I don't. As far as he knows I could have had AI."

"AI?" Kendell asked.

"Artificial Insemination," Dionne clarified.

"If Orlando knew, he'd fight for custody so he could get my money."

"But it's his child," Kendell reminded her.

"This is something you're going to have to work out. When I told Terrence about our son, he was very angry no one told him. I may not agree with you, but I understand."

"Alex you can't be serious?" Dionne looked at me.

"If Orlando had been an upright man, I'd try my best to convince her. However, he isn't. Chloe, you need to do what's best for your baby."

"Thank you, Alex."

"Remember whatever you decide, make sure you're willing to live with the consequences."

I thought if I did a little housecleaning or conscience cleaning I'd get the peace I've been desiring.

I really missed the mark on that one. As much as I don't want to admit it, I know where my peace lies. I looked at the picture of me and Moses.

I picked up my phone, scrolled through the contacts and landed on his name. I pressed the button and his face appeared. All I have to do is press the number, but what if he doesn't answer? What if he does...what will I say? Do I apologize, tell him I love him or let him go?

this is how it ended

"MORNING, ALEX"

"Good Morning, Bas." Not looking up from my paper work. "What's on tap for today?" He dropped the mail on my desk and didn't say anything. I looked up over my glasses and he was standing with his arms crossed in front of his chest not smiling. I wasn't quite sure what to make of his serious stance. "Is there something bothering you?" I sorted through the mail waiting on an answer. "Well?"

"I was wondering how much longer this idiot head phase is going to last?"

"What are you talking about?"

He sat down in one of the chairs in front of my desk and placed his right foot on top of his left knee. "You."

"Me?" I took my glasses off and looked at him. "What are you talking about?"

"I was talking to Moses and..."

"Let me stop you right there. I told you..."

"I know what you said and I know it's a lie."

"So not only am I an idiot head, I'm a liar as well?"

"Yes."

I got up and walked over to the credenza and refilled my coffee cup. "Sebastian, I don't know what's gotten into you, but…"

"I don't know what's gotten into you."

"Excuse me?"

"I don't know who's worse, you or Moses."

"I don't know what you're talking about. I haven't spoken to Moses in months."

"Ten to be precise."

I walked back to my desk and sat down. "You know that how?"

"He told me."

"My boyfr—I mean Moses told you that? When?"

"Yesterday."

"Why were you talking to Moses?" I sipped my coffee.

"He's my friend."

"Uh-huh, so he told you…"

"I asked him when was the last time he spoke to you and that's when he said he's been waiting on you to call him."

"If he wants to talk to me, then why doesn't he call me?"

"Funny, I asked the same thing."

"What did he say?" I took another sip from my cup.

"He said he told you to call him once things were settled with Terrence."

"He said that?" I leaned back and crossed my arms in front of my chest.

"Yep."

"Well, I just haven't gotten around to…"

"Save it." He held up his hand. "I don't think my ears can take another excuse from you."

"What did you say?"

He stood up and straightened his tie. "Save that lie. I'm sorry…excuse, for someone that doesn't know you." He turned and started towards the door and stopped. "If you don't want to get back with Moses, that's your business, but I think you should let him know so he can move on."

"Is that all?"

"That's all I think you can stand to hear." He walked out and closed the door.

The nerve of Moses talking about our relationship to Bas. And how dare Bas tell me I need to call Moses. If I choose to call Moses, I'll do so when I'm ready and not because his friend says I should.

What about me? If Moses is so concerned about the status of our relationship, then why doesn't he call me instead of talking to Bas. The nerve of both of them.

I sliced the letter open with the silver-plated letter opener still furious at Bas. Since when did he and Moses get so buddy buddy. --Waving the letter opener in the air at no one. -- I know one thing, I better not find out Moses still has that bodyguard following me. I took the letter out of the envelope and unfolded it followed by another sip of coffee.

If the bodyguard is around, it would mean he still cares. Maybe that's why he hasn't called. Maybe the bodyguard told him I was done with Terrence. Maybe he told him I come home every night and reread his books. Or maybe, he told him he heard me outside on the patio crying. Maybe Bas is right, I'm an idiot head. I wiped the tear rolling down my cheek and directed my attention to the letter.

Hey Alex, I know you're probably angry with me, but don't be. Going to Brazil was the best thing I've done since dumping that Gold Digging, Idiot Head ex-husband of mine. Apart from missing my girlfriends and American food, I'm fine and fat. I screamed the first time I saw my behind in a mirror while shopping for maternity clothes. You really should consider selling designer maternity clothes. You'd make a fortune.

Marcelo has been great. I wasn't quite sure how he was going to feel about dating a pregnant divorcee, but he's really embraced it. And before you ask, yes, I told Orlando I was pregnant. He said fatherhood is something he has no desire to experience. So, I am officially a chic single mother-to-be dating a gorgeous Brazilian man who gives me foot massages. Who would have thought?

My mother called me an Idiot Head, and she's right. If I had used the same principles I use in business in my personal life, I wouldn't be in this situation. At the same time, I wouldn't have Parker Alexander. Oh yeah, I'm having a boy. [See the enclosed picture of your godson.]

I decided to have the baby here, which means I expect you a week after Parker gets here. My mom is with me and my dad will be over when it gets closer to my delivery date. I still can't believe I'm having a baby. Every time he kicks, my heart jumps and my eyes fill with tears. I'm excited about possibly being a soccer mom. I know I'm getting a little ahead of myself, but I guess my mommy hormones have kicked in.

I was pretty angry with you for not telling us about your marriage and son. I'm sorry we made you feel you had to hide them from us. I was thinking. I've always been a little impulsive when it comes to my personal life and you've been a lot cautious. Maybe it's time we switched roles. I'll try being a little cautious and you should try being a little impulsive. Trust me, you need this girl.

How's Dionne? I bet she's as big as me by now. Has Bas proposed to Kendell yet? Don't tell him, but I miss my sparring partner. How about Taylor? Can you believe what she did? Give my love to your mom. I miss you guys. Love, your very pregnant friend, Chloe."

Okay, what's going on with Taylor? I opened her letter and almost fell out of my chair looking at the photo I was holding.

Hey Cuz, I know you've probably been worried about me but I'm okay. I got your messages, but I've been a little distracted. I don't know how much you know, but here it is in my own words.

Things had been going great with Jason. I thought his mother was fine with our dating. I mean she encouraged him to include me in family functions, but I was mistaken.

She invited me to lunch a couple of months ago, and something happened. While we were putting our cards on the table, a mutual acquaintance stopped by our table. Turns out we both dated the same man at different times in our past. How many women can say they have an old boyfriend in common with their mother-in-law? After a good laugh, we compared notes and swore to never say anything to Jason about, Mister X.

Afterwards, she made it perfectly clear she wasn't happy about my seeing Jason, but his happiness far outweighed her feelings about me. She also threatened to have me arrested if I made Jason or Zach unhappy. I told her what goes on between me and Jason is none of her business.

Jason said she told him she liked my spunk, and if he did anything to mess this up, she'd throw him in jail, [ha,ha]. So he asked what would she do if he said he wanted to marry me? She said, she'd perform the ceremony. A week later at Sunday dinner, she married us.

Get up off the floor, because you read that correctly. Your anti-marriage cousin is married and I have a teenaged stepson. In fact, by the time you get this letter, I'll probably be in Italy with my husband on our honeymoon. I know, I can't believe it myself. [See the picture.] Me, a wife and a step mom, who would have thought? I know I didn't! Gotta go. We'll probably swing by and see Chloe before coming home. Take care, Cuz, love ya, Taylor."

Next I opened the big envelope and pulled out the contents. It was a letter attached to another envelope.

Dear Lexi, I want to thank you for everything you did for me. I didn't want to admit it, but you were right. The purpose for our reunion wasn't to be lovers again, but to be friends. Something we really weren't. I know we can't be close friends, but we're something better, what exactly I don't know, but trust me, it's a good thing.

Blair and I are separated and she's apologized for deceiving me. We agreed to wait until after the holidays to file for divorce. I agreed to set up a modest trust fund for each of the children. And a more reasonable financial settlement for her. My cousin and his wife, that still sounds strange, have agreed to my terms and moved to the south of France. They felt they would be more comfortable living there. Isn't that ironic?

I don't think I could have gotten through this entire mess without you. I apologize for my behavior and that of my family. And I apologize for not being there for you and our son. However, I will not apologize for loving you, but I will apologize for not being the man you thought you married. You would be very proud of me, I found a great church and have rededicated my life to God. I am well on the road to discovering who Terrence Pierce is.

I desire only the best for you. You have proven yourself to be a good woman, friend and wife. I don't entirely regret my marriage to Blair, but I think if we had a tenth of what you and Moses have, we could have survived this mess. Moses is very blessed to have you in his life.

I know you offered to give me your Pierce Holdings shares without any compensation, but I can't do that. It wouldn't be right. Selfishly, I want you to keep them so I have an excuse to see you at board meetings. However, I don't think Moses would appreciate that. If you insist on my taking them back, I'll only accept them if you agree to the terms attached. Otherwise, I'll expect you at the next board meeting."

I reached inside the envelope and pulled out the papers and my eyes almost popped out of their sockets. My hand was shaking as my mind processed the amount of the check... fifty million dollars. I closed my eyes and quickly reopened them, thinking it might be a mistake or that I was still light headed from looking at Taylor's photo. I reached into my desk for my magnifying glass to get a closer look and it was correct. I was holding a check for fifty million dollars. I put it down and read the attached note.

I did a lot of Spring cleaning and got ride of some dead weight [did you get my joke regarding my cousin?], which made the company a nice piece of change. I know the amount of the check seems excessive, but it's a fair price for your shares. If you don't believe me, ask your uncle, he's been helping me get things in order.

The other check is not returnable. It's what I call back

alimony. If you agree to the amount for your shares, call your Uncle and he'll tell you what needs to be done. If you don't agree to the terms, send the check back.

The terms for the alimony check are simple. One, call me at least once a month. I want to know how you're doing. Second, enjoy your life with Moses. Have a lot of babies, grow old with him and let him love you the way you deserve to be loved…completely and unconditionally. I've seen how he looks at you. He loves you in a way I never could. Just like I know you could never love me the way you love him and I'm good with that.

Take both checks, and live. Love your, friend, Terrence. "

I didn't know what to do. I picked up my phone and pulled up my uncle's number, but I couldn't make my finger press the call button. Instead, I scrolled through my contacts and stopped at Moses picture and number. I wanted to press the button, but I didn't know what to say.

I stood up and started pacing. I picked up Terrence's note and reread it. I put the checks in the envelope along with a note to deposit them and put Uncle Wallis' name on the front. I opened my safe and saw the stack of letters. I put Uncle Wallis' envelope inside, took out the stack of letters, placed them in my bag, along with my laptop, iPad and phone. I picked up my jacket and bag and left down the back stairs.

I sat in my car trying to figure out where to go. I started the engine and pulled out of the parking lot. I dialed the one number I had no problem dialing. After a couple of rings, a familiar voice picked up.

"Yes?"

He was still pissed with me and I know why. "Bas, I need you to cancel the rest of my day and tomorrow as well."

"Where are you?"

"There's something I need to do."

"Why does it sound like you're outside?"

I honked my horn. "That's because I am. Call my Uncle and have him come pick up the envelope in my safe with his name on it."

"Why don't I just messenger it? It would be…"

"Dammit Bas, please do what I asked. I'll call you later. Bye." I pressed the button ending the call, reached into my bag for my sunglasses. "What the crap!" A piece of paper sliced my finger. I pulled out the offending paper and tried to read it as I drove. I put it down and finally fished my sunglasses out and put them on. When I reached the stop light, I picked up the paper, read it and knew what I needed to do.

I made a U-turn and got on the freeway headed to the airport. I pulled into the over priced airport parking lot, grabbed my bags, ran inside to the Delta Airlines terminal and bought a first class ticket on the first available flight to New York. This definitely falls under the heading of impulsive, exactly what Chloe suggested.

Eight hours later and I'm thinking a phone call would have been better. As the car made its way into the city, my hands grew sweaty and my mouth felt like cotton. Forty-five minutes later, the car pulled up in front of the beautiful townhouse on the Upper Eastside. The driver opened the door, and I hesitated before exiting the car. Standing at the bottom of the steps, I took a deep breath and began my climb. Before I reached the top step, the door opened and Mrs. Joseph was standing in the doorway waiting on me.

"Hello, Alexandra. How was your flight?" She had her short arms stretched out to greet me like my first time here.

"Fine. Thank you."

"Mrs. Bartholomew is in the parlor."

"Thank you." I walked inside, placed my bags on the bench by the front door and went straight to the parlor where I found the sweet but tough woman I hoped would be on my side. I approached the doorway and tried quieting my footsteps, but the clack of the heel on my Alaia boots against the mahogany floor gave me away.

"Alexandra, come in here." The voice from the parlor called out.

I stepped into the parlor and stood in front of her. She looked me up and down stone faced. I felt like I was being inspected. "Good evening ma'am, I mean Grams."

"At least you haven't been crying. I can't have you meeting my grandson with puffy eyes. Sit down."

I sat in the chair across from her. "Mrs. Barth—"

"Now is not the time to talk." I know she didn't just go there with me. "Alexandra, how much do you know about Moses' wife?"

"He told me she died during child birth and that she had an affair."

"That's all? You didn't press him?"

"No. I respect his privacy. I didn't need to know the details. Why?"

"Moses loved Natalie almost as much as he loves you. About six months after they were married she started things up again with some lowlife from her past. A few months later, she became pregnant. When Moses confronted her, she got angry and left. The man she was having the affair with didn't want children or a wife. Moses chased her and persuaded her to come home so they could be a family. There were complications during the delivery and she died. Two weeks later the baby died. He was devastated. He disappeared for quite a while and when he came back, he was guarded, distant, cold. Then he got back with that annoying Vanessa Toliver until he came to his senses. He dated a few women, but nothing serious and then he met you."

"I didn't know."

"You didn't know. Is that all you have to say?" She growled.

"What do you want from me?" I barked back.

"You had no problem telling him everything about your ex-husband and your son, yet, you didn't bother to ask him about Natalie and Allegra?"

"I figured when and if he wanted to tell me he would."

"I see."

"Mrs. Bartholomew," she didn't insist I call her Grams. I must have hit a nerve. Oh well, if I'm going down, I might as well go down fighting. "I don't know what it is you want me to say. I'm sorry I hurt you. I'm sorry I didn't pry into your grandson's marriage a little deeper. I'm sorry I didn't live up to your expectations. However, the only apology you're going to get from me is I'm sorry you feel you deserve an apology."

"Excuse me. Do you—"

"Now is not the time to talk." I sat up straighter. "I've done nothing to you that warrants an apology. The only person's forgiveness I need is Moses', and if he won't forgive me, then that's on him. You're right, I should have pressed Moses for details about his marriage, but how would that have helped us? He came looking for me, which meant he was ready to move on. Now if he doesn't want me, then I'll leave the same way I came, alone, and go on with the rest of my life."

"Young lady, no one has ever spoken to me like that and didn't have it followed by an impression of my hand on the side of their face."

"Well there's a first time for everything isn't there."

"I take it from that speech you've straightened out everything with your ex-husband?"

"Yes, ma'am."

"Grams."

"Yes, ma'am Grams."

"Now you're ready to go forward with my grandson?"

"Yes, ma'am, I mean Grams."

"Relax. What makes you think he hasn't moved on, after all it's been awhile since you last saw him?"

"I don't, but being in love means you take chances. Besides, if he had moved on, you wouldn't be chewing me out."

"You love him that much?"

"Ma'am, Grams, I walked out of my office over eight hours ago with one thing on my mind, getting back the man I love."

"I see." She nodded her head. "Wait in his office, he should be home soon."

"Thank you." I got up and started walking away.

"Alexandra."

I turned to face her. "Yes, ma'am?"

"I meant what I said when we first met. I like your spunk, but if you break his heart, I'll kill you."

"I did it all for him."

"I know. Good night."

"Good night." I continued down the hall wondering if I did the right thing coming here. The person I thought was my ally has sided against me.

I walked into Moses' office and found a spot to wait. Standing in the dark I kept rehearsing what I'd say. Three hours later, resolved he wasn't coming home, I went into the kitchen, wrote a note and left it along with the letters.

I heard the front door open and close, followed by footsteps coming towards the kitchen. I was trapped. There were only two ways out of the kitchen and one would put me right in front of Moses. I took the other way and landed back in his office. I couldn't see anything and stubbed my toe against the chair. I hobbled into the corner and stood quiet, hoping he'd bypass his office and go upstairs.

Unfortunately, the footsteps continued toward the office. I held my breath, hoping he changed his mind and turned around.

Instead, a bright light startled my eyes and I cursed before I knew it. I quickly covered my mouth, but I was too late. He turned and our eyes met.

"Alexandra."

He only calls me that when he's upset. "Moses." My eyes were trying to adjust to the light change in the room.

"What are you doing here?" He took his jacket off and placed it on the arm of the sofa.

As he walked around his desk, I got a glimpse of his tight behind and broad back as he loosened his tie. Lord have mercy. He took his tie off and unbuttoned the top few buttons on his shirt. My mouth was watering as I watched him get comfortable.

I saw his lips moving and then it occurred to me that he was talking to me. "I'm sorry, what did you say?"

"Why are you here?"

Not even a fake pleasantry…just, why are you here. "I… you look good."

"Thank you. So do you."

I see we're starting off this conversation with lies. I've been on a stuffy airplane and in the same clothes for almost eighteen hours. I'm wrinkled, ripe and know I look like crap.

He on the other hand looks like he just stepped off a runway in Milan. If he weren't a writer, model would be an easy fit, perfect bone structure, height, sparkling smile, hypnotic eyes and a behind so tight it should be illegal to view it in public even covered up with clothes. "Thank you."

"Did you see Grams?"

"Yes, we had an interesting chat."

"Really?"

"Why didn't you tell me the details of Natalie's affair?"

"It's not something I'm particularly proud of." He took his cuff links off and started rolling up his sleeves. "I met Natalie right after I broke up with Vanessa the first time. We met at a gallery, connected instantly and started seeing each other. We dated for almost a year before I proposed. Shortly after we were married, she tells me she's pregnant and in love with someone else. I went to Europe on a book tour and when I came home, she had gone to her parents' home in Atlanta. She was devastated because the baby's father didn't want children or a wife. I persuaded her to come home and we started over. While we were visiting her parents she went into labor and died, two weeks later Allegra died."

"I'm sorry."

He shook his head. "I chased her and swore I wouldn't do that again, but there I was chasing you. A woman attached to someone else."

"That's what you think?"

"What else am I supposed to think?" His voice was escalating.

"You're supposed to know I love you."

"How, by what your mother and Bas say, because that's all I have to go on. It's not like you ever said you love me."

"I just told you I love you." Both our voices were escalating.

"In a back handed compliment kind of way."

There's that bitter tone from the last time we spoke. "Wow."

"Tell me, how's your ex-husband, or is he your husband?"

"His name is Terence."

"Before you start questioning me about why I didn't tell you the details of Natalie's affair, you need to be honest with yourself about your ex."

"Terrence and I were married and I love him as a friend. If you can't handle that, then maybe you and I are better off being distant friends." It was time to leave. "I should have just written you a letter and saved myself the humiliation of this conversation."

"Why didn't you? It would have saved me the pain of having to get over you again."

"Wow. So was everything a lie or was I some sort of therapy to help you get over Natalie and Vanessa?" When the hurtful words are tossed about, you know it's over.

"Everything I said and did for you was because I love you. It's my fault, I thought you were available." He wiped his face with his hands. "I've moved on and I need a woman who loves me. I waited and waited for you to make up your mind. Every day for ten months I waited for a call, a message, a letter, something from you baby, letting me know how you felt, but nothing."

"Don't you think I wanted to call you?"

"Then why didn't you?"

"I was scared."

"Scared of what, me?"

"No, passion."

"Passion?"

"When I asked my uncle to help Terrence, before giving me an answer, he asked me how I felt about you. I didn't have an answer. When your grandmother asked me the same question, I knew how I felt."

"Seems you could tell everyone, except me, how you felt."

There's that tone again. If we make it through this, he is definitely going to have to do something about his temper. "You say I have nothing to be scared of, but I do. I'm scared of myself and the changes you made in my life. Before you came, my life was full, but you added passion and showed me there was still so much I hadn't experienced. I was excited and saw my life going in a different direction and that scared me because I liked it."

"Good for you. Is that all, because…"

"Dammit, Moses, I'm in love you? I love you so much, I put my life on pause so I could come and tell you." I covered my eyes with my hands, trying to calm down. I took a deep breath, slowly removed my hands and looked at him. "You said once things were settled with Terrence to call and you'd be on the first flight. Things are settled and instead of you coming to me, I came to you, but it seems I'm too late." I walked over and kissed him on the cheek. "Thank you for bringing me back to life and showing me how unselfish and passionate love can be." Just as my getaway was almost complete and my private crying session could began, he spoke.

"I'm sure Mrs. Joseph has your room ready."

I turned and replied. "Thank you, but I would rather leave with my dignity and what little respect you may have for me rather than spend another minute in this house." I walked into the foyer, picked up my coat and bags and left the beautiful memory filled townhouse on the Upper Eastside the same way I entered, alone.

Moses

I COULDN'T SLEEP ONCE ALEX left. It was four thirty and I'd been up all night staring at that picture of us at Courtney's party. I walked into the kitchen and spotted the plate of chocolate chip walnut cookies, her favorite. I poured myself a glass of milk and reached for a cookie remembering her first night here and how we stayed up talking and eating cookies. I spotted a stack of ribbon tied pink envelopes at the end of the counter and pulled them toward me. I immediately recognized the handwriting. I put the glass down and began reading.

> *Dearest Moses, I came here today to beg your forgiveness and thank you for helping me with Terrence. I don't know many men who would put their own feelings aside to help the woman they love, help her ex-husband. That's a mouthful. Grams said you were on your way home and I waited as long as I could before it became painfully clear, you weren't coming home. It's like you*

knew I was here. I'm sorry it took me so long to figure out what I wanted.

I have loved three men in my life, each one differently. With Terrence it was my first and it was nice. With Jonathan it was familiar and distractive. With you it was passionate and I was hoping my greatest and last. Unfortunately, it will be the hardest to get over. I want only the best for you and I hope you find the good thing you've been looking for. All my love, always, Alexandra. P.S. Maybe I'll see you in the airport. P.S.S. I did write you, I just didn't have the nerve to mail them."

There were forty letters, one per week since we last spoke with the last letter dated yesterday.

Dearest Moses, I don't know what I'm doing. Today, I left my office with one thing on my mind, telling you I'm in love with you. I got in my car and started driving and found myself at the airport. I tried to start my future with that old plane ticket, but it had expired. How apropos that one of the last things tying me to the past had expired a long time ago. Today is the beginning of the rest of my life. I want you to be a part of it. I'm no longer running and I like having you in my life. I'm ready, are you? Love, Alex.

I have shed tears for three women in my life, my grandmother Mary, Natalie, Allegra, and now the woman I forced to leave. She captured my heart and ruined me for any other woman. Even if I wanted someone else, I would always be looking for her.

I looked up at the clock and heard footsteps coming down the stairs. I wiped my face with my hands contemplating my next move.

"Have you been up all night?" Grams asked.

"This woman is…I…"

"I take it you read Alexandra's letters?"

"She…I can't do this."

"Do what?"

"Chase her."

"I see." She nodded. "Before you make a decision you might regret, I think you should read this." She handed me an Express Mail envelope.

"What's this?"

"Your reason to chase her."

I opened the envelope and pulled out a white letter sized envelope with my name on the front. I pulled the letter out and started reading. I was furious, excited and disappointed…in myself. I reread the letter and looked at Grams. "Did you read this?"

"Yes I did." She got up and turned on the espresso machine.

I shook my head. "When did this come?"

"Yesterday morning. Ironic isn't. The same day that arrives, so does she."

She dropped a pod into the espresso machine waiting for the strong hot liquid to fill the petite white cup. Once the cup was filled, she stirred in a teaspoon of sugar and placed it in front of me. I absorbed the entire shot in one swallow searing my throat.

"What do you think about this?" I placed the letter on the counter.

"I think, he means it."

"But she doesn't love him. She loves me."

She made herself an espresso and sat down at the table. "That doesn't matter. She's vulnerable and as soon as she blocks you out of her heart, she's going to take him up on his offer."

"She wouldn't do that."

"Yes, she would."

I started pacing back and forth. "I've got stop her."

She sipped her espresso and looked at me. "How? You don't even know where she is."

"I'll go to her house."

"That's a plan. Or you could just call her."

I stopped pacing and contemplated Grams' suggestion. I walked into my office, picked up my phone and pressed Alex's number. After three attempts all I got was voice mail. I know she's screening her calls. I wanted to throw my phone across the room. I scrolled the contacts and dialed the one person I believed would help me.

I pressed the button and waited for the voice to answer. Finally, after the third ring, a familiar voice answered. "Hello."

"Mom Connie." I was prepared for her to chew me out.

"What do you need?" Her voice was sharp.

"I need to talk to Alex."

"Call her."

"I did, but she's not answering."

"Tell me about the fight."

"How do you...," I walked back into the kitchen. "Let me guess. Grams called you?"

"Yes. And I also know about the letter from Terrence."

"Grams?"

"No. Wallis. Seems Terrence gave him that letter a couple of weeks ago and asked him to send it to you. I told him not to, but he did it anyway after he found out Terrence was sending Alex those checks."

"What checks?"

"Ah, she didn't tell you."

"Tell me what?"

"She gave back, actually, Terrence bought her Pierce Holdings shares for fifty million dollars. He felt bad about what his cousin did and gave her another twenty million as back alimony."

"What!"

"From what I understand, he sent the checks to her yesterday right around the time she left to come see you."

"Oh my God."

"After talking to Emma, seems you two had words and now you can't find her and want my help. Does that about sum it up?"

"Yes." There was no follow up, only silence. "Mom Connie, I...I..."

"Would you please open the front door."

"What?"

"Open the door, it's cold out here."

I pressed the button ending the call, walked into the foyer, turned the alarm off and opened the door. Standing on the porch was the older version of the woman I love. I wrapped my arms around her. "What are you doing here?"

"Seems you mucked things up."

I stepped back. "I wouldn't say..." She looked up at me. "I screwed up bad."

"I need coffee and a land line."

Alex

THE CAR PULLED UP IN front of a strange building. It looked more like an office building instead of an airport.

"Excuse me, where are we?"

"We're at the airport," the driver replied.

"This isn't JFK."

"No, it's Teteboro." He got out of the car, walked around to the rear passenger side and opened the door for me.

"I don't understand. My uncle said he got me on a flight."

"Miss, I was told to bring you to Teteboro for your flight."

I got out of the car. "I'm sorry, I don't understand."

"Miss normally, I would take you directly to the plane, but it isn't ready. If you go inside the concierge, will take care of you."

"None of this makes any sense." I reached inside my bag for my phone.

"Miss Miller?"

I looked up and a petite blond woman was walking towards me. "Yes."

"I'm sorry, but we're not quite ready for you."

"What's going on? My uncle said he got me a flight home."

She smiled. "He did. If you'll come with me, I'll get you checked in."

I went to tip the driver. "That won't be necessary. It's already been taken care of. Have a safe flight."

"Thank you." I followed the concierge inside.

"There's a lounge to the right if you'd like to relax. Do you have any luggage?"

"No."

"The lounge is right through the double doors. I'll come get you when your flight is ready."

"Thank you."

I opened the door and looked around. There were a few people sitting in the front and a large black bag sitting on a coffee table in the rear. I sat down by the window and started rummaging in my bag. My phone fell out and landed on the floor. I reached down to pick it up and a dark masculine hand reached down at the same time and handed it to me.

"Let me get that."

I looked up to thank my Good Samaritan. "Moses." I jumped up. "What are you doing here? Let me guess, Bas? He is so fired."

"Let me explain."

"What's to explain? Didn't you humiliate me enough last night? In fact, I believe you handed me over to my ex-husband with your blessing."

"You were right."

"About what?"

"I left because of the note your ex-husband sent."

"Is that why you're here, because you could have put it in a letter."

"Written words can't convey how sorry I am about my behavior last night."

An apology. Perfect, this just keeps getting better. I tossed my head back. What did I do to deserve this humiliation? I lowered my head and my eyes met his and a jolt shot through my body. My knees almost buckled. Damn him for being so sexy. "Why are you here?"

"Grams told me to come get you."

"How romantic. Now if you'll excuse me, I've got to go." I picked up my bags and began walking away.

"I love you!"

I stopped walking and stood with my back to him. I didn't want him to see the emotions dancing on my face. I knew if I looked at him, I'd start crying. God knows that's not the last image I want him to have of me, a teary-eyed stereotype, saying goodbye.

"I can handle being third to the stores, I can handle your being friends with your ex-husband, but I can not handle you not being in my life. The past ten months have been unbearable. Please…"

This is horrible, two grown people standing in the airport lounge killing what's left of their relationship in front of strangers. I've just reached a new level of humiliation. I turned and the gaze of those incredible light brown eyes aimed at me felt like a laser piercing my heart.

"It's too late. We had a chance as long as the window was open, but last night you closed it. I'm in love with you but…"

"Miss Miller, your flight is ready."

"Thank you…I…I have to go." My feet felt like lead. I took a deep breath hoping to stop the tears that were gathering. I turned around and followed the concierge out to the plane.

We approached the stairs leading up to the door of the plane and stopped.

"Have a safe trip."

"Thank you." She turned around and walked back inside.

"Alexandra Miller?" I looked up in the direction of the voice.

"Yes."

I walked up the steps onto the plane and it was beautiful.

Much nicer than the one my uncle rented to fly us to Napa. I stood admiring my surroundings and failed to notice the flight attendant had closed the door.

"Welcome aboard."

"Thank you."

"Have a seat. Once you're settled, we'll take off."

I took my jacket off and handed it to the attendant. "This is nice."

"The owner has excellent taste."

I sat down, strapped my seat belt and stared out the window hoping for one last glimpse of Moses before takeoff. "Excuse me. I'm a little confused. My uncle said he booked me a flight home, but this doesn't make sense. I know he wouldn't…"

"I don't know who booked the flight. All I know is we've been instructed to fly you to California. Now, can I get you something before we take off?"

"Coffee."

"Black no sugar or espresso with one sugar?"

"How do you know how I like my coffee?"

"It's in the instructions."

"Oh. Coffee, thank you." I took my phone out of my bag and called my uncle but there was no answer. Then I sent a text.

BabyGirl: *Uncle, I don't understand what's going on. Please call me.*

Uncle: *Did you miss your flight?*

BabyGirl: *I tried to call you. I think there's been a mistake. Please call me asap.*

Uncle: *I called in a favor and got you a ride home. Is there a problem?*

"Miss Miller. You need to turn your phone off. Thank you." He placed the white china cup and saucer on the table in front of me. "I was told to give this to you before we took off. Maybe it will clear things up for you."

"Thank you." I opened the envelope, pulled out the documents and began reading.

Hey Beautiful, seems I've made a mess of things. I was excited to see you standing in my office last night, but I was also very angry with you. Why did it take you so long to come back to me? Ever since I walked out of your office ten months ago, I've been imaging our reunion in my mind and dreams. In both versions, I swooped you up into my arms and reacquainted myself with your sexy lips. Definitely nothing like what happened last night.

I miss having you in my life. I miss hearing your voice every day. I miss the way you feel in my arms. I miss kissing you, protecting you and dancing with you. I miss you.

If you choose not to give me another chance, I'll respect that, but it won't change how I feel about you. You are that good thing I asked God for and like any good thing, you're worth waiting for. Love you now, love you later, love you forever, Moses.

I buzzed for the flight attendant.

"Yes, Miss Miller?" Smiling. "The envelope cleared up some things for you, didn't it?"

"I need to get off the plane."

"I'm sorry, but that's not possible."

"Why not?"

"We've already called the tower and been assigned a take off position."

"You gotta help me." I stood up and started walking towards the door.

"Miss, I wish I could but--" He rushed over and threw himself in front of the door.

"Move," I demanded.

"I'm sorry. I can't do that. We have to leave."

"Move."

"Miss, I'm glad whatever was in that envelope cleared things up for you. However, I can't let you off this plane. Once the door is closed and the tower has been called, it's too late. I'm sorry."

"Fine."

"Thank you. Now sit down."

"Excuse me?"

"I'm sorry I don't mean to be rude, but I need you to sit down so we can leave. Thank you."

I went back to my seat. Once he was in the back, I ran over, opened the door and the alarm started buzzing. The flight attendant came running out.

"You need to do something about that buzzing."

"What did you do?"

Then the phone started ringing. "Want me to get that?"

He cut me a sharp look and answered the phone. "Yes...I know...she tried to get off the plane...I told her, but she insisted... I'm not sure...okay...I'll tell her." He hung up, pushed the door open and waited for the stairs to be pushed up to the door. "The pilot says you have fifteen minutes. If you're not back by then, we're gone. Whether you're on the plane or not."

With my hands on my hips. "Does he know who I am?"

"Yes, we all do. You're the woman who will be sitting in New Jersey trying to find a way home if she's not back here in fifteen minutes."

"Fine." I hurried off and ran back inside the terminal looking for Moses. I was about to go back to the plane, when my eyes finally landed on him standing in front of the window.

I ran over, threw my arms around his neck, pulled his face down and crushed my lips against his. He slipped his hands around my waist, pulled me to his chest immediately taking control of the kiss. It was just as I remembered, passionate, dangerous, filled with emotion.

I couldn't get enough of him. He tasted like coffee and peppermint. His hands slid down my back and he pulled me deeper into his space ravaging my mouth. I could barely breath with his hard chest pressed against mine. He moved his mouth across my cheek to my ear and whispered, "Passion."

"Exactly."

He returned his soft lips to my mouth. The sound of clapping hands, interrupted our passionate reunion and we pulled apart. "I missed those lips."

"Me too." He leaned down to kiss me again and I covered my mouth with my hand. "Oh, my God."

"What's wrong?"

"We have to go. Get your bag." He picked up his bag and we walked out to the plane and the flight attendant met us at the door of the plane.

"You just made it," the attendant informed me.

I looked at my watch. "I still have three minutes."

He looked at Moses. "Is this why you ran off the plane?"

"Yes." I looked at Moses and felt a huge smile rising on my face.

"Okay. Let's get you two settled in for takeoff."

"What's your name?" I asked.

"Donté," he answered. "Okay then, buckle up. If we hurry, we can still make our slot, no thanks to Ms. Miller."

Once we were airborne, I looked around the plane and asked a simple question. "So what's with the plane?" Moses almost choked on his coffee.

"Excuse me?"

"So you owed my uncle?"

"What are you talking about?"

"My uncle said he called in a favor to get me a way home. And why wasn't Donté surprised to see you?"

He put his cup down and wiped his mouth. "The plane belongs to a friend and I've borrowed it a few times."

"Really?"

"If you don't believe me, ask Donté." He smiled.

"Donté," I called out and he emerged from the back.

"Yes, Miss Miller, do you need something?"

"It's Alex."

"Okay Alex, what can I do for you?"

"Mr. Adair, Moses, says he's borrowed the plane before, is that true?"

"Yes," he confirmed.

"Who does the plane belong to?" He looked at Moses.

"Tell her," Moses urged.

"I don't know."

"You don't know who you work for?"

"I'm going to the restroom." Moses excused himself.

"No. Like the pilots, we were hired by a lawyer."

"Excuse me?"

"We were hired by an attorney and told from time to time the owner will loan the plane out and when the time is right the owner will be revealed. Until then we've been instructed to treat every passenger as if they're the owner. That's how I know Mr. Adair. He's used the plane a few times."

Moses returned from the restroom and sat down, smiling. "Nancy Drew, did you find out who owns the plane?"

"No, and I'm very frustrated. Why won't you tell me?"

"Why do you need to know? It's not like it's going to affect your trip right now. Sit back and relax. I remember you saying something about getting your own plane. Well, pretend this one is yours and enjoy the ride."

"Miss Miller, I mean Alex, I need you to fill out the evaluation form before we land."

"Oh, you won't tell me who owns the plane, but you want me to do an evaluation. You sound like my assistant. He's bossy too. Where is it?"

"It's in the envelope I gave you when you boarded." He went to the back.

I pulled the large envelope out of my bag searching for the evaluation form. Behind the small white envelope from Moses was an envelope marked, "Evaluation Form." I pulled the paper out and began reading and then reread the paper two more times.

"Donté," I called and he came and stood next to my seat.

"My God woman, did the owner plant you as a test, because you are working my nerves!"

"Please explain this?" I handed him the paper.

He read it and looked at Moses. "Are you sure about this?" Moses nodded. "It says he bought the plane for you. Are you happy now?" He handed me the paper and headed to the back mumbling, "I know I'm not being paid me enough to deal with her."

"Moses, when did you…"

"I bought the plane when I got back from Napa the first time."

"I can't accept it. It's way too much."

"Then sell it."

"But, it's so pretty." I ran my hand across the arm of the seat and looked around the plane absorbing everything. I couldn't believe he did this. "Why?"

"I thought it would make a nice engagement present."

"What?"

"I said," He got up, walked over and got down on one knee. "I…thought…it…would…be…a…nice…engagement… present."

"Yes."

"I haven't asked you anything." He smiled.

"Oh."

He turned my seat so I was facing him. He took my hand in his. "Alexandra, before I met you I thought love at first sight was something we writers wrote to sell stories. When I saw you at that party, I instantly knew how Adam felt the first time he saw Eve. It was like I had just woken up from a deep sleep eyeing the perfect gift from God just for me. I read a book describing how Adam must have felt about Eve. How he took great joy in teaching her things, caring for her and being the one he could share the experiences of life with. I want that to be us. I want to be the one that loves you, nurtures you, teaches you, protects you and learns from you."

He pulled out a handkerchief with a black "B"

monogrammed on it and wiped the tears rolling down my cheek.

"I know you love God, I know you like chocolate chip walnut cookies, peonies and the color pink. I know how important your family and friends are to you. I like how you stand up to my grandmother and I love that you are in love with me. I won't make promises I can't keep, but I promise the only person I'll place above you is God. Alexandra Simone Miller, I am in love with you. It's time we stop messing around. Will you do me the honor of becoming my wife, my helpmate and my lover?"

With tears streaming down my face, I answered, "Moses Bernard Adair, I am in love with you and yes, I would be honored to be your wife, your helpmate and your lover."

I cupped his face in my hands and pressed my lips against his, kissing him like before in the terminal. I pulled back and those incredible light brown eyes were dark and sparkling. I brushed my thumb across his swollen lips. "I missed those lips."

"Me too." He smiled. "Maybe I should have gotten a ring instead of a plane."

I smiled. "We can go ring shopping before going to the townhouse."

"That's an option. Or…"

I smiled. "Or what?"

He pulled a small black box out of his pocket and placed it on the table. "Or you could wear what's in the box."

I looked at him, and then back at the box. "What's that?"

"Open it."

I opened the lid and my mouth dropped open. The large pale pink diamond ring barely fit the box. "Oh, my God." I covered my mouth. "It's beautiful."

"Good thing I got the plane and the ring." He placed the ring on my finger and gently pressed his lips against mine. He slowly pulled back and whispered, "Passion."

"Exactly."

the end

A sneak peek at the next book by Tracy Reed

The Alex Chronicles
WHAT MY FRIENDS NEED TO KNOW

PART TWO

TRACY REED

this is what happened next...

Moses

I QUIETLY OPENED THE DOOR, walked inside and heard voices talking about the last twenty-four hours. I stepped closer to the kitchen, trying to stay undetected. Unfortunately, my foot landed on a loose board giving me away. I looked up and all eyes were on me.

"Moses," Mom Connie announced. Her facial expression immediately went from elation to disappointment when she only saw me. "What happened...where's Alex?"

I took a deep breath and dropped my head searching for the right words to answer her question. "I...I uhm...I'm not sure where to start."

As a writer, you'd think I'd be very prolific when it comes to using words. However, when it's my private life, I always seem a little lost. I found myself faced with how much to reveal. I closed my eyes and tossed my head back, hoping for the right words. When I lowered my head and looked around the room at the people who love me, I knew what I had to say.

I cleared my throat and spit it out. "It was bad. I followed the plan and told her Grams told me to come get her and she wasn't too happy about that."

"You said that to her?" Grams asked.

"You get paid to write and that's what you said?" Mom Connie asked.

"Connie, that's a little harsh," Grams jumped to my defense.

"Emma, we gave him a failproof plan and he..."

"I know, but I'm not going to allow you to talk to my grandson like that."

She exhaled. "I'm sorry."

"Son, why would you say that? I know you can formulate a sentence. So what were you thinking?" I thought she was on my side. She seems to have sided with Mon Connie. "No wonder the poor girl turned you down. I would too. Idiot head."

"Grams..."

"What? Connie and I gave you a simple plan. All you had to do was speak from your heart, not say I told you to come get her. We even told you to write it down in case you forgot or got nervous." She wiped her forehead and exhaled. "How did you mess this up?"

"Emma, calm down. Son, did you at least show her the ring, because if you showed her the ring, you stood a chance of salvaging this thing," Mom Connie asked.

The ring. The jaw dropping ten-carat Asscher cut diamond with a hint of pink, sitting on a platinum band sprinkled with white diamonds. The day after I had lunch with Mom Connie and she told me to prepare for this day, I began searching for the perfect ring. I didn't want any white diamond. I wanted something extraordinary for Alex. The ring had to bare her personality. It needed to be a symbol of everything we'd been through and it needed to let her know how precious I feel she is. It needed to standout and yet be subtle. Although, I don't know how subtle a ring of that size can be.

"Yes ma'am." I dropped my head again, because I couldn't bare to see the disappointment in their eyes.

"Somehow I knew they'd muck this up," Mom Connie replied. "Emma, we need another plan."

"Hold on, Connie." Grams stood up and started walking towards me. "Son, what exactly did Alexandra say?"

I stood up straight and braced myself to answer her. "She said…"

"Yes." Shouted a voice. Alex walked around and stood next to me. "I said yes."

"Oh, my God," Mom Connie screamed, as she ran over and hugged my fiancée. She stepped back smiling at both of us. "Moses, you had us scared."

"You thought she said no?" I laughed.

"Moses, how dare you play such a trick on your grandmother," Mrs. Joseph chastised me.

"I'm sorry, Grams." I walked over and hugged her. "Forgive me?"

"Yes." Her smile covered her face. "Otis, get the champagne." Alex and I traded hugs and kisses with everyone.

"Yes, Miss Emma."

"So what are you four up to?" Alex asked.

"We've been waiting to hear from you two. Now that we see everything went according to plan," Grams said.

"Not exactly." I wrapped my arm around Alex's waist and she looked up at me with those beautiful dark eyes. "I wasn't kidding about it being bad. We stood in the middle of the lounge arguing."

"What?" Mom Connie shouted.

"Oh wait, it gets better," Alex replied. "I left him."

"Alex, you didn't?" Mom Connie shook her head.

"But then I read his note and knew I could either spend the rest of my life with my stupidity and embarrassment or with the man I love, so I got off the plane." She looked up at me smiling and I pressed my lips against hers.

"Thank God, you both came to your senses," Otis blurted out and we all laughed.

"So what time is the ceremony?" Mom Connie asked.

Alex and I looked at each other. "About that. We stopped by the City Clerk's Office on the way home and…," I looked at those four sets of eyes staring back at us and then at Alex.

"Please don't tell us you got married?" Grams begged.

"Go ahead, tell them," Alex urged.

"While we were getting the license, we figured why wait."

"You didn't." Mom Connie's words summed up the look on everyone's face.

We looked at each other and then at the four anxious faces staring back at us. "You guys are so easy. You should see the look on your faces," Alex laughed.

"We didn't get married. Neither of us had our birth certificates."

"I have Alex's," Mom Connie announced.

"Mama, why do you have my birth certificate with you?"

"I was hopeful for this out come," she smiled.

Alex walked over and hugged her. "I love you, thank you."

"You're welcome, baby."

"Thanks Mom Connie. In that case, I guess the wedding is back on for day after tomorrow."

"So where do we start?" Mom Connie asked.

I was unpacking when a tap on the door grabbed my attention. I looked up and standing in the doorway, was my fiancée. Looking at her immediately brought a smile to my face. "Hey, beautiful."

"May I come in?"

"Sure. How was your nap?"

"I couldn't sleep."

"What's troubling my fiancée?"

"I was thinking, maybe we should wait."

"Wait for what?" I asked.

"To get married."

We've been apart ten months, and I still know how to read her. I know the best way to handle Alex is to give her a little space while still nudging her in the right direction. I wrapped my arms around her and pulled her close. God, it felt good to have her back in my arms. I would agree to almost anything she requested, if it meant I could keep her close like this. I gently kissed her on the forehead and looked into those beautiful dark eyes filled with uncertainty. "What's the problem?"

She gave me a half smile. "Nothing really. I just think we may be rushing things."

"Uh-huh." I pulled her closer. "I thought you were fine with us getting married in a couple of days?"

"I was...I mean I am."

"Okay, then it's settled." I kissed her.

"I just think...I mean..."

I stopped what I was doing, sat on the bench in front of the bed and pulled her down onto my lap. I looked at her trying to get a read on what was really causing her apprehension. I wrapped her in my arms and braced myself for this conversation. "Okay, I am going to give you one opportunity to tell me what's really bothering you."

She bit her lower lip and my heart melted. "I think we need to get reacquainted. I mean it's been ten months since we last saw each other. Heck, we had more fights than kisses before you proposed to me this morning." I felt her body tensing up as she recited the laundry list of reasons why we should wait to get married. "And my friends, how do I explain having a husband, when they didn't know I was seeing anyone. I just told them I was divorced and lost my son. I'm still dealing with the fallout of those two secrets. And..."

I crushed my lips against hers. My ears needed a brake from the windfall of things troubling her. I slowly pulled back and kissed her again. "Shhh..."

"But..."

I kissed her again followed by a gentle stroke of her soft face. "Shhh...breath." She exhaled. "Do you know why I didn't put up a fight when you asked for a little space to deal with your ex-husband?"

"Space…really? I recall you hiding out nearby and let's not forget about the bodyguard." She smiled.

"That's not the point." I smiled. "You weren't the only one that needed space."

"What?"

"I was having a challenge being around you." She looked confused at my statement. "The first time I kissed you, I new I was in trouble. That kiss woke up feelings I had long put to bed. Every time I kissed you, I wanted more. I had convinced myself if I pushed things I could deal with the repentance. On a few occasions I was tempted to ask you to…"

Her eyes got wide. "What?"

"Hey, I'm not dead. You're an incredibly beautiful woman. That sexy little walk, those full tantalizing lips and…" I looked down at her breasts and back up. "…your other attributes have caused me a lot of lustful, sleepless nights."

"Is it warm in here?" She started fanning herself with her hand.

"I have had quite a few repentant nights and cold showers because of you. Now that we're engaged, I don't know how much longer I can hold on. I have dreamed about how your soft naked body will feel under mine. How your full breasts will feel in my hands as I gently caress them anticipating your reaction to my touch. About the tastes my tongue will be introduced to as it slowly glides along your body. How you'll sound calling my name as we…"

She jumped up and ran her fingers through her hair. "I…I, hum…" She patted her chest. "Are you sure the heater isn't on high, because…"

I grabbed her hand. "So when you ask me to wait, I don't think I can." I stood up and stepped closer as she stepped back trying to keep some distance between us.

"I understand your concerns, however…"

"Alexandra, you have two options. Marry me tomorrow or we're done."

The Alex Chronicles:
WHAT MY FRIENDS
NEED TO KNOW

PART TWO

excerpt from

the good girl

part one

chapter one

gabriella

I CONSIDER MYSELF TO BE smart. After all, I got my Bachelor's degree in three years, thanks to no social life, Summer school, and an extra load of classes. While my classmates were going to parties and football games, I was going to my internship.

I was fortunate to intern at Morgan Grant Holdings my senior year. I really like the company and the people. However, when I graduated and applied for a position, the only thing available was a Floating Assistant. I took it, because I know the company's policy is to promote from within. My parents don't understand why I'm so desperate to work for this company. I honestly don't understand it either. All I know is, it just feels right.

Morgan Grant has branches all over the world. I'm hoping wherever I land, I'll have the opportunity to travel and really make an impact. Since I've been floating, I've worked in nearly every department at their San Francisco headquarters.

I look at my job as a very long training program. During my internship, I was relegated to Mergers and Acquisitions. I liked the high powered energy and seeing deals go from inception to birth. However, as a floater, I loved the two weeks I was in Advertising. The creative energy there is like a drug. I love how they function as a group. If given the choice, that's where I'd like to be. Advertising works with all the departments and subsidiaries in all the offices. Creativity and travel...that's what I want. Until then, I'll keep floating and interviewing.

The Director of Human Resources called me early this morning, requesting I report to her office immediately for a special assignment. I quickly got dressed and headed to work.

I walked into her office and sat down. She handed me a card with only an office number. Before she could give me instructions, her computer dinged and she looked at the screen. After reading the screen, she grabbed her head, started typing and told me to go to the office upstairs and someone would give me details.

I took the elevator up to the twenty-third floor to the office number on the card. I've never worked on the Senior Executive floor. Most of the offices on this floor belong to the "big boys"... at least that's what I've heard.

The elevator stopped, the doors opened and my mouth dropped open. It was beautiful. It didn't look like an office, but like someone's luxurious living room. I looked around for a receptionist, but didn't see one. Maybe that's what I was going to be doing. I looked down at the card and it said twenty-three forty-two. I looked around and there were three doors. I searched for twenty-three forty-two and spotted the brushed steel numbers on the wall next to a hall. I walked down the long hall and stopped at the door marked, twenty-three forty-two.

I knocked on the door, but there was no answer. I turned the knob and the door opened. I walked inside and looked around the beautifully decorated black and white office with a view of the city. None of the spaces I've worked in had a window. Most of the offices with windows were reserved for executives. I thought to myself, "Whoever works in here probably prefers working at night with the lights of the city casting a sense of calm."

The walls were painted a beautiful glossy dark black. The white lacquered Parsons desk fit perfectly in the black and white space. However, the desk chair seemed out of place. It was as if whoever decorated the space forgot the assistant needed a chair, and grabbed the first thing they saw in storage. In front of the desk were two French-style arm chairs painted black with wide black and white stripe fabric. The only things on the desk were a vintage-style brass lamp, a telephone, large Apple iMac, MacBook Pro, iPad, and an iPhone. Seemed someone went a little crazy at the Apple Store. There was also two back-up drives and about a dozen jump drives. This was definitely the big leagues.

Behind the desk, was a white lacquered credenza with a huge arrangement of white lilies, art books, candles, a black tray with mineral and flat water, napkins with the company logo, jars of mixed nuts, pretzels, and black and white M&Ms. In the corner, was a small black velvet settee with black and white striped pillows like the chairs. Also, a small brass and glass coffee table with a stack of art books, a small arrangement of white roses, a very modern brass floor lamp, and a black and white geometric print rug.

The office was beautiful and unlike any of the ones downstairs. I looked around and thought how cool it would be to work in this space permanently. I sat down in one of the chairs facing the desk and waited for someone to appear.

Ten minutes later, the phone rang. I looked around and no one appeared, and the phone stopped ringing. A few minutes later it rang again, so I answered it. "Hello, Morgan Grant." I didn't know whose office it was so I played it safe. I knew I could always transfer the call to the right department.

"Great, you're there. I need you to familiarize yourself

with the leases for the D.C., Atlanta, Charlotte, and Dallas offices. Also, get the number of employees. I need to know if there are any open positions, and if so, how many. Call Estella in Human Resources and tell her what you need. Then, make a list of the top three commercial real estate brokers in London and Paris."

He was speaking so quickly, I never got a chance to tell him that whoever he was trying to reach wasn't there. I put the call on speaker, got my phone and recorded everything he was saying while jotting down whatever I could catch. I wanted to make sure I relayed the information correctly to whomever the office belonged to.

"Then go to Brockman's, ask for Cameron and pick up the things he has for me. Tony will pick you up tomorrow and bring you to the airport."

"When the assistant arrives, who should I say called?"

"Phillippe. Don't tell me I just gave all that to the receptionist. Human Resources said my assistant was in her office."

"I'm sorry, but no one was here when I arrived. I'm waiting on someone to give me instructions for my next assignment."

"What did Human Resources tell you?"

"There was an emergency. Then I was handed a card with this office number and told to report here for my next assignment."

He sighed. "Are you Gabriella Townsend?"

"Yes."

"I'm Phillippe Marchant, you'll be working with me."

"For how long?"

"Excuse me?"

"Usually, when I start an assignment, I'm also told the duration."

"This isn't a temp job. You've been hired to work with me."

"Oh, I didn't..."

"It's not your fault. I'll deal with Human Resources. I'm in Seattle putting out a fire. I'll see you tomorrow." Click.

I pressed the STOP button on my phone recorder and looked around *my office*. All my hard work and patience had paid off. I jumped up and down doing the happy dance in *my office*. I walked over and sat on my settee, my chairs and touched everything in *my office*.

I finally sat down in the odd desk chair and sighed. This is perfect. It's decorated exactly how I would have done it. "Wow, thank you God." I collected myself and got to work.

Just as I was about to head out to Brockman's, my phone rang. I picked it up and answered, "Phillippe Marchant's office."

"Gabriella."

Now that I know this is my office, I took the time to really listen to his voice. It was deep and sounded like smooth port wine. "Yes, sir."

"First of all, it's Phillippe."

"Yes, sir. I mean Phillippe."

"Call James Marshall's office. His number is in the Contacts on your computer. Let them know we'll be attending the gala and that I'll give James the check when I meet with him."

"Is there anyone else I need to inform about the party?"

"Excuse me?"

"You said *us*."

"Crap. Is there a black folder on your desk?"

"No."

"Go into my office and look on my desk."

"Hold on."

I walked over to the sliding wood door across from my desk, and pulled it back. My mouth dropped open again for the second time today. In the almost two years I've worked here, I've never seen an office like this one. It's not an office, but a loft. The very masculine scent greeted me at the door...tobacco, musk, leather and something spicy I can't name.

The walls were the same color black as the ones in my office, but in a flat finish. In the far left corner was a lounge area with a large black leather sofa, a couple of oversized brown leather club chairs, and a large square distressed wood coffee table with a large art book opened to a page on vintage cars. To the left of the door were shiny black bookcases filled with books, albums and a vintage record player.

In the other corner, was a large rectangular dark wood table with eight square black leather and brass chairs around it. Above the table, was a cool vintage light fixture expanding the length of the table. An antique brass open shelving unit was on the wall facing the conference table. On the wall above the shelving unit was a large, round mirror. An incredible plaster and iron sculpture sat on top of the shelving unit.

I stepped inside and the view of San Francisco took my breath away. The wall facing the conference table was floor to ceiling windows…a billionaire's view. I looked around and finally cast my attention on the large, sleek and shiny black lacquered desk. It looked more like art than a desk. The only things on it were a large Apple iMac, a telephone, a couple of black lacquer trays, and a small tray filled with black Montblanc pens and black old school pencils. The chair seemed out of place in front of the desk. It was black velvet, with a feminine shape to it.

It was clear Phillippe was an art lover. There were interesting pieces accessorizing the space. The large black and white print on the wall behind the desk was my favorite…a pair of hands. It was simple and dramatic. Instead of a light cluttering the desk, there was a cool, bubble bulb chandelier hanging over the desk. Behind the desk was a black vintage credenza with a tray of bottled water, glasses, napkins and three glass canisters…one with mixed nuts, one with black and white M&Ms and one with pretzels. I see Mr. Marchant likes to snack, which explains the identical set up in my office.

I walked up to the desk and inside one of the trays was a black folder with "Gabriella" written on it. I picked up the folder and went back to my office.

"I have it."

"Do you see an itinerary?"

I opened the folder and thumbed through the pages searching for the document. "No."

"Crap! I'm sorry. This thing in Seattle caught me off guard. You and I will be visiting the offices I asked you to get information on before coming home. After a brief break, we'll be heading to London and Paris to look for new office space. We have to attend the Marshall Pediatrics Spring Gala while we're in Charlotte. I apologize for throwing all of this on you at the last minute. Do you need a couple of extra hours to get packed?"

Couple of hours? How about a couple of days! The last time I had on an evening gown, was the prom. "That would help."

"If you need a dress, when you go to Brockman's tell Cameron I said to fix you up with whatever you need."

"That won't be necessary."

"I insist. Consider it my way of apologizing for the crazy first day."

"Thank you."

"I'll see you tomorrow at three."

"Bye."

phillippe

She probably thinks I'm the worst boss in the world. I hope she doesn't regret working with me. Truth is, when I read her resume, I was very impressed and didn't need to meet with her. Anyone with her intelligence willing to work as a floater until something becomes available, understands what it means to work here. She has the kind of loyalty I want on my team.

Tony's security check didn't turn up anything for me to be concerned about which pleased me even more. I would, however, have preferred someone a couple of years older, but her dedication to the company convinced me to give her a chance.

I hope she likes her office. I worked closely with my decorator to make sure it was filled with things she liked. Tony is thorough in his research. How he found out her favorite colors was beyond me. It was perfect that we have very similar tastes, because it makes for a cohesive work environment. Her love of art was one of the other reasons I hired her. We'll be doing a lot of traveling and I like visiting museums and art galleries. It will be nice to have someone I can share that with.

First things first, I've got to get this company healthy.

EXCERPT FROM

Generational Curse

1

KYLA PROMISED HERSELF SHE WOULD never be like the other women in her family, dating a married man and settling for the pennies he doled out.

She'd always felt she was worth more. She met Eric at a fundraiser. He smiled, she smiled and after the cocktail hour, they found themselves seated next to each other. During dinner they talked and flirted and once the evening was over, he asked for her number. She declined and while getting ready for bed, she reached into her bag for her phone and noticed that she also had someone else's phone.

She called the last number dialed and a vaguely familiar voice said, "I've been waiting for your call. So what time do you want to meet for breakfast so I can get my phone?" They both laughed.

They agreed to meet the following morning for breakfast. Two days later, they met again and included an extra slot for "therapy."

Making love in the morning seemed so decadent. She didn't think anything of it until she received her first black envelope a month later.

Eric said, "I'm tired of hotels. Rent a place and fix it up for us and keep whatever is left."

"I'm not a hooker."

"I didn't mean any disrespect. I want to keep seeing you, but my neighbors are nosey."

"Oh, you're married."

"No, I'm not. I just like my privacy. I like being with you, but—"

"I understand." She dropped her head and quickly began getting dressed. "I don't think this is—"

He noticed the change in her behavior and rushed to reassure her. "I don't want you to think I'm ashamed of you, but I also don't want you to think I'm monopolizing your time. You need your space and so do I. When we get together, it should be on neutral, comfortable ground and not some cold hotel room or a place filled with memories of past lovers."

He wrapped his arms around her pulling her to him, gently stroking her hair, inhaling her neck and gently placing a kiss on her soft shoulder. She turned around trying to read the expression on his face. Looking into his eyes, she wondered how many more love nests he had scattered around the city. She pulled his face close to hers and covering his mouth with hers, kissed him passionately. She slipped her hands inside the front of his pants while sliding her tongue inside his mouth, exciting him to the point of arousal.

She pulled back and whispered, "Once more before we have to go?"

He couldn't resist her. The soft seductive tone of her voice and the gentle touch of her hand, made him weak and willing to do anything she asked. Kyla knew if there were anyone else, they would have a hard time competing with her.

She got her education in how to manipulate a man by eavesdropping on her aunts' conversations. They were all experts when it came to being with and manipulating married men. She learned how to kiss from her high school boyfriend. And her college boyfriend, her biology professor, schooled her in anatomy and how to physically please a man.

Before getting involved with Eric, she had dated, but she only had two other semi serious relationships. Neither was fulfilling. The first was Thomas Smith. He was cute, but he lacked the drive to satisfy her physically. When they were together she found herself fantasizing about other men. Intellectually he was a genius, but no one really makes love to a person's brain. It was the other part of his body that needed more educating and she knew she wasn't a school teacher.

Then there was Alister Humphrey. The name alone intrigued her. She had never met a black man with such a stuffy name. In the beginning he seemed like the complete package. Model good looks, intelligence and his skills in bed were unbelievable. The first time they made love, the intensity of his being inside her brought tears to her eyes. Not because it was painful, but because she had never felt such pleasure. Alister knew exactly how to read her body. A skill that was the result of his blindness. What he lacked in vision, he more than compensated for in his other senses. But, he was a man and as they all do, he began making demands and that's when she called it quits. Mind blowing sex aside, Kyla was gone.

Her aunts always said, "Don't allow a man to make demands on you. You make the demands on him. Use what you have and any man can be controlled with the sway of your hips and the wink of your eye. And, showing a little cleavage wouldn't hurt either."

If she were going to marry, it would be to Eric. He was everything she wanted. Handsome, well educated, focused, rich and eager to please in and out of bed. But she also learned from her aunts, the wife always got the leftovers and Kyla didn't like leftovers or sloppy seconds. When Eric suggested the apartment, at first she thought, he was ashamed of her. But Eric's response to her kiss and touch convinced her, she was his priority.

She knew she was in charge. She eased her hand further down his pants pleading, "Baby, please make me sing again before sending me off to start the day."

She kissed his neck before dropping the sheet that was caressing her body and walked into the bathroom. He stood still contemplating the repercussions of being late to the office, when he heard the shower running. He looked at his watch and texted his assistant he would be late. He put his phone on the desk, striped, walked into the steam filled bathroom and opened the shower door to a wet and soapy Kyla, smiling.

"Are you ready to sing?" he asked as he leaned her up against the slippery tiled wall. He pressed himself against her and filled his mouth with every inch of her. He lifted her from behind and rode her like a beautiful long legged mare. The harder he rode, the louder she sang. One last trot, and he sang out too. He rested his head on her chest and she had her answer, "no," there was no one else, just her. She reached over and turned the hot water off. They both needed to cool down. "Baby, I'll do whatever you want, just don't leave me," he begged.

She smiled to herself and replied, "Whatever you say baby."

He pulled away and she turned the hot water back on and washed him like a newborn baby. Gently stroking every inch of him. He knew there wasn't another woman like her. No woman ever treated him like this. He stood still and let her soft hands wash him clean.

On his way to work, he called her. "You are an amazing woman." She remained silent. "Can I see you tonight?"

She thought for a moment before replying, "Only if you promise to repeat that shower scene."

"Your wish is my command."

Now more than three years later and countless showers and secret meetings, she's still calling the shots.

TRACY'S OTHER BOOKS

GENERATIONAL CURSE

THE GOOD GIRL
part one

The Alex Chronicles:
GIRLFRIENDS & SECRETS

LOVE NOTES
Words For Lovers

Thank you so much for taking the time to read my book. Your support means a lot to me. If you enjoyed this book, please recommend it to a friend, family member, a stranger, your book club, your social media posse, favorite bookstore or anyone.

If you haven't done so already, join Tracy's mailing list for free short story and novella downloads and advance notice of new releases and giveaways.

Subscribe to Tracy's Mailing List
www.readtracyreed.com